A CRY OF ABSENCE

A CRY OF ABSENCE

A Novel by

MADISON JONES

LOUISIANA STATE UNIVERSITY PRESS
BATON ROUGE

[redacted]

Manufactured in the United States of America

Louisiana Paperback Edition, 1989
98 97 96 95 94 93 92 5 4 3 2

Library of Congress Cataloging-in-Publication Data

Jones, Madison, 1925–
A cry of absence, a novel / by Madison Jones.—Louisiana paperback ed.
p. cm.
ISBN 0-8071-1579-7 : $9.95
I. Title.
[PS3560.O517C7 1989]
813′.54—dc20 89-8196
CIP

For Shailah
Also for Carroll, Percy, Ellen,
Michael and Andrew,
my beloved children whose unmuted presence
added to the difficulties

A cry of Absence, Absence in the heart

JOHN CROWE RANSOM

PART ONE

1

But, my dear, it's so provincial of them," Mrs. Delmore said with a pleading gesture that caused the silver bracelets on her wrist to click.

Hester disliked being called "my dear" only less than she did hearing "them," which included herself, called "provincial." Not that this, finally, was the one last straw. It was merely another in the series of offensive observations that Mrs. Delmore—and, for that matter, nearly the whole luncheon group—had been making upon the town of Cameron Springs. But the moment had come, Hester felt, when good manners no longer required that she maintain a cool, tolerant silence. With some dryness, and a little stress on the "we," she said, "Yes. But that's the way we do here."

Mrs. Delmore, however, was not of the kidney to be silenced by what she doubtless considered Hester's stratagem of including herself. With another clicking of bracelets she lightly said, "You will just have to change the way you do, then. After all, my dear, Negroes have the same right to the public schools that the whites do."

"They have their own public schools," Hester said, and then felt like biting her tongue off. She had meant only to declare herself, not enter into a demeaning argument with this woman. Fortunately Mary Lassiter, the hostess, in some embarrassment, stepped quickly between them with the big silver coffeepot, saying, "Let's talk about the weather, it's so beautiful today."

"Perfectly charming," Mrs. Rago helpfully said, in a gay, conspiratorial, northern voice. "Is September always this pleasant here, Hester?"

What was her first name? Making an effort to focus her whole attention on the rather sallow but pretty face of Mrs. Rago across the room from her, Hester proceeded to explain that, no, it was not usually this way, that as a rule the first weeks of September were as hot as August. The topic immediately became general, leaving Hester slack in which to reflect that none of them, perhaps not even Mrs. Delmore, had been conscious of offending her by their observations on the town. It was not an easy thing for her to comprehend, but she had noticed often in recent years this new habit of mind that regarded any place, even one's own place, as merely the accidental locale of one's present habitation. Cameron Springs was Hester's place, but it was hardly less theirs, by reason of a few months' or a year or two's residence. A place was nice or not so nice, according to a semiprivate standard, and what did the fact of its being one's own have to do with the judgment? Therefore if Hester took offense at their judgments, it could only mean that the standard she held was faulty and outdated. So now, with these last remarks, Hester stood fully revealed for what she was. Well, it was a revelation that made her feel more at ease than she had until now, not like a hypocrite anymore. She found herself able to give her first really genuine smile of this luncheon hour to Mary Lassiter, who just then, with a look of solicitude in her heavy-lidded eyes, was offering her the silver tray with cream and sugar for the cup she held on her knee.

Hester's being here was a natural enough mistake. She had met Mary Lassiter six months ago when Mary, new in town, had first started coming to the garden club. They had struck up a casual friendship that Hester, probably because of her increasing tendency to withdrawal, had not anticipated leading to anything beyond itself. When, last week, she had received Mary's unexpected luncheon invitation, she had accepted with a reluctance that was only partly because she, as the old member of the community, ought in courtesy to have been the one to make the first move: she would have felt reluctant in any case. Now she wished that she had abided by her impulse, for this past hour had greatly depressed her. Not that she had not known about the gulf between herself and the new people, seven of whom—wives of husbands who worked in executive jobs at the new industrial plants—surrounded her in the room. It was that she had not realized its depth, involving the something like scorn in which they held so many of the values that she and the town—at least as it *had* been—either cherished or regarded as the not-unworthy creations of necessity. And where scorn was too strong a word, ridicule was not. Like that earlier interval, difficult for Hester, when Mrs. Delmore had exercised her evidently much-admired wit on the crude, little Confederate statue that stood, gun in hand, on its tall pedestal in the square. The statue, too, Hester inferred, represented attitudes that belonged in the refuse heap. At times this luncheon experience had been a little like some she had had when reading those lofty and insulting comments on the South in newspapers published a thousand miles away. But this was in Cameron Springs, only blocks from her home, and it gave her an oppressive sense of being at bay.

Hester had no sooner articulated this thought than she resented her weakness in having admitted it. Very well, let them snipe: what was it to her? Who were these women, anyway, with their French twists and brightly lacquered nails and thoughtless, undisciplined postures that needed half a sofa for comfort? Who, especially, was Mrs. Delmore, at this moment gesturing with her scrubbed, milkmaid's arm on which the bracelets jingled, her mouth drawn up at one corner with the irony of an anecdote—something discrediting to the Baptists—that she was telling to the room at large. Vaguely tuning in on it, Hester wondered about the effect on Mrs. Delmore of announcing that she was herself a Baptist, which she was not. Mrs. Delmore gestured again, involving her head this time in a way that shook the frosted curls behind. The gesture produced general laughter, and Hester permitted herself a smile.

She was thinking now how glad she was not to have indulged the maudlin temptation to do her hair differently for this occasion, instead of in the loose bun at the nape of her neck. For this, the bun, was her style; this was the way Hester Glenn looked now, at forty-eight, with her hair going gray and with a vivid line between her eyes and visible crinkles at the corners of her mouth. But still, she thought with sudden pride, despite the several years she had on most of these women, she could have outmatched them all if she had wanted. Heels like theirs would have raised her taller than any of them and a sheer dress like some of those would have emphasized a waist not yet in need of corseting. Whenever she wanted she could still appear as what men had used to say of her—a stately and elegant woman. Perhaps over the years, fourteen of them since her separation from Thomas, she had grown too lax about these things. She had had her troubles, though, increasingly. Her thoughts ran to Ames, then to Cam, and there paused.

She was glad for the blue china dish with mints that intruded into her pause, and Mary's voice: "Try one, Hester. They're very special." Hester took one with a certain relief and then became conscious that once again, apparently at Mrs. Delmore's inspiration, the subject had got back to Negroes. Before Hester could get thoroughly tuned in, Mary, offering the tray to Mrs. Rago now, said, "Of course it's not only a southern thing, Nora. It's really a national problem."

"Now Mary, you just stop shielding Hester," Mrs. Delmore playfully said. "We are your guests, too."

"I just don't like to see you disagree," Mary said.

"But we are not disagreeing, are we, Hester?" Mrs. Delmore said, turning to Hester with a smile. Clearly this woman had not forgotten their earlier brief dispute and meant to have last blood. Hester matched her smile and said, "I really don't know."

"I mean we all have eyes and ears, of course," Mrs. Delmore went on, a little irony now showing at one corner of her smile. "No fair-minded person could help but agree that they are treated very badly."

Hester's smile was gone, but she throttled her angry impulse. In the coolest voice at her command she said, "Maybe I have just not been observant enough," and very deliberately turned her eyes elsewhere.

There was a moment of silence in which the other women looked uncomfortable. They were not very uncomfortable, though, Hester reflected, and soon enough they would have forgotten their outspoken friend's little lapse of good manners: after all, she was perfectly in the right. And once Hester was gone from their cozy midst they would say this, along with other things her presence had inhibited, offering Mrs. Delmore still further occasion for the exercise of her rare wit. Well, that would be soon now. Meanwhile, in a tone that gave no hint of hostile feeling, Hester made an amiable remark about the walnut tea cart placed in the circle before her, and so launched the general conversation again.

7

A few minutes later she was walking down the treeless lawn toward her car. Getting out of there, however, had not substantially relieved her depression. Partly, she supposed, this was because her eyes were immediately confronted by all these new houses that had sprung up, magically, in old Jake Tarver's cow pasture. Close her eyes and she could see his big herd of whiteface still grazing it, all headed one way and some of them at the crest of the slope detailed against the eastern sky. The houses were substantial ones, on large, sodded lots, but to her there was something strange about the way they stood there. In the bottom of her mind the shadowy notion remained that the next time she drove south out of town on Quincey Street and came to where the new extension began, these houses would not be here at all. Getting into her car, she wondered what it would be like to see life always as a kind of transient, with nothing much to reverence or uphold, like those women in the house. There were times when she could envy them their freedom.

She approached the square down Forrest Street, driving between shaded rows of houses reassuringly solid and venerable. Across from the white twin-columned courthouse the Confederate monument stood at the center of the square on a circular plot of grass, a polished cannon at each of the pedestal's four corners. As she drove around it she glanced up at the little soldier, made of concrete, holding his gun and gazing blankly south from his perch ten feet above the ground. The figure struck her suddenly as pathetic in its smallness, its exposure, and a flash of angry sympathy started up in her breast. What was it that woman had said, to the amusement of them all at her clever way of phrasing it? "That poky little cement savior." For just a moment she hated them all. She saw them as the first—no, not the first—wedge of that huge power that had been for so long gathering itself in the distance, waving scorn and accusation at her town, herself, her family. Even at her dead.

By the time she pulled up in front of her house at the corner one block off the square, her anger had subsided. Already she was ashamed of its violence. After all, she had often enough encountered this kind of attitude, in people and in print, and had learned long since to dismiss it. Why, then, should this occasion have so affected her? Maybe it was just the accumulation of so many repetitions, the slow drip-drop that wears through stone. Or maybe it was other pressures. Her sons came back to mind, but she quickly put these thoughts aside and got out of the car.

In any case, as a consequence of it all she stood here surveying the familiar street, the tall brick front of her own home, with a new self-consciousness. She saw a wide street running between rows of old, quiet houses unevenly distanced from the sidewalks and screened in part by dense maple or magnolia trees and swollen, black-green shrubbery that was boxwood or lush camellia. The Perkins house, close to the street like hers, caught the sunlight on its pair of columns. And two blocks down, above the sudden, drab stone wall of the old city cemetery, the crowns of a few taller monuments gleamed like bone. Her own house, only steps beyond the shoulder-high hedge that grew tight against the wrought-iron fence, looked oldest of all by reason of its time-blackened and empurpled brick and the colored fanlights in the arch over the wide front door. She did not know how another eye could fail to see it as hers did.

"Fine afternoon, ain't it, Miss Hester?"

Lucius was there, somehow, across the hedge from her, as if he had presented himself just now for her scrutiny. "Yes, it is, Lucius," she said, and mechanically added, "Have you finished clipping all those shrubs?"

"Yes'm. Fixing to go on home now."

He passed through the gate, tipping his battered black felt hat to her as he went by, and headed down the street. She watched him go, bent and limping a little, in a patched khaki shirt dark with sweat where the suspenders cleaved to his back and shoulders. He would keep on straight to the cemetery wall and turn left and, crossing the road into the colored district, go to the small frame house that she had built for him and his invalid wife whose four operations she had paid for. Did he secretly hate her for this, and for the other things, keeping it masterfully concealed from her family and herself for seventy-something years under a black mask of loyalty and cranky affection? And never a slip anywhere? She could not believe that. Indeed what had he really to be bitter against except a fate that neither he nor she nor anyone else had ever known how to alter. She thought that he understood this. So did most of the Negroes, she felt, even now, even with all the agitation going on among them and those court integration orders to breed delusion . . . And women like these to nourish it. She thought of the new "citizens' committee," of which Mrs. Delmore's husband was head. A little of her anger came back, and she went into the house.

Always it comforted her to see things in their places, to look left and right into the parlor and the sitting room and see the lyre-back chairs that had been her grandmother's, the towering walnut secretary in the corner, and on the mantel the ticking clock with brass pendulum swinging back and forth. It was a lovely, high hallway, leading back to a staircase that wound so gracefully up to the story above. But this made her think of her sons and made the crease stand vividly between her eyes. She listened overhead for several moments. Then she walked back through the shadowy dining room to the kitchen on the rear of the house. But Willodene was not there, gone probably to the grocery. Hester returned and, taking the mail from the hall table, went into her bedroom.

Removing her suit, she noted the severity of its cut and color and was vaguely glad that she had worn it. Had she grown too severe, perhaps? Had she, since her separation, been too severe with them—her sons? But she had seen enough of permissiveness in parents, leaving their children to grow up at the mercy of every mean and impure instinct. In her own training there had been none of this softness. But in those days, she reflected, there had been supports from outside, from the church especially, to strengthen what parents taught. This new young preacher Mr. Mabry at her own church, the Presbyterian—what was he about already except screwing up his nerve to sanction, without even his present guardedness, the same, loose attitudes that she had heard from those women this afternoon. No wonder the attendance of many like herself had become an occasional thing. She did not really regret anymore that she had not been able to keep her sons interested in the church.

She thought about her sons. For all their faults they were good boys, decent. There was a malice in people that liked nothing so well as to feed on some dirty, unfounded rumor. Like the one, now entirely discredited, to which Cam's name had been connected—about the McKendry girl who had had the illegitimate baby. Hester could not but believe that the prospect of the father's being "somebody," a Glenn and a Cameron too, explained its persistence even long after the actual father had been identified. Of course, she bitterly admitted, there was always the memory of her husband to add a look of substance to the rumor.

In her dressing gown Hester sat on the edge of the high four-poster bed and gazed at the lavender flush of sunlight in her drawn window curtain. At length she glanced through the mail lying on her bed table—two bills, an ad, a note from the Cameron County Heritage Society, of which she was the secretary. It seemed to her that she had left some duty unperformed, but she could not think what, and soon she realized that this was because she was pointlessly listening. She put the mail down and lay back on her bed.

For a while her eyes wandered along the cracks in the high, plaster ceiling, then down to her dressing-table mirror on whose face lay a glaze of lavender light reflected from the window curtain. Still listening, she dozed off and presently dreamed of footsteps stealing ever so softly past her door and on to the stairway, while she lay stiff with tension, hearing the footsteps mount and the creaking noises of the house in the night stillness.

There was a tapping at her door. When she answered, Cam, in spotless white T-shirt and tennis shoes, came in. Instantly her tension was gone. As always the sight of him brought a gust of pleasure to her breast. Graceful and strong, tall for seventeen, with loose auburn hair and cool gray appraising eyes, he seemed to her the image of what a young man ought to look like. And ought to *be,* also. How she wished that her mother and father, who had so much wanted a boy, could have lived to see him now.

"You feeling all right, Mama?"

"Just a little tired," she said. "Come and sit down a minute."

"Just for a minute. The game's tonight." With quiet feet Cam approached and sat down on the bed beside her. "This is the big one, with Alden. And I'm pitching. I've got to win this one for sure."

She reached out and touched his hand, feeling the roughness of calluses along his index finger. "I know you will."

"I haven't lost one this season, you know," he said, smiling at her. "Bainbridge was pitching the three times we lost."

There was nothing wrong with his kind of pride. She had wanted this in him. It was what all of her family had had—a just sense of their own excellence, their rightful place, that was in no way vulgar or ugly. He was like them, she thought again, looking at his clear, chiseled face and auburn hair—the epitome of them all. "Good luck," she said. Then a thought came to mind, and before he could move, she quickly restrained him. "Do you know the Delmore girl? Whose father is head of that 'committee'?"

"I know her when I see her. She's Ames's age."

"Is she like them . . . like her parents?"

"A troublemaker, you mean? Gosh, yes. She's in it big. The only friends she's got around here are niggers."

"I've told you many times not to call them that, please. It's offensive to them."

"I'm sorry, Mama," he said, pausing. He looked at her with grave eyes. Then, "What about her, though?"

"Oh, nothing, really." Hester sighed. "It's only that I met her mother at a luncheon today. It was unpleasant. I always feel depressed after I meet those people. They are such destructive people, so full of arrogance and contempt. They don't know or care what they break, as long as it's in the name of their 'equality.' To them the idea that we have anything worth maintaining is just ridiculous."

Cam was gazing toward the curtained window now. Hester added, "And it's hard to know how to oppose them. Or those Negroes they've stirred up."

For a few moments Cam continued to stare absorbedly at the curtain. This time it was he who touched her hand. "Don't worry, Mama," he said. "They won't break us." The quick smile he gave her as he rose from the bed left her, as always, comforted.

She heard the rumble of his old car backing out of the garage and, after that, for a while, nothing. Her window curtain stirred, admitting air like breath from the shrubbery out in the yard. Her drowsiness came back and the sound, later, of the kitchen screen falling shut, of Willodene returned, made a not unpleasant ripple across the surface of her sleep. But then:

"Miss Hester, you 'wake?"

She was suddenly on her elbow staring at the shut door. It was

Willodene, but her voice had reached Hester like the sound of an alarm. Louder than she intended, Hester said, "What is it?"

"You ain't heard the news, has you?"

Hester sat stiffly upright, saying, "What news?" her voice distorted in her tightening throat.

" 'Bout that Stevens. Somebody done killed him."

"Stevens?" She uttered the name with a blind relief that drained the stiffness from her body.

"That colored Stevens. The one been stirring the trouble up."

Hester's mind, so newly released from its first tension, felt a little sluggish. Stevens? What "trouble"? Suddenly she could feel the answer rising like an old threat on a flank neglected for the moment. She gazed at the lavender mirror glass, knowing that Willodene stood outside the door with her head cocked, her feet in the cut-up sandals firmly planted, her weighty underlip hanging in readiness to feed out only one at a time the fragments of her story. But what she wanted more, Hester imagined, was to trace in her mistress's expression the effects of each detail. Hester said, "Was it in town?"

"No'm. Out to the Grimley hills. Hunting dogs smelled him out, he were buried."

Willodene's eyes, showing white, would be turned up in her head with the effort to envision Hester's face. Hester got up from the bed, saying, "I'll be out in a moment, Willodene."

Hester heard her steps withdraw, the sandals flapping, and with deliberation she took her gray housedress out of the closet. Her arms felt heavy as she put it on. The image of Mrs. Delmore, bracelets clicking on her milkmaid's arm, came into Hester's mind, and she thrust it out with an anger that quickly gave way to a feeling of shame. What had Mrs. Delmore's opinion to do with this? Calmly she fastened the buttons up the front of her dress. Not all the trash in the world were white. Negroes could have done this thing, they had done worse. Stevens. She had seen him on the square once—a young, tall Negro who would have been nice looking except for his fixed, sullen expression. Was it really true? They were so given to idle rumors.

Still holding to this thought she stood, moments later, facing Willodene across the kitchen and saying, in a tone more formidable than she had intended, "How do you know this, Willodene?"

"From folks up on the square." Hester's tone had not put her on the defensive. From over the bag of groceries on the center table she looked straight back into Hester's face, her gold tooth showing above the slack underlip. "They was telling it *all* around."

"Who was?" Hester said, clutching her doubt.

"Plenty of folks. It ain't nothing but truth, Miss Hester."

Hester's little doubt collapsed; Willodene's evasiveness about names, she saw, was merely "their" instinct to privacy. It had been a small blunder, in fact, to have questioned her so. Hester, to gloss over her disadvantage, picked up a cooking spoon off the stove and hung it on the wall hook.

"That spoon dirty, Miss Hester."

She took it down again, looking at it. "You say he was buried?"

"Yes'm. Dogs dug him out. Seem like he been there a couple of days."

"Didn't anybody miss him?"

"I reckon they didn't. Say he was in and out a right smart. I 'spect his mammy just thought he was gone off again."

"Do you know her?" Hester, observing the spoon in her hand, allowed her face to be studied.

"I knows her to see. She's the one got that beauty salon back there on Bee Street. Little bitty, light-colored woman. You seen her. She ain't got no husband."

Hester put the spoon back on the stove. Willodene was waiting for her question. In the pause she began to remove groceries from the bag, muttering to herself in a way that did not deceive Hester as to where her attention was fastened. The question hung on Hester's tongue. Rays of sunlight spilled through yellow fig leaves into the west window and scored the linoleum at Hester's feet in mazelike patterns of vivid light and shade. "How was he killed?"

"Say they figures he was rocked."

"Rocked?"

"Yes'm. Had the marks all over him. Say somebody had just kept on busting him with rocks. Knocked one eye plumb out."

Hester put a hand on the stove, then took it away.

This time Willodene did not wait for her question. "Had a chain tied on his leg. Had him tied up by his leg so's he could dodge around while they throwed at him. They found the place where he was tied to—kind of small tree with bark all wore around. Rocks laying there." She took a head of lettuce from the bag and seemed to inspect it before she put it down on the enamel tabletop.

There were only the sounds of Willodene's movements, handling the groceries. The refrigerator cut on, whirring and clicking, and Hester, through an east window now and over the crest of the high hedge, saw the shiny top of a car glide past on the street. She found that in order to clear her voice she had first to swallow hard and then draw breath. "Who do they think could have done it?"

"Ain't no telling. But it's some mighty mean white folks lives out there at Grimley. Some of them millworkers."

Hester suppressed an impulse to deny it. Could it, after all, be anyone but white men? She watched Willodene, with shoes slapping the linoleum, move to the far end of the kitchen and place a bag of apples on a shelf. She was slow about it, settling the bag just so, as if it were a mirror in which she was focusing the image of Hester's face. She said:

"How come white folks does like they do?"

Hester's lips parted. Only a few, she almost fired back—only the scum. Then she did say, "I hope these will be hanged."

"Yes'm."

Her tone made Hester stiffen. Some light had come back into her eyes when she said clearly, "I don't think you have any reason to doubt that I hope it."

"I never meant that, Miss Hester. I knows the difference between white folks. I knows you ain't that kind."

Willodene had turned around, her black brow puckered, to say this, and for a moment Hester met her eyes straightaway. "Very few of us are that kind, Willodene," she said, ". . . whatever they may be saying about us now." She looked out at the clusters of yellow fig leaves, and added, "We will see them caught and punished." Then, "You had better put the roast on now," she said and left the kitchen.

For a minute or two she stood motionless in the hallway and listened to the ticking clock. Except to dust or to entertain, she rarely entered the parlor, but she did now, seating herself in one of the straight, lyre-back chairs that faced the hearth, the mantel clock and, above it, her dead mother's portrait. Hester was like her, people had said, about the eyes and the tense mouth that would straightly say its piece and then shut down; and like her also in the high-bridged arch of the nose. She wanted to think that in qualities of character as well she resembled her mother, for this was her house she was keeping. It did not seem to Hester that she had kept it very well. Maybe if her husband had been the man her father had been . . . A sound through the open front door interrupted her reverie and she got up quickly from the chair.

The *Herald* was lying on the steps. A glance showed her the headlines. Quickly she folded the paper again and, descending the steps, turned and walked among the shrubbery out into the side yard. Big camellias and sasanquas made a sort of bower for the birdbath and the yard chairs, and here she sat down. Two times she read the story through. Dropping the paper onto her lap, she sat with her eyes shut. Birds twittered vaguely in the bushes, clashing the leaves not far from her head. Hadn't she troubles enough, after all, without taking this one too as her own? In such a world, what could a person do except cleanse his house and shut his door against the stink of dissolution.

2

Ames had not gone home afterward. Instead he had had Larch let him off outside of town at Bracey's, and he had spent most of the afternoon nearly alone in the dim, barnlike interior of the place, drinking and throwing away his change in the jukebox and pinball machine. There was his usual reason for not going home. Disapproving as she did of his idleness, his encounters with his mother during the hours when people ought to be about their work were likely to be chilly. But today, against the other matter, this one did not weigh much. He would have had to tell her and he did not want to be the one. Seen through her eyes, ugliness not even comparable to this had a way of taking on its darkest colors, and already he was more upset than even this cause seemed reason for. At the time, in fact, he had been sick. He had ended by vomiting. And even now, hours later, thoughts of it shadowed him like lurid presences over his shoulder.

Ames had been fishing that morning, in the little swamplike backwater where Tad's Creek emptied into the Saugahatchee. He had fished here often during this summer vacation from college. It pleased him to get out in the stillness of daybreak and walk this whole four miles and then, as the sun rose higher and the heat gathered, to recline in the boat and feel the languid currents drifting him softly against mudbanks and the big, denuded sycamore roots. This morning, as usual, he had quit about ten o'clock and, in a pleasantly sleepy mood, walked back to the highway and headed toward town. It was shortly after that when he saw the revolving red light on Larch's car come streaking over the hill in the near distance.

He was not prepared for the car to stop at all, much less for the violence with which the driver hit the brakes, bringing it to a skidding halt only steps past Ames.

17

"Want to see a dead nigger?" Larch called from the window.

"I've already seen one before."

"Get in," Larch said. "Hurry up."

Ames got in and was instantly thrust hard against the back of the seat by Larch's takeoff. "What the hell?"

"Got us a killing," Larch said, glaring straight ahead as they gathered speed. His sinewy neck rose like a stalk from the buttoned-up collar of his khaki deputy's shirt. "Think it's that Stevens nigger. Another one found him out here while ago."

"Stevens? The civil-rights one?"

"We think so. Going to make a stink if it is."

In a gruesome, punning sort of way, Ames thought later, Larch had proved right on this point. It was clear the moment they approached, wading through yellow sage, a sudden beech woods where a small group of men stood around. The stink, dim at first, had an edge of sweetness that a few steps more made rank in his nostrils. Ames did not go very close. Unearthed from the dirt bank behind it, the corpse lay on its back, half naked, with one stiff hand and arm grotesquely lifted at its side. Ames could see that an eye socket was full of dirt and, next, despite the smear, a deep, black gash in the temple.

"Is it Stevens?" Larch quietly said.

Sheriff Venable nodded. He was standing close, hunched in his simian way, peering. He must have stood peering for a full minute or two without a sound from anyone. And suddenly Ames was conscious of the flies. They scored the filtered sunlight in streaks of glistening green, or sat like vivid beads on the mottled flesh. The stillness seemed to grow, expand, until the sound of the whirling flies was like the keening in a void.

"Been hit a lot of times with something," the sheriff finally said. "While he was tied up with that chain on his leg, I reckon."

Then Ames saw it, a chain bound tight around the bare ankle and winding back into the dirt bank.

"See can you find the place where he was tied up at," the sheriff said. "Ought to be close around."

They had found it fairly soon. Ames heard a call through the woods, and he hurried to a clear place where one small beech tree stood alone. The bark near the foot of the trunk was skinned around.

Lying about, there were some chunk rock as big as a man's fist and a few bare patches where sod had been torn loose from the earth.

"Had them some fun doing it," Sheriff Venable muttered, weighing a rock in his stubby hand. "Like one of them throwing galleries at the fair."

Ames's sickness had come on him suddenly, but he had managed to suppress it until he could get off by himself in the woods. Afterward, propped against a tree trunk, he imagined that the ringing in his head was the sound of green flies whirling.

The whole afternoon of sipping whiskey at Bracey's and watching lights flash on the pinball machine and flooding his ears with the squall of the jukebox had not displaced from his mind even one detail of it all. And he kept recalling the lanky figure of Stevens, Otis Stevens, as he had seen it more than once around town that summer. A handsome Negro, very black and straight, always scrupulously dressed—or overdressed—in pale green or lemon shirts and trim, flashy sport coat. To Ames, the arrogance of his posture, his manner of resting an unflinching gaze on whites he met, was not so much ominous as it was something between silly and pathetic. Two years at a northern college and, the story had it, he had come home to liberate his people. His efforts, however, had not produced any spectacular results: they appeared, in fact, to have been confined to exhortations at meetings in Negro churches and to instances of rudeness toward white people on the streets. But this kind of behavior was hardly uncommon these days, and such threatening talk as Ames had heard among whites had in no way singled out Stevens from others like him . . . But he *had* been singled out, by someone. And about one thirty Ames was watching through Bracey's window when Ted Diamond's old blue hearse passed by. Inside was its stinking burden.

The proprietor Bracey, as in every case, had not been surprised by the news. He too had seen the hearse roll past, and afterward, slumped on his stool behind the counter, he had taken the matchstick from a drooping corner of his mouth and said, " 'Course that nigger was asking for it. Folks are worked up."

Ames was downing another hot swallow of the whiskey. As soon as his eyes cleared he looked straight back at Bracey and said, "That's an excuse?"

"It's all the excuse some of them needs." Bracey pulled at one of his fanlike ears. "You don't reckon they're going to keep on taking all this stuff lying down, do you?"

Ames was just a little drunk now and the shadow at the back of his mind had all but lost its features. He felt merely angry, hostile. "Crap," he said. Something more violent was on his tongue, but another voice interrupted:

"Hell naw, they ain't." It was the only other customer, a man in blue denim at the opposite end of the counter. His voice did not have quite the tone of anger, but his flat gaze, out of a burnt-clay face, rested squarely on Ames. He had been in the process of rolling a cigarette. His tobacco sack lay propped against a beer bottle. "You can't push folks but just so far. I don't go with nigger-killing. I've knowed some mighty good niggers. But this here pushing keeps on, you going to see more'n just one. White people ain't going to set back and let everything they got be took over by niggers. And the 'gov-er'ment.' Gover'ment don't care no more about our kind than they do a cur dog."

"Is that right?" Ames said, feeling his jaws grow stiff with anger.

The man's face registered something, but he finished rolling the cigarette and licked it and held it up to his thin lips. "Might be you're a rich kid, though. Maybe your kind ain't got nothing to worry about. You can have your own schools, can't you? And you don't need no job."

"Glenn's all right. He's a good boy," Bracey said. "Now you all just hush."

Nothing more was said, though Ames could feel the man's flat blue gaze resting on him from time to time. Presently Ames went back to his booth at the far end of the room and sat looking out down the highway into town. His anger did not last. And soon even the whiskey's glaze had ceased to blur his thoughts.

It was close to five o'clock when he left Bracey's, stepping a little uncertainly. The walk into town sobered him, and by the time he reached the square he could notice the effects only in the throbbing of his temples. Pausing at the rack of newspapers on the sidewalk by the courthouse he read the headlines. Afterward he continued to stand there. It was about here that he had stood with Cam when Stevens, determinedly staring dead ahead, passed by so close that his shoulder had collided hard with Cam's.

Walking slowly Ames crossed the square. When he looked up next he was at home. He did not want to confront his mother just yet, and the side yard, with all its crazy profusion of heaped-up shrubs, offered him a temporary haven. Or so he thought, for there was no reason to suppose that he might find her at this supper hour seated in one of the metal chairs inside the screen of bushes. Yet there she was, her profile visible to him. She had a brooding look. And although his approach had rustled the big sasanqua, she seemed to be still unconscious of his presence. Thinking that he might yet withdraw unnoticed, he placed a foot behind him.

"Come and sit down," she said.

It was not a command; it had the tone of a statement almost unconsciously made. He noticed now that her nostrils, always expressive, were slightly flared and waxen-looking. They gave accent to her rather more than commonly vertical posture and the way her feet, in the scarred house shoes, were planted side by side on the clipped grass beneath her. When she did not speak again he entered and, passing by the chair in front of her, sat down in the one at the other side of the clearing.

"You know about this, don't you?" One of her hands rested on the newspaper in her lap. She did not look up at him.

"Yes, I know."

"It was that young Stevens Negro. Somebody rocked him to death."

It called for no answer and he gave none. A moment later he saw her head sink a little forward and remain that way, lifting the gray-streaked bun at the nape of her neck. She had a rather prominent nose, and the large bun was doubtless contrived as a sort of counterweight to give her profile the illusion of balance. But to Ames, instead of a contrivance it had always seemed her necessary style, the one inevitable expression of her character. Her present posture dispelled this illusion of balance, and this was why, just now, it vaguely distressed him to observe her so. He cast about for something.

"It needn't have been white people, you know."

"I wish I could believe it wasn't." She lifted her head, looking into the wall of boxwood that solidly hedged that end of the enclosure. The ray of sunshine resting suddenly on the crown of her hair made it appear an almost solid iron-gray. "No," she added. "They were white men. What kind I don't know. Evil white men."

Evil. Ames thought that nowhere else could he hear the word used as she used it, with all the color of its ancient meaning. It seemed incongruous that now there were birds sweetly twittering in the big camellia bush just behind her, rustling the leaves.

"Do you know what I have figured out?" she said, giving him her first glance. She let him hang for a moment. "It was Stephen in the Bible who was stoned to death. He was the first Christian martyr. This is what those men got from the story. What do you think of that?"

Ames felt a curious chill in his breast.

"Or was it just mockery?" she said.

Ames knew that she did not really expect an answer—the question was put to herself more than to him. He also understood that for her, with her rigorous, biblical piety, this view of the thing had compounded its evil. What he did not see was why it had brought this chill upon himself, like throbs of cold blood through his heart. He was suddenly moved to say, irrelevantly, "The Yankee newspapers'll get hold of it pretty quick, I guess."

She looked at her hand resting on the paper in her lap. "Of course." Then, "It makes all those things they are saying about us up north seem to be true. About how cruel we are to Negroes. All of us. Because of a few scum," she said, her voice hinting at her passion. "As if we were all scum and didn't hate such people as much as anybody else."

Her tone focused Ames's attention, for he thought that never before had he heard her sound defensive. It was a distress indeed that could make her speak this way. But there was more to come. It was about her father, that familiar incident of forty years ago when he had sheltered the fleeing Negro in his house and defied the gang of white men to set a foot on his doorstep. "Where justice was concerned, my father didn't know the difference between the races," she said, then suddenly hushed, as though she had been startled by the tone of her own voice. For a moment, with her lips uncharacteristically parted, she looked embarrassed. "We had better not talk about it anymore," she finally said, and with decision picked up the newspaper off her lap.

Intently Ames watched her as she turned through the pages, her eyes pausing for an item here and there. Birds twittered and rustled the bushes behind her and, soon, an evening scent of foliage had freshened the air. Increasingly everything seemed mended, but still he would not risk allowing his attention to wander from her. He saw her, after many pauses, come to the final page and saw her gaze drop to the left-hand corner. That would be the horoscope. She would read the day's predictions for Scorpio, Aries, and Cancer, which were her own and her sons' constellations. She did it unfailingly, though it was a habit he never had noticed until the past year or two. In her it was curious. Once, observing her absorption, he had asked her if she believed in the thing. "Not really, of course," she had answered. But then she had looked at him with a lift of her brown eyebrows that gave a certain weight to the lightly spoken words: "It is funny how close it hits sometimes, though." This had made him laugh, as he always silently laughed when he caught her in the act. But today, he discovered, it did not amuse him to watch her. Perhaps this was because of the intensity with which her eyes held the page, the set gravity of expression. He saw her lips in motion, as if she were carefully spelling out the phrases. Which of the horoscopes was it? He felt coming back again that sensation of cold blood pulsing through his heart. "What does it say?"

She removed her gaze from the page. "Nothing." She folded the paper and put it in the chair between them. "I guess I had better see about supper," she said and, getting to her feet, passed out of sight beyond the camellia bush. Ames took the newspaper and opened it to the horoscope.

Cam's was Aries. Ames saw immediately, with a relieved awareness of his own absurdity, that it contained the usual kind of vague counsel: a caution that the day was inopportune for new ventures, that circumspection was in order where money was concerned. What, indeed, had he expected? Yet his eye went through it again and, this time, fastened on the last, brief sentence. "Maintain serenity when affronted." Suddenly his mind blazed with the memory of Cam's face, his drawn mouth, that day on the square when Stevens had bumped against him. Cam's words had been inaudible, but not the venom with which he had uttered them.

The chill at Ames's heart persisted. At length he raised his head and stared, over the crest of the big camellia, at the high, upper windows of the house. The panes, reflecting the west, presented a solid sheen of luminous red-gold light. He realized that a face looking down from either of those windows would be invisible from here. Suddenly he was possessed by the entirely ungrounded conviction that Cam was up there and, more, that he had been there watching since the moment when Ames had appeared. The conviction grew so strong that Ames looked away self-consciously. When it seemed that time enough had elapsed, he got up and walked to the house.

From the hall, standing at the foot of the staircase, he could hear his mother's voice speaking to Willodene back in the kitchen. He could not hear a sound overhead. Keeping his steps natural he climbed the stairs to the upper hall. Cam's door, on his right, was shut. But it was always shut, like everything of Cam's. Except for the streak of sunlight under the door, the hall was all shadows, as quiet as daybreak. Preparing himself with a question, he tapped at Cam's door. Presently he tapped again, noting how heavy his arm felt. Then he opened it.

The sun in his face partly blinded him, and he started at the impression that his own reflection in the dresser mirror was Cam looking back at him. The room was empty, however. The unnerving sense of a presence was, he knew, his own imagining. Yet it was as palpable to his senses as the musk in a den and was the reason for the clammy feeling of his palm on the porcelain doorknob. Wasn't he afraid of Cam? The thought literally sprang into his consciousness, fastening there with the resonance of something shouted into his ear. His own little brother, a high-school boy, four years younger than himself? Yet in some way it was true. Had it not been true for a long time?

Ames stood surveying the room as if its features concealed an answer. Unlike his own room across the hall, it was kept with astonishing neatness—shoes aligned under a bed whose snow-white counterpane was stretched as tight as a skin, comb and brush lying precisely side by side on the massive dresser. Even the banners on the wall, trophies of Cam's athletic prowess, were hung in identical patterns of threes. Now, all washed in the orange glow of the sun's last rays, each of the room's separate features impressed itself upon his mind with a certain unnatural vividness. As he stood gazing, it came on him that he no longer could evade the thoughts that had been so obscurely dogging him all these hours. He knew what he had entered for.

At the back end of the room there was a deep closet, almost a little room in itself, with a narrow window. Even in his somewhat feverish haste, Ames had time to be surprised at the disorder that met his eyes—a torn, discarded baseball glove, old clothes, dusty toys of childhood, all scattered about on the floor. There was even broken glass. But he did not pause for reflection. His glances fell here and there until his attention stopped on a large, black trunk. It was not locked. It seemed to contain nothing much but items of worthless junk from which the dust rose into his nostrils as his hands probed about. One hand closed on something hard and smooth and he pulled it out.

It was the chipped, plaster figure of a dwarf a foot high. His hand searched out another one in the trunk, then fragments of a third and fourth and fifth. He remembered, or seemed to remember, them standing there among the prizes in the lighted booth. A throwing gallery at a little country fair. His memory unwound like a reel, showing him again, in all the vividness of those minutes, the grinning, black face in the target hole. And Cam, at twelve or thirteen, his lank, auburn hair afloat with a backward toss of the head as his lean arm coiled for the throw, then fired the ball straight into the target. Five times, for all his watchfulness, the owner of that face was not quick enough: the heavy balls thudded home and smashed his grin. At those moments the grin appeared on Cam's face, a small, hard, private grin that Ames already had memories of. That night at the fair he had seen it five times in succession, while the calliope shrilled and the octopus whirled other customers around and Cam, until the last of his money was gone, went on throwing with all his strength at a black human head. And these were the prizes, a little family of now-broken dwarfs that Cam had pointed to with an indifferent finger.

The sound of a voice startled Ames. He rammed the figures back among the rubbish in the trunk and shut the top. The voice sounded again, but then he recognized his mother's call.

3

There were two dead bulbs in the chandelier above the table and, mingled with afterglow from the windows, the light in the dining room had a vaguely yellow, nerveless quality. To Ames it was like an effect of their silence, something accumulating that made each new forkful of meat or corn on the white-rimmed china plate more tasteless than the last. Sometimes his gaze stopped on the empty chair opposite him. Finally he summoned the boldness to ask, "Where is Cam?"

"I thought I told you he's playing ball tonight." She seemed barely conscious of the delicate bites she took at extended intervals and chewed with almost imperceptible motions of her jaw. She might have been attending to the muted, throaty music of Willodene's humming beyond the kitchen door behind her.

"Is he pitching tonight?"

"Yes. They want to win this one. They always win when he pitches," she said, pride brightening her face a little.

Had she really seen nothing, ever, where Cam was concerned? No, the distress behind this brooding look of hers was no more connected with Cam than it was with himself or the Brookses next door. The reason for it was clear enough: the damage to her idea of Cameron Springs that she carried around like the Ark of the Covenant—and expected every one else to carry. How little she knew, even about her own sons. It was because she did not want to know and had discovered how to stop her eyes and ears against any near approach of ugliness. This left it to others, to him. The thought kindled, and suddenly he had an impulse to shout his fears at her. He did say, but quietly, "By the way, how is the Pilcher boy?"

She turned her level, brown eyes on him. "Oh, he's been out of the hospital two weeks. He's fine now."

Ames looked down at his plate. "That's lucky." He was conscious that she continued to look at him and presently he took another bite.

"Why did you say that?"

"Well, it was lucky. I've known of people getting killed by a baseball."

"It was the way you said it. Did you mean something?"

"No," he said, chewing. A moment passed, making audible Willodene's throttled humming.

"There are rumors, aren't there? That Cam *tried* to do it?"

"Oh, I've heard that once or twice." He was both sorry and not sorry that he had started this.

"Why would he?" There was an edge to her voice.

"It's not me saying it. What I heard was that Cam hated him."

"Why? Why would Cam hate him?"

Ames hesitated. Then, on a little surge of anger, he said, "They say because he was a better batter than Cam."

Deliberately he did not meet her eyes, but he knew just how they were fixed on him—wide, with a dark, vivid edge ringing the clear, brown irises. Retreating, he said, "Don't think I didn't deny it."

"How horrible of them," she finally said, her voice made faint with passion. Then, "I should hope you did deny it. I should think you would have fought them."

"It wasn't that kind of thing. I couldn't very well—"

The swinging door had opened and Willodene, her sandals scuffing, entered with a plate of biscuits. "You all sho' ain't eating much tonight, is you?" she said when Ames too had refused the plate.

"We are not very hungry tonight, Willodene," his mother said in quite her normal voice and appeared to consider carefully her half-empty plate until Willodene had withdrawn. Ames took another tasteless bite.

"I hope you at least answered them back," she said.

"I said I did." He knew that she wanted more than this, but he could not manage it. She looked at him, then looked straight ahead of her at the big sideboard where a silver urn and platter gleamed obscurely in the light.

"Sometimes I think you don't trust Cam. That you never have. Since he was a little boy."

He said nothing. He was thinking that this was a truth he had come to realize clearly only half an hour ago.

"You never talk to him . . . *really* talk to him. He's needed a father."

"So have I, maybe."

She did not dignify this with any response. "You could have helped. He's needed somebody to confide in. He still does."

"He never wanted to confide in me, since he was a baby. Or anybody else. Who did he ever confide in? Does he in you?"

He had touched something; it was barely perceptible. "Of course he does. I mean somebody else . . . not his mother."

But Ames ignored this, adding, "He's as secret as a stone."

"It's only his way. It's habit," she said. "It's why people misunderstand him. And say . . . such a thing." She hesitated, staring hard at the sideboard where the silver gleamed. "Such a horrible thing," she added, her voice close to breaking, and pushed her chair back and stood up.

Ames felt a start of pity. But his impulse to comfort her withered as soon as it sprang, and without a word he let her walk past him and out of the room. Afterward he kept sitting there divided between his pity and his wish to make her share this thing. Who else was there to share it with? At length his father came back to mind, the jaunty, romantic figure of Ames's early childhood. For that moment Ames saw him without the confusion, or the pain, that seemed always to darken these memories, saw him grin with small white teeth and extend a sinewy arm to tousle Ames's hair. Would he be this way still, after fourteen years? In Memphis, Ames thought. Doing what? Was it really his father's fault that all these years had gone by with hardly so much as a word to keep his memory alive in Ames's heart? Ames was not sure anymore. Nor was he any longer sure, in spite of what he since had learned about his father's unbridled conduct, that at bottom the fault was not somehow his mother's. There was a way she had of speaking, sometimes, a cold way that still raised frightening echoes from those early years. He could remember the look of his father at such times. And now he could remember where his sympathy had lain.

But all that was long ago. He ended by getting up from the table and walking straight out of the house.

Ames had nothing in mind except to walk, and, as he passed through the gate, it seemed to be merely the leftward cant of his body that turned him in this direction. There was deep twilight along the street. A few children were playing. Voices reached him from front porches behind the looming shrubbery, and once a laugh that must have issued from an old, dry throat. Two blocks down, at the cemetery, he turned left again. The gray-stone wall ran along beside him, and where it dipped he could see, by the stray light from Paxton's used-car lot down ahead, irregular companies of gravestones and a few low, black-roofed vaults. At the far end, standing in the glare of light from the car lot where plastic flags of red, white, and blue hung motionless from their wires, his eyes followed the highway out of town north past the textile mill. One week more and he would be on it, headed back to school. No matter what, he would be. Now he crossed the highway and went on vacantly down the opposite street.

Small, drab houses in crowded rows were interrupted by more solid fronts of brick and whitewashed board-and-batten, all close up to the pavement. Four Negro girls danced around a pole in the wan streetlight. Their glances at Ames made a momentary interval in the song that took up again as he passed by. Someone played a guitar in the darkness of a porch, resonant chords that all but drowned the undertone of a voice. He heard a call from another shadowy porch and had raised his hand mechanically before he realized that it was a catcall and not a greeting. Beyond the housing project was a brick grocery store, then a small frame building with a plate-glass window. A hanging sign said "Curly Locks Beauty Salon." The place was in darkness. Stopping, he wondered where Stevens's mother lived. Some Negro boys leaning against a wall watched him as he went on.

He stopped again in front of a yellow house with a sizable yard full of flowers. He stood there for a minute.

"Mr. Ames? Come on up here and set with us."

He pushed open the gate and walked up the path between the flowers and climbed the narrow steps to the porch.

"Set yourself down right here," Lucius said. He had gotten up from a nearly invisible chair.

"I'll sit here," Ames said, and settled against a post at the top of the steps.

"You been fine?" This was Ella's voice. He saw her shift her bulk in the swing and heard the chains creak.

"All right. You doing better now?"

"I's feeling a little better. 'Cept just for my blatter. It's done gone acting funny again. Keep feeling it jump, like, every little while." Her voice, threshing the matter fine, ran on in a hush only the emptier for distant children's voices and a cat meowing somewhere. Lucius's voice, entering now and then, was deep and mellow, a comfort in the dark. But there was an intrusion. Footsteps from inside the house were approaching the door.

"Matthew, thought you was gone off," Lucius said. "Come on out here and see Mr. Ames."

It was Lucius's grandson, whom Lucius had raised from a baby. Ames had not seen him for three or four years and had not even known that he was back in Cameron Springs again. Ames got to his feet.

But Matthew had paused in the doorway, a figure in silhouette, seeming blacker than he used to. Ames felt the pause, his nerves tightening. Matthew opened the screen, then, and came out, but his movements were slow. Ames, saying, "How long you been back, Matthew?" had a sensation of cold air on the hand he extended. The hand hung there, pale in the dark, for so long that Ames at last started to withdraw it. Then Matthew's hand appeared. But the contact was a mere brushing of flesh that communicated nothing. Trying to make his voice easy, Ames repeated, "You been back long?"

"Month," Matthew mumbled, the darkness of his face relieved by a small white flash of teeth.

"You've been in Detroit, haven't you?"

"Been everywhere."

Again, the silence.

"You boys set down and talk now," Lucius said, his voice conveying a little tension. "You all *old* friends. I 'member when you all used to play ball together."

Feeling the new pause growing, Ames sat down again. Matthew did not. He only leaned against the wall, a stiff, black shadow.

"Played in the field down there where the car lot sets at now. You all had some *big* games."

"I remember them," Ames said, forcing it. "You always played catcher, Matthew. You were sharp at that."

But Matthew said nothing. It was not possible to tell where his gaze rested. Lucius, shifting in his chair, finally said, "Sho' did. Yes sah, you all had some *big* ball games. That's where Mr. Cam learnt how."

Ames's breathing stopped. Sidelong he tried to make out the direction of Matthew's eyes, waiting, all the while, as if for a second blow to fall.

"Mr. Cam is some kind of good ballplayer, ain't he? Seen his picture in the paper two or three times."

"Yes," Ames said, releasing his breath. "He's good, all right." Matthew never had stirred, and in Lucius's innocent praise, what was there to shy at? Had Ames's thoughts been in his mind, Lucius would not have spoken so. And as for Matthew's hostility, that had no need of any such explanation. What evidence was there, after all? Still it was like trying to free himself of a nightmare.

"He better'n good," Lucius answered. "I seen him pitch. He ought to get in them big leagues. Throw that ball right in there where he want it just like a bullet."

Ames's eyes strained toward Matthew's face in the dark. Through an anxiety that he hoped would not betray him, he said:

"Are you back for good, Matthew?"

Matthew stirred and languidly straightened up. "Naw," he said, and followed it with, "Got to get on, now," in a voice just audible. In silence he stepped over Ames's feet and, descending to the walk, showed his indifferent back as he passed out through the gate.

He left silence behind him, in which Lucius creaked his chair and muttered. It was Ella who broke up the stillness, however. Again, with relief, Ames heard the slow account of her ailments proceeding out of the dark. Her soft voice helped him relax a little, thinking that Lucius, who had known Cam from a baby, obviously had imagined no connection. No, Ames thought, to mention the matter at all would be a mistake. Ames's mere presence here was a mute apology, something that both of them immediately had understood. This was enough. He listened, and presently Lucius was speaking again, the mellow, intimate voice that washed like memories across his consciousness. When he rose some short while later to take his leave, it seemed as if the voice had cleared his head.

"Come on inside here a minute, Mr. Ames."

Ames paused. The threat hovered again. Reluctantly he followed Lucius into the dimness of the living room toward the lighted kitchen door. A bare bulb hung from the ceiling and the sudden brightness flared like alarm in his eyes. But then he saw Lucius bend and, with a long slow arm, reach behind the wood stove, saying, "Something you like." It was a jug of pale whiskey, which he held up for Ames with a smile full of yellow teeth—a sort of apology of his own. "I knows you likes it."

Lucius fetched a jelly glass from an open shelf on the wall and, setting it on the stove, poured a long drink from the jug. While Ames drank, a small swallow at a time, feeling the whiskey sear its way down his gullet, Lucius stood grinning at him. Afterward Ames saw him in a blur, with the light shining on one glossy cheekbone and one corner of the grin. He drew a breath, and suddenly it came over him to say, "Who do you think could have killed that Stevens boy?"

He saw the smile fade out.

"I don't know, sah."

Ames set the empty glass on the stove. "It's bound to have been white men, isn't it?"

"Yes sah."

Ames had already felt the door shut between them. He was sorry he had spoken, and it must have been for his own comfort that now he futilely asked, "And you can't think of anybody that even might have done it?"

"No sah, I sho' can't. Just somebody mean." He dropped his gaze to the floor.

Two blocks from Lucius's house was the Negro residence where the whiskey had come from, and Ames, at the back door, bought a pint of it. Before he reached the high school he stopped to drink where he could see the aura of light from the ball field and hear the voice of the crowd. He did not go inside. He found a place in semidarkness along the fence where he could see, through the bleachers, the pitcher's mound, empty just now while the sides were changing. Once, in the talk from the crowded bleachers above him, he heard Cam's name. But the mound was still empty. The gap through which he peered, like a frame, held it in isolation, in a radiance brighter than day.

Cam appeared, suddenly standing there at center of the frame, with long, tan arms hanging straight down from the meager, gray sleeves, with shirttail to his hips and bare head from which the lanky auburn hair fell like a shadowy thatching upon his brow. All at once, as if he did not have to look, he picked a ball out of the air. Then it started: the poise of the body and back-tilted head, the slow, rounding swing of a long arm, the pause, and then the coil and downward strike of the arm discharging the ball like a flick of light across the tail of an eye—all one flawless pattern of movement. Three more times it happened, without variation except increase of tempo, and then the umpire's strident, "Batter up."

Ames felt the tension of his fingers on the wire and, then, the hot, dry balls of his staring eyes, as if the lids had not blinked in a long time. He did not blink them even now. He saw Cam's hair afloat with the backward toss of his head as the lean arm coiled, then fired. He saw the ball flash in, dead center, the grin blasted from the face of the Negro in the target hole. The grin appeared on Cam's face now, small and hard and private. There was a roar of voices, there was not any calliope, and Ames all of a sudden understood that he was drunk. He straightened up and, letting go of the wire, walked away uncertainly across the deserted school yard. Behind him the crowd gave another shout.

Ames did not remember much about his walk to Bracey's, but it seemed to have taken him a long time. Either he had lost or thrown away the bottle. He bought a beer with the last of his money and, propped against the counter, looked fuzzily around him. The long hazy room, blaring with music and voices, was already crowded with people dancing and bulging out of booths and shuffling around with glasses in their hands. He kept looking from face to face. Presently it became clear to him, maybe for the first time, that these people were all younger than himself, Cam's age. Where had his own crowd, who ought to be here, gone so suddenly? Or was it so sudden? Hadn't they been gone from here a long time—a year or two, or more—and left him alone? It seemed a huge dilemma and his mind reeled away from it.

But still he looked at the faces. It seemed that tonight he had come here just for this, as though he were looking for one in particular. Not Cam's. He was pitching. No, not Cam's. Something jabbed him in the ribs and, uncertainly turning, he saw a pretty smile, all white and orange-red, that he associated with the name Beth. She said something to him, but it seemed a hard thing to get straight. Before he could, she had already reached up and tousled his hair and walked away. Then he understood that she was laughing at him, this high-school girl. The thought was a blow to his dignity. He felt shame at first, and then resentment that quickly bloomed into a slow, impotent anger. The rest of the beer did not wash it away. The gaze he now turned from face to face had become a hostile glare.

At length a face arrested Ames's eyes, a long, beaked, and rather sallow face. Soon he was sure that this was the one, the Pilcher boy. The boy was standing close by, near the door, but when Ames let go of the bar he was not perfectly sure that he was going to make it with dignity. He thought he did all right, though, except for a negligible collision with a passing girl. Confronting Pilcher, he stood with feet spread a little apart and said into the surprised-looking face, "Want to talk to you."

"Huh?" Pilcher said, his voice just audible in the scream of jukebox trumpets.

"Outside," Ames said, gesturing weightily with his thumb.

Despite a wary look, Pilcher followed him out and was there facing him when Ames, putting a hand on the rough, board wall for assurance, turned around and said, "Why d'you go around saying my brother did it on purpose?"

A little above level with his own, the beaked face caught some light from the high windows. It looked puzzled for a moment, boyish. Then it hardened. "You're Ames Glenn, aren't you?"

Ames gazed steadily at him—steadied by his anger, he thought.

"I say it because it's the truth," Pilcher said firmly.

Trying to keep his words from slurring, Ames said, "What d'you mean it's the 'truth'? What d'you—"

"I mean he tried to hit me. He threw right at my head." Pilcher's furrowed brow implied the opposite of an apology. "That wasn't the first time, either. He tried to before that, but I was lucky and ducked it."

"It's a dirty, goddamn lie," Ames said, removing his hand from the wall. "Why would he try to?"

Pilcher looked squarely at him. "Because I outhit him. That's why."

Ames was conscious of the screaming music and voices from the windows higher up in the wall. He was conscious also of something unreal about his anger. Still, in the same angry voice, he said, "You got no way t'know that. Something you *think*. It's a low-down—"

"Hell I don't know it. I saw his—"

"You're a low-down bastard," Ames blurted. He had already decided to hit Pilcher, but when he swung, aiming at the beak, his blow seemed a listless one. He did not even care much that he missed. Pilcher's fist hit his jaw solidly, then his mouth. They were hard, jolting blows, but they were painless. And so was the ground on which he found himself lying. He knew now that he was not in the least angry, but he had an obligation, and with the wall to support him he struggled to his feet and swung at Pilcher. The same thing happened, the same pair of jolts to his head and the same horizontal ground, like a rerun. He got up in the same way, too, and prepared to swing again. But there was a difference now, there was no Pilcher to swing at. Instead there was a crowd of boys encircling the empty space in front of him. He flattened his back to the wall and looked from end to end of the crowd, but there was no Pilcher. When somebody said, "It's all over, Ames, you scared him away," followed by laughter, Ames realized that he was standing there with his fists still raised.

A couple of uncertainly familiar people tried to help him, but he elbowed them away and, presently, was out in the dark alone, walking. He walked slowly, very tired now, with a sense of something ominously heavy hovering above his head. What had his horoscope said for today? He had not even read it. It was Cam's he had read.

He had no idea what time it was when he approached his house.

The aura from the lamps illuminated streets as empty as streets in a dream. He made his way to the back porch door and fumbled for a time before he could find the knob. When he had got in and got the door shut behind him, he reached out for the wall. He must have been turned wrong, because he missed it in the dark, losing his balance. The fall did not hurt, but he knew it must have been noisy. On his hands and knees he crawled to the staircase and got a hold on the banister post. Then a light came on.

His mother stood at her bedroom door. He started to rise and, halfway, gave it up and sat down on the steps. She continued to stand there looking at him. Presently she said, "You might as well crawl on up to your room. You are nearly there."

He said nothing. He looked down, then propped his head in his hands. In a moment he heard her steps withdraw. They came back again, approached him, and he felt her hand on his head, lifting it, and a wet cloth firmly pressed against his face. For a while, as he sat with eyes shut, hearing her breathe, she continued to dab the cloth around his lips and along his cheek.

"What is the matter with you?" she quietly said.

"Had a fight," he breathed, knowing this was not what she meant.

"I take it you didn't win," was all she said, and took the cloth away and straightened up. "Go on to bed."

He did not move and neither did she. She stood there with her arms, bare to the elbow, hanging straight at her sides. "It's one o'clock."

Ames remembered that he had just now heard the clock strike. Its ticking loomed in the stillness.

"Have you seen Cam tonight?"

Suddenly he seemed to have no resistance against what he was about to say. He clenched his teeth. Then he said, "I think Cam was in on that."

"On what?"

"Killing that colored boy." He was staring at the floor where her bare feet stood. Presently he saw the toes of one of her feet twitch, and all of a sudden it seemed to him that he had just now uttered an unspeakable obscenity. He imagined her face aghast with it. He could not raise his eyes to look. Her voice came to him as quietly as something out of his own mind:

"How could you bring yourself to say such a thing?"

"Because . . ." He found himself floundering as though he had been caught in an act of incredible malice. "Because it's his kind of thing. I've seen him do things like that, just like it. And he hated Stevens. You don't know him . . . what he's really like. You *don't*. He's—"

"Be quiet!"

An oblique, retreating glance showed him a face he had not ever seen before.

"I know my own son. Both of them."

"But you don't," he said faintly. "You haven't seen him do those things. That boy was killed with rocks . . . that somebody threw at him. And the Pilcher boy wasn't any accident. Cam—"

"You *are* drunk, aren't you?" she said in a tone that stopped him cold. He felt his raw lips touch, and the hard contraction of his throat. Some moments passed, slow beats of his heart that he felt in the swollen flesh of his lips. Her voice was low, but the note of astonishment was plain:

"Do you really hate him that much?"

"I don't," he answered abruptly, lifting his eyes halfway, to where the knotted cord defined the hard slimness of her waist. His raw lips touched again. Quickly he put a hand to his lips and said, "I got this from Pilcher."

He heard the clock ticking. At length he saw one of her feet move slightly, but this did not lead to anything. It seemed a great while later when she said, "He didn't even have a reason to do such a thing. You're just upset. Go on to bed, it will look different in the morning."

He felt an immense weight of exhaustion. He reached out for the banister and, without looking at her, got up and started climbing the stairs. But halfway up, as he rounded the curve into the darkness, another impulse seized him. Gripping the banister he looked down at her and said, "Do you remember the last time we all went to church—all three of us?"

Her upturned face did not look blank. She was just waiting.

"A couple of months ago?"

Still she waited.

"Do you remember what the sermon was about?"

She turned her face a little aside, as though to remember. "No," she said.

"It was about the stoning of Stephen in the Bible."

There was a moment, time for three or four ticks of the clock, before she said curtly, "What of it? Most people know that story. Go to bed." She turned away and waited by the light switch at her door until he went on out of sight and the sound of his feet was audible in the hallway overhead.

4

It had kept Hester awake almost all the rest of the night. Not that she gave any credit to Ames's fantastic suspicions. These, whenever they came to mind, she rejected for the outrage they were, without a second thought. But how could he say such things? It was not malice. She knew him better than that. In any case, what could have been the purpose of such words unless he believed them to be true? No, he believed them. But how could he? What was the matter with him? He had been drinking heavily, of course, as she knew he often had this summer, but that did not explain it. It was better explained, she sadly thought, by a certain absence in him of a faith that ought naturally to have been there—faith in his family, in himself. He seemed, like so many others now, not to know what he ought to believe in. It showed up everywhere, in him and the others too, exactly as if they all had been born minus some organ that had used to be a part of the human anatomy. And so their instability before any stray wind of thought or opinion that happened to blow upon them. This explained it better. Given Cam's nature, and maybe a tiny bit of basis in some of those rumors, Ames simply had not had anything with which to defend himself . . . But Cam was his brother, still!

Brothers, she thought. The word did not mean much anymore, a cant word. How different the two of them were, so far apart. If she could but infuse in each one something of what the other had—more of devotion and loyalty in Ames, a greater openheartedness in Cam. Cam. There was no denying a secretiveness in him, a door somewhere that he would not entirely open even to her. And yet he loved her—she was sure of this—loved, and honored her in a way that Ames had never done. Almost as she loved him, she thought. And yet that secretiveness. And those rumors. She thought again of the Pilcher boy. "Yes ma'm. But he did hit me on purpose."

Between the drab yellow walls of a hospital room divided by a screen, he lay with his head in a white bandage against the whiteness of the sheet. The bandage covered his brow, almost covered his eyes, and appeared to be secured in place by the high, hooked nose at its lower margin.

"Please don't think that. It only seemed that way to you . . . He's awfully sorry," she said, repeating Cam's words to her as best she could remember them.

Presently: "He hasn't been here to say so, has he?"

"But he will be. He's coming this afternoon," she said, planning that it should not be a lie.

But she saw no response in the boy's face. When he spoke again, it was to thank her for the pot of roses that already had sweetened the air.

She remembered thinking, after Cam had paid his visit that afternoon, that this had ended the matter. But it had not. The ugly talk was still going on, and still, as she knew now, John Pilcher was the source of it. It must be that he was the jealous one, or he could not have ignored Cam's explanation. How could he? Was it only because of her years that the store of malice in her fellowmen seemed greater than it used to be?

About dawn Hester had fallen asleep at last and had waked up feeling somewhat better. In any case she was glad for the distracting chores that lay ahead of her this day—the shopping, the session with her lawyer, Aunt Minnie to be visited—and in order not to see the boys, she left early, taking the car. Although she felt a little tired, the morning's business revived her spirits. When noon came, she did something she rarely did, had lunch at Irving's down on Bayliss Street. Afterward, in the shelter of one of his artificial palms, she sat for a while chatting lethargically with the old man, bemused by the tic that kept his spectacles hopping on the bridge of his nose. When Mr. Irving started to bring up the matter of Stevens, she lightly dodged the subject. Even the sight of Mrs. Delmore, with another woman, strolling past along the street as if it were her private footpath did not spoil Hester's mood. Somehow, though, it did remind her that there was a meeting of the Heritage Society this afternoon and, further, that she had forgotten about the duty assigned to her.

Because of the nap she took when she got home, she arrived at the meeting a little late, in a sort of detached and fragile mood that cast on the most familiar things an unaccustomed light. It seemed to her, for instance, as she got out of the car in front of Mary Talbot's, that at some time she had seen precisely this house, with its pink brick and stained redwood front and its tubular bay window, in a picture show, or maybe featured in a woman's magazine. She had the same feeling when, assailed by Mary's welcoming chatter, she passed through the vestibule and down two steps into the long, rustic living room where a circle of some twenty faces, her age and older and younger too, greeted her with smiles. They were all long familiar. She knew something about even the history of expressions on certain faces, the darkness surrounding Edna Traynor's eyes, the drooping, painted, embittered lips of old Mrs. Halleran. Why, then, did she feel as she did—as though this meeting were something vaguely fictitious into which she had intruded, sitting down at a fictive table in front of the bay window and opening, in a businesslike way, an insubstantial minute book? It all seemed as if it might have some connection with a dream that had vanished when she awakened from her nap.

By the time Hester got her thoughts at least partly engaged, a new candidate for membership was already under discussion. Jane Willingham, the sponsor of whoever it was, was saying, "She's just the kind of person we want. And she has all the requirements. Her grandfather was a captain under General Hood."

"That's old Wayne Groat's granddaughter, isn't it? From out at Bethel?" Mrs. Halleran's voice was deep and powerful, silencing the others. She sat very erect, her black-satined bulk all but hiding the chair, and closed her eyes when she spoke.

"Yes, I think it is," Jane said warmly.

Mrs. Halleran closed her eyes. "My father told me he saw old Sam Groat the day he first came into this country in '65. He was carrying a peeled walking stick and a bag on his back." She opened her eyes again.

"Oh, I don't think so," Jane said, creases spoiling her tall, flawless forehead. "I'm sure you have him confused with somebody else."

"Hmn," Mrs. Halleran said and closed her eyes.

Hester deliberately allowed her attention to drift away from the argument. It was a rule she had never liked anyhow—that a member must have a direct ancestor who had fought in the war—one she had tried, if not very vigorously, to have abolished. After all, this was not the point. The point was . . . But suddenly she felt as if she no longer really knew what the point was. "To preserve our heritage." This was the assumption with which she had joined, under a little pressure from friends, when the society was organized two years ago; and this was the assumption which, ever since, she had vaguely entertained. Yes, this was the point. And these were her people, who had honored her twice by electing her as secretary, the keeper of their common history. She looked at the minute book, the pen in her hand. But nothing, it seemed, had yet been resolved about the candidate in question, whoever she really was. Obviously Mrs. Halleran, looking more erect than ever, was making a fight of it. Hester withdrew her attention a second time and began slowly turning back through the pages of the minute book.

"Resolved": her eye read, "that the Marker Committee is directed to place, on Highway 34 at Post Ford Creek, a plaque commemorating . . ."

". . . that the cannons around the Confederate monument be polished . . ."

". . . that Mrs. Andrew Biglow be issued a formal invitation to . . ."

". . . a plaque commemorating . . ."

". . . that the fence around the Confederate cemetery be . . ."

". . . Mrs. Wallace Morton be issued . . ."

". . . a plaque commemorating . . ."

Hester stopped turning the pages. She had remembered something unpleasant, something about the Confederate monument. It was at the luncheon yesterday. Mrs. Delmore's remark, quoting her husband, to the effect that the monument should be replaced with something relevant to the times. Hester shunted the memory out of her mind. She let her gaze wander to a picture on the wall above where Helen Cate, with her prematurely cotton-white hair, sat conversing in an undertone with Edna Traynor. Hester liked the picture. It was of a river tinted by rays of the evening sun and, on the other side, a rolling meadow that drew the eye into hazy, limitless distance. It made her think of hearing bells over water. Jordan, she thought, would look like that, with bells ringing from across on the other side. Wasn't it something like this that she had dreamed about today? Maybe the fields at Fountain Inn rolling down to the river?

"Hester's woolgathering," someone said.

There was some sympathetic laughter at her embarrassment, an embarrassment compounded when she realized that now was the time when she must confess her dereliction. She had been named head of a committee of three assigned the job of inspecting the old Brownfield house with an eye to buying it as quarters for the society. Being the birthplace of General Luther Brownfield it was desirable for historical reasons and was, in addition, close enough to town. *If* the house was still sound, and capable of renovation at not too great a cost. This, of course, was what she was supposed to have seen to and somehow had just forgotten. "I just plain forgot it," she said with a feeling of vexation not reflected in the courteous faces directed at her. At least there was the one redeeming fact that she had gathered a little information about the house from Mark Denny, the bank president. "Mark *thinks* it can be bought," she said. "It's heavily mortgaged and the Handleys, who own it, don't have anything. Of course he doesn't know that it can."

"It can," Mrs. Halleran said resonantly. "Money talks."

"Yes, but it doesn't talk to everybody, remember," Hester said. "That house is in their family, I think. They may be attached to it."

"Money talks to everybody," Mrs. Halleran said, closing her eyes. "Hold it out to them, they'll take it. Their kind can't afford sentiment."

"Oh, I don't think we have anything to worry about there," Martha Ludlow said. "People like the Handleys are not stopped by that kind of thing." On her long-fingered, silken left hand, drooped over the end of the chair arm, a pair of diamonds throbbed like stars. They engaged Hester's eyes unpleasantly all of a sudden.

"What *are* they like?" Hester said, trying to submerge her little rush of hostility beneath a tone that sounded merely listless.

"Oh, you know. Poor and trashy. Henry knows about them. Not the kind to turn down money for feeling's sake, anyway."

"Who *is?*" Jane Willingham said laughingly.

"I think you are, Jane," Hester said, conscious how her rather pious manner did not suit the occasion. "I think all of us here are."

"Oh, don't let them push *me* too hard," Jane said, ignoring Hester's tone.

This was banter, of course, and it was Hester's mood that made her thoughts fall with such weight upon the remark. Still, did it indicate something? She thought of the old Willingham place standing high above its surrounding fields, the finest of them all. There was the new rubber plant to come, that planned to locate somewhere on Jane's side of town. Suddenly, perversely, the someone her mind's eye saw on the Willingham's front veranda, flinging a braceleted arm about, was Mrs. Delmore. Hester said, "Well, if we mean anything real, we'll just have to push right back."

The remark fell all too weightily. It produced only, here and there, politely acquiescent nods.

"Hester's an old stick," Jane said, smiling to pass it off, and Mrs. Halleran took advantage of the interval to revive the question of admitting old Wayne Groat's granddaughter to the society.

Hester found, when the meeting ended, that she had written nothing in the minute book, for after that brief period of participation her feeling of remoteness had come back. Again she had the sense of something fictitious, and as she closed the book she had to reject the thought that the blank page for today was expression enough for what had fallen on her ears. But she would fix it later. It was her duty. And so, still, was the Brownfield place. But the feeling did not pass off as she stood conversing, over coffee and cake, with this or that familiar face. And probably it was this feeling that made her seem to perceive in their manners toward her an ever-so-slight reservation. Even in the goodbyes of Mary Talbot, she felt it, wondering, as she passed through the door, if she would enter this house again.

But of course she would. Nothing had happened. These were her people, as ever, she told herself as she drove along, turning into Forrest Street. It was only the stress of yesterday's events that was affecting her. Again she put these out of mind. Driving around the square she glanced up at the monument, the little Confederate facing south with his gun. She glanced at the cannons. Yes, they were polished now, shining black. But then, instead of turning onto Hampton Street, she completed the circle and headed back out Forrest toward Grimley Road. She would see to the Brownfield place right now. Thinking of Martha Ludlow with the pair of diamonds on her finger, Hester experienced a little pulse of new-risen anger that made her press down on the gas pedal somewhat more heavily than was her custom.

Not far beyond the city limits, on the other side of a gas station, the gravel road turned off. Across a field of bursting cotton she could see where the road bent sharply as it entered the woods, and very soon she had a glimpse of a house through the trees. Rolling to a stop out front, she looked it over. Except where the dirt lane entered and then spread out into a bare area close to the steps, the yard was solid weeds. There were several oak trees, two of them blasted and dying, and a large, full-blown cedar to the right of the porch. The house, with scarcely a trace of paint remaining, was winter-gray, but otherwise it was, like her own, typical: a pair of columns with balcony halfway up, a central hall with rooms to either side, and kitchen at the rear. The house looked plumb, she thought. She did not see a sign of life, but she drove in anyway and stopped in front of the porch. Then she saw a girl of maybe fifteen standing under the cedar, holding a baby.

"Is your mother at home?" Hester said from the car window.

The girl's cropped towhead indicated no. Her round, pink underlip hung slack, giving her face a vaguely startled look.

"Are you the only one here?"

"Yes'm," the girl said and looked down at the sleeping baby in her arms.

Hester made a few other inquiries, with uncertain results, and then asked if she might look around the place a little.

"Yes'm, I reckon it be all right."

Hester was uncertain what she had expected—surely not to find the place well kept. But neither had she anticipated finding such a condition as this, the kind of neglect that only the basest sloth could breed. Here and there a board was missing, like wounds in the side of the house. What window screens survived were rotten tatters, and many of the panes had been replaced by pieces of cardboard and rag. Around back she saw the remains of the kitchen steps lying detached from the rest of the house, in their place a chunk of yellow stone. On the ground lay refuse—tin cans, bottles, cobs, and blackened cabbage leaves—over which flies crawled and a few bantam chickens pecked.

Around on the other side, between the house and the ragged margin of weeds, she stopped and stood for a while. At length she decided that those fragments of stone protruding out of the weeds were the remains of what had been a fountain once, and somehow this impressed her as the saddest sight of all. A rooster crowed, a thin, quavering, far-off cry on which the stillness closed down again like a weight of cotton batting. Through oak foliage overhead, sunlight fell in tired gold spangles on the ground, and with clarity she remembered that in her nap today she had dreamed of Fountain Inn, her father's old home.

The girl, still holding the baby, was peering into Hester's car. As Hester rounded the corner, the girl stepped back guiltily and tried to appear absorbed in the business of rocking the baby in her arms. It was fretting now, a pale, thin baby in a soiled-looking diaper. Noting the bare chest and shoulders, Hester said, "It may be getting a little cool on him now."

"No'm, he ain't cold." The girl continued to rock him in her arms, looking gravely down at him, pouting almost.

Presently Hester said, "Has your mother ever taken him to a doctor?"

"No'm."

Hester paused. "Is your mother here?"

The girl shook her head.

"Does she work?" Hester asked.

"I don't know'm. I ain't seen her since I was just little."

"Oh," Hester said. And then, "You mean the baby is yours?"

"Yes'm."

Hester was still digesting this when she saw the blush that now had appeared in the diverted face, quickly suffusing the girl's cheeks and temples. Then she understood. Quickly her eyes took in the rounded softness of the girl's limbs, the full, pink underlip. A vague alarm, whose origin Hester herself did not instantly recognize, made her ask, "What's his name?"

"Billy," the girl said faintly.

Hester, observing the blush still in her face, dropped the subject.

The ridiculous little start of alarm she had experienced now lingered only in her memory, like a shame. To banish thought of it, she looked toward the house and said, "Tell me, was your mother a Brownfield?"

"Ma'm?" She looked up a little furtively with pale blue eyes at Hester.

"Was your mother's name Brownfield before she married?"

"No'm. It was . . . Baxter, I reckon."

Waiting, Hester gazed at the house, thinking suddenly that its weathered face was the very color her own mind cast over desolate memories. "And you don't know the name Brownfield at all?"

"I can't recollect nobody named that."

"He was a general in the Civil War," Hester said rather mechanically, looking at the house. "He was born here. You are some kin to him, I think."

"Well, I sure never known that," the girl said, shifting the baby. "The Silver War."

"That's why I'm interested in your house," Hester said, still looking at it, thinking that now her interest in it had no life anymore. But she had come to inspect the place. "Would it be all right if I went in and looked around?"

"It ain't very clean," the girl said, after a pause. "But I don't reckon it'd hurt nothing."

No, it could hardly hurt anything, Hester thought, as she stood, moments later, in the wide, bare, and gloomy hallway. There was as much lath as plaster showing on the walls and ceiling, and some new-fallen fragments of the plaster lay scattered about. In the scarred floor there were broken places, with rude boards nailed over them. The whole frame of the door on her right had been torn away, and the aperture suggested the work of a man with an ax. Thinking vaguely how the plan was exactly that of her own house, she went from door to door of the rooms, peering in at the few iron cots and beds, at chairs with missing arms, at staggering tables. Even the mantels over the hearths were gone—sold, she guessed, for their mahogany. There seemed to be little sense in her climbing the staircase, which lacked a banister. Just for thoroughness' sake she did it anyway.

Except for litter, there was nothing in any of the four upstairs rooms. The one she entered had a large ragged hole in the ceiling, and she discovered, by looking directly up from beneath it, some pinpricks of light in the roof. So the roof, probably, was rotten. Someday, she thought with satisfaction, it would come down on their feckless heads. She felt a board give beneath her foot and she quickly stepped forward, which put her in front of the window, where she stopped.

She stayed there at the window, looking down, a breeze through a broken pane touching her face. That was indeed the remains of a fountain down there. She could pick out other fragments of stone and trace its circular shape in the weeds. The quavering rooster crowed again. Her mood of reverie had come back and she closed her eyes, trying to form in her mind an image of how that fountain must have looked. What she got was an image of the one at Fountain Inn. When finally she dismissed it and turned around, there was a man leaning in the doorway.

The start she gave had left her quite mute. The man did not speak, either, and the little smile on his mouth did not reassure her. But even had it been a smile to trust, it would have been belied by the way his short, thick body blocked the door. As to his body, there was more exposed than she liked to see. His shirt was unbottoned nearly to his waist and through a bristly pelt of mingled rusty and gray hair the flesh looked sickly white. Still Hester pulled herself together and, with a fair semblance of coolness, said, "Your daughter told me it would be all right if I looked over your house. I'm not—"

"It's all right," the man broke in, in a voice that was pitched higher than she would have expected. "I don't mind a bit, just help yourself. I'm afraid it's not so clean, though, like your house is." His gaze slid down her and across the floor, and his smile took on a vaguely deprecatory shape. It was perhaps mockery. She observed the shrewdness in his puffy face, with signs of little dewlaps starting. She quickly said:

"I didn't come just for—"

"It's just I was mighty surprised," he interrupted again. "I never had looked to come home and find Miss Hester Glenn in my house. You're welcome, though."

Her body stiffened. Would he move if she made straight for the doors? Clearly shaping her words she said, "I'm only here in behalf of a group I belong to. They thought they might be interested in making an offer for the place if it was in good enough condition."

The man seemed to give a sigh, shaking his head and looking around him. "I'm afraid it ain't in too good condition. It's awful old and ain't been kept up good like yours has. 'Course I ain't had your money to," he said, letting his pause work while he looked up at the hole in the ceiling. "It's a right historical old house, though. It was a Silver War general borned here. Which you knowed, though. You could buy it and fix it up just like it was when the general lived here. Put all them pretty things in it like you got in your house." His gaze glanced off her face and roamed about as if he were picking locations for new furniture.

Still Hester hesitated. It was not only that her revulsion kept her at this distance. She also feared that her most determined advance would not be enough to move him out of her way through the door. In the momentary silence she heard, faintly, the girl's baby crying. The man, looking at her again, said:

"You got some pretty things in your house, too, I'll say that. Pretty as I ever seen."

She wondered what he was getting at, but she kept silent.

"I bet you don't even recollect me ever being in your house. I bet you don't even recollect my name, do you?"

"Handley," she said, for prudence's sake, feeling as if she were compromising herself.

"Hollis Handley," he said, with a little nod to introduce himself. "I done some painting work in your house once, two year ago. You don't recollect that, though, do you?" He paused a second. "I know you don't recollect me from a kid. You seen me plenty, though. You've rode by me a heap of times in that buggy with your daddy. Had a gray horse. I reckon you never noticed me, though."

"I have to leave now," Hester said with all the ice she could summon, and shifted her stance as if to move. Handley gave no sign of noticing. He stood exactly as before and said, in the same dubiously earnest voice:

"But you know, times is changed though, now. It ain't hardly the same like it used to be 'tween the poor and the rich people. The poor is still poor and the rich is still rich, but the young ones don't pay it much mind anymore. They're more democrat-like. Now you take that boy of yours." He paused. She stared at him.

"He don't pay one bit of attention to rich and poor. Him and—"

[redacted]

#5536

"Which boy?" she said, against her will.

"That baseball-playing one. Cam. Him and my boy Pike is thick as thieves. Come right in my house and set down and eat with us just like he was part of the family. Don't care no more than nothing about it being a poor man's house and things kind of run-down. Ain't been a week since he was here. So you see, you ain't the first of your family in my house. And welcome, too."

A feeling of weakness had seized her, and the idea of forcing her way through the door was suddenly an impossible one. She seemed to have the strength only to stand here listening for that baby's cry again. Was he listening too? There was no change in his posture and no sign except what his deliberate pause might or might not be telling her. But the cry did not come. Now Handley shifted his posture and, putting a bare, hairy arm up against the doorjamb, said:

"Naw, it ain't the same anymore. The rich and the poor is teaming up. Got to. Else the black niggers be taking everything over—yours and mine, too. Getting more smart every day and the gov-er'ment right in behind them shoving. No ma'am, we got to see to it—all of us has. 'Cause it's going to have to be some niggers showed a thing or two." He paused again, slowly blinking eyelids which, as she noticed now, looked thin and membranous, as if when shut they might only inhibit his vision. "We already done showed the first one, I reckon you noticed."

Who did? Hester's mouth said, but it did not make any sound. The sickness rising in her quickly reached a point at which she knew she must in some way act—scream at him or thrust him bodily out of her way through the door. Instead, in a voice whose constraint astonished her, she asked the question aloud: "Who did?"

"Well now, I couldn't say about that . . . 'Course I got my ideas, but I ain't—"

"What ideas?" she said, her breath faltering.

"I wouldn't want to say," he said, looking at her more intently than before. "Unless I knowed for sure. But whoever it was, they was shore-God doing all us white people a favor."

"I have got to leave now." This came from her suddenly, on the same burst of impulse that set her moving straight toward him—a first, a second, and a third step. It was then that the board gave way.

[redacted]

She recognized as pain the harsh sensation in her ankle and felt only the jolt when her knees and one hand struck the floor. Then she was being lifted up by her other arm, hearing his voice as from a little distance. There was something about her ankle. Looking down, she saw blood, the stocking lacerated. "Ain't but just a little old scratch," he said. "And your stocking tore." This was when she became suddenly, vividly conscious that he had bent down and put a hand on her ankle. Violently she snatched her foot away and, though she staggered a little, found the doorframe with her hand and gave herself a steadying push into the hall toward the stairs.

Hugging the wall, she descended at a pace that she knew to be reckless. But he was behind her. She heard his footsteps, gaining, and then his voice close to her, as unruffled as if he were squiring her down at his leisure, saying, "You better take some care down these steps, Miss Hester. Wouldn't do for a lady like you to have a fall . . . in my house. Let me he'p you a little bit, Miss Hester."

She reached the lower hall and then the door and the porch steps down into the late sunlight. And then her car. Somewhere he had left off his pursuit, but the vision of him at her elbow, with a mock-courtly hand to assist her entering, did not pass until she felt the car door shut tight against her side. He was standing on the porch. She saw that without looking. Whatever it was he called out to her was obscured by the sound of the engine. Yet she knew, as she drove rapidly away, that his words were an invitation for her to return.

Where the sign at the highway said "Stop," she made herself obey. There, staring into the rear-view mirror at the straight road behind her, she sat waiting for her pulse to recede. It did presently, but this left her mind not much clearer. Impressions hovered in a sort of opacity and kept yielding to irrelevant details of the landscape—the hanging, orange sun, the field of cotton, a truck passing by on the highway in front of her. Gradually she became conscious of pain in her ankle and she noticed again the blood and the torn stocking. She could not go home this way. Remembering the gas station just down the highway, she set the car in motion once more.

It was a dim rest room in the side of the building and here she removed her stockings, placing them in her purse, and with paper towels washed the blood from the cut on her ankle and also washed the place where his hand had touched. Over the washstand was a tarnished mirror which, as she stood combing her hair, reflected an image strikingly pale and ghostly. And the bright lipstick she applied, accenting its pallor, made her think of a spirit with painted lips. For a minute or two she stood wholly preoccupied with her reflection, oppressed by it. Then, heavily, she went back to her car.

By the time Hester got into town there was something very definite on her mind, a thing that had seemed irrelevant at first. Now it quite seized her and caused her to miss her turn onto Forrest. When she did get back to the square, she parked in one of the spaces along the curb and sat there in the car trying to deal rationally with her new compulsion. Presently, yielding to it, she went into Lawson's drugstore, to the phone booth at the rear. It was but a moment until she had the Pilcher's number. But then, standing tightly enclosed in the narrow booth, she listened for a space to the humming over the wire before her finger sought the dial.

At the second ring, a male voice answered. "Is this John?" she said.

"Yes ma'm."

But her name brought silence. She could envision how his mouth had gone sullen, as it had that day when she had visited him in the hospital. The wire hummed. Faltering, she said, "I didn't call about what happened last night." And then, against his silence, "I was just wondering . . . You are all right now, aren't you?"

"Yes ma'm, I'm fine," he said faintly.

"I was just wondering . . . if my son Cam ever came to visit you while you were in the hospital?"

"No ma'm."

"Are you sure?"

"No ma'm, he didn't come."

There was another silence.

"I thought he had," she said finally. "He was going to."

"He didn't, though. I haven't seen him," John said in a low, sullen voice.

Hester wet her lips. Then, with an effort, "Please don't . . . don't think he did it on purpose."

But there was no answer.

"Goodbye," she said.

She did hear a dimly audible goodbye drifting back to her as she took the receiver from her ear and placed it on the hook. Afterward, she stood for a long time in the soundlessness of the booth.

5

Where's Mama?" Cam said. He was standing in the door from the dining room to the kitchen, wearing a T-shirt with the word "Cougars" printed on it. His clean, pale blue jeans fitted like skin to his trim hips and thighs, and his spotless white socks and tennis shoes gave a sort of radiance to his feet and ankles. It was the tennis shoes, Ames thought, that made him walk so like a cat.

"I don't know," Ames said, over the plate of scrambled eggs he was eating at the kitchen table.

"Where's Willodene?" He had a folded newspaper in his hand.

"It's Wednesday," Ames said and went on eating.

"So, no supper." Cam hesitated, his gaze on Ames. He entered and, dropping the paper on the table, walked around Ames to the refrigerator. Ames was conscious again of how quiet his footsteps were. It seemed that he had heard only the plop of the newspaper and, now, the click of the refrigerator door as it opened.

"What's here?" Cam said.

"Eggs," Ames said in a murmur. The sun had gone down and the ruddy afterglow from the west window was diffused among shadows gathering out of the corners of the room. And just now, Ames felt, there was some way in which he would have preferred that Cam not be behind him. Yet this was foolishness. One moment's listening to Cam's irritable puttering among the contents of the refrigerator expelled the feeling wholly. All day it had been so with Ames, tides of apprehension giving way almost suddenly to release. He wished that his mother would come home.

"Crap," Cam said and the door clicked shut. There was a rattling of paper and then Cam appeared with three apples and a butcher knife clutched in his hands. He deposited them on the table at the other end from Ames and, sitting down, began to carve the apples. His blade moved deftly, flickering with light from the window. Each apple was halved with exactness, the core sectioned out, and then the halves were split. But there was a little slip. Cam cursed under his breath. Then, for just a moment, both of them sat gazing at the small runnel of blood that appeared on Cam's left index finger. Cam raised it to his mouth and held it there thoughtfully. Then he returned to his surgery on the apples.

"Did you see me last night?"

"A few minutes of you." He heard Cam bite into a piece of apple. The remains of the egg were hard and getting cold.

"Gave up one hit," Cam said, chewing. "Went to sleep on that one." Then he said, "Look," and unfolded the newspaper and pushed it down the table to Ames. It was open to the sports page. There was Cam's name in a headline and, underneath, an action picture of him with his hair flying.

"Who won?" Ames said.

"We did. It says right there, doesn't it? Four to nothing. I made one of them. And two other hits."

Ames pretended to read the blurring print. Cam was chewing audibly. Ames could see his clean, muscular arms resting on the table and see his face bend down to the piece of apple in his hand. His teeth showed white when his mouth opened. As he chewed, lean cords of muscle straightened and sank relentlessly in his jaws. When Ames pushed the paper aside without comment, Cam looked at him for a moment and said:

"What happened to your mouth, anyway?"

"It got hit."

"Yeah. Who hit it?"

Ames hesitated. "A friend of yours."

"Who?"

The remnants of egg on Ames's plate looked knotty and unpalatable. "John Pilcher," he softly said.

The sound of chewing stopped. Then it started again. "That son of a bitch," Cam said. "What were you fighting him about?"

"The family honor, I guess."

Cam's brow knit, drawing a faint line between his eyes. For the moment he looked a little like their mother. Then he laughed, the small, dry, gusty laugh that seemed to be the only kind he had. "That was noble of you. You lost, though, it looks like. To a high-school kid."

Ames was silent. He knew Cam's contempt for a loser.

"I guess he was saying I tried to kill him," Cam said, still smiling.

After a moment, "Did you?" Ames quietly said.

The smile went away. He looked level at Ames, his face cold in the gathering twilight. "Don't start that shit with me."

It made Ames pause. He found that he had to summon a little boldness to continue: "That's what he's sticking to. He says you had tried to get him before . . . Because he was a better hitter than you."

"I don't give a goddamn what he says. Or you either. Or anybody." He picked up another quarter of an apple.

"What about Mama?" Ames suddenly said.

"She doesn't think that." He was holding the apple short of his mouth. "Does she?"

"I don't know," Ames answered. He was increasingly conscious of the growing dusk.

Cam bit into the apple and chewed for a moment, the working of his lean jaw muscles now almost obscured. "He'd better stop saying it, though." He swallowed. Then: "He's not a better hitter than I am. I've hit .386 this season. His is .379. So he's lying. He'd better stop it."

All this was said in a calm, explanatory voice that somehow increased its effect on Ames. For a space he put off saying what he now intended to say. "What if you had killed him?"

"I'd have cried," Cam said.

Ames sat looking at his plate and heard again the sound of Cam's white teeth rending a piece of apple. From the cold place around his heart he felt already a new impulse rising. He glanced at the newspaper. Then, as a diversion, he got up and scraped the remains of his egg into the garbage pail and set the plate on the counter. "I wonder where Mama is," he said vaguely. There, an arm's length away, was the hanging light above the sink. All at once he reached out and switched it on. Cam blinked at it. Deliberately Ames walked back to the table and, seating himself at an angle to Cam, proceeded to turn through the pages of the paper. He found it at the bottom of page one.

He did not read it. He sat with his eyes fixed on the heading, calculating his words. Then he opened his mouth and said, "I see they buried Otis Stevens this morning."

"Yeah," Cam said. "So what?" He stuck the last bite of apple into his mouth and chewed it.

"So, they buried him."

"They always do that to dead people," Cam said, and swallowed.

Ames kept looking at the newspaper. "You know, I was out there right after they found him. With Larch."

"You were, huh?" Cam rose and picked up the apple cores off the table.

"Pretty gruesome," Ames said.

Cam stepped to the garbage pail and dropped in the cores. He took a dishrag from a hanger over the sink and proceeded to wet it. "How'd he look?"

"Rotten. With a chain around his leg."

Cam squeezed out the rag. "I wonder who did it."

Ames paused. Then, "Some scum," he said and felt how his throat had stiffened.

Cam finished squeezing out the rag and came back to the table. Picking up the knife, he began intently to wipe the tabletop where he had been eating. "Well, whoever it was, you can't say they didn't do us all a favor."

"The hell I can't." Furtively he watched Cam's face.

"I haven't seen you crying. Or anybody else."

"You haven't looked, then."

"Shit," Cam said. "Who? I mean white people."

"Most of them. Mama, for one."

Cam took one more swipe with the cloth. "No she's not—not inside," he said and turned back to the sink.

"In fact I never saw her this sick about anything," Ames said, raising his voice a little.

"Not down inside, she's not." Cam turned on the water and with the rag started to wash the shining blade of the knife. "She hates them. It hasn't been a week since we both heard her cussing them."

"You know better than that. You know what she's done for them. That was about school integration."

"Same thing. Down inside she's not sorry." Cam dried the knife with a towel and put it carefully in the rack, then proceeded to wring out the dishrag. Ames watched him, that cold feeling now a sickness at his belly. And it was this distress that made him say, with a bluntness he had planned to avoid:

"Well, anyway, they're going to catch them. Venable's already got a lead."

Cam had been arranging the dishrag neatly on its hanger. Now his hands stopped. "Does it say that in the paper?"

"Larch told me," Ames said, untruthfully.

"What kind of lead?"

"He wouldn't tell me. Just that they had somebody in mind."

"Who?"

"He wouldn't tell me that, either."

Cam's hands now rested on the edge of the sink. After a moment he turned on the faucet and began to wash them in the stream. Just above the sound of the water he said, "It sounds like a bluff to me. Anyway, Venable's not the kind to push a nigger killing. He hates them too. He'd lose his job if he did."

"I think he will," Ames said. "You don't know him. And he won't lose his job, either."

Cam went on washing his hands. Then, "Crap," he said, but he said it in a subdued voice. He turned off the faucet and with his back to Ames stood for a little while carefully drying his hands on the towel. But when he turned around, his face told nothing. Once more it was quite the boyish, arrogant face Ames knew. "Well, I don't give a shit one way or the other," he said. "I'm going to get a hamburger." With this he turned and went out the kitchen door, banging the screen behind him.

Moments later Ames heard the car door shut and then the blast, magnified within the garage, of the unmuffled engine. He followed the sound of it onto the street, past the kitchen window and then, with a surge of noise, around the corner toward the square. To get a hamburger. The tension in Ames's belly was a rejection of the thought. Was that where Cam was going? Or out to find his buddies, whoever they were now, for an evening's drunk on Rafe Quinn's moonshine whiskey? No, not "drunk"; Cam was never that. He might come home and fall asleep in his car, as Ames had found him several times, but this was almost the only outward sign. Somehow he seemed, when he drank, only the more himself . . . Whatever that was.

Ames stood up. He felt a need to do something, and his answer was to switch on another light in the kitchen. It did not help. For the first time since those childhood nights in the dark hollow stillness of his room upstairs, where he had been forced to bear it alone, he imagined the house ever so dimly astir with presences too feeble to utter themselves. Where *was* she? He thought of the telephone in the darkness of the hallway, and hesitated just for a moment. But no sooner had he taken a first step toward the dining-room door than he heard her car turn into the driveway.

When she entered he was seated again, pretending to look up from the newspaper under his hands. She stopped inside the back kitchen door, the crease vivid between her eyes, and blinked a little at the light. He thought she looked pale. And the way she stood blinking, her purse dangling from an arm that hung straight at her side, made an attitude hard to associate with her.

"Have you had anything to eat?" she said in a voice unexpectedly normal. It was his own that seemed altered:

"Yes. Did something happen?"

"Isn't Cam here?"

"He went out a minute ago. To get a hamburger."

"I'm sorry," she said, letting her gaze come back to him. She meant, he realized after a second, that she was sorry for her neglect. "Have you had enough?"

"Yes."

He saw her draw a breath. Then, more like herself, she walked across and set her purse on the table. The crease between her eyes was like a bloodless open wound.

"Did something happen?" he repeated.

"A little something that upset me," she said, looking toward the refrigerator. "There are some frozen chops. I can thaw them in a minute."

"What was it that happened?"

"It doesn't concern you." She went to the refrigerator and took a package out of the freeze compartment.

"I don't want anything else," he said almost angrily.

She unwrapped the package nevertheless and, moving to the sink, held the frozen meat in the stream from the faucet. It was then he noticed the cut on her stockingless ankle.

"What happened to your ankle?"

She did not answer. Instead, as though it had taken this much time for his earlier protest to reach her understanding, she suddenly turned off the faucet and wrapped the hunk of meat in its paper again. Putting it back into the refrigerator, she said, "Do you know somebody, a boy, named Pike Handley?"

Ames thought a moment. "I might. I think he's Junior Handley's little brother. Why?"

"You've never heard of his being a friend of Cam's?" She continued to gaze into the open refrigerator.

"God, I hope not," Ames said, barely conscious of the offensive expletive, which she did not seem to notice. "If he's anything like Junior."

"What about Junior?"

"Just sorry. Every way. I think he's gone from here now. Where did you hear that?"

"I heard it," she said and at last shut the refrigerator door.

"Why won't you tell me what happened? If it's about Cam it concerns me." He was conscious again of the crease, like a bloodless wound between her eyes.

"If there was anything to tell you, I would." She picked up her purse and, showing him her straight back, went out the dark doorway into the house.

It was his dismissal and squelched his impulse to call after her. In a moment he could not hear her footsteps anymore. Getting up, he walked nervously to the screen door and stood there. A breeze came, fanning his cheeks, cooling the breaths he drew into his hot, tense nostrils. A sudden poignancy, as if that breeze came from a long way off with its hint of frost and late roses and tawny, falling leaves, emptied his mind of thoughts. What and where was this place that teased his memory so? He could walk out of this house, this town, and not ever set foot in either one again.

He did go out of the house and to the garage, but it was with Cam on his mind once more. The keys were in her car, deliberately.

In the darkness he felt them with a kind of oblique and distant rage at her steadfast rejection of the facts. He backed the car out and drove to the square and turned left. Three blocks down Beech, he stopped in front of The Pit. There were half a dozen cars parked on the asphalt lot outside the building. None of them was Cam's. And the same thing was true down the street at Wally's.

Ames was unsure, but he could not afford to ask. His first turn off Grimley Road was a mistake, and somewhere on a pitted gravel road, between a thicket and an empty field of sage, he turned the car around and drove back. His next try, beyond the gas station, struck him at once as more likely. Soon, through trees, he saw a light. Driving slowly, he rounded a curve. And there it was, a pale hulk in the starlight, one window dimly aglow. But he dare not stop and the darkness prevented all but the perception that there was some kind of a car parked in front of the house.

At a safe distance beyond he sought a place to turn around, or to stop. Almost immediately he saw, on his left, the surviving traces of a lane into the thicket and he quickly slowed and turned in. Then he gave a start that made his foot slip from the clutch. The motor choked out and, in the stroke of stillness, he sat staring down the beams of his headlights. Through a thin screen of weeds and brush the blue rear end of a car was visible—Cam's car: the decal of the cougar's head stared back at him from the window. Presently, not far away from his face, leaves rustled in a gust of wind. Then the thought that Cam—and Pike Handley too—might be watching him from the woods came like a second alarm. In one flurry of movement he started the car and backed it onto the road and drove off in the direction that took him away from the house.

It had seemed to Ames, in his room that night, that he had heard his brother come home not once but many times—had heard his car enter the garage and, moments later, his footsteps on the stairs and the crying boards of the hall outside his room. All but one of these, of course, he had dreamed in his fits of sleep, but he still did not know with certainty which time was the real one. It was not the time when he had seemed to hear his own door stealthily tried. He had dreamed that, he knew, because for many minutes afterward he had lain there in the dark, raised on an elbow, listening for a sequel that never came. And when was it that, watching from the closet window at the rear of his room, he had seen his mother? Here was another of the night's confusions. He was still not entirely persuaded that he really had seen her out there at the entrance to the garage, in her bathrobe, made visible in rays of streetlight filtering through the leaves. Doing what?

It did not matter. What mattered now was a plan that had come to him in the first minutes of daybreak. It had taken hold and had become, finally, a kind of obsessive game, like a puzzle, of which his mind would not let go. Fully dressed he paced about his room or perched nervously on the edge of his bed. A curious and, as he knew, false elation came at last. In the end it was purely accident that he did not encounter anyone as he made his abrupt exit from the house.

But how to find Pike Handley? It was only by analogy with Junior that Ames supposed him to have quit school long ago and to hold a laboring job somewhere. He turned out to be right, but without risking inquiries he had to look until past noon before he found the place. It was Curry's lumberyard on the west side of town, one of the last places he could think of to look. Later, recalling those moments as he had approached it, he reflected that it was, in any case, the last place he would have tried. That strange, perverse enthusiasm had quite deserted him by then. For a long time, as he walked on from place to place, he felt it draining away. Now, approaching the lumberyard in a kind of flat exhaustion, he looked it over like a man who fears that a missile may strike his naked eye. Reflecting the billows of rain clouds overhead, occasional tides of shadow darkened the earth. And just as he drew near, the towering stacks of lumber were veiled in a sudden, stark-gray light.

He could hear the big saw screaming on the other side of the yard, but the stacks of lumber blocked his view. They made a shelter, suddenly. He stopped and, resting a shoulder against a rough wall of boards, thought that he would just stay here a while. The sun came out again, a splash of light. He heard a clatter of boards and then a voice. He had to remind himself that he was not hiding, and this seemed to be his one reason for moving on down the avenue between the stacks to where, in an open space, three men were loading a truck. One of them was white—and he was not yet quite a grown man.

Ames's impulse now was to retreat. He thought he might have

done so had not the boy, for some reason, turned around and looked at him—with a look that narrowed as it touched Ames's face. Ames knew him. It was Junior again, thinner, but with the same low, bushy hairline and tight ears and small, keen eyes. Ames did not think that he made any overt sign, but the boy, after that moment of dead pause, seemed as if he had perceived one. He started walking across the space toward Ames. The two Negroes, after a second's half-curious scrutiny of Ames, went back to loading the truck.

The boy stood facing him. The yellow crowns of his lower teeth showed above his lip, and beads of sweat stood all over his hairless face. His eyes, set on Ames's mouth, had right now the intensity of a bird's. Ames found that he had forgotten his own speech.

"You want me?" the boy said softly.

"You're Pike Handley, aren't you?"

The boy just stared at his mouth.

"I'm Cam's brother."

The small eyes blinked. "I thought you was," he said, in nearly a whisper.

A clattering of boards seemed to drive away the words that had almost come back into Ames's mind. To fill in he said, "Cam sent me to tell you something."

The boy's gaze lifted a degree, seeming to fasten on the point of Ames's nose. Ames's words came back to mind:

"He said get rid of your shoes—right away. The sheriff found a footprint out there."

The boy looked suddenly down at his shoes—big, scarred brogans loose around his sockless ankles. When he looked up his face seemed pale, but his small eyes gazed straight into Ames's own. "I don't know what you're talking about," he said in an undertone of defiance.

A clatter of boards sounded again. But it seemed to be the saw, screaming from across the yard, that dissevered his thoughts from each other. All of a sudden a cloud shadow enveloped them. "Out there where he found the nigger buried. You'd better get rid of them right now."

The boy's gaze had recoiled, shifting away, but it came back again. "You're crazy. Cam didn't tell you that."

"You'd better believe me," Ames said.

The small eyes, glaring with what looked as much like fear as outrage, did not waver this time. "I'll go ask him . . . Soon as I get off work."

"Hey, Pike," one of the Negroes called from the truck.

"What you think you're doing?" the boy said harshly, still in an undertone. He broke the pause by turning suddenly and, with a kind of stiff deliberateness, walking away toward the truck.

Ames watched his tense back for a second. He withdrew and, circling the lumberyard, stopped in sight of the space by the office where three old-model cars were parked. But half an hour later, Pike had not appeared. Did it make any difference that the boy was wary, sharp like all his kind? No, his face had been enough. The desolate certainty with which Ames walked away was not any the less because his trick had produced no final proof.

6

It had come suddenly upon Hester in the night. For the first time since she had lain down, the restless stirring of her limbs had ceased, and afterward she had grown as still as if the thought had impaled her on the bed. Other thoughts, the ones that had possessed her until this, merely hovered now, or approached and retreated before its intensity. Not even the lack of faith with which she had charged herself, which she had deplored in Ames, raised any guilty scruples now against the action on which her mind was fastened. Lying still in the darkness, while the clock ticked on, she waited. And presently she heard him, the sound of his car and, soon, heard his quiet footfalls on the back porch, entering, and up the stairs and in the room above her.

Later, with her small flashlight, in soft, stealthy slippers, she had made her way out of the house. Then she did feel a little guilt, for when had she ever stolen about, like a thief in her own house, while the others were sleeping? But this thought only touched on her mind and was forgotten as soon as her hand had let the screen door close behind her. A few deliberate steps and she stood before the garage in back of her car. She would need her key. In the narrow space between her car and Cam's, where fumes from his engine still tainted the air, she opened her door and felt in the dark for the switch. Taking the key, she went back to the trunk. She had trouble directing the key into the lock, and in the faint glow drifting from the street, she saw that her hand was trembling. The key went in, the lock snapped, and the trunk door rose of its own accord. She had the little flashlight in her hand. Its beam showed her the spare tire, the tire tools fastened in place, and nothing else. The tow chain was gone.

It had not been in Cam's trunk either, or inside his car, or anywhere on the floor or hanging on the walls of the garage. There was no mistake. She had looked again in first, full daylight, even climbing the perilous wooden rungs up to the dusty attic overhead. And this time she did not neglect the toolroom on the back of the garage or, at last, the basement of the house. There was no mistake. The old chain that had been in her trunk was nowhere on the premises.

So, what now? Nothing? But this was the very thing she could not endure. Until midmorning, however, pursuing her daily routine about the house—dusting and sweeping and making beds in a sort of daze that made her think of someone acting the part of himself in a play—she did endure it. Then a decision sent her quickly to her room for a change of dress, and half an hour later she was turning into a parking space beside the courthouse.

The sun appeared from behind a cloud and flushed the courthouse wall a dazzling white, and Hester did not know who it was that spoke to her as she walked around to the rear of the building. The door to the sheriff's office was three steps down. Entering, she had immediately the sensation of having passed into an underground vault where torches low overhead gave down a meager, uncertain light. As her eyes focused, a figure appeared. It was a woman facing her from behind a counter, waiting upon her expectantly.

There was no delay. She was led past several desks and a uniformed man who nodded at her. In a moment she was seated in a little room, the door shut, gazing with some confusion at Monk Venable who was still courteously standing beside his desk, and saying, "Well, Miss Hester, I ain't seen you to talk to in a coon's age." He was a small man, with stooped shoulders and a face whose simian features the years had rather accented. "Like I see you around a lot and keep thinking, I'll just go up and talk to Miss Hester, about old times. But seems like I never do." He smiled warmly at her.

His slow, country way, in no hurry to get to any point, had half distracted her. It made her think of their school days, of little Monk with his country talk and his patched, outsize hand-me-downs. Even now, she noticed with feeling, his khaki shirt was a bit too large.

"You know, Miss Hester, I was thinking about you just the other day. You remember that time at school you pulled Hank Turner off of me? Saved me a *real* licking." He smiled again.

She smiled, herself, now, nodding. The single window, at ground level, was blocked by a dense laurel bush, and somehow the room, for all its cluttered desk and steel filing cabinet, made her think of a hiding place in deep-green, summer shade. There had come a sudden poignancy that almost obscured her intention.

"You were mighty good to me. Looking out after me all the time. A little old hick like I was. I appreciated it, too."

"That was a long time ago," she said, still wanly smiling.

"Yes, it was." He settled a hip on the edge of his desk and thoughtfully stroked the bald scalp over his forehead. "It was. And you look at the difference now and it seems even longer. You don't know anymore what to look for next. We even got new kinds of meanness."

So suddenly did her consciousness respond that he might have touched a raw place in her brain. She took a breath and, noting how the room had closed in tight, said, "Are you going to catch the people who killed the Stevens Negro?"

"If I can, I am," he said, his smile fading. "With some luck."

She chose her words. "But you are trying?" Immediately she saw the reproach in his flat, blue eyes and she felt wounded by her own cunning.

"You know me better than that, don't you, Miss Hester?"

She nodded, checking her eagerness to assure him. Lying was not so easy a thing.

"I hope you do. It being a black man wouldn't make me lay off. This here was a *mean* thing. Mean as I ever saw."

She felt her tongue grow thick. Shifting her gaze, she tried to draw some calm from the laurel bush at the window. Monk helped a little by getting off the desk and seating himself in his chair.

"Do you think you can catch them?" she said with an effort.

Monk looked down. "Tell you the truth, Miss Hester, I ain't got hardly anything to go on." He picked up a quartz paperweight and stroked it with his thumb. Intently she observed his thick, discolored thumbnail. "They didn't leave nothing. Nothing but that old piece of chain there." His thumb gestured. Instantly, as if the chain had been a snake coiled on the bottom shelf against the wall, her gaze hit upon it. Then she could not take her eyes away. Faintly she said:

"That's what they had him tied with?"

"That's it. On his leg. Tied to a tree so they could bust him with rocks. Like it was done for sport. That's what makes me think it might have been boys that done it."

For just a second she thought that she was in danger of fainting, but even then she did not take her eyes away. It might or might not have been her chain: chains all looked alike.

"But there's a heap of boys around here. I questioned some, but it didn't turn up nothing."

She made an effort that seemed as great as any in her life. "There's no way to trace that?" she said, and looked straight at him.

"The chain? No, ma'm. You can't hardly run down an old piece of tow chain, been used a lot."

She looked at the laurel bush. "Then you really don't have anything to go on?"

"I'm mighty afraid I don't, Miss Hester. So far. I'm just counting on something turning up. I hope so, there's a lot of mad colored folks around. It's a bad time for something like this."

Hester felt now how tightly her hands had been clenching the handle of the purse on her lap. Had he noticed this? . . . his eyes were quick. With a cunning that even now made her feel shame, she said, "That's what I was thinking. I just wanted to talk to you about it. It's upset me a great deal."

He nodded his understanding, and lest they be too much, she held back other words that were rising to her lips. He said:

"You let me do the getting upset, Miss Hester. I get paid for it."

She felt a kind of gloomy warmth approach and withdraw before her tension, and she gave him a smile that felt vaguely like a spasm of muscles in her cheeks. "I'll try," she said.

The time had come: despite the fear of her weakness she got to her feet, managing it fairly well. She was careful not to glance at the chain again, and she thought that she made no boggle as he opened the door for her and from the doorway bid her goodbye in his courteous, country way. The outside door had closed behind her before she felt the extent of her weakness, and the three steps up required an effort that made her pause for a minute or two with a hand on the blinding courthouse wall.

It was curious how her mind had stopped working. On every other subject it was fluent enough, but here, on this matter of Cam and the chain, it met a kind of barrier. The effect, however, like a blind spot right at center of her vision, did bring a certain release, finally. Before going home she had even done her grocery shopping and, at the cash register, had stood listening to herself exchange pleasantries with the ruddy and benign Mr. Fitzhugh. At home, after her brief lunch, she set Willodene to polishing silver in the kitchen, standing by for a little while to oversee the process. Even to Willodene's "Well, they put po' Otis Stevens in the ground for good yesterday," she responded only with a moment's pause and the quiet words "Yes, I know," in a tone that ended the subject. The boys were not at home. But even to this knowledge she responded with only a vague sense of relief.

She found, however, once she had lain down on her bed for a nap, that her mood had deceived her. She was tired, more than tired enough. But what she now discovered was that she feared to surrender consciousness to the sleep that was stalking her, untuning one by one all the nerves of her body. For consciousness seemed her one defense, and she opened her eyes and forced the sleep away. There were things, daily matters, to engage her mind. But these did not come. Instead she watched the changes of light in her room as drifting clouds veiled and unveiled the sun. Filtered through the curtains, the grayness brightened into a rich lavender that her mirror caught and held like an oval window opened against an exotic sky. For a space of only seconds or, again, a minute or two, the glow would persist; then it would die out, revealing once more in the mirror's gloom images of a bedpost and a woman's bare, severed foot. In time she heard slow steps on the staircase and, recognizing that they were Ames's, went back to her musings again.

Later, perhaps much later, there was a knock so faint that it barely intruded upon her. She had not said anything when the door opened. There was Ames. He closed the door behind him and faced her in the shadowy light. She did not know what started her pity, but it came in the form of an impulse to embrace his lean, uncertain head, to hide between her breasts an expression that had troubled her too often. He was a child again, coming in to confess to her the little sins on his conscience. Rising onto an elbow, she held out a hand to him.

Ames approached, but he did not take her hand. Then the sun came out, and she saw that his face was not as she had seen it in the shadows. It made her heart pause. Waiting upon his lips, she saw how their tension left them spare, drained of their color. He started to raise one hand, apparently, but he did not. In a low, harsh voice he said, "He did it, Mama."

She looked away from him. The mirror's face shone lavender again and distantly she thought of such an impossible sky.

"He did, Mama. He and the Handley boy." His voice kept on and the words were clear enough, but still they fell as against a barrier that stopped them short of the center where all their meanings could come together. She heard his voice falter, then resume. In almost the same words he was saying it over again, telling about last night and today. His voice, however, was different this time. His tone was a plea, and her pity came rushing back. Looking at him, she reached out and took his hand. It was limp, and maybe the throbbing she felt was the beat of her own pulse. After a little silence he said, "What are we going to do?"

"About what?" she said, and gripped his hand. Immediately it seemed, as by a mere contraction of her will, that a calm had closed on her tremulous nerves. She found she could speak almost with conviction. "It's not true. You don't have any proof, nothing but suspicions. Imagination builds things up, sometimes. Because of other things. He could not have done this."

Ames's gray eyes looked as if dilated. She knew how she must have sounded. Letting go of his hand she said, with all the conviction she could master, "But I'll find out for sure, to put you at ease." Then, on inspiration, "And I don't want you worrying, I want you to go on back to school."

He continued to look at her that way. "How, find out?" It was a low, curious voice, almost scornful in its tone.

"I'll find out," she repeated. "And I want you to go back to school. This afternoon."

"You know I can't."

"This afternoon," she said. Summoning her strength, she sat up on the side of the bed, causing him to step back a little. She saw him blink. "It would be much better for now. So please go on."

He blinked again. She saw his lips twitch, but nothing came. Abruptly she stood up, facing him with an air of command meant to be intimidating. His gaze declined very slowly from hers. Without speaking he turned and walked to the door. But there he stopped, his body going rigid all at once, and in the same instant she heard footsteps outside and then a voice, Cam's voice: "Mama."

"Yes."

"I won't be here for supper. We're playing the last one tonight."

Ames stood with a hand still poised above the doorknob. "When will you be here?" she said.

"I don't know. After the game."

"All right."

They listened to his steps and heard the screen door shut.

"Will you please go now?" she said to Ames. "Go back to school."

His hand came to rest on the doorknob. He did not look at her. There was only the nod he gave as he opened the door and went out.

In the past hour thick clouds had covered the sun, shedding through the windows a gloom like winter twilight. From the kitchen she heard Ames leave, without stopping to say goodbye, heard the front door close behind him. Already, because Hester had not wanted to face her, she had let Willodene off for the day, and now she was alone in the empty house. It brought her no comfort. In fact, as she soon felt, it seemed a strange emptiness, suggesting a deserted house, or one into which she had merely intruded. And her pacing from dusky room to room felt in some remote way like a violation of each separate threshold. She considered going out into the yard, but then she remembered that Lucius would be there. What if he should come to the door? She would not answer his knock. Or any knock . . . But it could not be true. Cam had not done this thing. She would discover in time that he had not.

The irony of what happened a little later appeared to her, in the moment when she opened the door, like something designed by her fate. She had meant only to get her newspaper, which would be lying just outside on the steps. Instead she confronted a woman there, with hand upraised to knock. Recognizing Mrs. Delmore, Hester could not say anything at first. Mrs. Delmore, however, if she noticed, seemed entirely unruffled. She smiled, showing large, even, milk-white teeth. "I was by and just thought I'd drop in and see you a minute. *And* your house. I hear it's *so* lovely."

Hester could only admit her, with some words of hospitality that barely did achieve utterance. While Mrs. Delmore gave voice to small but repeated exclamations, Hester led her into the sitting room and then across to the parlor. The bracelets on Mrs. Delmore's wrist tinkled with her gestures and the little curls at back of her head seemed newly frosted. From across a sort of distance these things registered on Hester's attention. And so did Mrs. Delmore's immaculate fingertips which, as if instructed by her words of subdued praise, brushed lightly over the backs of chairs and table surfaces and frames of pictures on the walls. But the moment was approaching. On the back of the massive walnut chair by the fireplace, Mrs. Delmore's hand stopped. "It's almost like a throne, isn't it?" she said with a smile. "May I sit in it?"

"Of course," Hester said, and watched Mrs. Delmore seat herself with her hands on the carved armrests.

"It is like a throne." She smiled up at Hester. "Is this where the 'Old Massa' sat?"

"I suppose so," Hester said. She read this as the opening shot and found that she was standing with her arms folded across her breast, her mother's posture. There was a certain strength in this last thought, but almost immediately it was dissipated by Mrs. Delmore's saying, "Do sit down and let's talk."

There was nothing for Hester to do but seat herself in the lyre-back chair facing Mrs. Delmore and wait with tightly folded hands. Justly or not, she felt a certain effrontery in the way this woman's eyes surveyed the room.

"This *was* a plantation house, wasn't it?"

"No, it was my great-grandfather Cameron's town house. He built it in 1850."

"My! A hundred and seven years old," Mrs. Delmore said, looking around again. Perhaps the irony that Hester thought she perceived was not really intended; in her anxiety she felt unsure of her impressions.

"Was all this his furniture?" Her gesture made the bracelets tinkle.

"Some of it was," Hester said.

"Everything certainly seems to be in perfect condition. Was the house built by his slaves?"

"Yes," Hester said.

"How many slaves did your grandfather have?"

"A hundred or so, I think. My great-grandfather."

"Heavens!"

The way this was delivered made Hester think of a small, contemptuous puff of breath in her face. The woman had come for this. Not only this, however. There was more in the offing, and the realization of it was what now brought down on Hester a kind of helpless feeling she had known in dreams when nameless things were overtaking her. It was why she could not make any response to this small display of malice. She only sat there with her mouth dry and waited for the thing that she knew would fall upon her at last.

It was a little while coming. There were disjointed remarks about the town and the weather before the topic of Tuesday's luncheon appeared. By this time Mrs. Delmore had leaned back in the chair and extended one plump leg out onto the floor. She smiled complacently, speaking of Mary Lassiter's discomfort at "our little disagreement about Negroes." Hester waited, feeling in some indistinct region of her mind hatred for this woman, and then heard her say, quietly, "I'm afraid events have supported *me,* though. I have never heard of anything more brutal than that murder. What kind of people would do such a thing?"

For all her preparation, Hester was not equal to the moment. She thought her face must have paled and she knew her eyes had retreated, kept retreating, under the woman's gaze. "I don't know," she said, but she said it feebly.

"Something will just have to be done in the South, you know. We simply can't have this kind of thing in our country."

All the replies standing ready in Hester's mind seemed now without any weight. Even this house did not support her. Features of the room as familiar as her own hand had suddenly an air of exhausted arguments, as if her touch had worn them all past use.

"Will they try to catch the ones that did it?"

"Yes," Hester said almost mechanically. "They are trying now. Of course."

"I haven't heard about it." She looked straight at Hester now, without even blinking. "Would the killers be punished if they were caught?"

Hester looked back at her. The woman's gross effrontery had made an impression somewhere in Hester and it seemed to be the cause of the answer she gave with more firmness than she had anticipated. "Yes. Of course they would be punished." She was about to repeat it, even, when Mrs. Delmore said, with a lift of her plucked eyebrows:

"Well, I hope so. Kirk Qualls is going to publish a piece by my husband in the *Herald*. Horace is chairman of the Citizens' Committee, you know, and they want to see that something *is* done about it."

It's been only two days, Hester thought to say, and did not say it.

"Everyone is invited to join the Committee, you know," Mrs. Delmore added. "I hope you will."

She waited, but Hester's only answer was a murmur intended to be obscure.

Mrs. Delmore, with a little click of her tongue, pulled in her leg and suddenly stood up. "Well, sorry to stop in and be such a bore. I love your house."

Hester managed to rise with at least a little dignity and show her out.

The door was shut now, the house was empty. Yet, standing there, Hester had some moments of curious uncertainty as to whether Mrs. Delmore was not still with her, still seated in the walnut chair. In fact, to see that the chair was empty she had only to look at it there in the parlor, standing thronelike near the hearth in dismal cloud light from the windows. Nevertheless the image of the woman survived with such a clarity in her mind's eye that Hester need but look away to believe her still seated in it, with a plump leg thrust out into the floor. The effect was distressing to Hester. She knew that she could not, as long as the image persisted so, cast off this feeling of displacement. She actually entered the parlor and shifted the chair to the other side of the hearth. It did not help. Indeed the altered balance within the room seemed only to intensify her sense of loss. Several times she shut and opened her eyes, as if this might purge whatever haze was disturbing her perspective.

It was the thought of purging that all at once put the words back into her mind—words that her own lips, not many minutes ago, had solemnly uttered to Mrs. Delmore: "Of course they would be punished." She uttered them again, and again saw the plucked eyebrows in response skeptically lift. "Well, I hope so," the woman's cool voice had said. The shame of it rushed upon Hester. Details of the conversation flared on her mind with a lucidness that sent the blood into her neck and face. To be helpless before such a person, shamed by her in one's own house!

But what of Cam? To think of him taken publicly. To see this thing that she was suffering, that now had fastened like something alive upon her brain, dragged out for all the world to gaze on. Cameron Glenn. That name in headlines? Bear it? She did not think that she could. . . . And not only she. Aunt Minnie, her cousins Lance and Sarah, all the Camerons and Woodruffs and Glenns in Nashville and Montgomery, wherever they were. The dead ones, even. Might not they, her father and mother, in some way know, know what had come to pass in their house? The image of what her father's wrath would be made a vivid pause in her thoughts.

No, it could not be true! The denial came rushing up inside of her. What followed was like the slow recession of a nightmare, and in its wake a brightening. Where was the proof? An old chain missing from her trunk? Did she not know her own son, her Cam, who had been her baby? It was not possible that he had done this thing, not Cam. She who in her mind had so reprobated Ames—where had her own faith gone? Here was shame upon herself. But this thought gave her no pain. With an almost wild exuberance at her heart she turned and hurried back to the kitchen to fix Cam's supper.

7

The western sky partly cleared in the minutes before sundown. Against the violent blue, great billowing clouds were hues of pink and indigo and gold. The kitchen streamed with light. Enamel surfaces had a tint of rose and her bare arms the kind of glow that belonged to a young child's flesh. There had been such evenings at Fountain Inn. There had been emerald hills after rain at sunset and flaming roosters on the fences crowing and haystacks far out in the fields like heaped-up crowns of brazen hair. It was as if, by God's own hand, reprieve had fallen upon her in the kitchen at sundown. After all, Cam had not done it. She knew this now, knew with a mind as cleansed and lucid as the evening air.

She would fix his supper. There were things he relished in her pantry—smoked ham with the rich heart not yet touched, late corn from Lucius's garden, tomatoes so bursting ripe they glowed in the shadows behind the pantry wall. And he would come in with his tanned flesh also glowing, and his radiant feet, and devour plate after plate, while she looked on and felt her heart swell with a pleasure that ached inside her breast. With a burst of enthusiasm she set to work, shucking five ears of corn, making biscuits, carving the big ham. It was a violet twilight that gathered on her busy hands, and then a denser, silver gray. Not until the last daylight had faded did she remember, suddenly, that he would not be in for supper.

Leaving things to lie as they were, she paced the kitchen. It would be late before he came, interminable hours. If only he would enter now, to laugh away or to banish with his anger the last, insubstantial doubts that she now realized still were hovering in back of her thoughts. She would not mind his anger, his justified reproaches. She would humble herself. What she could not face were the hours of waiting alone in this empty house. Without another pause she went out to the garage and got into her car and drove away.

There was no one on the square. She passed around the lighted monument and headed south into the street down which the soldier's blank, concrete eyes were gazing. It took her past the rows of venerable houses, shadows with luminous windows, set back behind intermittent screens of maple and magnolia foliage. A turn brought her, at length, up past Prince's Chapel and the Beasley house and then Darnley's Cannon in its little sanctuary at the crest of the ridge. To avoid the area of new houses, built and building, called Darnley Estates, she turned right onto Morgan and issued finally into Grimley Road. She crossed the railroad tracks and passed the city limits sign and still drove on. Where was she going? Turning the car around, she drove back into town.

She stopped finally, after driving past her own dark house, at the Torbert house and sat there undecided for a minute or two. Aunt Minnie would be at home. She was always at home, snug in her two little rooms. The old lady had an air of living like a small, dim sea creature in the confinement of her rear apartment, and it was this, partly, that made the thought of her presence comforting to Hester. She was Hester's father's elder sister, a spinster, who had survived all her family. Now she sat with her crocheting at the window all day and looked out at a birdbath and an elderberry bush, and remembered. Sometimes she would interrupt herself to fix tea, on a delicate silver tray, with tiny hand-painted cup and sugar bowl, painted by her own hand years ago. Or if Hester was there, Aunt Minnie would produce an identical cup for her, crooning her pleasure in the service, recalling teas of fifty years ago. Hester got out of the car and walked around to the apartment at the back of the house.

Because it was night there was no view through the window of birdbath or elderberry bush. The old lady, however, was all the same at her eternal crocheting, as though she had whole families of trembling souls to keep in scarfs and sweaters and hoods. The gooseneck lamp she used had a powerful bulb and a drenching light that set her small, intent figure in vivid isolation from the relative gloom surrounding her. It made her white hair radiant, put a sheen on folds of her black satin skirt, and caused the texture of her frail wrists and hands to resemble the ivory of old piano keys.

"You look beautiful tonight, Aunt Minnie," Hester said, feeling her anxiety withdraw before her surge of emotion.

"Heavens, child. An old woman like me?" But she looked pleased, letting her hand pause a moment. "No, I'm afraid beauty is something we all get over having after we're young."

"That's not true," Hester said. "You have it. More than they do. A kind they don't have."

"Well, you are sweet to say so." Aunt Minnie set the hook in motion again. A silence fell. The lamp accented the palsied trembling of her head and her fragile, tedious hands, as if the life still left to her was a flickering sort of thing, a candle in the wind. Any gust might put it out. Hester's anxiety welled up again. She said, "What are you making?"

Aunt Minnie, at some little expense of trouble, held it up for inspection—a muffler, in dark green. "It's a muffler. I'm nearly through with it. Do you like it?"

"I think it's lovely. What do you do with them all, Aunt Minnie?" Not that this was really a problem. At her rate of work, what with all the unraveling required, each piece was a kind of Penelope's web for the old lady. She completed successfully maybe ten in a year.

"Oh, I just make them for the family. I think I'll give this one . . . to . . ." She broke off, and Hester could imagine the names, some those of dead people, flickering across her mind. Which were the living ones? In the thought of Aunt Minnie's confusion there was something warm for Hester, as if kindly spirits were hovering very near. Aunt Minnie said, "I think I'll give it to Cameron."

"I know he will be pleased." Her anxiety would not keep in abeyance. "He likes pretty things."

"Though he never comes to see me anymore," Aunt Minnie said, crocheting again. "I wish he would."

"You know how it is with boys that age. Always too busy," Hester murmured, thinking of him.

"He's such a fine boy. So handsome. And smart."

"He won the scholarship prize in his class last year, you know," Hester said, her pride flaring briefly. "And he's the star of the city baseball team." He would be playing now, throwing the ball with such great speed that no batter could hit it—dangerous speed.

"He is a Cameron, all right. Like all the Cameron men. It's Ames who is like his father." Aunt Minnie hushed with a kind of abruptness, and Hester saw the dim, timid glance that stole her way. She did not mind now. She had rather that even this be the subject.

"Yes. He is a Glenn. He looks like Thomas's brother Henry Glenn."

Aunt Minnie crocheted on for a moment. Presently something stirred her lips, and when the words did get uttered, her voice was faint and apologetic. "You don't ever hear anything about *him* anymore, do you?"

"No. Not in years. He could be dead now, for all I know."

"But his family would have heard."

"He dropped his family a long time ago. And most of the Glenns are gone from here . . . Anyway, it doesn't matter," Hester added, sorry that even now she had permitted this topic.

Aunt Minnie sighed. "Such a pity. He seemed to be such a nice, gentle boy. He could have been—"

"You know what he was," Hester said in a voice that made Aunt Minnie turn to her crocheting again.

It seemed to Hester now that, except for this one she could not keep back from her mind, there were not any subjects left. She was grateful, after a minute or two, suddenly to hear Aunt Minnie's voice start on another topic. It was a matter of the church. "They want to move it. Out, somewhere. I don't know why. I voted against it. I know you did."

Hester had heard something of the wrangle. Now she remembered that it had been brewing even months ago, reminding her that for a long while she had not been paying much attention to the church. Her own ballot must have come in one of those recent letters she had not opened, but she nodded anyway, because she would vote no.

"Why do they want to move it? From the old building?" Aunt Minnie said, looking with bewilderment at Hester.

"It's that same crowd. And that young preacher," Hester said. "They only live for something new and different. But you won't have to move," she went on. "There are plenty who won't. And there are plenty of other preachers. It's probably the best thing that could happen to the church, to be rid of those people."

Aunt Minnie seemed comforted, and soon she had slipped back into memories of earlier days. But somehow Hester could not follow her any longer. The words came and went in her ears, leaving filmy images soon dissipated on currents of her anxiety. It was a surprise when she saw the muffler, suspended at two corners by Aunt Minnie's tremulous hands, held up for her approval. "It's all finished. Do you like it?"

"Very much."

"I hope Cameron will like it. Will you take it to him for me?"

"Of course I will," Hester said, taking and carefully folding the muffler with hands that also were a little tremulous.

When Hester entered her house that night she did not lay the muffler down. As she waited, moving with restless steps from room to room, she carried it still. And even when she wandered out into the yard, the folded muffler was in her hand. She would offer it to him and say, "Aunt Minnie sent you this." And then . . . What would she say?

In the space where the yard chairs were, she finally sat down to wait. This was the place where she usually came in times of distress, but it brought her no comfort now. In fact it seemed strange and curiously ominous that here, closed in by the shadowy masses of shrubbery higher than her head, there should come to her ears with clarity sounds not audible in the past. Dim motors hummed from unexpected directions, and there were voices that could not have come from only the residential blocks surrounding her own. Even the sound of a B&N train clear out at Rainbush was once audible to her for a minute or so. But the strangest thing of all was to hear, finally, the clock on the parlor mantel strike eleven. Never before, she was certain, had the sound of it reached her out here. There was something unnatural in all this, as if the acuteness of her ears had exceeded the human limit.

The clock struck again, eleven thirty, before she heard him coming. It was precisely as she had so many times already imagined it—the rumble blocks away of his unmuffled engine, louder as it entered Hampton Street, approaching, with flicker of headlights through the foliage as he passed by out front; a lapsing of sound from beyond the house as he turned left at the corner; the rumble loud again, flare of light in the trees, and, finally, in the garage, sound dying away in the echo of one outrageously magnified blast. An interval of weakness held her back for a minute.

He was already upstairs when she entered, and light from the hall above drifted down the stairwell. Standing at the foot of the steps she heard his tread, heard it cease. The interval seemed long, with only the ticking of the clock, before his steps resumed—slow, uncertain steps that approached the head of the stairs. She saw his white feet, and, for some moments, nothing else. They moved again, his legs and torso descending into view, and then his head. He saw her at once. With a hand on the rail, he looked down at her from the high curve of the staircase and said, "Where's Ames?"

"He went back to school," she said, quite clearly.

"I thought he had another week."

"He wanted to go on."

Evidently he could not see her very clearly. She perceived in his face the effort to do so.

"Kind of sudden, wasn't it?" he said.

"Yes. He had some reason."

Cam had quit trying to read her face; he appeared to be looking at his hand on the banister. "I wonder what?" He added quickly, "I had something to talk to him about."

"Was it important?"

Again he made an effort to read her face. "Oh, just some stuff," he abruptly said. "I'm going on to bed now." He turned and started back up the stairs.

"Wait a minute." Then, "Here's something for you," she suddenly said, raising her hand with the nearly forgotten muffler. "Aunt Minnie sent it to you." She let it dangle from her fingers.

His head was out of sight and he had to stoop. "Good-looking," he said. But he did not start down. "Just leave it there on the banister. I'll get it in the morning."

"Don't you want to see it? She made it for you."

"I will in the morning. I'm tired, Mama." His head vanished again and a foot moved up to the next step.

"I want to talk to you."

Still he continued to stand there, a trim white body without any head. Then she was on the stairs, climbing, seeing that he obliquely watched her, watched perhaps her weighty feet mounting from step to step. She motioned him on. When, breathing as if it had been a long climb, she reached his open door, she could not see him in the darkness of the room. Her hand found the light switch inside.

He stood with his back turned, his bare arms resting on the tall chest of drawers, and in the mirror before his face his eyes regarded her. They had a dull, resentful expression, exactly as if her intrusion was an abuse of his rightful modesty. This disturbed her, somehow. It brought a pause in which the room itself, in all its perfection of tidiness and order, took on a vaguely frightening aspect. She said, "What did you want to talk to Ames about?"

"Just some stuff, like I told you."

She drew a tense breath. "Was it about the Handley boy?"

The eyes in the mirror regarded her.

"Your friend. You've been to his house for meals. His father told me that yesterday."

"Well," Cam said. "That's not anything." He was now looking at the three china monkeys on top of the chest. His fingers rested on one.

"Ames told me about talking to him this afternoon, at the lumberyard."

His fingers held a china monkey. His eyes were veiled, but the line of his mouth was very straight and still.

"Is that why you wanted to talk to Ames?"

There was no change at first—except one that barely registered at the margin of her consciousness: it seemed that the stillness of the house had got into her ears like cotton. Cam's fingers lifted the monkey slightly off the polished surface, but this was all, for a moment. "Yes, that's why. I want to know what's the matter with him. What does he think he's doing? He's crazy . . . I don't know what he might have got you thinking." Except in the mirror he had not looked at her.

"He said you went out there last night, to the Handley's. Right after he talked to you . . . about . . ."

He seemed to be waiting for her to finish, not even watching her in the mirror now. Finally he said, "Well, what of it? I've been out there two or three times. Just for kicks. There's nothing wrong with that, is there?"

Neither one said anything for a space. The stillness in her ears seemed to get into her mind all of a sudden, blocking the passage of thoughts. It was like something she would have to break through, and what came from her mouth seemed to have escaped before her mind could formulate it. "I had a chain in my car trunk. It's gone. The best I could see, it looked like the one in Monk Venable's office today."

The eyes she saw in the mirror were lidded now. His voice, very low, said, "Did you tell Venable that?"

"No." She felt a tide of weakness come and felt as if she literally had taken a step backward when she said, "I couldn't be sure, of course. I only went to see if he had found out anything . . . About the Stevens Negro," she added, bringing it out like some impediment in her throat.

Cam's fingers still held the monkey slightly off the surface of the chest. "Had he?"

"No."

Gazing at the monkey he said, "It couldn't very well be your chain. I took yours out to the river. It's out there on a boat . . . if you want it back. Old chains all look about the same."

The stirring at her heart, which she would still have restrained, seemed to make room for the first real breath she had drawn in all these minutes. In spite of herself she said, "Yes, I suppose they do. I couldn't tell."

"I don't know what Ames has got you thinking," he said presently. "Or why. Unless just because he hates me."

"No. He doesn't hate you. You are his brother."

"Yes he does. He has for a long time. He's jealous of me. That's why he's been telling you lies about me."

"They are not 'lies.' Not on purpose."

"I hope he's not going around telling them to other people."

"Of course he's not. How could you think that of him? He said those things to *me*. It's unjust of you."

"Yeah," Cam said. He turned the monkey slowly in his fingers. "What did he tell you?"

"He was only worried, afraid. Things upset him so."

"Yeah, but what 'things' did he tell you?"

For all her distress she was conscious of a relief that actually had misted the dry lenses of her eyes, and it was this that now made tremulous the hand she put for support on the corner post of his bed. She did not remember the steps that had brought her here; she had drifted, somehow. There was a question to answer. She said faintly, "About how you hated Stevens. His being killed with rocks. Things like your going out to Handley's last night, little things."

"And that's all?"

Still more faintly she said, "And things they say you did. Like the Pilcher boy."

A moment passed. "Yeah, he'd believe that. Or anything about me . . . Got you believing it, too, it looks like."

"I was only afraid," she murmured. "Because he was. I had to ask you."

"All right." His fingers shifted the monkey, arranged it to form a triangular pattern with the other two. "I'm answering you. I didn't do it. I don't even know who did."

A second flush of weakness came, a second breath deep in her lungs. She knew, a moment later, that he had not repeated these words, but it seemed as though he had. Her ears retained the most vivid image of his voice in speech. Still holding to the post, she let her body sink onto the bed. Almost dreamily she answered, "I knew you couldn't have."

For the first time he had turned his head to look directly toward her. He had already turned away again before she understood that his irritable expression was not in reprobation of her lack of faith in him. It was because she was mussing his counterpane. This impressed her; it seemed like something she would remember later. For now it seemed merely a curious interruption. He said:

"I'll bet I know what really got him last night. Me telling him whoever did that, did this whole town a favor. I'm not going to act like I'm sorry it happened. He's a hypocrite."

"That's not fair," she said, trying for a note of reprimand. "And it's not true. That was no favor to anybody, it was horrible. It's . . . *wrong* of you to say that."

His head turned a little and from the corner of his eye he sent a glance her way. "Mama, you can't tell me you're really sorry it happened."

"Please don't say such things. You know better."

"All right."

There was a still moment, a troubled moment that contended with her feeling of relief. Suddenly Cam said:

"Ames is not really on our side. I wouldn't trust him a foot."

"There are not any 'sides' in this. Please hush."

Cam bent his head forward and went on standing there, his eyes in the mirror glass lidded. Presently he said, "Anyway, I didn't do that. And I didn't do those other things, either. Like Pilcher lets on. I didn't hit him on purpose."

Hester averted her eyes, then looked at him again. "Why didn't you go to see him in the hospital . . . as you said you had?"

"Because I didn't want to hear him say that. I wasn't going to beg him not to. Would you have, Mama?"

She did not answer at first. No, Cam would not beg, she thought, feeling her relief bloom up bright in her mind again. "He would have believed you, though."

"Heck he would. People are always telling lies about me. You've heard some of them. A long time ago they said I pushed Tommy Calvert off of that roof. They've been telling them ever since . . . You know why, Mama? Because I beat them at everything. They can't ever beat me, and they hate me for that. So they sneak around and tell lies on me. And people believe them. Everybody does."

"Not everybody," Hester said. Compassion had sprung as suddenly as a stab of pain in her breast. "I don't believe them."

His head was still bent. "Don't believe any of them. A bunch of rotten lies—the whole world is. It didn't used to be, but it is now, Mama." He hushed, stood motionless for a time. "I wish I never had been born in it." She saw that his eyes were shut. When at last he opened them there were tears on his underlids.

She got up from the bed. A step behind him she halted and stood there aching with the impulse to take him against her breast. "Don't think that. It isn't true. You'll see it isn't."

He did not move, and now she did reach out and rest a hand high up on his back. After a while she murmured, "Forgive me." And later, when still he had not moved, "Go to bed now. You're tired."

"All right, Mama."

She remembered the muffler still in her hand. She placed it on the chest beside his arm. From the door she heard him say, "Mama, you quit worrying about all this stuff."

"I will," she said. "Good night." And she heard his faint "good night" in answer as she drew the door tight shut behind her.

PART TWO

8

When Hester was a very young child she had imagined that the Lord had laid it out with His own hand—the patterned garden beside the house, the orchard behind, a fence here, and there a swooping meadow half shady with water oaks. Down the incline toward the gate, as it had done from the beginning, the drive divided itself to pass around the first and greatest of pecan trees. Boxwood balanced boxwood along the front walk and twin urns stood like counterweights at ends of the broad porch step. Who but the Lord could have raised those columns up—and so long ago that the big crossbeam now faintly sagged in the intervals between them? For all his antiquity and his looking, with clipped beard and smoky eyes, a little as the Lord must look, her grandfather was not even born in that far-off time.

She thought that nobody was born then. When God made the house and set down in their places behind it the barn and the smokehouse and the four log cabins across the field in a stand of chinaberry trees, there was not a sound in all the world. Then he made birds and chickens and cows, so that when he made people the sounds were already here, whistling and crowing and bawling in the fields. Then he made people: the white ones first, to live in the house, and then the black ones, to feed the stock and farm the cotton that the white people showed them how to plant. It was all exactly as His hand, in that original silence back at the beginning, had made it to be.

Summer days at Fountain Inn seemed in her memory all one endless day, beginning with roosters. High up in the house she waked to their shrill voices streaming like the banners of sunrise through her tall window. And soon, the bell, its silver resonance soaring over the fields. There were other sounds—thuds and clink of harness, Negro voices wordless and mellow like echoes in a drum, someone calling.

There were so many sounds of morning. She could hear Ben's ax at the woodpile and the slow creak of the well pulley. At the barn was a tingling or rasping of milk in a tin pail, and a crunching of corn in big mules' teeth behind the shut stall doors. From the cabins out in the field came the cries of colored children playing. She would be there soon, with Link and Annie and Della May, all on their knees in the deep dust at the shady side of a cabin. "You be de princess, I be de knight." Around them in the fields and the chinaberry trees was the crying of locusts and meadowlarks.

The afternoon droned and clucked with chickens. Old Burtie stumped about the kitchen or ironed on the back veranda where Hester lay on her belly, bare feet against the rail, and listened to inexhaustible tales of Burtie's wonderful life. The high parlor was cool, always. Her grandmother sat here, darning or sewing with wrinkled, miraculous hands, tall and straight in her walnut chair, and told about Hester's father when he was a little boy. About other things, too, old things, in a time that she said was different from this. There had been the War, she said. Before it, there had been a life they would never see again. But Hester doubted. She knew that it had been a real war. Over the mantel hung the shining cavalry sword that her grandfather had used in it. But *how* had the war been lost, for where was the difference it had made? The life of which her grandmother spoke seemed faraway only in time, and that sword looked as bright and flawless as any victor's sword. And the tales of glory she had heard, of Lee and Forrest and Jackson? Whatever was lost seemed sad to her only because they had lived so long ago.

It was being old, Hester thought, that made her grandfather sad. His hands trembled upon pages of the Bible and other books he read, and sometimes, when he turned around, the gaze resting upon her would make her think of filmy smoke in the hollows of his eyeballs. But then he would smile and, if she was close enough, put a dry hand on her head. Most afternoons he sat in the summerhouse by the fountain, reading through silver-rimmed glasses that straddled the peak in the ridge of his nose. At times he would read aloud to her, about Abraham and Moses and the children of Israel. His voice was younger than the rest of him. It still came to her memory fused with a gentle splashing from the fountain outside, where the mouths of four little angels sprayed water into the circular basin around them—cold water, spewed up from deep in the earth. Picking and chewing at stems and leaves that grew in through the lattice, she listened and thought of the children wandering in the desert. The desert lay beyond the ridge where she had never gone. Right here was what they had been seeking—this green land where the fountain flowed.

Somehow Fountain Inn had seemd always to be at the center of Hester's childhood. In fact this was not so. The weeks and summers spent there barely counted against the years at her home on Hampton Street. Nor did the figures of her grandparents compete in her mind with those of her mother and father. Still there was a way in which Fountain Inn seemed more her home than this, as if she had lived there a dimly remembered primal life before this present one had dawned. And it was true, in a much more reasonable way, that this life here on Hampton Street did derive from that one. Her father did, and the house itself, so many years ago.

And so, in a lesser way, did the life of the town, for Hester. For one thing, there was its history, which she knew even in childhood—how the name and the land both were the gift of her great-grandfather Cameron. It was only natural that her father had been the mayor more than once, and that, until his last years, he had been one of the powers to say what would and would not be in the town. There were other powers, of course, names like Traynor and Willingham and Qualls, which she recognized. To her, these were names of lesser magnitude, but they too, she imagined, had come from places almost like Fountain Inn. In her more contemplative moments she saw that not only her house and its people but the whole town was like a birth from this primeval source. The town also, for all its differences, had its dusty roads down which the cotton wagons rattled, its quiet old houses in droning summer heat, its Negro cabins in deep backyards, and women in head rags and black children in hearing distance. The fields were not far. Milk cows driven by Negro boys passed by her house at morning and evening, and, in the season, murmurous gangs of men and boys with cotton hoes swinging and glancing over their shoulders. Lucinda in her kitchen was a younger Burtie, with tales not much less wonderful. And Poss, in her yard, was as old as Will. Hester was not sure which ones among the white people were her real kin. There were so many she called by the name of Uncle or Aunt or Cousin, whose houses she could enter as she entered her own. There was not any house, white or Negro, whose people she did not know at least by name, and no event or change of scenery that had for long escaped her notice. There were differences enough from Fountain Inn, all right, but underneath it all was the pattern that the Lord's hand had shaped.

This was how the world was, she thought, and changes were no more than the wrinkles and passing tumults that wind could raise upon the face of things. She never had forgot the first occasion when this ground seemed to quake beneath her feet. Old Dr. Phillips, the Presbyterian minister, was much in her house, for meals and for sick calls, a stern, ascetic man with gray moustache and a voice that was habitually a little louder than other people's. He did not look so much like the Lord as her grandfather did, but Dr. Phillips's sudden death, when it came, was like the most vivid of challenges to every right and permanent thing. Righteousness itself seemed threatened. If such things happened, why not to drunk Bob Wakefield, who went on staggering about the streets? But still the shock was in no way equal to that she felt a year or so later when she saw her grandfather lying like a figure of wax in his coffin.

In a little time, of course, her wounds healed over. And probably these were among the things that had prepared her not to be so conscious yet of her father's distress at what was beginning to happen in the town. It was something, he said, that had come in with the motorcar, and the noise and the dust they raised on the unpaved streets. She could see the motorcars, all right, though there were not yet so many of them; and, with his opinions in her mind, she imagined that she could perceive something of the new spirit that he was always describing in words like "aggressive" and "licentious" and sometimes even "wicked." But Hester's mind was so busy elsewhere, then. Already, at thirteen, she was in love with Thomas Glenn.

It had happened, she always remembered, on Confederate Memorial Day. There was the usual parade of creakily animated veterans in their faded uniforms marching four abreast around the square, with dust and banners and rebounding strains of "Dixie" and "The Bonnie Blue Flag" that excited the flesh like wind from distant battlefields.

She saw him all at once, as in a burst of light. Among the spectators were many men on horseback, but he, he and his sorrel mare, stood literally heads and shoulders above the rest. It was becasue his horse had reared, reared and stood there. In her memory of it they never had come down. They were still poised there like a horse and rider just on the threshold of soaring into flight. Her beloved, too, was in uniform, full regalia that looked as if it had been made for him, and a shining saber was at his side. Standing straight in the stirrups, as tall as the horse, his golden head bare because the cavalry hat had fallen onto the back of his neck, he seemed to her as blinding bright as the sun in a morning sky. She was madly in love with him.

He was not as tall as he had looked then. In fact, as she discovered in later lears, he was barely an inch taller than herself. From the distance at which she worshiped him, however, she thought he would have to stoop his head to walk through an ordinary door. But her love was a secret she kept very close: for years she never breathed a hint of it, not even to her mother. The reason, besides that of her childish modesty, was the reservation that she felt in her parents' attitude toward the Glenns. Certainly the Glenns were numbered among the people who counted and, in a way of speaking, they were friends of her parents. The friendship, however, was only of a kind based on mutual position and respect, and mainly was expressed by occasional visits to each other's homes on Sunday afternoons.

Probably no real intimacy had been possible between the two families. It was not a difference that had anything, or anything substantial, to do with class. Rather it had to do with temperament, and might have been epitomized, in that day, by the difference between the Episcopal and Presbyterian churches, to which, respectively, the Glenns and the Camerons belonged. On certain matters, they simply had irreconcilable attitudes. Hester's parents' reservations about the Glenns—which she had quite naturally sensed—were grounded largely on the feeling that the Glenns were of a kind deficient in full and appropriate moral earnestness. As for the Glenns' feelings, Hester was uncertain whether, behind a facade of perfect manners, they were not smiling at the abundance of this quality in her parents. Anyway, in her childhood, this thought, like thoughts of wickedness, was vaguely titillating to Hester and added to her fascination with Mr.

Glenn. She had considered him to be the handsomest man who ever lived. With his confident posture and streaked gray beard, he was the image of the Confederate cavalry officer . . . And his son was like him, she thought later on.

No doubt it was what Hester felt in her parents' attitude toward the Glenns that invested Thomas with a certain indefinable air of the forbidden. This was what caused her not unpleasantly shuddering fancies of a dark and mysterious side to his character. But dare one ever marry such a man? Above all, her mother had told her many times, be sure of goodness and honor in the man you marry. Then worry about his other qualities. How, therefore, could she marry him?

Of course, in actuality, these girlish fantasies were based on nothing—or nothing except her sense of her parents' feelings. And these, a few years later, she saw for what they were, a matter not to be taken with any great seriousness. It came to this: the Glenns were rather worldly people. These, in fact, were her mother's very words when it became apparent, in Hester's nineteenth year, that Thomas's courtship of her daughter might conceivably end in marriage. But as for their actual moral comportment, she knew nothing against them. It was, then, merely the matter of temperamental difference between the families, and Hester could have wished never to have been marked with even the inclination to suspect that more was behind her parents' feeling than now appeared. Because of it she had to make a certain effort in order to dismiss unpleasant rumors that sometimes reached her ears. Still, she was a woman now and no longer so ignorant where the ways of the world were concerned. She would not believe such rumors, but what if there was some truth in them? Young men away at the university, not yet bound by clear ties of honor, were often given to follies. That was the way of the world. To balk at this was prudery. By the time he proposed marriage to her, during her last year at the women's college at Blanton, her old reservations were nothing but memories infrequently recalled.

Yet, as she finally had seen, she would have done well to take warning from those prudish girlhood instincts. Had they not, perhaps, been premonitions, really? There was a kind of moral refinement that often, in certain realms, could sense an evil not yet even out of its germ. Her mother had had this quality, Hester thought, and maybe had passed it on to her daughter, in vain. But whatever the source of those feelings, they did appear prophetic at last. Indeed, on her honeymoon, even, for all the strange excitements of her flesh, she had experienced in Thomas's very knowing embraces a consciousness of old specters rising into her mind again. It was a last, late warning, and, as her body grew accustomed to such use, she had dismissed it.

Concerning Thomas, what would she not have dismissed in those earliest years of their marriage? Always attentive, with small gallantries and presents and inquiries after her comfort, he had left her in no doubt about his love. Nor had she any reason to doubt that what she saw reflected in those polished manners and fine, gray, responsive eyes was the real character of her husband. He was all she could have asked for. She was as proud as if he had been shaped in the very pattern of what a man ought to be.

What had happened to him? It was as though, after six years of marriage, one day the wind had changed. Or rather, more likely, she had all of a sudden waked one day to a change long since in the making. There was the matter of the kind of friends he now had come to prefer—rude, irresponsible people, loose in their fidelities. But even before this she had begun to notice the decline of his manners toward herself. There was no longer the old rush to arrange her chair or to have her coat held ready when she was preparing to go out, and no longer the old lighthearted, mock-servile gallantries, calling her "my queen" and "your ladyship." Somewhere his private, pet name for her, "Queenie," had got dropped forever. In its place—though this was later on—he produced on occasion another one, which he delivered in a different spirit. "Saint Hester," he would call her, sometimes in a tone that gave her genuine pain. For whatever her faults, there was no justice in this. She never had been self-righteous, and he knew it. And the proof, if any were needed, was the years in which she had performed veritable feats of agility to pardon his increasingly open waywardness, until it became an intolerable insult to her.

Early on, as Hester watched his manners and even his sense of responsibility decay, she had been inclined to blame his father. In late years, since his wife's stroke and the further decline of his fortune and position, the old man had turned cynic. Nothing was safe from his mocking eye—not Hester, not even little Ames. The house was

Hester's by then, since the deaths of her mother and father, and old Mr. Glenn would come every time to her back door, in simple, open mockery. He would find some cutting word for everything, everybody, as his eye happened to fall, while Hester sat blushing with a rage she had to restrain by force. "Is that boy of ours still minding well, these days?" he would say, meaning her husband. "I expect that he's 'predestined' to be a deacon pretty soon," he would say, referring to her husband's choice of membership in her church, the Presbyterian. And it got worse with time. Beyond all, her husband's prosperity, the fruit of Hester's father's lumber business, was prey for the old man's crude sarcasm. Remarks, to Thomas, prefaced by such words as "Now that your manly talents have brought you so far . . ." and "Now that you have become supreme master of such an empire . . ." were a common thing in his last year or two. But the old man had died, and where then was the cause?

No, it was not any seeds of discontent the old man might have sown. Many a husband owed his success to the property of his wife. This was not its origin. No, the seeds were there from the start. She had been warned and, in her romantic passion, had not listened. What, then, could she have done? Nothing but what she did do. Endure the grossness she saw bud and slowly flower in him, watch it waste and tarnish things, suffer the indignities—and try to pardon. Had she not, down on her knees, prayed for ways to strive against it? And pardoned and pardoned until the day when she could not pardon any longer. In human decency there was nothing more she could have done—not even if there had been no children three and seven years old to raise.

Hester remembered well how his departure had been like a purging of her house. When he and the last of his things were gone, not only from the house but the town also, it seemed to her that for the first time in years she breathed an air that had no taint upon it. Her babies, too. Her anxiety for them diminished as one with her fading sense of his presence. The scandal, the gossip that reached her, she dismissed with hardly a thought. She had been living with that already. What mattered was her babies, that they grow up in a home kept clean of all that was ugly and sordid, where only the decent things of life should ever meet their innocent eyes. She would give them this. With all her strength she would try to.

And she had tried. Where was her fault, her neglect? When had she been infirm or too indulgent, or failed by word or example to instruct them in the duties of goodness and reverence and honor? There had been times, surely; she was human. But could these have been so many? Or had she failed in the love she owed them? Thinking of Ames, she had sometimes been troubled by this question. Cam, from his birth, in a time already poisoned for her, had seemed so much her own. She feared that he had taken away a part of what was rightly due to Ames, who seemed by this the more his father's child. But in so many ways, indeed, he was his father's child. How could she help her feelings? Could she help, in her dreams of the future, that always it had been Cam whom she saw grown into the perfect image of a man.

But if she had slighted Ames in her love, she had not slighted Cam. Before he was born, from the time when she felt in her womb the first small spasms of his life, she already had loved him in a way new to her, with a kind of all-enfolding love that might have been waiting all her years only for this conception. Her troubles with Thomas were by then a worn, familiar story. The end, if still obscure in the distance, already was in sight. Through the last months of her pregnancy she spent much time in the upstairs room that would be the baby's when it came, that was the room in which she herself had grown up and to which she had brought her husband home three years after their marriage. Here she sat by the window, alone, sunk in the kind of musing autumn brings. The infant stirred within her body. Down on the street the yellow leaves were falling, and through her window the yearning breeze tingled upon her lips and in her hair. Sometimes it seemed that all wonders had converged upon her. To be here in this house, bearing life inside herself as she in her turn had been borne a generation past; to think of her small self tottering and falling upon its floors, and the hands, extended to raise her up, whose touch she never would know again. It all made a mystery whose signs she felt stirring under her heart. She felt like something other than Hester Glenn—old without age, without affliction. And also new, as if she stood at the unchanging origin of things.

During his birth she held tight to consciousness and afterward, for nearly an hour, would not let the nurses take him out of her sight. At home, even for the first few weeks, she refused to accept any help with him. She kept his crib beside her bed where she need only extend her hand when he began to cry. In the dark of night, his fierce mouth upon the nipple of her breast, she held him cradled in a hollow of arms and thighs and experienced again that blooming, drowsy consciousness of a self transcending the fleshly dimensions that held her in space and time. When finally her husband's complaints had forced her to move the crib upstairs, the baby's room came to be like her own. In fact, in the unhappy last year of the marriage, it did become her own, for always she slept there, taking the little boy into her bed, against her breast, to keep him, and her own heart, warm.

But had she failed him later on, in a way unknown to her? She could not discover it. If, reviewing his life, she could have remembered in herself indifference or neglect, times when affection languished; if she could have recalled occasions when indulgence had spared him any punishment or any reproof he had earned; then she might with reason doubt the knowledge of what her love and guidance had planted in his heart. But when a record of all his days would have shown no page unmarked by her diligent attentions, how could she have doubts? There was a secret fault in herself, a pride that had blinded her to some cause in her own life? Retracing her life, like turning over all the stones as far back as memory could reach, she found pride, all right, and selfishness and failures of justice and charity—all the faults to which she was humanly given. But where, under what invisible stone, was hidden such a fault as this?

No, she was looking much too far afield. Her fault was as close as the doubts that had haunted her all these past two days. It was only this fault, her lack of faith, that need haunt her now. Lying in her bed that night she purged her mind of those doubts, and the silent words she uttered into the dark were a vague prayer to be forgiven.

9

Day's afterglow in the elms along the street had tinted their leaves a fragile and poignant gold. In his room upstairs on a front corner of the fraternity house, Ames would not hear anything at all for long intervals. And just now, seated at the desk with his American history book lying open before him, the stillness suggested a sort of last exhaustion, a final aftermath of last night's riot that had left the house in a rubble of whiskey bottles and broken glasses and collapsed beds in private upstairs rooms. Or else suggested a void . . . with an ache in it, that was himself. Raising his eyes from the nearly invisible print, he looked down into the street again. How like him to be here, an old member of this particular fraternity, when all the others, prospering, had moved from these shabby houses into the row of new ones along Greenwood Street. And like him, too, to be here for reasons of sentiment, because a great-uncle of his had helped to found it.

On the open page before him was a particular paragraph that he had read through several times, but now, when he tried again, the print was entirely obscured. Somehow his effort produced instead the memory of his mother's letter once again. "Dear Ames," he had read, a week ago now, in his mother's bold, upright script:

> Your fears were entirely unfounded. I am now certain of this. The one seemingly solid detail that had persuaded me to take your fears with some seriousness turns out to have been grounded only on an inexcusable suspicion of my own. I found this to be the case with each one of the details that troubled you and am now thoroughly ashamed of my doubts—as you should be of yours. It was a lack of faith on our parts. You may depend on my assurance. So let us forget this matter entirely and not even so much as speak of it again.
>
> It was probably just as well, however, that you went away when

you did, because he was naturally angry to learn of what you had done. Such things are perhaps best mended at a distance. I do suggest that you write him a letter apologizing, and when you come home next you may find, I trust, that all of this has passed over. After all, you are brothers, and I am the mother of both of you.

I think it best that you destroy this letter.

Affectionately,
Mama

He had destroyed the letter, but only after he had read, studied it many times over. Late that night, in the silent fraternity house, he had watched it burn to ashes in the metal trash can here beside his desk. He wished he could burn the words, burn everything out of his memory. It would be like that moment after he had read it for the first time, when relief like a kind of swoon had fallen over his mind. But he had read the letter again, and then again.

Until this weekend the house had been empty most of the time. It had been a haunted kind of emptiness, as if the hush of each moment had just then fallen in the wake of voices and laughter, and this, instead of his thoughts, seemed to be what kept him awake at night. He read, with attention that flickered on and off, books for the classes he would take, and magazines and *The Cameron Springs Herald* which he walked ten blocks each day to buy. He lingered over this, turning each page, scanning every column with his eye.

In Monday's *Herald,* a day old, he had found something. It was a letter to the editor from Horace Delmore, written in behalf of the citizens' committee. It was a harsh, indignant letter that on first reading made his bristles rise. There were phrases like "What kind of people . . .," ". . . in a so-called civilized country." The words "savage" and "barbaric" appeared, and the barely qualified suggestion that nothing was being done to apprehend the murderers. Finally there was the invitation, extended to all "decent" people of the community, black and white, to join the committee in its struggle to achieve and maintain social justice.

Ames's own indignation had not lasted even until he reached the end of the letter. He had put it by with a sensation of nausea coming on, thinking of Cam, seeing him in his white T-shirt, with glancing white feet. And then his mother. She would have read this, too. He could envision the tightening line of her mouth, his nostrils' flare, and the gesture with which, in silence, she would put the paper aside. But would it be still the same, without even a quake of uncertain virtue in her? Her letter had said so.

And could not *he* be wrong? Was there behind his certainty one piece of solid evidence? There were whole hours when he clung with apparent success to this view of the matter, and lesser intervals when it seemed that the last of his fears had left him. They had not. One by one they drifted back, becoming certainties again. Often at night he walked, following a route almost the same each time, down block after block made desolate in the aura of wan streetlamps, through neighborhoods where the houses gazed from blind, despondent windows.

Yesterday, as he had walked across a campus suddenly populated again, he had encountered a boy he knew from Cameron Springs. Ames had no chance to avoid him. The boy, Sneed, in red skullcap and glasses, was coming on directly in his path. He stopped in front of Ames and said, "Did you see the ruckus?"

"What ruckus?"

"Yesterday. Back home. About had a riot. Didn't you know about it?"

Ames had stood almost silent to listen, his gaze drifting absently from Sneed's rather raw, pink lips to the ground and up to the face of the tower clock visible through foliage of a hackberry tree. He could see it happening, the double column of Negroes—and a few whites! Who?—fifty or sixty, including women and some boys, filing out of Cox Street onto the square. Rudely inscribed pasteboard placards weaving and tilting over their heads, they slowly circled the monument. Traffic had stopped. Astonished white and Negro faces, too, looked on from the sidewalks, and a raggedly plaintive hymn, like a spiritual, echoed in the quiet that now had fallen. They were rounding toward the courthouse, the sheriff's office, to deliver their protest face to face. And then the glint of a bottle arcing through the air, exploding on the pavement. Then the swell of voices, catcalls, other missiles sailing over into the welter of shifting, bobbing heads. Someone was down, a Negro woman, her open mouth streaming blood down onto her white shirtwaist.

The violence had lasted only a very brief time. They had taken the woman off to the hospital and arrested four or five Negroes and several whites in the crowd and cleared the square. On the pavement lay shards of brick and bottles among which occasional passing cars threaded their way with caution. Later, people reappeared on the sidewalks, but among them there was no black face to be seen. These were clustered along the streets in the Radney and Tulip sections of town, faces with fleshy underlips thrust out and red anger in their eyes.

Ames had got very drunk at the fraternity party that night. He did not remember much about it except that he had stood propped in the corner space beside the piano and sung songs in a loud, seemingly melodious voice for what might have been an hour or two. At some time during the evening he had been in a bitter argument, but with whom and about what he could not recall. The haze that obscured his other, more substantial memory made him especially grateful. Late, after the party had ended, he had taken some girl upstairs. He remembered that he had been helpless, that she had laughed at him, and that he had taken a swing at her. He did not think he had hit her, but this was as much, thankfully, as he could recollect.

But over this matter there was no veil. The night that had gathered in his room, this hush as of exhaustion, seemed only to intensify the lucidness of these thoughts. He switched on the small desk lamp and, sitting there in his pool of light, read over the same paragraph in his history book.

> Seen thus objectively, in the unbiased light of modern statistical and other research, these facts necessarily explode virtually all of the romantic illusions about the Old South. That such a society, based squarely upon a crushing exploitation of the Negro, with its largely rude, oppressive, and anti-democratic characteristics, should give rise to so many dearly cherished fairy tales is a classic illustration of the hollowness of most of our myths. It scarcely needs saying that the persistence of myths like these, playing havoc as they do with the rational conduct of life, gravely reduces the chances for the achievement of truly free and just societies.

It did not anger him anymore. The effect was more nearly that of colliding, at the end of the paragraph, with a barrier at once solid and insubstantial. It made his mind flicker, go out for a moment. Before it could make a recovery he took his jacket from the closet and left. He walked a long way for his supper. Afterward he kept on walking and when, quite late, he got back to his room he had made up his mind to go home in the morning.

It was Sunday. He had known this, of course, but what made the fact real for him suddenly was the emptiness of the square and the glazy hush that hung like a kind of nimbus upon the white courthouse and monument and shut doors in weathered-brick storefronts—a remembered air, Sunday's special light. It was as always. Even the gleaming bits of glass he saw in gutters had not yet chastened his mood, and he was halfway up Hampton Street before his steps slowed down at last to a halt.

What had he come for? ". . . best mended at a distance," she had written; ". . . not speak of it again." She would not welcome him. And Cam? From where he stood Ames could see the house, and more and more he felt as if hostile eyes were trained on him from the windows. What released him finally was the sight of his mother's car, with two heads visible inside, appearing from beyond the house and vanishing down Bainbridge Street.

The Presbyterian Church was an ancient building—time-empurpled brick and stained high-crested roof and spire that soared like a rusty lance above the near horizon of trees. In deep magnolia shade across the street he stood, an hour later, waiting. Because he had seen her car parked down the block he knew she was in there, seated, as he remembered her always, in light that filtered down from the green-glass figure of Abraham in the windowpane. This was a childhood memory, though. She did not go often anymore and her being here today seemed in some way meaningful. He was not entirely sure of what his purpose was until he saw, as if on a peal of organ music, the doors swing open. Then he stepped behind the tree trunk.

His mother was one of the first in the doorway, taller by half a head than the woman in front of her, looking straight out before her into the street. For a second Ames thought she was alone. She was not, and it was Cam. The yellow checks of his sport coat drew Ames's eyes like a banner. Holding his mother's arm, Cam guided her attentively down the steps, while she, as if no care of her own were needed, continued to gaze straight out ahead. Was it shadow from the brim of her navy-blue hat that made her face seem paler? Really he could not tell. Nor could he tell whether there was an unaccustomed languor in the way she let herself be escorted down the sidewalk with Cam still holding her arm.

The crowd thinned out and then was gone, but Ames continued to stand there for a while. Perhaps, if he waited long enough, he would find her at home alone. He did wait, killing time over coffee at Pitman's Café, and then set out toward his house. But what was he to say? A mere dumb compulsion kept him from turning back.

They had not come home yet, for as he approached the house from the rear, on Bainbridge, he saw that her car was not in the garage. He walked across into the side yard and sat down among the big camellia bushes where he could not be seen from the upper windows. On and on he waited, and still they did not come. Rays of the sun through the waxy leaves grew warm upon his flesh. A twittering and a languor of insects slowly purged his mind, and, after a while, stretched out with his head on his arm, he fell asleep.

For a time before his eyes popped open, there were voices in his sleep. He waked up already tense, and heard, like a voice from beyond a curtain, his mother saying:

"And you might tell Mark hello for me. I haven't seen him in a while."

There was no audible answer. A car door slammed.

"Do call me, please. I like to know when you're coming."

"Okay, Mama, I promise." Cam's voice. And then the grind of his starter, the reverberance of his engine in the garage.

Until he heard the engine's rumble die away down the street Ames did not move. It was as though he had dreamed the brief exchange of voices and now, waked up, could explain to himself his own troubled response. Mark would be Mark Waller, anything but a friend of Cam's for quite a long time now. And his mother's voice? Or was it only the screening foliage that in some way had altered its timbre? He heard the back door fall shut.

Ames was on his feet, but still he hesitated. Somehow it had gotten to be midafternoon and there was a bus at four. He could make it easily. But his feet took him toward the house, slowly, and onto the back porch as if he were an intruder stealing up. Then, through the screen, he saw her. She sat at the bare kitchen table, in profile to him, her head a little bowed in that disturbing way that seemed to create an imbalance between the projection of her nose and the bun of hair behind. Still she did not see him. "Mama," he said. She started as if he had touched her.

"Ames. I didn't know who you were." But she was still looking at him as if he were an apparition.

She did not get up when he entered, and her look, he saw, had changed from one of alarm to almost stern appraisal. In fact his impression of a moment ago seemed like an illusion now. Uncertainly he said, "I wanted to talk to you."

"What about?"

He halted well shy of her. She had quit watching him. She looked straight before her, into the dining room, it seemed, without any suggestion now of that disturbing imbalance about her head.

"You know."

She let a second or two go by. "I told you in my letter. Very clearly. I want you to put it out of your mind . . . as I have. And not ever speak of it again."

"We've *got* to. What *he* said doesn't prove anything."

"Nobody except you has accused him of anything. And you have nothing to go on but ugly suspicions," she said, still gazing as if at some object in the dining room.

Her tone left him speechless for a moment. He was trying to call up an answer when she added, "I will not go into it again. I made sure, and I told you you could depend on it. I wouldn't have told you if I didn't know. So let's not talk about it anymore, *ever*."

Her last word had come down with an edge that kept him mute. Silhouetted against the window beyond, her profile had a chiseled immobility suggesting stone, cold to the touch. Then her lips moved. "I asked you to write to him. You haven't."

"And say what?"

Now she looked at him and maybe the hint of pallor had just now appeared in her face. "That you are sorry. That you are ashamed of your suspicions now."

"How can I write him that?"

"It *should* be the truth."

Her eyes were accusing him. In spite of himself his gaze faltered, as did his voice when he answered, "I'm sorry."

This left a hush and the weight of her eyes on him. Abruptly he turned and walked behind her to the sink. He ran water into a glass. Without wanting it he took a swallow or two and went on standing there.

"Why do you hate him so?" came to his ears, in a changed voice.

"Do you really think that's the reason? Even if I did 'hate' him?"

"I'm afraid it is the reason . . . Why?"

"It isn't," he only murmured, putting his hands on the sink, propping his tired body.

"Is it because of me?" she said softly, and waited a space. "Because you felt that I was partial to him? I have thought about this so much lately." Again she waited.

"No," he murmured in a voice that perhaps was not audible at all. At least she gave no sign of having heard, for she went on:

"I'm afraid it was my fault. I think I didn't realize, when Cam was a baby, that you might feel forgotten. Especially during the time when your father and I had ceased to have any marriage. It was all that, all the trouble and strain with him, that made me so blind. And afterward, too. I think it got to be a habit. Because you seemed so much older . . . But I loved you, too. I wish I had shown it equally." She finished in a low, regretful voice and left a silence for him to speak in.

He started to and did not answer. It seemed not worth the effort to deny this—if it should be denied—or to repeat himself again. Besides, in this moment he felt a certain pity for her.

"I so much want you to love each other, to be friends . . . Can't you be?"

Leaning there against the sink he tiredly pondered an answer. "Would it do any good if I were to write him that?"

"I'm sure it would. If you would mean it . . . He doesn't hold grudges for long," she went on in the same voice. "If you would just try to know him. People misunderstand him, the way he is. They blame him for things and it makes him more that way. It hurts him. He's not like most boys. I can see so much of my family in him. Underneath the shell he feels much more than you'd think."

Ames's grip on the edge of the sink had tightened. Suddenly he said, "Where is he now?"

"He and Mark Waller are going somewhere."

Only the ensuing pause could have indicated that she had sensed anything in his question. He decided to let the matter drop, and he heard her continue:

"I think it would be better, though, if you didn't see him yet a while. Write to him. Give him time to forget about it."

He had not intended to answer this at all, but something in him bolted. "Time heals everything, you mean."

"It heals many things," she said with a coldness that was a response to his tone.

There was silence, and when at last he turned for a look at her she was sitting exactly as before, head sternly trained toward the dining room, inanimate hands lying not quite at rest on the tabletop. He said, "I hope it heals things like that business on the square Friday. The colored people won't forget that very soon, either."

"That was inspired by white people. That Delmore crowd. Their Citizens' Committee," she said, her voice biting down on the title. "They put those Negroes up to that."

"I doubt if it took much putting. They don't like being murdered any more than we would."

In the second's pause he imagined that he could see her nostrils tensing. She said, "Monk Venable has done everything he can. There has always been killing in the world. You know that."

He checked his tongue. The quiet went on and on, and presently he took his hands off the sink. "I had better get going. I can still catch the four o'clock bus."

He heard her chair creak faintly. "I could fix you something to eat," she said in a softened voice.

"I'll have to hurry. I want to be gone when he gets back." Without looking at her he walked to the door.

"It's only for a little while," she said. He heard her get up from the table. "Until all this blows over. This is your home, too."

Was she waiting for him to come and brush her cheek with his lips? One glance at her face told him that he could not—even if she would welcome it. "All right, Mama," was all he said as he pushed the screen door open.

The bus had just pulled out when he reached the station. It meant hours of waiting, but there was nothing to be done. He sat down on a bench. Later he wandered up to the square, scanning it briefly before he entered. There were a few cars parked, a group of boys passing across, and over in the courthouse yard some country men lounging under the trees. Still no Negro face—bits of shining glass against the curb reminded him. The faces there in the courthouse yard were mostly the color of clay or else tan like old dry canvas, with seams and furrows and rheumy eyes that gazed around the square with all the inconsequence of cattle. Hats of battered felt or straw, necks like chickens or fattened shoats rising from denim collars. They would be talking, as usual nowadays, about the niggers, with, on this special weekend, a little gratified laughter. A surge of something like malice moved Ames suddenly to walk across the square and sit down on the low concrete wall in earshot of their voices.

Yes, he had been right. Listening over his shoulder, he soon made out that they were talking about Wendell Pitts, the young Negro lawyer who had led the march on Friday. One thin, nasal voice was especially clear:

"Yes sir, that's half your trouble, right there. The biggest part of them just follows him."

From the tail of his eye Ames had a glimpse of an old man seated at the end of the bench. The bald head was nodding agreement. But another voice said:

"Naw he ain't half of it, neither. The doggone gover'ment's about nine parts of what's making this pot boil. Gover'ment's the reason why one of them like Pitts can come up and spit in your face."

"It ain't just the gover'ment, though," a third one said. "Look at that Committee bunch. And they're white people. *Look* like they're white. Trying right now to get the mill to throw out the whites and hire niggers in their place. My boy out there, he ain't going to stand for it. He ain't about to have his kids grow up the way I had to."

Now, Ames thought, all their heads were nodding.

"It's some hometown white people in that with them, too. And several of them's preachers, by golly."

Again the thin, nasal voice: "Well, it's some hometown white people had about all they're going to take, too. I wouldn't be surprised if I know some of them."

Ames got up off the wall and walked back across the square.

He kept on walking. Without any special intention he followed Cox Street for a while, observing, as he went, the well-remembered places of his childhood—Miss Milly Bradford's leaning tree, the Langley's high stone wall. But these seemed mute to him now. He found himself more often considering the works of construction and demolition underway in the town. He paused for a long time at what had used to be Hardy's old cotton gin down by the railroad. It was nearly gone. Amid a rubble of gray lumber stood the big, yellow machine that would root out the last of its foundations in the next day or two. At the north edge of town, where the interstate would come through, he spent another while trying to imagine what it would look like without Buck's ancient general store and the run-down houses with their chinaberry trees and the little green oasis that was Julie's spring where the neighborhood Negroes still got their drinking water. But he paused longest of all on the high ground close to where Darnley's Cannon stood, contemplating, over the hill beyond the edge of town, smoke from the textile mill.

Later on, after a sandwich or two at Wally's drive-in, Ames had a little encounter. It was deep twilight and, recklessly, because he was not in the habit of thinking this way, he had drifted into the edge of the Negro district. He was first made conscious of the fact by a quietness that seemed unusual for a September Sunday evening. Except for some lighted windows along the rows of small, tightly crowded houses, the street was dark. Nor did he see anyone just now. There was music from a radio somewhere, but no voices, and he felt suddenly an atmosphere of brooding all around him. The next turn left would take him out. He stepped up his pace. This was when the bottle hit the pavement in front of him, showering glass across his legs, and one fragment struck his hand.

"What you doing in here, white boy?"

Ames made out the figures of three men, or grown boys, seated on the steps of a storefront to his left. A night-light inside the store dimly illuminated the crown of one black head. "Just walking," Ames answered.

"This here niggertown. Us niggers don't 'low no white boys in here."

"I'll get out," Ames said.

"Yeh," another one said. "They stinks too bad."

"Us niggers fixing us a jail, too," the first one said. "Going to put white boys in it when they gets bottles th'owed at them."

There was a pause: "We're not all like that," Ames said.

"Listen at him. He ain't like that."

A light went on across the street and a Negro man appeared on the porch. He stood silently watching.

"You better haul ass out of here, white boy."

Ames nodded. Turning, he walked away at a steady and measured pace toward the next corner, conscious of his exposed back. But the only thing that pursued him was a low, derisive whistle and then a loud voice saying, "It smell better around here already."

Ames ended up out at Bracey's. Despite the Sunday ordinance he had no trouble buying beer, which he sat and drank in a booth at the far end of the long, dusky room. The beer only made him sleepy. When the time for his bus approached, moving seemed too much trouble and he kept on sitting there. A few customers came and went. The last were a group of country boys and girls in embossed T-shirts and tight, iridescent slacks who danced energetically to nickelodeon music until the place closed down.

There would not be another bus, Ames thought, until around two o'clock. He walked slowly into town and once stopped to rest at the foot of a tree in somebody's dim front yard. Now and then a car went by, but mostly the town seemed lifeless; he listened to the click of his shoes echo in the hollow quiet along the streets. A little more than a block from the square, he heard the explosion.

Reverberating among the still houses around him, it sounded as violent as a cannon shot. Already running, he turned the corner into a street that opened onto the lighted square ahead. He saw two figures. He saw them plunge into a car and saw the car, with a crying of tires, take off from the curb at the end of the street and come flashing past him. The streetlamp showed a Negro face at the window.

Ames was not the first one on the square. Already there were two policemen, one of them Larch, and within a minute a man and a boy in pajamas appeared, coming from the south side. He could hear Larch cursing, but the first few sweeps of his eyes around the square did not show him anything out of order. Then he saw where Larch had stopped. It was the monument. On top of the high pedestal stood the fragments of two legs, broken off at the ankle and at the knee, while just above them, beams from the four spotlights down on the grass converged in a bright nimbus of empty air.

"Goddamn them," Larch said clearly.

Ames had stopped at the edge of the circle. In front of him, scattered on the grass and on one of the narrow concrete walks, lay chunks and shards of the soldier. Its head lay under a cannon. By now there were a dozen people standing around the circle, quietly swapping views, and Ames could hear the voices and footsteps of others approaching.

"Anybody *see* anything?" Larch said loudly, belligerent, craning his tall neck around. "Any car getting away? See any niggers?" His eyes came to Ames, maybe paused, and passed on. Ames felt his jaws clamp down tight.

"I *heard* a car," someone said. "High-tailing it, too."

"Well, where at, goddamnit?" Larch barked.

"Heading up Cox. Right after it happened."

"Didn't nobody *see* it?" Larch shouted.

There was silence. Ames stood with his jaws clenched.

A patrol car cruised onto the square, grinding its siren a little to clear the way. Larch approached it at a trot. Then, its siren screaming, the car headed across into Cox Street.

For the number of people already present, the crowd was curiously subdued. Even from across the circle isolated comments were clearly audible:

"Pretty nervy of them. Right out here in the light this way."

"Had to climb up there, too."

Someone said, "Here's a dynamite cap," holding it up. A group knotted around him, mumbling. Presently a white-haired man—it was old Andrew Keith—stepped onto the grass and, bending down, pulled the soldier's head out from under the cannon. Afterward he stood holding it wrapped in his arms like a melon against his belly, his head bowed, looking gaze for gaze into the blank concrete eyes as if he expected something. This went on until a policeman, in an irritable voice, told him to put it back where he had got it. Mr. Keith shook his head, but he obeyed, putting it with scrupulous care back under the cannon.

The people were still coming and Ames had got crowded back from his place in the front rank. Then a shift in the crowd opened a gap for his eyes. Suddenly he saw, across the square on a corner of Hampton Street, the still figure of his mother in a dark garment. Close beside her was Cam, as still as she. The gap closed. He kept himself concealed in the crowd for a while, and presently, when he looked again, they were gone.

Ames withdrew from the crowd and walked back down to the bus station and sat down on a bench in the corner. When his bus passed through an hour later, the square was entirely deserted. The nimbus where the beams converged above the shadowy pedestal made him think of a spirit reluctant to pass on into darkness.

10

Hester was a long time in getting back to sleep again that night. It was as if the sound of the explosion had left inside her skull a little hollow place where the soldier used to stand, and to which her attention repeatedly came back with a kind of dull surprise. The soldier had been there always, she realized, a fixture of her mind. Its absence was somehow like an impairment to her clarity of thought. Broken stumps where legs had been. Higher up an aura of light illuminating nothing. She remembered her feeling of need to take Cam's arm as they had walked back from the square.

But what was it Cam had said to her? "Don't worry, Mama, we'll put it back." The thought of his words touched her once more, made her feel the pressure of his arm. How well he knew her heart—as she knew his. How could she have doubted him, then, even for a moment? And Ames? They were not to be borne, those thoughts of his, like ugly specters that had lingered after his departure today. Mere blind suspicions. Or mightn't she call them wicked? If his will was not in it, how could she make him see?

But didn't she have herself to blame, her own blindness as a mother? And also, maybe, this lapse of hers that had seemed to countenance Ames's suspicions. Since then, how many times she had wondered at and condemned herself—times like that moment tonight on the square when Cam had said those words to her. And their Sunday afternoon at Fountain Inn last week, hours that had purged from her mind the last abiding stain of any doubt. Already she felt them stored among the memories that never would cease to be like balm to her heart. That afternoon had shown her the boy whom even her own eyes rarely saw laid bare. Not by words. His quietness, his sympathy, spoke a far more eloquent language. There were times when he had seemed almost to be a spirit communing at her side. As when they had stood leaning upon the rotten split-rail fence, gazing where the house had been and across the brown cornfield that had been meadow, far down to the fringe of trees where the river was. There was gusty wind, bringing an early chill of autumn and tang of woodsmoke from a distance. High against a sweep of mare's-tail clouds flights of doves crossed over and drew the eye to a horizon like a tall rim of the world's edge. She told him about the house, led him among the weeds and the gray chunks of stone that had made its foundation. She showed him the few gnarled apple trees where the orchard had been and still-surviving shoots of worn-out quince and camellia. Where the summerhouse had stood, marked by a single leaning post, they stopped longest of all. From the wreckage of the fountain, water still ran, trickling, and Cam scooped with his hands for a drink. It was here that he had said, "I wish I could have seen it, Mama. The way it used to be."

She could see it. And she could see him in it, with the house and the fields behind him. His quietness, the way he looked about him with eyes lingering where she pointed, bespoke the way she felt—at one with him and with this place where memory raised up again the house and the cabins and the old, low, sweet voices. His words, when he said anything, seemed to come like thoughts of her own mind calling the visions from this deep. And when her gaze came back to him again, to his clear tan skin and vivid jaw and lank auburn hair that the wind riffled, she would see a Cameron standing where they all had stood. When at last they started back toward the car, she had had him take her arm.

If only he could show others the self that he had showed to her that day, and so many days. The world saw a front of toughness that was not real. This was why people misjudged him, blamed him sometimes for things he had not done or meant. Now and then, moments when she had run against it herself, she understood how they felt. One's instinct was to recoil and not reach out anymore, imagining that the coldness outside went all the way to his heart—unnerving even for her at times. Was it not deliberate in him, a mistaken point of manhood? She had tried more than once to speak to him about it. At supper the other night she had tried, for there had been occasion.

Evidently, in one of those unaccountable moods of his, he had meant to shock her. Anyway, into his freshly emptied plate, he had said musingly:

"They're still carrying on about that Stevens nigger. White people, too. Like *they* cared."

Her blood had made a little pause, barely felt, a mere late symptom of last week's derangement. "They *do* care. Of course they do."

"It's fake," he said, slowly dragging the tip of his fork across the plate, gazing at it. "It's something they put on for each other. Makes them feel 'good.' "

"Please don't say that, it isn't true. I told you that before. Don't say it again in my presence."

He went on silently moving the fork, as if he were drawing patterns in the empty plate. Under the chandelier, the smooth topknot of his head was mahogany colored. She could hear, in the kitchen beyond the swinging door, Willodene rattling dishes.

"It is true, too. They can't fool me. *Every*body's glad of it." His glance touched her face.

She put her hands on the table to rise, but then, seeing this, he said, "I'm sorry, Mama. Don't get mad."

So she had kept her seat, taken her hands from the table and busied them with folding the napkin on her lap. Presently she said, "You sound so cynical, sometimes. And cold."

"I was just talking, Mama," he faintly said in a voice that did sound regretful, and went on tracing invisible patterns with the fork in his bare plate.

"You *make* people misunderstand you," she said. But she had stopped with this. His reverie had seemed already to withdraw him beyond reach of the little lecture she had intended.

The exchange had left her, for an hour or so, in a state of something like distress. After that she thought she understood. He had not forgotten that night of the week before, and this was a kind of small retaliation, a striking back at her and at everybody for their lack of faith in him. It was one with his appearance—on the day after that night—holding the chain and announcing to her, in a cold curt voice, that he had brought back the real "murder chain." It made her aware, with new sorrow, of the vicious circle that caused him to be as he was:

his cold, proud responses to every show of distrust seemed only to justify more of the same. She knew this. But how could she help him to see it, or make others see beyond an appearance intended to hide his feelings from their eyes?

But he was young yet, he would learn. And learn or not, *she* knew him and felt a pride in him that never had really faltered since his birth. He was *her* child, a Cameron. No use to deny that she loved him more than Ames. And loved him more than ever, now, as if her lapse had been only a step in bringing her closer to him. He seemed to feel this, too, and the few distressing intervals had been but trivial pauses in the flow of their sympathy. He was more attentive than in the past, discussing little matters with her, telling her of his day at school. There was always some small triumph, an A+ on an algebra test, a game of touch football won by his catch. What kind of sport coat should he buy for fall? A light tan one, with shoes to match? And there were weightier matters, new instances of unrest or conflict in the town. She relied on him for this information, and every day for the past week there had been something—an exchange of words or missiles between white and colored boys, some gratuitous effrontery or insult cast at whites. He knew, the day after the night it occurred, about a meeting that had been attended by some whites as well as Negroes.

"The Delmores?" she had asked. "They were there, of course?"

"Yes. There were some more, too. Somebody named Bottenger I never heard of." Cam was sitting perched sideways on the kitchen stove, the tip of one white tennis shoe resting lightly on the floor.

"I know who he is," she said, over her ironing. "Another one of those new people at the Whitney plant. There are so many new people now. And there will be more when this next plant comes." She turned the slip on the ironing board, and paused. "I wouldn't mind that. I never did before. But they are different now, so many of them. They care nothing about us. They value one thing—equality. Nothing else is sacred. They sum up all justice and virtue in that one word." She put her fingers on the handle of the iron, but she did not, after all, lift it off the rack. Cam was watching her intently, an intelligence in his face that looked both sad and ardent. It was one of those moments of communion she had felt with him lately and she was moved to go on:

"To them everything we value is foolishness, or worse. Old superstitions that they have nothing but contempt for—just more signs of our 'savagery.' Whatever bad happens here is because of our values. . . . We do have our bad, but we have much more good—more than they do. That's why we fought them before. They want to destroy what we have."

Just as before, he continued to gaze at her, with only a mild blink of lids when her eyes came squarely on his.

"I want you to understand it," she said. "I want you to know what we are, why we hold onto it."

And she thought he did understand, without her needing to tell him. It was in his blood to know. She could sense the warmth of feelings shared with her, the movements of his sympathy, his starts of indignation. No, there could be no doubts of a son whose heart was like a mirror of her own.

No, it was Ames who should concern her. There was no reaching him anymore. Somehow he was like a part of what was happening in the world, even in this town of hers. Among her friends, even? She had been thinking about this, too, sometimes, since Wednesday's meeting of the society at Jane Willingham's old home. It was not a new thought. It was merely that circumstances had made her more acutely conscious of it that day at Jane's. At the time she had even struggled against it, seeking comfort in her friends' familiar talk, the little, muted wrangles and the vanities exposed, the booming and tyrannical declarations of Mrs. Halleran. It was all as in the past, nothing altered. She was with her kind, like her family, and all their loves and hates and sad stories and animosities were also hers. There were comforts, too, in the big living room where she had sat so often, in the height of the ceiling and the crystals of the chandelier, like massive raindrops frozen as they fell. She loved the great ebony mantel and loved the floorboards of polished ash so wide that nearly every one by itself would do for a table leaf. And out the big windows the swoop of the lawn, and then the pasture, the white oak grove. Then what was different?

Perhaps it had started only with the talk about the new rubber plant. The plant was to locate on this side of town, they said, and this was what had called to her mind Jane's remark at the meeting the week before. Had Jane really meant, despite her jesting tone, that she might sell this home of hers. On top of this thought there fell, uttered by someone, the name of Delmore. It brought what felt like a flush to Hester's neck and then the same vision as before: she could see the woman, with plump, braceleted arms and frosted curls, possessively lounging on the Willinghams' front veranda. What was the woman doing now, she and that "Committee"—plotting what destruction?

But these were mere accidents of conversation, no one's doing. No, it was not so much in the substance of what had been said—or not mainly that. In the fact itself that Helen Cate had dropped a piece of news that angered Hester, there was nothing remarkable. Brought suddenly to attention, Hester had heard:

"They think it should be removed. They say it reminds the Negroes that they were slaves. So it helps to keep them down," Helen said with a kind of resigned irony.

"Want *what* removed?" Hester said.

"The Confederate monument, Hester."

There was a pause. "But that's so silly," someone said. And Mrs. Halleran gave a resonant sigh. But what Hester had missed on all their lips and faces was the kind of response she had felt in herself and partly had expressed. The thing she encountered instead was the same air of ironic resignation that she had noted in Helen's manner. It was not different in other cases, either, when matters related even in distant ways to this one were discussed. A sort of cavalier withdrawal followed each mention of unrest in the town, and bejeweled Martha Ludlow, to nods of agreement, quoted her husband: "Henry says we simply can't afford to have trouble. He thinks it would be ruinous to business. He says it would throw us back ten or twenty years." And vaguely assenting murmurs followed her words. Hester had fallen completely silent at last. There with her minute book, making an entry now and then, she had felt more and more like some one recording deliberations acted on a stage. . . .

But now there was this, an explosion quite shocking enough to sweep the euphoric haze from their minds. She would have liked to think that every one of them had been jolted out of bed and faced, on the square, with that nothing where the beams of light converged above the pedestal. And how, now, could they ignore the real source of this act? Not the Negroes, though Negro boys no doubt had performed it. It was more than clear enough—dramatized for every eye at the center of the square. A costly slip for the Delmores and all their reckless crowd. But what finally had soothed Hester to sleep that night, and lingered in her sleep, was the thought of old bonds made strong again in the face of this threat to them all.

The mood in which Hester had gone to sleep was with her still the next morning. In fact she went about her daily business with a lightness of step that was not the common thing for her, as if some undefined but pleasant event was in store. When the grocer called at ten o'clock she hurried to the telephone in the expectation of hearing Jane's or some other familiar, female voice. Her disappointment did not last long. Somehow the irrelevant call had only sharpened her expectancy and she kept imagining familiar hands, hands that had not done so for a long time, dialing her number. Or someone at the front door, maybe more than one, old friends who until recent years had needed no invitation to appear. In the mild glow of her morning mood it seemed as if already these years of near estrangement were at an end.

Fall, the season she loved best, had already touched her yard. The elm and the oaks behind the house had begun to turn and, in the side yard, boughs of pyracantha rose in flame against the black-green massiveness of boxwood and camellia. In the blue dome of the sky, high up, bullbats wheeled and darted, and a dry, limpid sunlight fell without its summer weight. The quietness, too, was coming on, an undertone of lowered insect voices peeping and whispering among the shrubbery. In all seasons except winter, Hester spent much time in her yard, directing Lucius or puttering among the shrubs. But today had a special serenity. Her mood, the season, the click and rustle of an invisible Lucius working his shears among the foliage somehow called to mind with uncommon vividness memories full of old faces and mellow, sibilant, autumn days from her youth at Fountain Inn. Some of these shrubs, the three now-massive boxwoods and a few of the hydrangeas and camellias, had come from there, brought by her mother in Hester's girlhood after the old house had burned. Some of the others, too, had been planted originally by her. She had valued them greatly, and tending them still gave Hester a sense of rendering her mother a very personal service. But Hester loved them in her own right, also. In fact she had, herself, planted so many more shrubs that her mother's old pattern, except in Hester's mind, had got quite obscured. Really there were too many, and from some angles the side yard suggested a lush jungle of irregular, if well-trimmed, foliage.

But Hester liked it this way. She liked the green and private bowers it made and the narrow lanes that opened like small surprises beyond the density of a bush. But something, this morning, had given her an idea. Coming suddenly upon Lucius bent down over a little sasanqua, she said, "Do you think you could build me a summerhouse, Lucius?"

"A which?" Lucius straightened up and looked at her sideways. His underlip hung slack, in apparent vexation.

"A summerhouse. You remember the one at Fountain Inn."

"What you want with one. You wouldn't never set in it." He had let the hand with the shears fall straight down at his side.

"Could you build me one?"

"I might could. Where you going to put it at? Got bushes everywhere."

"We could put it where the chairs are. I think I'll call Mr. Crane and ask him about lumber. And have him find me some old board shingles, too," she said and walked away, hearing Lucius sigh, feeling the weight of the high-noon sun lying with a pleasant warmth upon her bonneted head and naked arms.

Inside, she called and arranged about the lumber, except the board shingles, which might be hard to locate nowadays. She ate her little lunch, set Willodene washing windows, and afterward went to her room for a nap. But still her telephone had not rung. In the afternoon paper there was a news story on last night's event and Kirk Qualls's brief, noncommittal editorial deploring the vandalism, mainly in the aspect of its destructiveness to community harmony. But this was all. And the telephone remained silent. Later she tried calling up Jane Willingham, but there was no answer. When, before sunset, she walked down to the square, it seemed to her that the people she saw went about their business or on with their conversations as casually as if the soldier were still there on his pedestal. She had walked down here, she now realized, in a sort of cloudy hope that somehow since last night it had been mended and put back in its place. Once again she felt its absence like something torn from inside her skull.

But of course it would take time—maybe a month, even. A new one would have to be made. And was there one good reason why she should have received a call? Besides, Cam assured her that evening that the boys at school were angry—a certain indication of their parents' state of mind. Her doubts, then, had no foundation. She pushed them firmly out of her mind and, the next morning, with little more than the kind of buried uneasiness to which she was growing accustomed, went as always about her daily tasks.

Tuesday's paper had nothing on the subject. Indeed, why should it have, she asked herself, unless the vandals had been found? But Wednesday's paper did have something. It seemed at the time almost as if she had anticipated this, somehow prepared by the mere, trivial fact that the society meeting for today, to which she had looked forward, had been unexpectedly called off. There were two items, but her eye ran first to the letter signed by Horace Delmore on behalf of the Citizens' Committee. Its effect was no more than a momentary kindling in her breast of a feeling for which there was no name but hatred—momentary because one knew what to expect of those people.

The other item, the editorial, was what struck Hester with such force. It was not only that Kirk Qualls was owner and editor of the newspaper. He was also a member of the city council, and often, in an unofficial way, a sort of spokesman for it. And here he was, a Qualls, an old family of the town, in timid half-endorsement of what the Delmore letter said. Only a partial endorsement, of course. He recommended merely that restoration of the monument be postponed, and not that it be replaced by something more "acceptable." But his timorous arguments read like echoes of the letter's much bolder ones. At present, he said, feeling was running high among Negroes—and with much justification. Not, of course, that such acts of vandalism were to be excused, but the fact was that, *at this time,* it would be better to avoid any occasion that might give the appearance, however mistaken, of ignoring or defying the feelings of colored citizens. And then his real point, what really frightened him. What of Cameron Springs's industrial growth if serious racial disorder should develop?

In such a climate, would the new Hastings plant come to Cameron Springs? Already there had been rumors of some second thoughts on their part . . . And so it went, through the whole column, the whole editorial space.

But it was not so much the opinions of the man Kirk Qualls that disturbed her. She had seen enough hints in previous editorials and knew enough about some of his more recent associations not to be too surprised. Hadn't he, ever since his father's death, been veering as much as he dared toward the other side? It was not him, or even so much her fear of the influence that he might be able to exert. What did disturb her was his having nerve enough to publish this opinion at all. He was not a man to take any step without first making the most canny assessment of its effects upon himself and his newspaper. That he had done this indicated strength. But strength from where? Did she not know this town, her own town, at least as well as he? Except for only a few, she was sure the people all felt in their hearts just about as she did. No. For once, anyway, Kirk Qualls had nodded. And yet, envisioning off and on the pedestal with its broken stumps, she continued to pace slowly about the sitting room and across into the parlor.

Thirty minutes later, in the brown tweed suit she wore for lesser occasions, she was being ushered by a secretary through the door of Kirk Qualls's bright and greatly altered office just down the hall. Kirk Qualls was standing up, a thin, hollow-chested young man with ascetic mouth turned down at the corners. He was in his shirt sleeves and his cuffs were rolled back, exposing the stalklike leanness of the arm held out toward the chair he was offering her. "Have a seat, Mrs. Glenn. What can I do for you?"

His tone had a spare kind of cordiality such as one might offer an unfamiliar client. "Mrs. Glenn," he had called her. Sitting down in the chair and saying, "I hope I haven't interrupted you," provided an interval that Hester needed.

"Just winding up, anyway," he said, seating himself at his big, flattop desk and taking time out to shift a light that hung near his head from a movable arm above. He was terribly at ease with her.

"I want to speak to you just a minute about something," she said.

His smile further tightened his lips at the corners. "I expect I know what, don't I?"

"Do you?"

"About my editorial, isn't it? I've had a couple of calls already," he said, ending on a just-perceptible chuckle. His manner suggested the way one handled cranks and old people.

"Yes it is," she said. "It's something I have strong feelings about. The whole community does, in fact. I just wanted you to know how we feel. We—"

"Oh, I know how *you* feel . . . Mrs. Glenn." She thought he had almost said "Miss Hester." "You consider it knuckling under, compromising and so forth. And a lot of people will. But the *whole* community? I don't know about that."

"Virtually the whole," she said. "You'll see that they do."

Kirk Qualls leaned a little back in his chair. The good-humored, faintly ironic expression on his mouth had not changed. She was struck with the difference in everything since she had been here last—with the slick, green-painted walls instead of old chipped plaster ones, this desk instead of the battered rolltop, radiant light instead of glare. And most of all with this cool, sophisticated young man instead of the ruddy old one who had called her "Miss Hester" and laughed loudly at anecdotes he told about her family. This one took a cigarette from his shirt pocket and said:

"Of course I'm not in charge of the thing. This is only my personal opinion. And we have to grant people that, surely."

This was a small score. It made her suddenly conscious of her disadvantage. He rolled the cigarette between a thumb and finger.

"I only want you to realize," she said, still firmly, "that the town is strongly against you. We very much want it put back right away. Among other things, we don't like what you call 'knuckling under' to violence."

Kirk Qualls rolled the cigarette, watching the process as if it might result in something mildly amusing. "All I really said, of course, was to postpone it for a while. Don't you think that makes pretty good sense, if it might mollify the Negroes? After all, they are quite rightly angry. Maybe you don't realize how upset they are, Mrs. Glenn."

"I realize who is keeping them that way," she said, feeling

suddenly surer of herself. "This was not their own idea, even. That Citizens' Committee put it in their minds. Those people have been saying that it ought to be removed. You know they have."

"Our 'agitators,' you mean." The hint of amusement deepened at the corners of his mouth. Still rolling the cigarette, he said, "But they are part of the community now, too, Mrs. Glenn. You'll have to admit they are contributing a great deal. Surely the textile—"

"They are contributing, all right—to the chaos. They inspired that 'march' the other day. The Delmore girl was in it. Those people have nothing but contempt for our life. They despise us. They were delighted to see the monument blown up."

After a pause, Kirk Qualls said, "Mrs. Glenn, the real contributors to chaos were the home folks who murdered that Negro boy two weeks ago. And the others who know who they are and do nothing. There's where your chaos comes from."

She felt her strength, inexplicably, receding like blood from her heart. Watching his hand pick up a silver lighter from the desk and put it to the cigarette hanging from his lips now, she stifled this inane weakness. "There are people everywhere like those that did that. We need not abolish ourselves because some . . . devils are born among us. Other people have theirs, too."

Smoke, coiling in the radiant light, drifted between them. Kirk Qualls did not respond to her words at all. What he said, in a voice as detached as before, was, "Mrs. Glenn, we just can't have this kind of thing anymore. Aside from—"

"We have not had 'this kind of thing,' " she interrupted.

"Aside from other considerations," he went on imperturbably, "we can't afford it now. We have got to move ahead, and we *are* moving ahead. But racial conflict could hurt us bad. It could ruin us. We are absolutely dependent on industrial growth now, or the town will dry up. We have a most advantageous situation for industry here, if we can keep them coming. But this kind of thing will stop them. They want a desirable social situation or they'll go elsewhere for it. It's a matter of life or death for us. So why not make a small compromise? Further ones, if necessary. After all, Mrs. Glenn, what does that monument mean to Negroes? It means the defense of the very evil they have suffered so much from, slavery. It certainly isn't any promoter of unity. We have to think about these things now."

Her momentary lapse had passed quite out of mind, and she, hands tightly folded upon her lap, sat observing him with a contempt that she had no wish to veil. He saw it. His mouth at the corners contracted a little and he took a drag from his cigarette.

"I wonder if you realize how much things have changed, Mrs. Glenn. Even in the last five years, in this town. In ten more, you won't know it. And I must admit I think it's about time. We haven't exactly been practicing equality, you know."

"Which is justice, of course," she said with tight, bitter lips and picked up her purse from the floor beside her. "But I don't think the town has changed so much that we will put up with this."

"You might be surprised, though. I've talked with a good many people. You might find that 'we' includes quite a few that are of the other opinion."

"Your friends, I take it," she said, gripping the purse tightly in her fingers.

"Oh, the 'agitators,' you mean," he said, his irony more apparent than before. "Well, it's true that some of them are my friends. But I have others, too—among the natives, you might say. Some rather influential, in fact, that you might want to include in your 'we.' No, Mrs. Glenn," he said, letting his irony recede, "I really think the town as a whole will be persuaded to go along quietly, in its own interest . . . That is, unless somebody starts demagoguing the red-necks," he added resignedly.

There was a cold place, like an object near her heart, that seemed the reason why her passion was suddenly without words. She felt herself master of only one response: she stood up. "We will see who is right."

Rising now, he stepped with some alacrity ahead of her to the door. "I wish I could persuade you to see it my way."

She looked at him flatly, then at the door. "Thank you for your time."

"Not at all." But the door latch seemed hung, and he had to turn the knob back and forth, saying, "It's got some mysterious ailment," before it responded.

"Maybe it's your father's ghost," she murmured.

"Maybe so," he answered, laughing, and added a slight, casual bow as he let her out.

It was now dusk and the lights around the square were burning—all but the spotlights in the center circle. There were no people in sight. Lingering, she gazed across at the empty pedestal standing in the central gloom. It seemed so strange. It almost frightened her. What she had felt, and had concealed, just at the end of the conversation in Kirk Qualls's office, was like the preparation building for this—and this the epiphany. That pedestal was like a tomb in a place of desolation. A sound of voices across the square was a sudden, blessed reprieve, and she hurried on into Hampton Street.

11

Hester's depression had not lasted long after she left Kirk Qualls's office. That night on the telephone Edgar Lashley, a member of the city council whom she knew better than the others, made light of her fears. It had been just three days, he reminded her. The only question was one of a little time, he was sure, and she needn't interpret Kirk Qualls too literally. A call to Jane Willingham, on a pretext of society business, assured her further. And so did bits of conversation she had next day with tradespeople in stores where she shopped. Her feeling of isolation, then, had no real basis in fact.

And yet, despite such assurances, the feeling would not pass entirely away. There were times when it dogged her like a persistent but unobtrusive shadow or, again, asserted itself in little fits of conscious apprehension. On the second night it came in a dream of the town deserted but for herself, in which she observed herself walking, past the ruined monument, first, then down empty silent streets where all the houses were curtained and shut, and the doors resounded like drums to blows of her loud knocking. At the Farnsworth house she had called out in desperation, and this was what had waked her up.

And then there was the interval after she read the letter in Friday's paper. The letter was written by Wendell Pitts, the young Negro lawyer whom she had seen around town—a quite literate letter. She was reminded at once, by certain turns of phrase, by its demanding, self-righteous tone, of the one on Wednesday from Horace Delmore's Committee. There was the real source. In all probability they had planted the idea, urged it on Pitts. And on others yet to be heard from? These two letters already suggested a sequence in the making. It would be with Kirk Qualls's connivance, too. He had been silent today and yesterday. Wasn't he only waiting to let "the public" speak and then, when he dared, come out with the voice of wisdom and prudence in support of what the Pittses and the Delmores had proposed: that a World War II memorial replace the old, anachronistic one?

Again that evening she was assailed by the impulse to seek assurance from others. They would think, as Jane had, as Edgar Lashley had, that she was making too much of the matter. Was she? But why could they not see the issue, and its importance, as plainly as she could? The very complacency she had met, the comfortable assumption that the thing, that everything, would happen in the expected way was perhaps the deepest reason that her confidence kept faltering . . . Or was it? There were pale, unobtrusive doubts, like whispers just out of earshot, that her consciousness rejected as quickly as they impinged. In spite of her restlessness she did not call anyone.

That weekend, what she gathered from leading remarks to acquaintances on the street told her nothing new and the newspaper did not mention the subject. Why could she not dismiss it, then? Obviously it was absurd to suppose, as she did in irrational moments, that something behind the faces she had queried, behind the friendly voices and even the pages of the newspaper, was being withheld from her. These moments were not many, but each one unsettled her confidence again. More than once she went out for a walk in hope of finding someone to whom she could mention the subject.

She might have discussed it with Cam. Several times she started to, but an obscure reluctance made her draw back. And each time he expected something. His brow would faintly knit. Once he said, "What's the matter, Mama?"

"Nothing important."

But why not have answered him? Better than most, better than anyone, perhaps, he would understand her feelings. Did she not owe him this confidence? When finally, at Sunday dinner, he asked her another such question, she answered him in detail, in a clear deliberate voice. He looked at his plate while she spoke. Afterward she waited for his response with an unexpected anxiety.

He looked up, looked level at her. "I wouldn't worry about it, Mama. The town wouldn't stand for that. Kirk Qualls is just one man."

Why had she been reluctant to confide in him? The gratitude she felt lifted her confidence again. "He has the newspaper, though."

"Who pays any attention to that old newspaper?"

"A lot of people. He has more influence than you think."

"Just on things nobody cares about. Not on this, he won't."

"And a lot of influential friends, too. That's what worries me most."

"I never see him with anybody but those new people. They never were on our side. Nobody's going to listen to them."

She sighed, but she felt like reaching out and touching his hand that lay in a fist on the table edge. "I hope you are right." And then, "But I wish I was sure. Sometimes I'm not so sure anymore who is on our side."

"Everybody is, that counts," he said. "You'll find out they are. I wouldn't let it worry me."

Her confidence that Sunday afternoon, only because of this brief conversation, seemed entirely restored. In perfect late-September weather, amid the sibilant hush of shrubbery that made a bower of her sitting place in the yard, she felt the sunlight's mellow weight thawing the tensions out of her body. One regret hung lightly in her mind: Cam had not been able to go for another ride in the country with her. It would have been beautiful at Fountain Inn today, watching the slant of evening light take on its autumn bronze. There were other places, too, that they might have gone: Danally's Hollow, where the air smelled of springwater, and virgin oaks made a tunnel of the passage through; Sulphur Flat, the hunting ground; Granny Lunn Pike, where the old lady had fed the fleeing Confederates. And there was the great, sweeping bend of the Saugahatchee between the white bluffs below Grimley. These scenes stirred her memory now like sleepy wind in a tree.

Presently her eyes flew open, her lids blinking against the glister of light in the green foliage. The voice had come in her dream, she thought, a high male voice whose image lingered. Then a sort of jolting perception, whether of eye or ear, snapped her body upright. There was a man with her, speaking again, saying, "Miss Hester." And then, "I never went to scare you."

Unable to rise, she stared at him. He was standing to her left, where the passage through the shrubbery opened toward the back of the house. She knew perfectly, and had known from the instant of that startled perception, who he was. And this despite the improbable difference in his appearance. He wore a tweed suit coat too tight around the trunk of his body and a gold-spangled tie fatly knotted between the widespread lapels of his collar. In both hands he held, against his stomach, a small, green, felt hat, like a tourist's. It was his voice, speaking again now, "Taking you a little nap, wasn't you?" that had so sharply identified him to her. It had an abrasive keenness that she remembered well from that day at his house.

Still she could not rise from her chair, but she did manage firmness enough to say, "What do you want, Mr. Handley?"

It was curtly said. It made his eyelids flicker. In a wounded voice, "I just come thinking maybe I could do you a favor, Miss Hester. Fellow told me you was wanting board shingles and I know where some's at. They ain't easy come by, anymore, you know."

She only stared at him, uncertain as yet what he was talking about. His mere physical presence, his garments and vaguely puffy face and hair like sparse tobacco threads, still held her in a sort of thralldom.

"For your summerhouse, I mean," he said in response to her stare. "That's the lumber for it laying out yonder, ain't it?" He gestured behind him with his head, exposing unlooked-for sinews in his throat.

Remembering now, she said, "Yes," nodding stiffly at him. Was this what he wanted?

"Well, if you want them, I got them. They ain't new, you can't get no new ones. But I guarantee these is good. How big's your summerhouse going to be?"

She had utterly forgotten, but he answered her blank gaze with: "Well, you probably need around a hundred fifty to two hundred board feet. I'll come measure when it's framed up. Give you a good price, too . . . We got a deal, ain't we?"

Her answer, "No," came from her mouth with a harshness that she had not intended. Somehow its echo in her mind was vaguely frightening. But what had she to fear from him? Deliberately stiffening her posture, she added, "Mr. Crane is already taking care of it for me."

He shifted one foot—in a scuffed, two-tone shoe—but he did not turn to go. "He ain't found any yet, though. Might can't. And I already got some. Fact is, I'd be glad to build the whole thing for you, Miss Hester. I built several in my time."

"I have someone," she said. And as if his term of familiar address had only now reached her ears, she added coldly, "And I am Mrs. Glenn."

Her reproof made his gaze fall, curtaining his eyes behind lids that once again suggested membranes, as if they might only cloud and redden his vision. "Yes ma'm. I never went to sound for'ard. Just seemed like I had knowed you so long." He hesitated, as if musing, and now the fancy that his eyes were cloudily watching her through the lids half-prepared her for his words: "Got boys is good friends and all."

She thought of getting up. But he seemed too close, blocking, as on that other occasion, the path of retreat. Keeping her voice hard, "If I need your boards, I'll get in touch with you."

"Yes ma'm, I wish you would," he said. He moved and partly lifted the hat, but this was all. Her heart was beating. He said, "You know, I'm right proud of them being friends like they are. That's a fine boy you got. He's a pleasure to you, I know."

She was not sure whether she nodded in response.

"Now, my boy, he's a good boy too, but he does worry me a little bit, sometimes. Your boy's a good friend for him, I know. He ain't steady like your boy is."

She mastered herself and looked squarely at him. His gaze met hers for just one intense instant that started a coldness gathering at her heart. Then it slid away and his lids veiled it.

She got up suddenly. "I have to go now," she said and stepped forward with a purposefulness that forced him to move from her path. She passed through the shrubbery, approached the back porch, but behind her she heard his footsteps coming on. She did not hesitate outside the door. Entering, she shut it firmly and did not pause again until she had reached her bedroom.

It was nearly dusk before she got up from the bed and went into the kitchen to fix supper.

Hester bought a tin of aspirin and took three of them there in the drugstore. The sunlight striking her eyes as she came out onto the sidewalk sent another stab of pain through her head. Back in her car she sat with her eyes closed. It was worse this afternoon, but she had had the headache off and on for three days, since Sunday night. In a way she associated it with Hollis Handley. Not that her shock and revulsion, obviously revived from her memory of that day in his house, were the immediate cause; his intrusion seemed merely the preface that had shattered the serenity of her mood. It was later, as she reflected upon the presumption of it, seeing it as yet another mark of this decay in the whole order of things, that her former tension had come back with a vengeance. And then to have her fears confirmed, as it were, on Aunt Minnie's tremulous lips:

"Do you know what he meant, Hester?" The old lady's hair was radiant under the lamp; her brow was lifted in bewilderment. She was talking about the preacher's sermon that morning, which Hester had not heard. "About a monument to 'brotherhood?' "

"Exactly what did he say?"

"Oh, that we ought to build a new monument to brotherhood. It sounded to me like he wanted to take the Confederate monument down and put up some other kind."

Since she did not know about the monument, Hester did not tell her. She left it a puzzle for the old lady and went home with this ache already vivid in her head. Cam was at home by then, eating at the kitchen table the supper she had left in the oven, but she did not mention the matter to him. All she did say, before she went into her room for the night, was:

"You don't see the Handley boy anymore, do you? You told me you wouldn't."

Cam, for just a glance at her, paused over his food. "Why do you think I have?"

"I don't. It's only that I don't want you to again. I don't approve of him, for you."

"Don't worry, Mama. I haven't seen him in a long time. I just went there those times for kicks."

Hester had gone to bed with her headache and since then it had never really left off. But today, as midafternoon approached, it had grown to a new intensity. Now, sitting here in the car with her eyes shut, she had some moments of feeling that never again could she bear to open them in the harsh, unshaded light of day. She would not go to the meeting. Her pain was ample reason. She would close herself in her shadowy room and lie with her head on the cool pillow until sleep darkened everything.

But these moments passed. No, she would go on, of course. It was what she had been looking toward these last three days, and longer. Strange that now it should seem so like a thing required of her by her fate. When the pain seemed a little less, she opened her eyes slowly and let them rest for a moment on the seat beside her where lay her minute book and the pages torn from the newspaper.

It seemed the rawest of ironies—another small stroke of her fate?—that when she first looked up, the person she instantly saw passing along the walk, with animated gestures toward a companion at her side, should be Mrs. Delmore. Hester watched her go by, in a suit of yellow velveteen and slanted, duckbill hat, free hand extended in a gesture as broad as any fishwife's. She turned the corner out of sight, but on the air behind her a little peal of laughter rang. In Hester's ears it carried an edge. She felt how tight her jaws were clenched, as if locked at the hinges, and her sudden move to start the car was a reflex of her body that took her by surprise. The moment passed. Wondering at herself, she backed with deliberate care out into the street and drove slowly around the circle, without a glance at the monument, into Forrest Street.

Hester had expected her first feeling as she entered, a little late, the circle of women already seated around the paneled walls of Laura Sharpe's big living room, to pass off in a moment. It should have been only a matter of time for attention to drift elsewhere. But even after she had taken her seat at the card table beside the plate-glass window where Marlon Bryce already sat presiding and had opened the minute book, her feeling persisted. She knew, as well as she knew these faces, that nothing hostile to herself had been stilled by her entering the room. Beside the minute book on the table lay the folded pages of the newspaper containing those letters to the editor. Here was the cause. But they, every woman in the room, surely felt as she did in this matter: Jane Willingham there in the rocker, with hair parted old style down the middle, seated in her attitude of unconscious grace that was the gift of her family; Mrs. Halleran, in skirts like widow's weeds, substantial and blunt as a fortress. The reflection steadied Hester. Clearing her mind, hand at rest on the folded pages, she waited for a pause to fall.

It was not to be for a while. Hester's first chance, as her fingers closed on the pages, was snatched away. From her seat across the table, Marlon Bryce suddenly said, "You have a report on the Handley house, don't you, Edna?"

The question brought a stop in Hester's mind. Staring across the room at Edna Traynor's face, she heard, "Not much of a report, I'm afraid. I asked Martin Leith to go out and examine it. He says we really shouldn't take the risk. Apparently the roof has been leaking for years and he thinks the building has been seriously damaged. He's very competent, you know. He says it would be most unwise for us to take the chance."

Hester watched her face until it turned aside for a question. Her own eyes moved elsewhere, avoiding faces now, fastening at last upon a vase of fluted burgundy glass beside the door. There was much colorful glass in the room, on tables and delicate shelves along the walls, glowing rose or emerald or amber in rays from the big plate-glass window at Hester's back. But the sight did not lift the pressure from her heart. Why should it be beating so, more than ever now?

"Well, that's that," Mrs. Halleran boomed, "history or no history. I suspected it all along."

This was the time, while the pause lasted, for Hester to enter the matter in her minute book. Instead, with a sense of plunging recklessly, she picked up and unfolded the newspaper pages. "Have you all seen these . . . these letters to the paper about the monument?"

"Do they concern this society?" Mrs. Halleran said.

"They ought to. Along with Kirk Qualls's editorial. I have the feeling they are part of a campaign that's getting under way. Let me read you this one." She began without looking at them, reading in a voice maybe louder than was necessary the whole letter through and then the name, Wendell Pitts. Looking up now, with a sense of pressure from the still faces watching her, she said, "I think we should act right away to make our feelings known. Before this thing gets up any more momentum. And bring all the pressure we can to see that the monument is put back as soon as possible. Start a petition, maybe."

There was a silence. Perhaps, in spite of her effort at restraint, her tone had been a little urgent, demanding. She felt in a throb of pain the headache reasserting itself.

"But that's only one letter, Hester," Jane Willingham serenely said.

"Here is another one, from the Citizens' Committee, saying the same thing. And Kirk Qualls's editorial, really backing them. I think it's part of a campaign and Kirk Qualls is in it."

"Oh, but Kirk only wants to postpone putting the monument back," Edna Traynor said. "Not replace it. He's just worried about it starting some more trouble."

"I talked to him about it. He's friends with those people, he agrees with them. I'm quite sure of it." Her tone, she knew, had grown militant. Deliberately she softened it. "They will replace it, too, if they're not opposed. They gave those Negroes the idea of destroying it in the first place. You mentioned the matter week before last, Helen."

Helen Cate, in an armchair close by, gave a nod of her white head. "Hester may have a point, you know," she said. But she said it meekly.

"Aren't you making a little too much of this, Hester? I'm sure they'll put it back." Jane's hands lay restfully folded on her lap. There were murmurs of assent.

"I'm afraid I'm *not* making too much of it." Hester heard the edge in her voice and tried again to soften it. "But even postponing it—which is really only the first step for them—is compromising with violence. It will only encourage more of the same."

"But Kirk's idea is that waiting will help to discourage violence," Edna Traynor said.

"That's what Henry thinks." Martha Ludlow's silken fingers toyed with the rich pearls of her necklace. This, instead of her face, was what Hester watched, hearing her say, "He thinks it's very important that we make some concessions now. He's very much worried about the new rubber plant, that it might not come here if there's more trouble. He's talked to some of the people. It would be quite a blow if it didn't come."

"That's what my husband says, too," someone offered.

"We do have to think about these things now, Hester," Jane said.

Hester was still gazing at Martha's hand fingering the pearls. She heard:

"This is a matter for the city council to decide, not this society," in Mrs. Halleran's resonant contralto. The old lady sat with an appearance of great weight, her hands squarely placed on the arms of the chair, and her black eyes looked severely at Hester. Hester thought of the Halleran property, acres and acres of it stretched along the north edge of town. Mrs. Halleran added, "I propose that we get along with our *proper* business."

"What is our proper business, if this isn't?" Hester said, hearing anger suffuse her voice. But she did not regret it enough to withdraw her level eyes from the now-snapping black ones of Mrs. Halleran. "How do we know what the council will decide, without pressure? Kirk Qualls is on it."

There was a moment of silence. Mrs. Halleran had turned her disdainful eyes elsewhere. Then, "Walter is too," Edna Traynor said faintly, of her husband. It was barely audible, spoken, Hester gathered, in a mock-pathetic tone. And from some quarter of the room another, obscurer comment issued.

Hester saw that she had erred. Sitting stiffly, with blood tingling in her face, she had a moment's consciousness of herself as a mere spectacle for their attention. But her anger came back quickly. To no one in particular she said, "What *are* we for? Just to put up plaques over nothing? If that's all, we are not 'preserving' anything."

"But isn't that the same thing you want to do, Hester? Except with a statue instead of a plaque?" Jane said with a mild expression, as gracious as ever.

Hester merely gazed at her for a second, across a space that seemed even physically greater than before. "You really think it's the same thing, Jane? You couldn't." She added, "Don't you see the kind of thing this is? It's an attack on us—on the way we do and the way we think. Only the first one, there will be more. They want to make us forget what we are. They want to make us over again, their way. It's to destroy what we are. They are not any 'friends' of ours."

The silence that followed she recognized as one of embarrassment, at her passion. Only Helen Cate and Jane did not avoid her gaze. Finally:

"But surely Kirk's a friend of ours, Hester," Edna Traynor said. "He was born here just like you were. Like all of us."

Hester said nothing.

Martha Ludlow said, "I think you're being awfully unrealistic. Things aren't like they used to be anymore, we have to face the facts." There were murmurs of agreement, and she added, "After all, it's only a little thing Kirk is suggesting. And it might save us a great deal. Think what a blow it would be if after all—"

"The new plant didn't come," Hester finished, from a tight, angry throat. "I would be glad if it didn't."

"This is all nonsense," Mrs. Halleran abruptly proclaimed. She had shifted her chair so as not to be facing Hester. "I propose that we get on with this meeting."

In the pause Marlon Bryce, across the table, glanced uncomfortably around the room and said, "Shall we?" But Jane, in a quiet and gentle voice, with a smile that had no trace of irony, said, "After all, Hester, we lost that war."

"We didn't lose everything, though." The sensation of blood suddenly rising in her face again made her look down at her open minute book to say, "But we seem to be up for sale now. 'Being realistic' nowadays, I see, means just selling out."

Hester's words had brought a real silence down, every eye upon her. It hardly mattered to her now. Somehow this was the moment that, in a vague compartment of her mind, she had been anticipating for at least these last few days. No, much longer.

Mrs. Halleran was moving to rise from her chair. "I will not be subjected to impudence. Since the meeting has no business, I must go home."

"Please, Mrs. Halleran." Marlon Bryce had almost got up from her own chair. "There is some business. I think we can get on with it now, can't we?" she said, with an uncertain glance of appeal at Hester.

What Hester felt was not anger now. It was more like need to be through with a part played nearly to the end already. "I just want to be certain," she said. "I take it that nobody will support a resolution to the city council . . . that the monument be put back right away? Will they?" She looked around the room at the still faces, at Jane's, then at Helen Cate's. Because she saw sympathy there and Helen's lips parted, Hester thought she was about to speak.

"Is there a second?" Marlon asked in a faint, harassed voice.

There was none. Helen, after all, was silent. Mrs. Halleran, with conspicuous exertion, got up from her chair.

"Please, Mrs. Halleran," Hester said courteously, "I'm the one who must go," and rose, leaving the minute book on the table. She at first resisted, then gave in to her compulsion and said, "I think it's time to put up a plaque for this society."

"Oh, Hester," she heard someone murmur—Jane.

With all their eyes upon her, Hester walked out of the room and straight out of the house to her car.

PART THREE

12

Ames had not been enjoying the party anyway, and when he saw her enter the fraternity house, with her swaying date and another couple, he had taken his drink and his bottle and gone back into the empty card room. She had seen him, recognized him, he thought, for on his way out he had received a special glance from her stern, wide-set, brown eyes. Except that she was Horace Delmore's daughter, Libby, he knew almost nothing about her. In the year or two since she and her family had moved to Cameron Springs he had nodded to her in passing maybe half a dozen times, evoking only stoical responses. He did not want to know anything more. Certainly he did not want to encounter her now—or anyone or any news from there.

And so, an hour later, when he looked up from his magazine and saw her standing in the card-room door, it flashed upon him that his luck contained an element of somehow conscious malice. Moments later, despite her appearance of surveying only the features of the room, he decided that it was not a matter of his luck. She had found him out on purpose. She kept up the pretense, however, scanning, as if he were not present, the leather chairs and the low, littered table where his feet were propped. He had a chance, covertly, to observe her. Except for the severity of expression, accented by the width of her face, she was not bad looking. He reflected that in other circumstances he might have thought her large brown eyes intelligent and her chestnut hair, though too short, unusually handsome. But what did she want with him?

"You're Ames Glenn, aren't you?" Her voice, with its midwestern edge, seemed vaguely masculine. As if she had dropped the question out of indifference, her eyes continued to wander over the room.

"Yes," he said quietly. She had not really entered the room and he did not rise. But now she did enter, drifted in and across to a shelf where a small, silver tennis trophy stood. She put a hand on it and picked it up. "I thought you were," she said.

The edge to her voice, he realized now, was sarcasm. She said it as though she had confirmed something distasteful about him. He kept still, glad he had not risen. Yet he was keenly conscious that in her eyes, which only appeared to study the trophy she held, there would be an expression of scorn.

"I'm a Cameron Springer, too, you know."

"I know," he said, then wished he had not answered.

"A grand old place. Real Ole South," she drawled.

He did not reply.

"Where all the 'niggahs' stay in their place." She put the trophy back on the shelf and turned her attention to a picture of a fraternity group beside it. On the wall to her left was a picture of General Lee and, despite himself, he sat waiting for the moment when her eyes would fall on it. He made an effort to summon in advance an icy retort to the inevitable. Certainly she had earned it. But why did he not get up and leave?

"And there's ole Marse Robert," she said, on schedule.

Yet all he could answer was, "Anything wrong with that?" Immediately he felt ashamed at his lack of spirit.

With hands on hips that drew the plaid skirt taut across her rump, she stood gazing at the picture. "It's even in the frat houses, isn't it?"

"What is?" he said with an edge to his voice.

"Ole South."

"Maybe. . . . Did you come in here just for this?"

"I guess I did. I'm one of those meddlesome Yankee bitches."

He did not answer, and as if to demonstrate her nature she sat down in a chair at the other side of the table and took a cigarette from a package in her skirt pocket. A sudden blare of music came from the front of the house. She gazed at the open door as if the sound disgusted her. "I get very burnt-out, sometimes."

"So you picked me."

"Well, you're the real thing, aren't you?"

"I don't know. Am I?"

"Your family is. Your mother. I don't imagine you're trying to convert her, are you?"

He said nothing.

She lit the cigarette, which he had made no move to light. "I don't imagine, for instance, you tried to stop her when she started that petition around."

"What petition?"

She blew a cloud of smoke and then fastened him with an expression of irony. "Oh, come now."

"I don't know what you are talking about," he said. "I haven't been home in three weeks. Or heard anything." It was true—or almost true. He had tried to shut even thoughts of the place entirely out of his mind. The one brief note from his mother had said almost nothing, except that he must write to Cam, words she had underlined. "What kind of petition?"

"You should keep up," she said. "You knew about the monument getting blown up, didn't you?" When he nodded she took another puff from the cigarette and leaned her head against the back of the chair. "Well, your mother seems to have decided the bad guys were winning the argument by default. So she wrote up a petition. All by herself, apparently. In very stirring language, too. Though it was more like a call to arms than a petition. All full of phrases like 'the threat to our way of life,' and 'our heritage.' And 'those who want to destroy all that we are.' She even suggested that the town was full of scalawags in high places, just crawling with traitors." Libby paused, regarding the cigarette held between her thumb and forefinger. "A little demagogic, I'm afraid. Also paranoiac. Though the two things go together, of course. A part of the syndrome." She waited, evidently to leave a space for angry objections, and dragged at the cigarette again.

But his anger was little more than a froth, something he ought to feel. "That doesn't sound like her," he said.

"It sounds very Southern to me," she said and looked indifferently at the ceiling. He was conscious that she would be glad to incense him, but he was not really thinking about her anymore. When he did not answer she said:

"There do seem to be a surprising number of scalawags, though

—including a lot of important ones. Of course it isn't a matter of conscience with most of them. They're just the ones who see where their bread is buttered. The effect is in the right direction, though, so that much is encouraging. Apparently your mother couldn't even enlist her pals, the old Confederate gentry, who are playing it cool, which has helped to keep the bourgeois in line. So she decided to aim her pitch at the plain folk." Libby stopped again, as if she still was waiting for some kind of an outburst.

He murmured, "Meaning what?"

"Meaning she set out to stir up the red-necks. Mostly that's what have signed it. Some of the names on that 'petition' look like hen-scratching," she said harshly. "My father has seen copies."

"You can't blame her for that." Ames's anger remained at the surface only.

"Can't I? How about her picking out the ones to ask? She knew who to go to. She had your little brother out in the country taking it around to them. Of course it snowballed out there. She knew exactly what she was doing."

"Those people are part of things, too, aren't they?" he said, in defense of what he did not feel like defending.

"Oh, yes," she said. Her mouth had curled a little. "Only the 'niggahs' are not part of things. Which accounts for there being no Negro names on the petition, probably. Or is it just because they're all too dumb to write their names?"

Ames let this pass. He said, "You still haven't told me what difference it's made—the petition."

"Oh, yes," she said. "I forgot." And then, "You *really* don't know anything about all this?"

"I told you I don't."

"You must be another 'neutral.' There are lots of you. At least you ought to take the hometown paper. But I was there yesterday. Your mother has been a success, so far. In a kind of way . . . Out in the country, anyway."

He just waited. He was thinking that his glass was empty and that he wanted another drink. They were drinking out front, where he could hear voices raised in song.

At the end of her rhetorical pause Libby said, "I don't mean she's been a success in making them put the monument back. Not yet, anyway. I just mean she's got the bullyboys out. She is already getting the violence she wanted."

"What violence?"

"Oh, just a couple of beatings. A few Negro houses shot into. Some threats in the middle of the night. Nothing much, so far. One of the houses they shot into was Wendell Pitts's. You probably don't know him because he is a Negro. He's been fool enough to speak out for Negro rights."

"I know who he is," Ames said, inadequately. He forced some conviction into his voice. "But she didn't want those things to happen. You can't blame her for all this. They would have happened anyway."

"Possibly," Libby said with a sarcasm that ought to have set his teeth on edge. "But I don't quite believe that excuses her—even if she didn't want 'those things' to happen. She did want *something* to happen, evidently. Don't you think?"

"She only wanted support. The way everybody does. The way you would, in her place."

"She's getting it. And she's just as much to blame as if she had done those things herself. And you know it. All of you really know it." There were little pinpoints of indignation in the large eyes she had fastened upon his. He met her with a gaze from which he tried to exclude all his feelings.

"Except you lie to yourselves," she went on. "That's the way it is with your 'upper class.' You let your red-necks do your dirty work. Then you blame them for it. The things they do are never what you 'meant.' That's the way they are, and it isn't *your* fault. It's the Yankees' fault for stirring them up." She broke off suddenly to grind out her cigarette in the ashtray on the table.

This was when he felt, from somewhere, a hot blaze of anger surge in him. It made his mouth come open, with some envenomed answer already at the threshold of his tongue. Yet her voice was able to check it, saying:

"You know, actually, it's just like with children. They always see what you *really* mean, down underneath. So when *they do* what *you mean,* it doesn't seem quite fair to blame them, do you think? But you don't think it's the same case, do you? If there is another murder, it won't be your fault, of course—or your mother's."

Where his anger had been, there was now a blank. He could not even look squarely at her, much less utter whatever words had been on his tongue. In fact it seemed that in this moment of pause, his mind had stopped working. He did not see, but he heard her, at last, stir and say, in a softer voice:

"Well, I've been the Yankee bitch long enough. My date may have sobered up to where he's missed me."

The sound of music from out front filled his mind for a moment and seemed to be the reason that his attention came back to her again. She still lingered, as if she had intuited something. She said:

"I know I've been very nasty. I just felt like unloading on someone."

"I guess I can understand it," he said, conscious of the change in her face. Her brown eyes had softened and now, in her gaze, there was a sort of consolation for him. It was as if she would have taken back some of the thrusts she had delivered. And in fact she said:

"I'm sorry if I've been unfair. It was just the impression I got—that you didn't feel anything one way or the other. Like a lot of people I've met."

"It doesn't matter," he said. He saw that she would not leave yet and he found that he was obscurely glad.

"Are you on your mother's side or not?"

He had turned his eyes away from her, but this did not help. Her question, her gaze, continued patiently to insist. The voices and music he distantly heard were no diversion, but he still did not know what he would answer until he actually said, "Not in this. Maybe not in a lot of things I used to think." He felt as if he had said something that should have stilled the sound of the music.

"Then you are against her, aren't you?"

He was so long in meditating his answer that finally she said, "God, I'm glad I'm not you. All this family stuff. When will you ever be free so you can be yourself? You are at least twenty-one, aren't you?"

He nodded.

"And you know she's wrong. It wouldn't make any difference if her being wrong was harmless, but it's not. It's destructive. And you know it is." She paused for a moment. Then, "Your mother thinks we want to destroy her 'way of life' and she's right. Wouldn't it really be a favor? To you, for instance? You can't even follow out your own convictions, apparently. So you have just retired into a kind of sad neutrality."

When still he did not answer, she continued, "Don't you see what a trap it is? The South is a trap. I've read everything I could about it. That's why you need us almost as much as the Negroes do—to help you get out . . . Or does that sound too terribly arrogant to you?"

"Maybe not," he said quietly. "Not if you're right."

"If I am, then you ought to join us, oughtn't you? If that's what you believe."

It was a subdued challenge. He never did quite meet it, though his eyes shifted to her face.

"That's the only kind of moral obligation I really have any respect for," she said and then, suddenly, stood up.

It may have been only the turmoil of his thoughts that made him neglect to rise also, though later he reflected that perhaps this was because their conversation had seemed to leave quite empty all the accustomed forms of his experience. And in the doorway she had stopped and turned around to say to him, "Believe it or not, you are welcome at our meeting tomorrow night."

"What meeting?" he blankly asked.

"The Citizens' Committee. You could call me at my father's house tomorrrow evening, if you want to go." Then, without even another glance, she had vanished down the hall toward the sound of the music.

13

It seemed to Hester that her pain magnified the sound of Lucius's hammer blows out in the yard. She had always been a healthy woman and this recurrent headache, two weeks old, had become a serious annoyance. On occasion it was more than this. Then it seemed to work like intermittent thrusts of a blade straight back from the center of her forehead. Once or twice, for brief intervals, it had all but incapacitated her. And just now was another time, just when she had almost made up her mind to go outside and see how Lucius's work on the summerhouse was progressing.

She knew well enough the cause of the headache. It was strain, accented by the events these last few nights had produced. People, her old friends, were blaming her for these things. She knew this. Their silence had told her, a silence whose meaning the editorial in yesterday's paper had surely given utterance. That the editorial had not in fact called her name obscured nothing. Her petition was mentioned—and branded not only as superfluous but also as having "incendiary effect." Clearly she was the one meant by "those who seek to force their will on the community" and "thoughtlessly contribute to a climate of violence." It appeared, she bitterly thought, that the truths that she had stated with perfect exactness were, like that many obscenities, not to be spoken where the public could hear—not anymore. But was she to keep silent because there was risk in speaking what she so clearly saw? Were they blaming Horace Delmore for *his* part in these things?

Her friends? They had used to be her friends. But how deep had these friendships really been when a rift like this, on the very ground of all their common feeling, was possible? The many ties, after all, were merely bonds of sand. For how else could they, her old friends, shed with such a readiness, with such ease, feelings that had been real in the past? It seemed to Hester now that she had not known them at all, not really. Not even Jane. Hadn't Jane's visit last week, on the day that had followed Hester's "scene" at that society meeting, made this clear enough?

Until then, Hester remembered, she had not yet been entirely able to accept the truth as it was. All through the night before and up into the afternoon there was a little game of deception that she had played with herself. It involved an expectation that there would be a call on the telephone or maybe a letter in favorable response to the urgent one which, on the previous evening, she had dropped into the door box of the room where the city council held its Wednesday night meeting. Or else—or maybe also—at her front door a delegation from the society come to tell her of a change of heart. Hence, when Jane's knock came, there had been a moment in which Hester had felt a surge of joyous confirmation. Even when she saw that Jane was alone, her satisfaction had lapsed only to the extent of supposing that a single spokesman had been judged sufficient.

But after all it was only Jane, bearer of nothing except her own concern at Hester's "stubbornness." It was expressed in Jane's mild and graceful way, her family way, at tea in the quiet, nostalgic air of a parlor not commonly entered now by anyone but Hester. The ghost of an old friendship—When had it really ceased to be?—presided over their talk, and words that at another time would have embittered Hester were charged only with sadness. The bitterness had come later, afterward, when she reflected on what the words actually had meant. Here in Jane's presence, in a medium made warm by her voice, her grace of gesture, her vaguely antique style of hair and dress, Hester found herself responding as if this were merely some unhappy matter to be disposed of without risk of any breach between them.

"You know how I feel, Jane," she said. "You, of all people."

"But everything is so different now, Hester. We can't possibly go on living the way we did in the past."

"We can go on being *what* we were in the past. Or we won't be anything." She noticed herself reflecting with part of her mind on Jane's familiar posture in the big mahogany chair—head leaning a little sideways, one corner of her chin propped on tips of stiffened fingers. And she wondered about the suit Jane wore, whether, for all its shapely fit and scalloped lapels, it was not an old one now converted to approximate the newer style.

Jane gave a sigh, moved her head. "But it's so fruitless. There's nothing you can do. I hate to see you just withdraw. And this is only a little thing. Really, it isn't worth it, Hester."

Hester had thought later, with bitterness, that this was what they all said, always, on every new occasion. It was never worth it. Was there anything worth it, for them? She remembered thinking this question at the time, though not in bitterness then. And she remembered pausing at it, or something *about* it—a pause in which, forgetful of Jane, she had looked out through the window as if some kind of an answer was about to shape itself against the sun-gilded maple foliage. She had missed what Jane was saying, and when, moments later, her mind had focused again, she heard a difference in Jane's voice.

"I hope you won't think of us as just 'selling out.' " On her face was a sort of wry apology.

Hester hesitated. "Your house?" she said, as if a magic had put the words on her tongue.

"The plant will be right there close, you know—when it comes. It won't be the same. The place will lose so much value. And with Ward gone now . . ." she said of her son, breaking off for a moment. "I believe even you would, Hester. Now, wouldn't you?"

"I don't know," Hester said, for she did not want to talk about it anymore—or any of these matters. There were other subjects, out of their common memory, that she was suddenly hungry for. "Let me give you some more tea," she said, to open the way, her hand insistent for the cup resting on Jane's knee.

Her small hope had not been answered. For all their mutual effort the conversation went but haltingly, and it was only minutes until Jane, not quite at her accustomed ease, was taking her leave. Only then did Hester's bitterness start to come upon her. She was still standing there behind the shut front door, in the silence of the house, when her idea had taken for the first time the shape of a definite intention. An hour later she had sat down to compose the petition.

No, she had not done wrong. Were not the people, all the inarticulate ones, entitled to be made conscious of the truth? Was it not their life, too? If those who ought to defend these things declined to make even the effort, then surely the people had every right to be told. And she had told them only the truth, nothing distorted or inflamed. Had she not seen to this? There were words, written in the first heat of her passion, that she had changed for gentler ones, references she had deleted. Less would have been untrue. Was she then to be blamed because a tiny few had responded with some acts of foolish violence? Certainly she was not the one who had driven them to their present pitch of frustration, a state of mind so fragile that her small voice could send them over the edge. If indeed her words *were* the cause. Did not her critics have reason to be grateful for the relative puniness of all these recent events?

No, she would do it again, the same way. Or nearly the same. Perhaps, in spite of pride, she should herself have done the work of distributing the copies. It was Mr. Fitzhugh, at the grocery where she always shopped, who, on her very first attempt, had caused her to change her mind. His barely veiled reluctance as he pinned the petition up beside the door had been more than a little humiliating for her. But should she not have had the courage to go on risking such moments? Not that Cam had required any urging. In fact he had assumed her part with as much willingness as if this thing had been his own conception, discussing it with her, checking voluntarily to see if new names had been added to copies already posted. This very day, for instance, he had gone to check at a store clear down near Mabry. So perhaps pride still was behind her wish that she had refused this show of his devotion. All the same she obscurely wished it.

And she did have another regret—for a somewhat better reason. Silence where there had been the sound of Lucius's hammer reminded her, for she thought that now she could go out for a look at the summerhouse. And surely this was because the silence told her that she would no longer have to encounter Lucius. It was no use trying to hide this fact, however irrational, from herself. She did not want to face Lucius now, even old Lucius, who all her life had been a part of the ambience in which she moved. It was a feeling that had come over her only this morning, suddenly, when she heard through her bedroom window the first sounds of his day's work under way. But this would pass. It was just another effect of a bad month. Meanwhile, lying upon her bed, she waited long enough to be sure that the stillness had not deceived her.

But it had deceived her. She did not discover this at first, because Lucius was seated in the partial shade of a shrub to the left of her and because her eyes, squinted in pain against the noon sunlight, were taken up with scanning details of the unfinished summerhouse. It would soon be done, she thought, somehow comforted by the thought. Four of the six sides were already closed with crisscrossed lattices, and the low, peaked roof lacked only the shingles that Mr. Crane had not yet found.

"Thought I'd get done with the latticing 'fore I leave," Lucius said.

She gave a start. Lucius was putting a last bite of something into his mouth and, chewing it, he said, "If I don't run out of lattices. Them there's all is left."

She gazed with a helpless feeling at the pile of lattices near her feet. Perhaps he was watching her. She walked on and entered the shade of the summerhouse and stopped. This consciousness of his scrutiny, however unjustified, did not diminish. With another, small start she heard him close his lunch box. "Why didn't you come to the kitchen for your lunch?" she said.

"Willodene ain't in there on Saturday no more."

"I would have fed you. I always have."

"Well, it don't make no difference."

She waited a moment. She took a step or two and with the latticework between them now looked through one of the gaps at his face. He was not watching her at all. He had picked up his big felt hat, and was shaping it on his lap. His thick underlip hung loose, all right, but not in sullenness. It was all her own foolish imagining.

"You ain't got them board shingles yet, have you?"

"No. But I will," she said, and with a feeling of almost joyful release began to pace slowly around inside the summerhouse, touching with her hands the posts and the latticework.

She even stayed a little while to watch him work, watching his deliberate black fingers place a strip of lattice and tack it with measured blows of the hammer. Presently he stopped, letting the hand with the hammer sink down against his leg. She saw that he had stopped *for* something. It was as though she felt it coming, because her gaze already had fled when she heard him mutter:

"They done some more meanness last night."

Finally, into the hush, she said, "What?"

"Caught a boy out on the road and beat him up."

He was waiting. She said, "Badly?"

"Tell me, busted his arm. Face all chopped up."

"Do they know who?"

"Three white fellows in a car, is all." He began hammering again.

For appearance's sake she waited another minute or two before she turned and passed through the narrow gap in the shrubbery and entered the house again.

Two hours later, in her car, she crossed the railroad tracks and passed the city limits' sign and drove straight on out Grimley Road. Beyond the scattering of gas stations and honky-tonks and small frame houses backed up to plum and locust thickets or acre patches of corn or cotton, she climbed Granny Lunn Ridge. Over the crest the land, the whole Saugahatchee valley, opened out below her in a great fan-shaped expanse of fields and yellow and russet woodland. There were spreads of ripe cotton bursting in a froth, green of new-sprung rye and barley and, away at the farthest reach of the valley, the shoulder of white limestone bluff in the river bend. Viewed through the haze of October light, it seemed to come upon her like a dream gathering in her mind. Thoughts of her mission, as she descended the long incline, almost escaped from her grasp.

She had not forgot, but her sense of urgency had receded. It seemed no more than part of her plan when she turned off onto an unpaved road that divided a cotton field. It led to where Bo lived, the one place he had always lived since days at Fountain Inn. How long since she had been here? She passed a standing chimney and, beyond a beech woods, came to a cabin where the name "Camron" was scrawled on a leaning mailbox. Obviously there was no one at home. She put ten dollars into an envelope and, after thinking about it a moment, did not sign her name. But this was vanity. In any case they would know. Half a dozen dogs, spotted brown and black and white, came boiling out from under the cabin to examine her as she entered the gate and approached the rickety steps. On a table just inside the screen, in a dim, fly-buzzing room, she put the envelope.

There were two spreading mimosa trees that half concealed the cabin from the road. All over the bare-swept front yard they cast a solid shade. Across the fence a field blinding white with cotton rolled away in the afternoon sun to a distant rim of woods, and eastward she saw doves flying against an intense blue sky. Close around was a purring and clucking of chickens in the yard. She seemed to hear Negro voices, low and thick and mellow, like the human undertone in all this outreaching quietness. Already it was picking time. Far out in the field, so far that her vision blurred, she seemed to see their straw bonnets faintly dip and rise, barely in motion, like yellow ships on a sea of cotton foam. But her lids were shut now. She saw with other eyes, while the slow beat of her pulse went on like an ache that never could stop.

Hester stopped one other time before she reached her destination. On a paved back road she pulled up beside a square, concrete-block building that was the new Huggins's grocery, which she never had seen before and went in and bought some aspirin. She remembered the old man at the counter, Mr. Huggins, with his pouched, doleful eyes and his dewlaps. But he showed no sign of recognition and she did not identify herself. Looking around, she saw the gaudy advertisements on the walls, the shelves stacked only with cans and bottles. Her petition, the reason she had stopped in, was tacked up beside the door under a Coca-Cola ad. There were maybe thirty signatures, some of them in rough, nearly illegible scrawl. Above them were her own words, in single-spaced type on a detachable sheet, and these were what held her eye. It was strange to see them here, disquieting. Somehow the tone had an unpleasant dissonance in her ears.

"Lady in town put those out," Mr. Huggins suddenly volunteered. "Got a good many names on it."

Hester nodded and, without answering, quickly left the store.

Herman Butterfield's house, small, white frame, a good deal the worse for wear, sat back in a close-cropped and almost treeless pasture with some cows grazing nearby. She could see him on the porch watching her open the gate. He was still watching, or staring, when she stopped behind his pickup truck and got out of her car. His spectacles blazed like mirrors reflecting the sun. As she approached, "By God," he said and stood up with a suddenness that did not quite throw caution away. "Miss Hester. Come to see Herman Butterfield. You come on up here and have a seat on this swing."

Mr. Butterfield had moved to the head of the steps, but she noticed that he put one hand on the post before he reached down with the other one and took her own. He was thinner, too. But next she was reassured. Now that the sun no longer glared from his lenses she could see the vivid blue of his magnified eyes. "How long's it been, Miss Hester?" He put her down in the swing. "Right after I come back from Congress? Six years?"

"I don't see how it could have been that long," she said.

But he established it; he recalled the time, the place. It was a funeral, old Major Wiley Danforth's, to which the whole county had come. Mr. Butterfield sat down in his chair now and, seated, his gestures appeared to have lost hardly any of their old, youthful strength. Except that the fringe of hair circling his bald dome was all white and that his overalls had the worn look of a regular uniform, she was hardly aware of any difference in him. The warmth of the sun was on her cheek, and, intruding upon the sound of his voice, she heard the rip of grass being cropped by a cow tethered close to the porch. For the moment she felt almost happy. She could only have wished to see, through lenses reflecting the sun's glare once again, the vividness of his warm blue gaze.

"But I bet you got a reason for coming all the way out here to see old Herman Butterfield, ex-congressman."

She was reluctant. She hung back for a moment.

"You know about these things in town, don't you? . . . the beatings and things."

"Yes ma'm. Heard about them."

"Who is doing it? Do you think it's millworkers? Some of those from Grimley?"

"It's right likely, Miss Hester. I expect some of them's in on it, all right." His bony hands, very still now, lay loosely folded upon his lap.

"Can't they be stopped?"

"I wish I knew some way to tell you. Those things ain't helping any."

"But isn't there *somebody* who could stop them? Who they respect?"

"Yes'm. There's some that could. But there ain't any that *would.*"

"You could," she said, leaning toward him suddenly. "If you would. You've always had more influence out here than anybody. They all voted for you. Nobody else had a chance."

Mr. Butterfield pursed his thin lips. "There was a time when what you're saying was right, Miss Hester. And it ain't been long, either." He paused and the glare on his heavy lenses came and went. "But it's been long enough. Naw, there was a time when I could tell them, and they'd stay pretty well told, most of them. I reckon because I kind of saw what they was *really* after . . . But that time went by. I saw the writing, but my kind of eyes couldn't read it. I never did know nothing but to stay right on the 'coon's track. When the time come the 'coon split up and went different ways, I was done. Naw, Miss Hester, in this here mess there wasn't a thing to do but jump on one side or else the other, yes or no, and not any in the middle. That's when I bowed out."

She gazed far across the pasture, where other cows were grazing, to pinewoods like a solid wall.

"I didn't suit them anymore. They got something to take my place, though. But it's a different kind of dog. I'm *ex*-congressman, Miss Hester. You might say, around here I'm sort of like ex-Herman Butterfield."

The sound of the cow's grazing had stopped. Even when he moved a little in his chair she did not look at him. She said, "They are blaming me for the things that have happened. Even my old friends. You know about my petition, don't you?"

"Yes'm. Saw it up at Huggins' store."

"Do you think that might have helped cause these things?"

"Well," he said, "it might have, some. It don't take much, nowadays. They get set off easy."

"Do you blame me?"

"No ma'm." Looking down, Mr. Butterfield took off his glasses. He set to wiping them attentively with a pocket handkerchief. "You were just doing what you saw it to do. You wasn't meaning to set them off."

"We have a right to fight back. We have to. When people want to destroy us. We can't just let them. I can't."

Still cleaning his glasses Mr. Butterfield nodded, but it was too long before he said anything. Then, "You stop in Huggins' store and look and you'll see my name on there, too."

She regarded him uncertainly. "But why, if you think I was wrong?"

"I never said that, Miss Hester." He was still tediously wiping his lenses. "I just don't know. All I know is it's got mighty hard to tell what you ought to do, where folks are concerned. What you can count on. You can start a thing off pure as Jesus and have it turn ugly as old Satan on you before it's through. It's hard to know when it's not the best thing just to let nature be."

"But you signed it," she said. "You must have thought I was right."

Mr. Butterfield shook his head slowly. "You might have been right," he said. "But I reckon I really signed it because it was yours, Miss Hester."

"Then you shouldn't have," she said gently . . . "just because of me. Not if you didn't really believe in it."

"I don't know why not. I believe in Miss Hester Glenn. If there's anything as much worth trusting as an old friend, I don't know what it is." A slow, playful smile formed on his lips. "That might be about the only principle I got left," he said.

His smile, like his words, had moved her. Her emotion, however, quickly gave place to another, keener one. He had looked up at her. Now he was putting on his glasses again, but it was too late. A glimpse had been enough. His naked eyes told a story far different from that of the vivid ones behind the deceiving lenses.

14

Shrubs growing at the corner of the Delmores' yard afforded a kind of screen against the drift of light from windows and front porches along the open street, and here Ames paused. It had been a day of pauses—sometimes more than pauses. There had been the interval this morning at the station where he had stood with ticket in hand not many steps from the door of the waiting bus. And longest of all had been the one that followed his landing in Cameron Springs. Literally for minutes, half blocking the door out onto the sidewalk, he had felt himself caught up in a sort of half-lucid daze.

That was in the midafternoon. It had taken another half hour before he brought himself to enter the telephone booth on the square and, with a feeling of stealth that kept him glancing out at passersby, call up Libby about the meeting that night. Of course no one had been watching him. Country people, mostly, farmers and laboring men, they ambled past indifferently or stood around in groups of three and four, and the accustomed, idle Saturday crowd was assembled in the courthouse yard nearby. The feeling of difference was in himself, as though his mind required a jogging. It did not seem strange that the pedestal at center of the square bore no soldier, or that Hampton Street across on the other side was like a street with a barrier for him. And although he was spoken to, and once, by old, nearsighted Mr. Bradshaw, obliged to answer a few well-meant questions, a notion that he was not really recognized hazily persisted. And in fact all this made a kind of sense. His earlier feeling of guilty stealth seemed quite expunged by a consciousness that he was no longer the person he used to be.

It was not that easy, however. The mere coming-on of night in a square that was almost empty raised thoughts like solid shapes in his mind's eye. He imagined in the walls of his mother's house the softly luminous windows, and light falling outward upon the still, green billows of shrubbery. He saw her in a window, her slim body in silhouette. These images were still with him when he walked past the old houses down Forrest Street and turned up Quincey and entered, finally, Meadow Hills where the trees left off and the road began to wind between rows of neat, new, suburban houses. Once or twice he stopped dead in his tracks. It was not only because the road branched several times and the ways looked much alike. It was also because his thoughts were running in a maze of both new and old uncertainties. But one of these thoughts, the one that had called down this pause beside the clump of bushes, stood alone when his mind had focused again. It caused him to see that after all he could not go through with this.

He stood for a long time, however, aware how his brother's image went on pacing like a figure back in the dark wings of his mind. A car approached and turned into the drive at the other side of the yard, and two Negroes got out and entered the house. Once he saw Libby. She must have been looking for him, because she stepped out onto the small front porch and stood a minute or two, in a pale blouse, framed in the lighted door glass. But he had only pressed closer against the bushes. There was a wide picture window with a curtain drawn across, and sometimes he imagined he saw upon it shadows cast by heads of whites and Negroes side by side, gravely conversing. Of course he could hear no sound at all of voices, could only guess at what they had to say. But he knew that he could not have faced them. He went away.

At the noisy café where he sat alone with his beer, he thought of calling Libby. He would tell her . . . all he dared to tell her. When nine thirty came he did call, but no one answered. So there was no real purpose in retracing his steps out Forrest Street and back up Quincey to Meadow Hills. Two cars going his way passed him in a hurry, fanning up gusts of chill air in their wakes. There seemed to be more lights on now. Up the long incline to his left patterned rows of houses stood out in bright relief.

He was conscious of voices, first, and then, over the crest ahead, of sudden illumination in which a redness throbbed. Topping the rise he saw the revolving light of a patrol car, other cars in a tangle along the street and figures starkly detailed in the beams of their headlights. He was still running when he turned in beside the bushes at the corner of the yard.

Most of the crowd was massed around the Delmores' front porch. Up on the porch was a small, round-shouldered man, Sheriff Venable, intently scrutinizing in the ray of his flashlight the concrete floor around his feet. Shards of glass were scattered about. Several times the light crossed a mark like a large stain where something black had hit and spattered and broken a chip from the concrete edge. A moment later, Ames noticed the door, standing half ajar. It was like a picture frame, empty except for the few splinters, shattered teeth of louver glass along the edges.

"I guess they threw it from the street," someone said. "Probably dynamite."

It was then, gazing into the dim vestibule where a chair lay overturned, that Ames felt his heart begin to pace. Over a shoulder almost touching his chin he faintly said, "Did it hurt anybody?"

A black cheek, like a small shock, presented itself to his eyes. "Girl got cut bad. Sitting by that door."

Before Ames could speak again, the Negro had disengaged himself from the crowd of shoulders and started away. There were plenty of others to ask, but Ames did not. An instant later he hurried after the Negro, followed him around to the far door of a car parked in the driveway. Turning, the Negro looked at him, looked him up and down with eyes in which the white was unexpectedly distinct. "You want something?"

"What girl got cut?"

The Negro kept looking at him. He wore a dark suit, maybe black, like a preacher. "Horace Delmore's girl," he finally said.

"How bad?"

"Looked like real bad."

"Did they take her to the hospital?"

"That's right." The pale eyes continued to study Ames.

Presently Ames said, "Anybody else hurt?"

"A few little cuts, is all."

Ames shifted in his tracks, but finally did not turn away. "Did you get any kind of a look at who did it?"

"Naw. Heard a car getting away." The Negro seemed infinitely patient, and watchful.

At last, Ames said, "You're Wendell Pitts, aren't you?"

"That's me."

Ames was more than ever conscious of the white eyes. He mumbled something indefinite. Abruptly turning, he headed out into the street and back toward town.

The hospital, a clinic, really, sat among residential houses three blocks from the square on Stewart Street. Ames doubted that he could have brought himself to enter had he seen, through the glass door, anyone in the stark waiting room. As it was, he entered like a trespasser, crossing the tile floor with steps that did not alert the nurse in the cubicle beyond the waiting-room window. The back of her white-capped head was toward him. Despite his subdued voice, she jumped a little when he said, "I want to inquire about the Delmore girl. They brought her in a little while ago, I think."

The nurse, presenting a craggy profile over her shoulder, said, "The doctor is still with her. She is getting a blood transfusion."

"How serious is it?"

"I really don't know. The doctor will be out in a little while. You may wait, if you wish." Showing him the back of her head, she resumed her work. He could hear her pen scratching. He did hear a voice from somewhere, but muffled, as if through cotton, and presently he turned away. It was his turn to be startled.

Ames did not know how, in this quietness, the man could have entered without his noticing. But there he was, holding a lighted cigarette and looking at Ames with an intensity whose force might have stemmed from the knots of muscle in his jaws. Even in other circumstances, Ames thought, his width of face and quick, severe brown eyes would have identified him as Libby's father. There was no chance for retreat. Horace Delmore said to him, "Aren't you the Glenn boy?"

It was a tough, curt, public voice, one that might have been intended for the nurse as well as for Ames. Indeed Ames could not any longer hear the pen scratching. Nodding, he said in a voice that sounded, and was, weak by comparison, "How bad is it?"

"She'll be all right. Deep cuts in her cheek and neck, she may need a little surgery. But it could have been her eyes, of course." This, left hanging, must have been meant for Ames to contemplate. Meanwhile Horace Delmore, his muscled and tight-knit body neatly fitted into a suit of gray seersucker, continued to stand there like something planted in Ames's path, as if he intended physically to defend the exit behind him. It was not only his gaze. It was also the disarray of his yellow tie, pulled sideways and soiled with irregular, dark blood smears, that conveyed his look of barely disciplined outrage.

"If I can do anything . . ." Ames said.

"There could be something," Horace Delmore quickly said. "Why didn't you come to our meeting tonight? You told my daughter you were coming."

For the first time Ames's gaze declined. "I decided against it," he said at last.

Waiting, Horace Delmore lifted the cigarette and took an impatient draw. "Come over here," he said abruptly, walking across to the other side of the room. There was a row of chairs against the wall and he settled down in the first one, by the door. It was not that he wanted privacy, for he barely moderated his voice when Ames, given no alternative, seated himself in the next chair one short step away.

"My daughter tells me you seem to have a mind of your own. *Seem* to," he said, not quite ironically.

Ames only waited.

"Do you?"

"You mean, about all this?"

"You know what I mean. About this racist society you have here. We've seen a good specimen of it tonight. Don't you agree?"

Ames was slow, but he did, had to, nod his head. He was conscious of the nurse's white cap above the window ledge and it took a conscious thrust of his will before he could shift his eyes away and nod more decisively.

Horace Delmore did not look satisfied. "I really don't see how any decent person can help but agree. If he has any sense at all. Look at this situation. A closed society, ready to kill dissenters. Hatred of the minority group. Repression and violence the only solution. It's fascist, really. Surely you must have observed some of this."

Wasn't it true—or some, enough, of it true? Then why did he not give voice to his answer?

"And your mother, can't she see it at all? She's a woman of some education."

He shook his head again, with more decision now. "She doesn't see what you see. She would say you are wrong . . . That most of it's in your mind," he added.

"And *believe* it?"

"Yes, she believes it. It's not hypocrisy. It's her faith."

"How could she believe it? What will she say about this, tonight? That it didn't happen?"

Keeping his voice low Ames said, "That things like this happen everywhere, sometimes. And that you're making them happen here. That you're making it worse. She would say the monument's getting blown up was your fault." And she, Ames suddenly realized, was making his tongue defend her. In anger he clenched his teeth.

"Good God," Horace Delmore breathed. The cigarette, which he had been merely holding, was about to burn his fingers. He dropped it to the floor and with brief violence ground it beneath his foot. "How many times have I heard that kind of thing. That, and all about how I 'don't understand.' I understand perfectly well what I've seen with my own eyes—and heard firsthand from reliable sources. In eighteen months of watching this town I've seen enough racial injustice to last me a couple of lifetimes. Insults, petty oppression, beatings, murder—you name it. I've had a bellyful."

He had thrust his face toward Ames as he finished, a posture that tightened the skin of his neck and better defined the knots of muscle in his jaws.

"I'm not trying to fool anyone. It's not *only* that I want to help these poor Negroes. This kind of thing is a slap in the face to the whole ideal this nation stands for—equal justice for all. That's what this country is all about, it's *our* ideal. And I am just as outraged to see it trampled and spat on as these Negroes are."

The white cap was motionless, and Ames imagined that the intensity of Horace Delmore's voice had carried his words not only there but even back into the room where, the starkly supine on a metal table, his daughter lay absorbing into her veins the runnel of bright new blood. The clear gaze, which Ames had felt upon his half-averted face, now scanned the room as if in search of other faces to challenge.

A little more quietly, without preface, Horace Delmore said, "No, tonight proved it to me. The time has come for a serious confrontation, not just half measures. We don't want violence, but we will have to risk it. Of course, we have it already. When a man's family is not safe in his own house. In the last four nights there hasn't been one without some kind of violence. Something will have to be done . . . Wouldn't you agree with that?"

Even now Ames's tongue barely assented.

Satisfied or not, Horace Delmore went on, "Actually, though, I don't think there's too much to fear. An outburst or two, maybe. From what I've seen, a lot of people around here are doing some fast second-thinking. That's true, isn't it? . . . They have finally started to notice that everything is against them. The government. Economics. This town is more than one-third Negro. What they need now is to be shown our power in some unmistakable way. They've already begun to crack. It's time to go ahead and break them." He watched Ames for a second. "But I still don't know which side *you* are on."

To gain yet another minute, Ames murmured, "How do you mean, 'break them?' "

Horace Delmore withdrew his gaze. Impatiently he took a package of cigarettes from his coat pocket and shook one into his hand. "I just mean, by pushing them all the way. Exactly 'how' is up to the Negroes. It's their show, fundamentally. But I hope they will do what is already being done some places—go into the white restaurants, the churches, movie houses. All the public places where they have been excluded. Break down the barriers once and for all, whatever it takes. If it's going to cause violence, then let's get it over with."

Quite unexpectedly Horace Delmore stood up and put the cigarette in his mouth and lit it. He did not even look at Ames when he said, "The only real choice for you is whether to go quietly or not. Of course it would take some guts to come in with us." Turning, he crossed the room and passed out of sight through the swinging door in the wall. Moments later Ames rose from the chair and left.

He did not go farther than out to the street. For a while, smarting, he stood in the gloom beneath a tree and turned in his mind a notion of going back to answer that parting taunt. Had he not earned it? He recalled his muteness, his half-dissenting nods, his unwilled and fatuous apology for what this last event had proved to be past all defending. And yet he had defended it—or his voice had, uttering arguments already as dead as chaff in his mind. There in the darkness, he shook his head. The anger that slowly gathered in him was, at first, directed only against himself.

He was walking again, faster as he went on. The dark fronts of the houses faintly repeated the click of his shoes on the pavement, but a louder thing was the stroke of his pulse driving the angry blood against his eardrums. On the square he stopped and stood in a kind of furious immobility, a tension like the fierce grip of his muscles upon the bone—stood long enough to watch a tedious car enter the square to his left and circle the naked pedestal and turn at last onto Hampton. Watching its lights diminish down the street, he suddenly felt that his way had been opened up for him.

Swiftly approaching the house he saw that his mother's light was on. She was there, awake in her room. In the grip of this one clear thought he entered the gate and turned, from habit, into the path that led through shrubbery around to the back porch door. But beyond the clump of massive boxwood he almost collided with something that loomed up in the glow from her curtained window. Though he barely paused, his hand reached out and touched it, touched the latticework. A dim astonishment surfaced in his mind. It was a summerhouse.

The back door was unlocked, as always, the bulb in the kitchen shedding its light on the spotless tabletop. A second pause—he had not intended it—was for the silence that waited inside the house. A sort of lunge carried him on through the dining room and into the half-lit hall. His mother's door stood open.

"Cam?" The lamp beside her bed was on. She sat, in a colorless gown, propped up against the black headboard, her still hands lying upon the covers drawn over her lap. Just sitting there, as if nothing could touch her.

"It's me." He had stopped in the door, forcing her, because of the light, to peer at him for recognition. Even now a little effort was needed to make him enter without her bidding; he did it abruptly and only stopped near the foot of her bed. He saw the question forming on her lips take another shape.

"Is something the matter?"

"Yes."

She waited, her eyes wide, her lids not quite motionless.

"They bombed a house, this time." Deliberately, to strengthen it, he added, "I was there."

One of her hands moved, nothing else. Presently she murmured, "What house?"

"Horace Delmore's." He was conscious of something like a shock on the air. He saw it register on her face. To make it stronger still he said, "It was a Citizens' Committee meeting."

But nothing followed this.

"The Delmore girl was badly cut. They took her to the hospital . . . She'll have to have some surgery."

"I am sorry." It was a murmur, accompanied, for gesture, by one slow blink of her lids.

"It's not their fault she's not dead." He put a hand on the foot-post of the bed. His impulse was to break it from its socket. "Is that what you wanted?"

"You know better." Her barely audible words were followed by a movement of her head in slow denial. Then, "And you were there?"

"Yes, I was there. The Delmore girl invited me and I went." Lie or not, saying it flatly into her face gave him a feeling of vague triumph. He completed the thing. "There were Negroes there, too. I'm glad I went."

But she only gazed at him. It was this, bye and bye, that gave the new twist to his anger. Deliberately he said, "Do you know where Cam is?"

It worked. It flickered across her face. "What do you mean?"

"Is he here?"

"No, he is out on a date. Please say what you mean."

"How do you know he's on a date?"

She had not only stiffened, her pale cheeks had colored. "I will not have this, Ames. You are in my house."

"Then I'll get out." He started to move, but he did not. The stillness seemed measured now by the distant tick of the parlor clock. Literally between his teeth he said, "How long are you going to lie to yourself?"

But the question made nothing happen.

"You know he killed that Negro. You know he did. All this stuff is his doing. And you've made it worse, there'll be more. And you always talked about truth and honor . . ."

"Please leave this house." She not only had sat up but thrust toward him a face he never had seen before—a mask, white-lipped and ribbed with fever streaks of red.

He did retreat. He turned and stalked three paces to the door. But there, abruptly seized by his anger again, he wheeled around. "You can't get rid of it by running me off. Because he did it . . . I'll prove it to you."

Her lips moved. They must have repeated the same command, but he ignored it. "What if I prove it to you?"

There was no more movement of any kind. The last of the color receded from her face and, presently, as if in exhaustion, she let her shoulders sink back against the headboard. The effect calmed him a little and his voice was quieter. "You've always talked about doing the *right* thing. The right thing for you to do is turn him in. It would stop all this stuff if he was caught. The thugs couldn't keep on after that, saying the 'niggers' did it. And the Negroes just want justice."

Her white face merely watched him.

"You could make him confess it. You could make him do anything," he said, and stopped, hearing again Libby's voice in his mind: *"They do* what *you mean."* He only added, "You know that." He saw his mother draw a breath.

"I will not ask him to confess what he did not do," she quietly said.

"You mean to stick to that?"

"I asked you twice to leave."

He ignored this, his anger rising once more. "You're going to stick to it, aren't you? And keep yourself believing it. Like you keep yourself believing all those other things, so you won't have to face the facts. All about our fine old Southern heritage. And Cam is part of it, isn't he? Pure as a lamb." It must have been her unshaken rigidity, as if her eyes were compelled to observe a display of obscenity. With all the harshness in him Ames said, "He even defends it for you."

He stood there in the aftermath of his voice, like a hollow place in which he could again hear the clock ticking. Yet her face had not changed, and still had not when suddenly she pushed the covers back and put her bare feet on the floor. He did notice that when she stood up she lightly held to the bedpost just for an instant. Then she advanced straight toward him, blotting the light behind her tall, draped figure. He could not but step back across the threshold. The door slammed shut in his face.

He heard only the clock. Presently he said aloud, though in a voice imperfectly controlled, "I'll prove it to you." Then he hurriedly left the house.

He had meant to keep on going, but he did not. Passing where the glow from his mother's curtained window silvered leaves of the shrubbery, he stopped. Exhaustion, it seemed, had fallen upon him as suddenly as a blow. After some minutes he felt compelled to sit down. Looking about him for the chairs, he quickly discovered one inside the summerhouse close by. Here, the night chill stealing upon him, he sat and gazed at her window. Once, perhaps, her tall shadow appeared on the curtain, but he was not sure, and finally her light went out. Later came the sound of an unmuffled engine and then an aura from headlights reflected in the trees around the garage. The engine coughed, went out with an echo in the hollow garage, and the car door slammed. There were footsteps on the walk. The back door shut with a just perceptible click, but except upstairs, briefly, no light came on, then or afterward. At last Ames fell into a kind of cold and rigid sleep. When he woke up, shivering, and departed, the whole world seemed as soundless as a tomb.

15

When Ames first opened his eyes, he was bewildered to see overhead the blackened stub of an old gas jet and a ceiling streaked with water marks. Realization came slowly, like a burden hard to lift. But not even his waking memory of last night was able to banish the strangeness that came with understanding where he was. Below him was the square, lying empty in the glaze of an October morning, observed from the elevation of an upstairs room in the old Perkins hotel. The room was small and desolate, its carpet worn thin by the transient feet of salesmen and other passers-through. His own feet, now, had added their bit to its threadbare meagerness. It seemed to him fitting that he should be here, where he never had been before.

But even within the few minutes while he stood there at the window, the weight of his depression began to lift. If Hampton Street, whose entrance he could see, was not *his* street anymore, then why need *that* matter still be his affair? All he could do, he had done, and the door had been shut in his face. It was not his to deal with anymore. At last he could belong to himself, be what he thought and felt, and chose to be. A rush of exaltation seemed as if it would lift him bodily from the floor. Soon, for the last time ever, he would be on the bus heading out.

The event itself, however, did not much resemble his anticipation of it. From the moment of his abrupt decision to go and visit Libby first, he had felt his mood begin to darken. He had got as far as a phone call to the clinic, where he was told that she had already gone home. After that he had merely paced the room or stood at the window gazing into the square. Yet he might have gone through with it still, except for an accident. Or a *sort* of accident, for its fitness half persuaded him that his own conscience had called it into being.

His mother's car had appeared, the one car moving on the square. Cam was with her. Circling the monument, they glided beneath Ames's hotel window and stopped at the curb a little way beyond. Her head was wrapped in a gray bandanna. Of her face he could see nothing except its pallor. Cam appeared, the sun on his hair and white T-shirt. A few lithe steps, the hint of a pause at the mailbox there, and he was out of sight again under the green car roof. She must have spoken to him, for Ames saw only the gray bandanna now. Then, at the corner, they were gone, vanished into Hampton Street. And Ames, at his window, stood trying in vain to purge them from his vision.

On stationery he found in the room he wrote Libby a letter. There was little to write, for how could one be honest only up to a point? ". . . Believe me when I say," he wrote, bending over the scarred tabletop, "that I am ashamed of what happened last night, and ashamed of not having come, as I said I would. In a different way, last night was probably almost as painful for me as it was for you. It made me see, in a light I never saw them in before, the ugliness and the falseness of things. So that bomb did have one good result, at least. It completed my own emancipation. At least I know now which side I am on . . ." He quickly sealed the letter and, only minutes afterward, posted it in the box outside of the bus station.

Later he regretted this letter, for after all he had put a lie in it. Completed his own emancipation? How far was this true when each direction of his mind led him finally to that identical impasse? Always, between him and his freedom, there stood Cam, as if the thought of Cam inhabited every point of his mind's compass. Yet there were other directions. In his bed that night he thought about them, dreamed about them in his sleep. Beyond the puny flyspeck that was Cameron Springs lay a whole world of choices and nothing to prevent his making any one he pleased. There were great cities. When at last he did fall deeply asleep, a city's jagged skyline stood out against the darkness.

Such thoughts, despite that they kept coming all the next day, never did take on substance for him. A moment's scrutiny and they were gone. But why, when these choices were as real as any other? He did not even try very hard to answer his query. He simply watched the bubbles come, and burst, and felt his gaze draw inward to the darkness where Cam stalked or his mother's face appeared or the shade of her form upon a window curtain. Again and again, over the protest of his will, one or the other or all together kept appearing to him. Nothing banished them for long, not even the whiskey he drank that night until he was staggering. And later he waked up in his bed believing not only that he had screamed his rage into her face but also that he had started to inflict some violence upon her.

Ames's schoolwork went badly. A test placed in front of him at history class that Tuesday morning might as well have been inscribed in an unfamiliar language. It was the same with the textbooks over which he sat slumped in the library much of the afternoon. He had little memory, when he left, of the pages he had covered. He was making still another try at it in his room later on when the telephone call came.

He had not wanted to see her. Only his confusion had thwarted the invention of some usable excuse. Afterward he was not sorry. His meeting with Libby had brought him within an hour to a decision that might have been painful days in the making.

"I'm not a bit sorry it happened," she said, touching with her fingertips the white bandages on her cheek and neck. Indeed she looked anything but sorry, and the half of her face illuminated by a sunray through the big glass window beside their table had a sort of russet tone. "A few little scars won't hurt anything. Something like this really needed to happen. Did you see the *Herald* Sunday?"

Ames shook his head. Music, loud in the confinement of the student center snackbar, filled in for him.

"I saved it, I'll show it to you. A really perfect editorial. I didn't think Kirk Qualls had it in him. He finally rose up."

"I'd like to see it," Ames said, bending to sip from his glass.

"Oh, he gave the town hell. My father thinks this could be the turning point. They'll have to look at what they've been 'preserving.' "

"I guess it could," Ames said. He just could meet her brown, level eyes. "For a lot of people." Letting his gaze drift out onto the lawn where some boys in sweat suits were passing, he felt her watching him. The low sun glared through a niche in russet foliage.

"Have you seen your mother since it happened?"

"Yes . . . I saw her that night. Afterward."

"What did she say?"

"That she was sorry."

Libby waited as if she expected more. "Nothing else?"

"I guess there wasn't much else she could say. Being the way she is."

"You don't think it will make any difference?"

"No."

The music had stopped, and he was distantly conscious of a scrap of conversation about politics from a couple seated near the swinging door. He saw Libby's full but unpainted mouth straighten a little, tighten at the corners. She said, "I know she's your mother, but what *does* she think she's doing? Besides 'keeping the niggers in their place,' I mean? I know she *thinks* there's a lot more to it. Just exactly what is it . . . that really exists?"

Some hazy answers flickered across his consciousness. In the utterance, how empty they would sound. For an instant Cam's name stood silently on his tongue. Might he not speak it out, be rid of it? The thought was like air as limpid sweet as grace drawn suddenly into his lungs, a heady feeling. On the table Libby's hand, stained russet like her cheek in the filtered sun, was all at once an object of desire. He imagined his own hand laid upon it. Then it moved. As with a hard contraction of his mind he said, "Nothing. Except what's in her head. And a few old monuments."

He saw, gratefully, approval in Libby's face. And what he had said *was* true, wasn't it? That much was.

"I think that's it exactly," she said. "It's a sort of dream world. It makes me think of Sleeping Beauty or something. If it was as harmless as that. If it wasn't all based on keeping the Negro enslaved. My father thinks that's the whole thing, really—a kind of romantic embroidery to prettify something ugly, so they can stand themselves. They have to be liars because they can't afford to tell themselves the truth. Even their manners show it. 'Much obliged to you, ma'm,' " Libby drawled. She paused. In a softened tone she said, "You know I don't mean you. I think you're an honest person."

He tried to make some kind of mute acknowledgment. Still she waited a moment longer.

"I'm afraid I'm being insulting about your mother. I don't mean her in particular. You've all been victims of the social system."

"It's all right," he murmured, a little late, coming back from where his thoughts suddenly had fastened.

"Are you still on good terms with her?" Libby presently asked.

"No. Not anymore."

Libby nodded and a voice from across the room rose suddenly in passionate conviction.

"It's too bad," Libby said. "But I don't see how you *could* keep being friends with her. If you really mean what you think. I would find it impossible."

He lifted his eyes, looked straight into her clear brown gaze. "I mean it," he said, and saw by her expression that she believed him. And one thing more showed him that she did. Just as she started to rise from her chair, she extended her hand and let it rest briefly on the back of his half-clenched fist.

It seemed to be this, the moment's touch of her fingertips, that had given the first real impulse to his decision. In any case the decision was made by the time he entered his room that evening, and such uncertainties as he later experienced were related to nothing except the details of his plan. Beyond a point he simply could not define them. All the hours of that restless night were not enough. And even on the road next morning, driving a borrowed car, he still was trying in vain to bring these details into focus. It made no difference, despite that he drove with a sensation as of plunging half blind on his course.

Entering Cameron Springs he did not even pause on his route to the lumberyard. His first pause came when a Negro at work loading a truck told him that Pike Handley had quit a week and a half ago. The Negro knew nothing else. Pike simply had not showed up that Monday, to the disgust of the foreman.

So now, what? Ames felt a sort of panic gathering as he drove past warehouses along the railroad and past the storefronts down Battle Street. There was no use telling himself that this was not some last, desperate hour, that the violence of his feelings made no sense. It had to be now, this morning. The time was something drawn to a pitch as tense as the string of a bow. More than once he restrained an impulse to stop and recklessly question people who stood along the streets. When at last his patience broke, he made a sudden left-hand turn and drove as fast as he dared through town toward Grimley Road.

The woods beyond the cotton field were tipped with yellow, like flame in the noon sun. They appeared to fade with his approach, and brown and russet foliage darkened the bend of the road from where he could see the house. It stood beyond the fringe of woods, bleak gray in the sun and patched with colorless tree shadows, and the window squares looked black. There was no car. His hesitation at the entrance to the dusty drive lasted long enough for him to reflect that, even so, he should not risk an approach as reckless as this. But his patience broke again. He turned in suddenly and stopped in front of the house.

There was no sign of life. Moments later he climbed the steps and, peering through the torn screen, saw a gloomy desolate hallway and stairs at the far end winding without a banister up to the floor above. His tense knock, rattling the loose screen door, produced nothing but echoes. The musty smell from within, the cracked and fallen plaster, more and more suggested to him not only abandonment but abandonment a long time ago, and he was unable to account for the cold feeling that he was under the most intent observation. With a start, he turned his head.

Pike was standing at the corner of the house. He did not say anything, he merely stared at Ames from under the thatch of hair low on his forehead. Streaks of sweat on the sleeveless, khaki shirt indicated that he had just come from work somewhere.

Ames turned and descended the steps. Even now, confronted with it, he did not know what he meant to say. Pike's eyes, never still in the small sockets, searched his face, but for a moment Ames could not find any words. Then, as softly as if his mouth were thrust up close to one of Pike's tight little ears, he said, "Is anybody in the house?"

Pike heard him. A twitch of his head seemed to mean no. "What you want with me?" he murmured back.

"My mother wants you to come talk to her."

The eyes widened. They were about the color of cork. "What you trying to do?"

"She knows about it. She's got something to tell you."

"You crazy?" It was as if a threatening movement on Ames's

part had made him take a half step back. "I don't even know what you're talking about. You come once before, talking like this. You must be crazy."

"I'm talking about the dead nigger. That you and Cam killed. That's what she wants to talk to you about . . . If you don't, you'll be caught before the week's over."

Pike's mouth twisted a little. Clearly his lips had lost a shade of color. Beyond the stillness contracting around them Ames could hear faintly the cackling of a hen. "She can't come here. She sent me to bring you to her. Right now, before it's too late . . . It's not a trick."

Pike's eyes had grown bright with wariness. "That other time was." Then, "Some kind of a fool trick. You're up to something."

"Think a minute. Why would I do this if I wanted you caught? I'd have told the sheriff. That other time I was trying to find out for myself. I found out another way. The same way—"

"You're lying. You never found out nothing on me." His face had gone chalky now.

"I found out the same way my mother did . . . From Cam."

Pike stared at him. In a voice barely audible he said, "You're lying."

"She got it out of him."

Pike's lips repeated his last words, but they made no sound this time. All at once, as if he were bolting to run, he turned half around. He did not run. He put his hands on the side of the house and leaned there with his head bent.

"She's got it worked out," Ames murmured. "How you all can keep from getting caught."

At last, so softly that again Ames could barely hear him, he said, "How?"

"She'll have to tell you. Come on."

"Why can't you?"

"It'll have to be her, she's got it figured. You'd better come on. You haven't got much time, Venable's on your track." Ames took a few steps toward the car. Turning back again, he said, "This is your last chance."

Slowly Pike took his hands from the wall. "I got to pick that cotton."

"It'll keep for an hour."

Pike advanced toward the car like someone drawn at the end of a leash.

Ames followed a roundabout way, along the edge of the colored district and up past the cemetery to the lower end of Hampton Street. He gave hardly a glance at Pike, who sat there as limp and speechless as if he had been clubbed into submission. What now absorbed Ames were thoughts of all the possible obstacles and mischances somehow neglected before—his mother's absence, Willodene in the house, Cam himself home early. Ahead of him, at the corner, the house loomed up like a shape envisioned until now in a dream only. In a sort of astonishment he turned, and turned again innto the short driveway. The garage space beside his mother's car was empty. Here, in a dazed silence that followed upon his cutting the engine, he sat staring at the blank rear wall.

"I ain't going in that house." It was Pike's strained and muted voice.

Her car was here, she was at home—and Cam was not. "Stay here," Ames said and got out.

Stopping shy of the porch he could hear nothing but the hum of locusts and the secret undertone of crickets peeping. From overhead where bronze and tawny foliage trapped the sun, a leaf came floating zigzag down the air and landed without a sound. But this was no time to pause.

The kitchen was empty. So was all the house, he saw, and his bold steps came to a halt back in the kitchen again. His blood was pounding. For just a second he stood still. Abruptly he went out the back door and turned into the gap between the shrubs.

He saw the summerhouse, first, like something remembered from a hazy dream, and then he saw her. A glimpse, of her form in a reclining chair, was all he stayed for. Back in the garage he yanked the car door open. "Come on."

"In that *house?*"

"Come on," Ames said.

Stiffly, Pike got out. Ames steered him by an elbow and stepped behind to drive him into the gap.

Ames believed afterward that his mother, before even a single word was uttered, already had read in full the meaning of this figure thrust in front of her and wilting there as if her gaze were hot. Until Ames spoke, belatedly, she did not take her eyes off Pike. When Ames did speak and drew them to his own face, he thought of eyes struck blind in the dazzle of midday light. He had only pronounced Pike's name to her. Now it seemed that he would not be able to speak again. In fact, as he thought later, he had not really needed to speak again.

To his astonishment it was Pike who spoke, his voice breaking flutelike at the end: "He said you knowed a way to help us out."

Ames saw him swallow hard, and there was a moment's interval before that appearance of wilting came back over him, as if her gaze had started to burn again. Now, his voice a sort of violent whine, Pike blurted, "I swear to God Cam done the most of it. I never throwed but two or three rock. I told him to stop. I swear to God . . . it was Cam killed him."

Yet nothing about her moved. The rigor of her posture seemed to defy even the need for breathing. Was it possible she had not heard him? In the very hush around them, the secret voices of crickets all of a sudden tingling in his ears, there was something that appalled Ames. Pike's voice again, subdued:

"He said you knowed a way to keep them from catching us."

"She doesn't," Ames said. "I just wanted you to tell her you all did it. So she would believe it."

Pike looked at him. He looked at Ames's mother, then back at Ames again, and now his mouth was open. "You said she knowed—"

"I was lying."

Ames was not even conscious now of the silence where Pike stood. And when the voice, a coarse whine, came in again it sounded as irrelevant as a voice overheard from a distance. The first words went past him. He did comprehend the final question. "So what you going to do?"

Watching his mother's stark face, he did not answer.

"They'll catch him same as me," Pike said. "I'll tell on him. I'll sure God tell on him. If they catch me, they'll catch him too."

She might not even have seen him: her eyes still gave that illusion.

"It was his doing, I swear to God. He was—"

"Go away!" Her voice silenced him. The cloudiness was gone out of her eyes, and between her brows the crease resembled a pallid, unhealed wound. Already Pike had retreated until his back was against the foliage.

In exactly the same voice she said, "Go away from here! Now!"

Pike's mouth came open. For a second he looked as if he were balancing himself. Then he stepped quickly in back of Ames and into the gap between the shrubs. "I'll tell on him if you do," he said, almost crying it, and the sound of his hurrying feet was audible for a space.

Conscious that what he had been feeling was remorse, Ames feebly said, "I'm sorry, Mama. I had to. You wouldn't believe it."

This called her eyes to him. The fierce crease between them had brought a kind of darkness over her brow. "I want you to leave, too."

Her harshness did not touch him. He stood his ground. "There's nothing you can do but turn him in."

In a voice perfectly cold and possessed, she said, "It is my business. He is my son."

Ames had some moments of uncertainty. Her meaning, or what she appeared to mean, came on him all of a sudden, and seeing her get up from the chair with that stark, chiseled face not even turned his way was like the confirmation of it. "You mean you're not going to do anything?"

Without a word she walked past and around behind him into the gap through the shrubbery. To her stiff, retreating back he said, lifting his voice, "You're really not going to?"

Then she was out of sight. There was nothing left of his remorse, and sudden rage was the impulse that sent him hurrying after her.

He caught her at the back door. Stopping in a patch of sun short of the porch, he said to her, "What if *I* do?"

She let the screen go shut behind her. Through the wire, like a veil, she gave him a glance that maybe did just pause on his face. "Then I hope you may be struck dead."

She was gone, but Ames kept standing there. What finally gave clear shape to his thoughts was the realization that someone back in the shadows of the kitchen was looking directly at him through the screen. It was not his mother. What he could see most clearly was the subdued radiance of the feet. Pretending as if he had not noticed, Ames turned and walked deliberately out to the garage. Cam's car, he saw as he backed into the street, was parked there beside the curb.

16

At sunset the wind had risen, lashing the bronze and tawny trees, and in the night it began to rain. Off and on next day and through the succeeding days and nights, the rain continued until water ran deep in the gutters and the green lawns stood in puddles and the boughs of trees hung loaded and dripping under a lowering sky. Hester, as she watched the streams of water sluice down from the eaves, knew that the Saugahatchee was swelling in its banks. But this—mid-October when cotton and corn stood ripe for harvest in the fields—was not the season for any such rain. It seemed to her a disjointing of nature's rightful procession, and the sound of drumming rain on the roof was at times like a herald of some all-obliterating event. She thought of the Saugahatchee rising, swallowing the fields. Where would it stop? For the first time in her life she went about in the fear of a natural thing.

And yet, in another way, she was also afraid for the rain to stop. The intervals between, the dripping silences under the solid arch of cloud, threatened her with shocks of sound about to explode in the distance. The tight-shut doors and windows seemed to offer no defense. It was as if her ears were always gaping for rumors of these sounds, and there were times when she stood for whole minutes like someone poised for the blast of an opening gun. Only the drumming rain was defense, and this brought its own kind of fear.

Hester would not so much as glance into the newspaper now, and when she noticed it lying, by Willodene's hand, on the hall table, she would drop it quickly into the trash basket there. She ignored appointments she had made with her lawyer and her dentist, and ordered her groceries by telephone. But still there was Willodene. Her eyes, those watchful Negro eyes so practiced in the language of a white face, seemed to follow Hester's movements everywhere about the house. There was no fooling her with words. She had caught at once the tension in Hester's voice. Sometimes she muttered to herself, and Hester, pausing, would strain to distinguish the guttural words from one another. But Saturday came, and at noon she was gone. And on Sunday, as if heaven had decided to grant to Hester this one small favor, Willodene telephoned with the news that her daughter was sick in far-off Louisville. So at least the house was all Hester's now, and Cam's.

She saw little of him. Standing there in the kitchen that terrible afternoon, as warily still as an animal, he had looked into her face as she passed through. It had been enough. Even without that other later encounter when, hours afterward, she opened her bedroom door and saw him halfway up the stairs crouched in shadows and peering between the banisters at her, she had known with certainty that he knew. "Listen, Mama . . ." he said, and she had paused for a little, a second. But nothing had followed, and she had crossed the hall below him and passed on through the door.

For two days after that she had seen him only by glimpses once or twice and heard his steps sometimes. Those nights, she sat alone at the dining-room table, trying to eat, trying not to let her eyes wander to his plate and empty chair. Then, on Friday night, he appeared for supper, his old self so well acted that at times she nearly forgot and all but uttered a motherly question or remark. He watched her. From across the table she could feel his studious, wary glances on her face. Once he said, "Some niggers tried to eat at Irving's today. Old Irving threw them out quick."

Rigidly, feeling the cold at her heart, she stared at her plate until she felt his gaze die out like a candle.

He did not try the subject again. After that—and she really saw him only at the supper table—he stuck to casual matters, facts about his day at school or small events from his childhood in which she too had shared, rattling on with a kind of tentative and watchful assurance that appalled her the more with each successive night.

"Remember when I fell out of that big apple tree? Right in front of you? You thought I was dead, for a minute," he said and smiled with a certain wistfulness at her. Or, actually laughing a little bit, "Aunt Minnie really did think it was a boy. The way that dog sat up there at the table with my coat and hat on."

What Hester had realized all too soon was the fact that he was waiting, merely waiting for her to forget this thing, and that all his chatter was guilefully designed to hurry it into oblivion. Sometimes this monstrous impudence would fairly choke her into speechlessness. He was merely waiting!—with only a certain discretion that showed in table manners a bit more staid than in the past, in reflections and comments all too transparently innocent. He needed new shoes, for the tan-and-brown ones would not hold a shine anymore. Had she, because the school dance was next weekend, had his good suit cleaned? At such times his handsome, youthful face would regard her with brief but startling candor. Nothing was changed, his manner tried to say. He was the son and she was the mother still—*his* mother. These were the moments when she felt not only the constriction stopping her throat, but also a sensation as if her whole face had turned to ice.

Still, there were the times when, lifting her gaze suddenly, she surprised the uncertainties passing across his face. In some way it consoled her to know that he was not really sure. The doubts showed in his lengthening absences from home and in his steps at night in the dark as he made his way to the stairs. And late Sunday night she had found him, reeking with whiskey, dead asleep on the seat of his car. She had had to leave him there all night, while the steady fall of drizzling rain whispered in the bushes outside her window.

A sort of blank, like a wall without any windows or doors, came whenever she thought of action. The accustomed thing at such moments was that her mind would suffer a small displacement, like a change of balance, and her doubts would rise. Perhaps he had not done it at all. Could it not be some curious or insane kind of misunderstanding, a perversion of her own thinking? Indeed it had to be, for nothing else was possible—not for the child she had carried under her heart and suckled at her breast and raised up in this house among images of respect and veneration until he seemed the youthful likeness of her own father. And what of all those times she had kissed him and told him things and led him by the hand? What of her pride in him? It was not possible. It was in herself that the evil lay.

These thoughts would come and stay a little and die out all at once. She would feel the blankness again. Wandering through the house, repeating chores of sweeping and dusting floors and tabletops, she watched with anxiety gray rain at the windows. Through silent intermissions it fell in swollen drops from the eaves. Once, from a front window, holding her breath for many seconds, she saw Monk Venable in his car come cruising down Hampton Street from the square, slowing as he approached her house, and then turn east onto Lanier. The telephone stood on the table in the hall and sometimes when she passed it she would envision holding it in her hand and Monk at the other end of the line, his quick eyes motionless in his head, listening. But here the blankness would come down. It fell on ever so many of her thoughts, on her brightest memories, even, and blurred whole pages of her Bible when she tried to read. Her late gardenias bloomed in the rain, but for once their suffocating poignance failed to touch her mind. She experienced a growing sense of helplessness, as if she were losing her grasp on solid things.

Twice, on Monday, people knocked at her door. The first knocked only a few times and then went away. The second was Lucius. From her bedroom door she saw him step onto the porch and thump at the kitchen screen. He waited, a little stooped, dripping water from the hat in his hand and the long tattered coat. Through the glass of the rear hall door she could see his face clearly and from more than one angle, for after he knocked a second time he kept cocking his head, turning it a little her way. What was not right? It was Lucius, certainly. And yet she was conscious of watching a face that was black, a blackness that somehow made the face appear anonymous to her. She felt disoriented, and it was some moments before she could recall that this was his day to work in the yard and to have his lunch in the kitchen. But she did not move. When at last Lucius turned his eyes directly toward the hall door, she felt a curious chill and stepped back into her bedroom. He came to the hall door and knocked again, finally calling out, "Miss Hester, you home?" It was a long time before he gave up and went away through the drizzle.

Those intrusions she had been able to stop at her threshold. It was not so with the third, the fated one. Indeed, in that way which had been growing upon her mind, she thought of it precisely as an event already established by her fate, requiring that on this night at some minutes after eight o'clock she should be in her kitchen alone, seated in a posture of dazed and aimless waiting in front of a door that somehow was not even shut. It was raining again, gusting a little, and yet she had not thought to close the door. Nor was she really startled to hear a step on the back porch. She did not even turn her head. But the step was followed by no second one, and this did make her look, staring with heavy eyes. There was a figure on the porch, back from the screen. A voice carrying just above a whisper said, "Miss Hester, you by yourself?"

She did not move. She thought that perhaps she could not, had she tried.

The figure stepped up to the screen. "Got to talk to you. Nobody else around, is it?"

It was the pitch of the voice. Even before she could make out through the screen any feature of his face, she knew that the man was Hollis Handley. She might have got up and slammed the door. All she did do was move her hand and grip the edge of the table.

"Don't want nobody to hear us," he said. "I better come in."

She could not utter the denial on her tongue. She could only sit and watch him, like an apparition already expected, open the screen and stop there before her with water dripping from the brim of the small, now-wilted green hat and slick rubber raincoat glistening in the kitchen light. He looked toward the dining room. "Anybody else home? I didn't see no lights, much," he said. "Might ought to turn this'n out, too," gesturing upward with his thumb.

She forced her lips to say, "What do you want?"

"Need to talk about them boys of ours, Miss Hester—me and you."

It appeared to be the scent of his rubber raincoat that faintly sickened her. He looked toward the dining room again, exposing those unlooked-for sinews like thongs tensely drawn through the loose flesh under his chin. He took off his hat and his eyes came back to her. "Me and you, we got to put our heads together."

Already knowing the futility of it, she murmured, "What are you talking about?"

A sort of lugubrious sympathy softened Hollis Handley's expression. "Now Miss Hester, it ain't no use to let on like that with me. You know what them boys done. Killed that nigger. That'n of mine finally let it out . . . after I pushed him a little bit. I been halfway knowing it all along. That business with you the other day give him a real bad scare."

She could only watch his face, watch his lips make words.

"I got him ca'med down some, now. I told him you wasn't going to tell on him, and your boy in it too. And that other'n of yours, neither. He wouldn't tell on his own brother."

This seemed to be an inquiry. She did not think that she responded in any way, yet after his pause he went on just as if she had affirmed his statement.

"But he's still one scared boy. He's a mighty nervous boy. He ain't steady as your boy is. Got hisself thinking that sheriff got his eye on him. Worries me."

There had been, somehow, an unaccountable lapse in Hester's attention, for now she observed, suddenly, that Hollis Handley had moved closer and stood next to the chair at the end of the short table. His hand rested on the chairback. By leaning sideways she could have touched it and she thought it would be cold to her fingers, like his raincoat. All at once she said, "Why did you come here?"

Hollis Handley put his hat down on the table. Then, like something in a dream she was having, he pulled the chair out and sat down facing her. On his scalp, among the strands of reddish hair, seeds of perspiration gleamed in light from the bulb overhead. He said, "Didn't nobody see me, don't you worry. That boy's what got me worried . . . nervous like he is. What you reckon I ought to do with him?"

He waited, his eyes wide and moist with anticipation of her answer. "Reckon it's been time enough so he could leave out of here?" His hand came off the table and slowly, as if he were not conscious of what his fingers were doing, began to unfasten the buckles of his raincoat. There, as the coat parted beneath his chin, was the same gold-spangled tie, fatly knotted between the lapels of his collar. Hester did not know why it was this that made her say, all at once:

"What is it you want? Is it money?"

Except for the sound of steady rain, everything had stopped. Hollis Handley's face was changed. His mouth sank at the corners and a look of injury darkened his eyes. "I don't know what kind of a fellow you think I am, Miss Hester. Like I was just a plain, common blackmailer don't even care nothing about his own boy," he said, shaking his head as if to rid himself of the vision.

"Then what *do* you want?"

"I might be poor folks. And *from* poor folks. But I ain't no trash." A little glint crossed his eyes. "I never had nothing and never had no education much, like you. But that don't make me no low-down scum. My mama taught me some principles same as yours did, and I got my pride, too."

There was something so convincing in his manner that, for all her assurance of his duplicity, her gaze faltered. But what did he want? Was it merely some idea, proclaimed by the gaudy tie and laundered shirt, to force her acceptance of him as an equal? Or could his show of anxiety possibly be real?

Hollis Handley had allowed a moment for his words to sink in. "It might be I ain't got all the reason you got for being proud, but I don't want to see my boy found out no more than you do yours. 'Course it ain't like my family got any name much, but we ain't never had one up in the pen. And I ain't wanting to be shamed, no more than you."

Certainly this note was false. She could only look at him, seeing the way he had sat back in his chair with a dignity that was half ludicrous.

"No ma'm, Miss Hester. I got my pride, too. And I already tried to tell you what I come for. I ain't looking for a thing from you but your *ad*vice. And helping me is helping yourself."

He looked earnestly at her. She did not think she had made any response, much less uttered the vacuous question "Why?" But this was the question he answered.

" 'Cause that boy'll tell everything if they catch him," he said, and let his pause work for a moment. "But you know that well as I do. Reason I want your *ad*vice, Miss Hester, is I got you figured for a mighty smart woman."

His expression had changed again. From appearances it was an expression of the most genuine admiration.

"But I don't have any advice," she murmured.

"I just want to know what you think about this one thing. Which I already asked you. If you think that boy ought to pull out of here. You reckon it'd look funny?"

She felt an immense unwillingness to speak, and yet, as the watchful, eager look of his face more and more impressed her, a fear to deny him. But what could he do to her? She wet her lips. "I have no way of knowing."

The darkening of his face lasted an instant. "You got to help me out, Miss Hester. You're in it with me." The insistent eagerness was back again. "I just plain got to have your *ad*vice on this. Now what ought he do?"

Oh, what did he want? What difference would her words make? "I should think not," she breathed. "Not yet."

Hollis Handley's relief, or satisfaction, was apparent instantly. He looked away, vaguely nodding, appearing to meditate her answer. "You're probably right. I 'spect you are. He better stay around here a while yet."

She did not know what she had done. In the minutes left of Hollis Handley's visit, she sat there in the feeling—a feeling not unlike one of panic barely checked—that she had made some undefined but ominous commitment. Was not this the meaning of what she saw in Hollis Handley's face, heard in his voice that was comforting her now, saying, "You just quit worrying, Miss Hester. Everything going to be all right." And finally there was the moment, as he got up from the table, when he reached out and boldly touched the knuckles of her hand. She jerked her hand from the table, stiffened in her chair, but it seemed as if her will had responded too late to make any difference. Saying, in a voice like her old voice, "Don't ever come here again," sounded equally futile. And from the doorway, fastening the buckle under his chin, he answered in the same composed and kindly tone:

"Whatever you say, Miss Hester. But I'll be around if you need me."

Then he was gone in the rain.

It was as if Hollis Handley's visit that night had worked a subtle and curious change. At first she had thought the difference one that an hour would efface—a difference abiding only in the remembered smell of his raincoat, the cold impress upon her knuckles where his fingers had touched. Later she washed her hands at the sink and after that stood breathing the gusts of wind from the open door. But it was more than these things. Her night's sleep, compelled by the capsules she had ordered that day, merely refined her sense of this new distress.

She opened her eyes next morning with an unaccountable feeling that she had waked up in a strange room.

The feeling did not pass off. All day it followed her, pursued her even into sleep that night, and was there again when she opened her eyes in the grayness of another rainy dawn. The feeling was one that she could not perfectly define, but it had to do with a muteness of things, as if her sense of hearing had curiously lapsed. Not that she failed to hear the sound of her own movements or the clock ticking or, from outside, the rain falling and wind sweeping under the eaves. This was a much more intimate experience, like a flat cessation of the nameless and muffled resonances to which her ears had always been accustomed. In her lifetime she had entered many old, abandoned houses. Now, at moments, there would flash upon her mind's eye a vision of one or another room in her own house with scarred and naked floor and crumbling plaster and emptiness that purled like motes of dust in her brain. But the greatest silences were those Cam's footsteps left behind whenever she heard him enter and mount the stairs.

It was in the parlor, under the vivid eyes of her mother's portrait, that she felt her loss most heavily. On Wednesday she did not enter it at all, not even to dust the cherry cupboard or the flawless mahogany chairs. But she did enter during the night. She woke up at some late hour and went in and deliberately, with a feeling almost of violence, sat down on the sofa facing the mute and stolid shapes in the gloom. Much later, although she knew she had been asleep, it seemed as if something shameful had happened to her. She was not naked: the weight of her nightdress lay against her cold flesh. Nor was it the presence of her mother, who had stood outside the doorway with arms severely folded, that had so convicted her of shame. She remembered something, an odor. It was in her nostrils now, the smell of a wet raincoat, and on her knuckles were prints of fingers colder than her skin . . . Hollis Handley was seated in her father's chair!

She was on her feet. There was faint dawn light in the room, and her father's big mahogany chair, empty, loomed from its shadowy corner by the hearth.

Once during that day Hester did actually pause beside the telephone and linger for a minute or two, shaping the words she might use. But the words were not utterable. She went back to the work she had taken up on this day, laboring with brush and pail and cloth and wax until floors and woodwork gleamed and sweat blinded her and pain grew as fierce as brands searing the muscles of her back.

Cam did not appear at supper that evening. He did not come in at all that night, even to sleep in his car in the garage, though it was morning before she discovered the fact. For an hour after this, Hester experienced a sort of bewildered relief, as if everything had been somehow mysteriously resolved. But only the bewilderment persisted, and even this was dissipated when Cam, looking haggard, appeared again in the evening. She prepared his supper and did not inquire where he had been.

17

Except that it was at some time after Cam's return last evening, Hester did not know when it had happened. The thought had lodged itself like an object, a crystal of ice, say, exactly at the center of her mind. Other thoughts would displace it for the moment, but even then she could feel its presence at the margin, pressing back. And the passage of each new thought would leave it settled as before, squarely at center of everything.

This was why, for the first time in more than a week, she had not avoided even a glance at the newspaper. In fact she had sat down in the chair with today's paper and, finally, as if she expected the print to burn her eyes, allowed her gaze to fasten on the page. Yes, there had been more violence. Beyond the print it shaped itself in a vision of bodies locked in struggle, of bleeding, contorted faces. Something about a restaurant. She did not read on to comprehend it. And yet she turned the page, and then another. There were indignant, accusing words. Was her name mentioned? Her eyes followed line after line, but it was not there. There were other names. One, at the end of a letter, was Delmore, and her eyes, compelled back up the column again, picked out the bitterest of his phrases. One word, like an oath, stood out among all the rest. It was the word "savage," used twice.

Hester did not know, at first, what outside thing had distracted her. Because of having turned in her chair to get light from the window, she had not seem Cam enter and stop on her right, a little behind her range of vision. The discovery came almost as one with the resurgence of that cold thought in her mind and she did not remove her eyes from the paper. Many seconds, ticked off by the parlor clock, passed in this way, with his presence registering like silence in the hollow of her ear. He said, "What's that?"

He was looking over her shoulder at the paper. Without shifting her eyes, she handed it back to him. The paper rattled and then was still. Soon she heard him drop it onto the sofa.

"Mama."

She did not answer.

"Mama," he said again, dimly. "I guess you hate me, don't you?"

She found the knob of a dog iron in the fireplace to fasten her gaze upon.

"Don't you?"

"No," she barely murmured.

"You act like you do." When he got no answer, he added, "I think you wish there wasn't any me."

Her heart gave a bound and went on hammering in her chest.

"Don't you?"

She could only shake her head. The silence stretched out, and presently she began to have doubts whether he was still there behind her. But then he said, "I never did like anybody but you. I don't even like Ames. Or anybody. Except you. You won't believe me, but I always did like I thought you wanted. As much as I could."

"And you did this," she said in a hoarse murmur.

After a moment, "You know you hated him, Mama. And all those people."

"Please go away from me."

There was another long silence, silence in which that crystal of thought diffused itself like a chill throughout the darkness inside her skull.

"Do you want me to go away? Clear away? For good?"

Go away? she thought. Vanish? Her heart gave another bound. No, it would not help. And it would only point the finger to him. "It wouldn't do any good."

This time, because of the cold that had invaded her mind, bringing an interval like a doze, she thought he *had* gone away. She started a little when his voice said, "Well then, there's not anything I can do, is there?"

Go to Sheriff Venable, she thought. But the words would not pass beyond the thinking.

"Then how long are you going to keep on being this way, Mama?"

She shut her eyes.

"I've always tried to be the best, like you wanted me to. And I am the best." His tone brightened a little, with pride. "You know I am. I'm the best at sports and school and everything. Everybody knows it."

Hearing his disembodied voice say these things in the darkness behind her shut lids, she thought it was like a dream, and she opened her eyes again. But he was still behind her, out of sight, and the voice was the same disembodied voice still complacently reciting the reasons she should have pride in him. "I never made anything but A's at school. And I was all-state pitcher this season. They were even scouting me, all the colleges were, and I was just a junior. And I'm good to look at, too—you know I am."

The horror, like something poised in the depths of her, surfaced for an instant and made her think, but not say, What are you, where did you come from? How did you come from my blood? Or the blood of your father, even, who, for all the filth in him, was a Glenn and a human being? For a little moment Hester imagined a bodiless creature barely staining the gray daylight behind her. She did not know why she now forced her listless voice to say, into the hush that had fallen:

"You really think these are the things I wanted?"

"You acted like you did," he said sullenly.

"And not the other things? The things I tried to teach you? Goodness and honor and respect. And loyalty."

"I never have been disloyal. I want the same things you want. And I've got respect, too. Most boys don't respect their grandfathers, and all the old things, like I do. Like you taught me."

"And you did this," she breathed.

He paused. After a moment, "If those old people were still alive, you know they'd be glad it happened."

She drew a breath but never tried to put it into words. Closing her eyes she waited with a kind of dread for him to continue, imagining again that his voice would come from a shape barely visible against the gray daylight. She waited a long while.

"Are you going to keep on being this way? There's nothing to do about it. Why can't we go back being like we were?" He paused once more. Then his voice sharpened a little. "What do you care about the man that wrote that stupid letter to the newspaper. He's one of those people you hate. I hate them, too. They ought to crawl back in where they came from, they're nothing but stupid troublemakers. They just want to ruin what we have."

She lacked the force to respond in any way. He stirred, presently, but it did not lead to anything and she sat just as before, with her eyes shut.

"Can't we ever?" he said.

There was silence.

"I'm the same as I've always been. I can't help being the way I am." He waited, and then said, "I'll go away if you want me to. I'll do whatever you want me to."

There was something so pallid and human in his tone that hope gave a little start in her. She lifted her head and looked around to see him standing with head bent and real tears on his brown cheeks. She said, "If I asked you to, would you go to Sheriff Venable and tell him everything you know?"

Very slowly his head came up. His eyes blinked. He looked away toward the window. "There wouldn't be any sense in that, Mama. You don't want me to do that. I can't do that."

She watched just long enough to see his red lips tighten. Turning back toward the hearth, she let her eyes fall shut once more. "Then go out of here, please. And leave me alone."

He did not try again. A minute later he left the room so quietly that only the creak of a board or two betrayed his mute departure.

After a while the clock struck, and some habit of response stirred her mind and made her look around. The hall and the parlor beyond were empty. Although she had heard no sound, he probably had gone out. He might have gone away, clear away for good, safely beyond her reach. She looked at her hands and felt astonishment to think that he might not be safe within reach of them. They were the slim, still-shapely hands of a middle-aged woman, a mother, and not strong. How, then, could they be a threat to the child they had raised? It was not *his* strength, though, however many times greater than her own, that made him safe from them. It was what the hands remembered, the configurations that fitted precisely the shapes of what his small head and rump and calf had been. They knew the feel of the iridescent skin, wet and dry, and where all the tiny wrinkles were, that needed powder. So how could they do any harm to that small body, even grown up great . . . and evil?

Unless there was some way she could put her hand upon him softly, while he slept, and extinguish his life like a candle. Or lie beside him and in some way draw it back into herself. Some gentle way. Gentle. But here her mind simply stopped, a cessation as if a pulse had failed. And all of a sudden she realized that this idea which for so many hours had been lodged in her consciousness was as empty as any bubble. Departing, it left the blankness over her mind again.

At last she got down on her knees and tried to pray. Her lips made whispering sounds, but this was all. The empty room, the ticking clock, annihilated her thoughts. There was no compassionate ear above. As she knelt it came upon her, a remote surprise, that her faith was gone—and not just for the time. How long since it had been really with her, as it always had used to be? But the thing that brought her up off her knees was a sound from somewhere in the house.

The sound was not repeated, but she stood there nervously, listening. Above all things she did not want to encounter him again. Quickly she went to the front door and went out and closed it softly behind her. She walked around the side of the house opposite to his room. Yes, he was still inside: his car was there next to her own in the garage. Getting into her car, she backed out into the wet street.

It was still cloudy daylight, but the square was deserted. There was not even the soldier, now, to keep her company. There was only the pedestal, which she circled past and left behind as she drove on down Forrest Street. Once Ames came suddenly to mind, and a moment later she had slowed the car in order to turn around. But then, speeding up, she went on as before. There was another such interval when she was thinking of Aunt Minnie, seeing the little apartment door at back of the Torbert house and, in the pool of radiance under the lamp, Aunt Minnie's serene white head. For a moment Hester seemed to feel on her knuckles the grain of the door, to hear the approaching shuffle of Aunt Minnie's feet. But these thoughts also died out of her mind. Where was she to go?

After nightfall she sat for a long time in her car outside a drive-in restaurant. She had a cup of coffee, barely noticing when she raised it to her lips that the coffee was cold. Most of the time she sat with eyes fixed straight ahead upon a neon sign that flashed off and on, alternately white and red, advertising something. The sight grew absorbing, finally. It seemed to get inside her skull, the flare of red and then of white, like throbs of different colored blood along the channels of her brain. The effect continued even after she drove away from the restaurant. And it seemed to be the reason that, although she passed along familiar streets, she more and more had a sense of moving in a world of hallucination.

For hours, maybe, she simply drove, back and forth through the town and out into the countryside. The feeling did not pass off. There were indefinite intervals when she grew convinced that she had lost her way and wandered into a town she did not know, for many streets and houses had scarcely a feature she recognized, and others, as if a great land swell had silently occurred, seemed to stand in an altered relationship. To come first onto Morgan Pike and after that the Beasley house seemed the wrong order of things. Darnley's Cannon, also, in its little sanctuary at the crest of the rise, had somehow got transposed to a different outskirt of the town. And how could Prince's Chapel face west? Even her own house, finally, she came on by surprise, unprepared, wondering to see it located here and with all the windows dark.

She turned in. But afterward, in the empty garage, her engine still running, she continued to sit there half suspended in the uncertainty whether this really was her proper home. Of course it was. And he was gone. Maybe he was gone forever! The thought made an interval not different from those she had often known when balanced just on the precipice of sleep. She had only to put out the lights and shut her eyes. How deep she would sink. But no, he was coming back. From her bed, late in the night, she would hear him enter and climb the stairs and tread about overhead on stealthy feet. But she had to sleep again sometime.

Heavily, she switched off the engine, then the lights, and got out of the car. In the clean air outside the garage her nostrils instantly were filled with the musky sweetness of gardenias blooming. She picked two of the blooms, like stars in a darkness beside the walk, and put them in a glass of water on the table beside her bed. She took a sleeping tablet, then a second. Soon, lying in the dark, drowsy now, she drew the poignant fragrance of the blooms deep into her lungs. It seemed to cloud her mind, at last, bringing her unsubstantial glimpses of tranquilly bright or shady childhood places—places like bowers where no wind could carry the fragrance away. These faded and, later, after what must have been an extended period of sleep, she dreamed again. But this dream was in fragments. Only a single image, already fading as it appeared, had survived intact. It was of her mother, looking stern, displeased, with arms rigidly folded across her breast.

Hester was awake and conscious of something that slowly grew lucid in her mind. Cam was out there. It was the noise of his car entering that had blasted her dream and waked her. She waited for his step on the porch, waited stiffly, until the scent of gardenias on the table seemed to turn rank and sickly, like the smell of noxious weeds. At last, just as she had begun to feel that she would stifle with waiting, it occurred to her that he was not coming in, that he was asleep in his car. She felt at least a part of the rigidness pass out of her body.

The clock struck once. Later she heard it strike again, still once, but now she was seated upright on the side of her bed, rigid as she had not been rigid before. And it seemed to grow more intense by the moment, as if this were death's rigor in her joints, inhaled with the stifling odor of the flowers. Her mind was not impaired, however. In fact it worked with a special clarity that did not fail to record even the most irrelevant impression on her senses—the sound of wind that had risen outside, the sheen on her mirror when moonlight appeared, the chilling draft that touched her naked feet. And then the sound of the clock again, still a single stroke. Time had stopped. It was frozen like her body and waiting upon a thrust of her will to set it on its course once more. She drew a breath. She stood up.

She did not feel stiff anymore. Indeed she felt rather light in her body, her movements directed by a will that seemed remote from its usual seat. With a certain mechanical accuracy she put her feet into her slippers and drew on her dark bathrobe. The boards of the floor were quiet beneath her steps. The back door yielded to her hand with only the faintest cry. But the wind outside was rude, with drafts that entered where the robe hung loose and tingled over the flesh beneath.

It whispered in the bushes, and the foliage above her bent and heaved against a broken sky.

She was already cold when she reached the garage and stopped behind his car. The cougar's snarling head, dimly visible, glared at her from the window. Then a gust of wind slapped the skirt of the robe against her leg. She entered the still garage and peered into his car through the driver's window.

It took her eyes a moment, but then she made him out. He was lying sideways across the seat, his head, defined by the pallor of his face, propped against the opposite door. With her face in the open window she could hear his heavy, whistling breath and smell the fumes of the whiskey. Suddenly she felt a swelling around her heart. It filled the whole cavity of her chest and ended by taking all her strength away. If only she might not have seen the pallor of his face in the dark or heard his helpless breathing. No, it was not her hand that could do this. She took her hands from the door and stood up straight. She would leave him here, as before, and morning would come and he would appear and nothing would be changed. Perhaps she would grow used to her knowledge. Perhaps at last she would cease to notice his almost soundless footsteps in the night. Outside, beyond the stillness close around her, the wind blew, heaving the branches in bleak streetlight. Standing stiffly, she hugged her breast against the cold. But she did not move and, presently, she began to feel a self-consciousness that came to focus at last upon the stern, familiar posture of her own body. It set her pulse beating again. Her hand trembled, but she put it back on the car door, then the other hand, and bending her face to the window, she whispered, "Cameron."

There was no change. She spoke his name again, louder, and after that reached in and shook him feebly by the hip. Still the breathing came and went. Her hand discovered the handle and, calling on her strength, she drew the door open. Reaching into the darkness, feeling along the dashboard, her hand came on the key to the switch. But the gear: the car would have to be out of gear.

She saw, with a quickening of panic, that she must get inside to do it, but now she did not hesitate. There was space between his rump and the edge of the seat, and here she perched herself, touching against him, while her foot pressed the pedal and her hand slipped the lever into neutral. And then the key. Her fingers trembled on it. Hesitating, she imagined a stroke like a gun's blast. And it would wake him. He would sit up, alarmed, and she would invite him into the house, to his bed. She turned the key.

A grating noise and then the engine resounded. It was not the shock she had expected, for she saw that he had not moved. She stared at the paleness that marked his head, propped against the door, and listened how the sound of the motor had achieved a kind of subdued and rhythmic beat. She would turn it off. The impulse moved her hand back to the switch, but she checked it there.

"Mama."

It was barely audible. She had stiffened, holding her breath. Later:

"Where we going?" he mumbled, ever so faintly.

She thought of answers, but all were mocking answers. To Fountain Inn, she thought. To see them pick the cotton. Minutes later she was still silent, frozen, hearing the hollow throb of the motor. Were those not fumes she smelled—already fumes—entering his nostrils on the long breaths he drew. But this was his body still warm against her side, his rump whose shape in infancy seemed even now impressed upon her hand. It was the hand that rested on the switch. With a sudden twist she turned the key. The motor coughed and died, and she gave a lunge that carried her clear out of the car and left her hanging upon the open door in a kind of swoon whose soundlessness was that of a void into which she had fallen.

But there was a sound. She did not have to turn her head to see that he had moved, that his face was turned to her now. "Mama," he said again, in a strange questioning voice.

She fled from the garage, but it was a slow, stumbling flight, as in a nightmare, with pauses to direct her steps. Even on the walkway she paused once, and before she could put her foot on the porch, a burst of wind made white gardenias reel in the darkness of a bush. She shut the back door, but the image stayed with her. In her room, even as her hand sought out the sleeping capsules and put them dry into her mouth, it was there before her eyes, an image of terror now. The covers in which she buried her face, her tight-shut lids, did not so much as blur the vision. And all night long, under the drugged black sleep into which she at last had fallen, gardenias went on reeling like stars broken from their orbits.

Full daylight, searing her open eyes, was the element in which, once more, she heard his footsteps stealing into the house. She closed her eyes, and this, in fact, shut out the sound—shut out every sound except, from her window, the voice of a towhee singing as if in the confinement of a hollow place. But Cam was there in the hall, still there. Her mind perceived him like a specter poised in the morning light outside her room. And presently she fancied the shape of him approaching her door, passing in through the solid panel with spectral hands held out to her. The faint footsteps resumed, however. She heard them, ever so soft, on the stairs and again in the room overhead. Nothing was changed.

Finally she got up and dressed herself and performed some tasks that afterward she could not remember having done. When she saw how the sun had climbed, she realized that it was midmorning and that no breakfast had been prepared that day. Neither, she thought, had she heard Cam's footsteps again. Without reason she became possessed by the idea that he was not in the house anymore and, all of a sudden, she walked to the stairs. She climbed halfway, with a sense of wielding her body, and there stopped. His door was shut. It was sealed, she fancied, and there was only emptiness behind it. At length, having climbed the rest of the way, she laid a stealthy hand on the porcelain knob. No, there was only silence. Quietly she opened the door.

He was not there. For many seconds—or minutes?—staring at the flawless cover tautly stretched upon the bed, at the marshaled order of chest and chairs and the patterned banners on the walls, she was conscious of a terror in the perfection of it all. Second by second she felt this terror growing, mounting with her heart, in strokes like thuds of a dull drum. Out of it, finally, came the sound of a voice. Later she understood that someone was calling her name and pounding on a door, and she turned and descended the stairs.

Then she was staring into a black face and white eyes that looked as if they could not bring her clearly into focus.

"Miss Hester," Lucius faintly said, words that left his mouth open without sound. Only his hand, gesturing, pointed her eyes to the garage. She drew a breath and stepped out onto the porch.

The brightness of morning waited outside with pitiless blades of light, and trees above her head held leaves of a fierce and smoldering yellow. There was no breeze, not a breath to stir a leaf, but the towhee in the big elm was still there, still singing. Even as Hester stood motionless at the entrance to the garage, she continued to hear its song, though muted and strange, as if experienced in sleep. For a space the object that held her gaze had a quality not much different: she thought that maybe she was dreaming it. She was a long time understanding that what she saw hanging from the partly opened door of his car was a real arm with stiffened fingers reaching shy of the concrete floor.

PART FOUR

18

It had frosted a little the night before, and early sunshine had not yet melted the rime on certain shrubs in his mother's yard. Ames noticed this fact as though it meant something. It did not mean anything and his stopping there on the sidewalk short of the gate was merely to make a delay like all the others he had made since the news had reached him last night. He had thought of not coming at all, or else of appearing only at the hour for the funeral when he need not confront her alone. Sooner or later, though, this had to be.

At last he entered the gate and, staring at the wreath of evergreen on the door, turned left and followed the path through the shrubs around to the kitchen. As always the door was unlocked. Quietly he let himself in.

The scent of flowers took him by surprise. Of course there would be flowers. But he had not anticipated, as he entered the dining room, advancing toward the hall, that their sweetness would come like an assault upon his nostrils, making his brain reel and his lungs skip a breath. From the doorway he could see them, the heaps of bloom in the hall and parlor, all the hues of lily and gladiolus and rose. But there would be no coffin yet. The oppression of flowers seemed to wane, and after that he could breathe again. He saw that his mother's door stood partly open.

A step or two, finally, put him where he could see her. She was seated by the window, fully dressed, looking out. Her folded and motionless hands rested upon the bed table. Just as it occurred to him that she must have seen him pass through the yard, he heard her voice:

"Come in."

He went slowly and stopped just over the threshold. The bun of hair in back of her head, arranged with its usual tidiness, appeared an almost solid gray.

"You know the details," she murmured, not in the tone of a question.

Apparently she had heard his faint answer, because she did not speak again. He kept standing there, and he began to hope that she had forgotten about him and that he might retreat for now without having to look her in the face. But then she turned around. His gaze wavered but hers did not. Her face was quite pale, in a way that suggested the pallor of aged china plate. Also it had less flesh than when he had seen it last, as if some days of hunger had sharpened the nose and chin and cheekbones. But what struck him most vividly was her expression of composure. In fact, with the furrow between her eyes nearly erased and the whole impression reinforced by her hands, which she now had folded across one knee, there was a sort of curious serenity in her face. She looked at him with dry, bright eyes very still in their sockets and, to his dull astonishment, said, "You know, I still own that farm out at Rainbush."

He could only return her gaze. In the same quiet, sober way she proceeded to add, "Our family were always farmers and planters, until my father's generation. And we have this farm. It's a good farm. You could go back to it."

"Go back to it?"

"You could, you know. What do you plan to do with your life?"

Still feeling a kind of haze over the subject he said impatiently, "I don't know."

"I want you to think about it."

Think about it? Now? A sort of cold violence moved him to say, "Who found him?"

He watched the brightness die out of her eyes and watched her, at last, turn back toward the window. "Lucius."

"Was the motor still running?"

"I don't remember."

There was stillness again, a stillness that he was tempted to break with yet another punishing question. He did not, and after a time in which she seemed to have forgotten his presence, he left the room and quietly went upstairs.

Cam's door was shut. An impulse made him try the knob, but the door was locked. She had locked it. He went into his own room and stood by the window looking down into the street. Soon they would bring the body. He would see it in the casket, a last glimpse. Once more his mind went back to that night four days ago and again he could see, in his room at the fraternity house, the figure of Cam standing beside the chest of drawers near the window. Light from the bent and hooded gooseneck lamp struck him only to the waist, leaving wan his head and upper torso, with a vaguely spectral look.

But he had been no specter then, for all the shock it had given Ames to open the door and find him there. For some moments Ames had been unable to speak at all. Neither had Cam said anything, and Ames had had time to imagine himself threatened by the flat stare in his brother's eyes. Then:

"I've been waiting for you," Cam said in a voice that sounded much more distant than the little space between them accounted for.

"I see you have," Ames finally said. "What for?" He had not shut the door. He put off shutting it now, only listening, as with one ear, for any sound out on the landing behind him.

"Have you got any money?"

"A few dollars. Why?"

"I need some. I need more than a few dollars."

There was no threat in his voice. It was barely even insistent. In fact, as Ames saw now, he had the look of someone cornered after a chase. His haggard eyes looked warily from hollows under his brow, and his hair, so neatly kept always, was a ragged nest of tangles. Nothing was tidy about him. His creaseless pants and dingy T-shirt appeared as if they might have been slept in the night before. And no white feet. Ames started to, and yet did not, reach out and shut the door. "What do you need money for?"

"To live on. I'm not going back home."

Making his voice still lower, Ames said, "Don't you think that might look kind of funny?"

"I don't care. I don't care how it looks. I don't care about anything . . . She's through with me, Ames." He broke off short of some other utterance. He was squarely facing Ames, and his eyes alone caught the brightness that fell upon his legs from the hooded lamp. It might have been, but was not, a glare of intense ferocity.

Ames turned and shut the door, but when he turned back to

speak, it seemed as if the room had grown somehow vaguely menacing. At a whisper he said:

"Why did you do it?"

The glare had gone out of Cam's eyes. He took a while to answer. "I don't know."

"Did you think you were doing it *for* something?"

Cam looked away. The stirring of his head neither confirmed nor denied it.

"Did you?" Ames asked. "Did you think she really wanted that . . . down inside?"

"I don't know, I told you." Then Cam looked at him. His body had stiffened, his eyes kindled again. "Why did you tell her?"

Ames resisted an impulse to take a step back, for the moment was one in which he really did fear that Cam might lunge at him. And the door was shut. Cam's expression, if anything, grew more inflamed by the second.

"She wishes I was dead, Ames!"

It was a quick, passionate cry. It lingered on and on, like an echo trapped in a hollow place. For a long while Ames could only stand there in his gaze, until it drifted away from him toward the window. Ames said:

"You're crazy. She's worshiped you from the day you were born. You know that."

"I think she does, though, anyway." The passion was gone from his voice. He turned aside and, hanging the fingers of a hand on the edge of the chest of drawers, stood in front of the window looking down into the street. Ames regarded the motionless figure, like something haggardly sketched and suspended in the pale window frame. And suddenly he felt again, in a way more vivid now, that sense of distance intervening between them. It was a feeling that comforted him; he responded to it by saying:

"You could turn yourself in."

"That's not what she wants," Cam murmured, almost inaudibly.

"Are you still sure you know what she wants?"

"*That's* not it."

At last, across the distance, Ames said, "You're the one that has to live with it."

"I could live with it."

"If she would just forget about it," Ames said with harshness. It was a harshness he half repented of as the moments drew on and the hush gathered and the haggard figure stirred no more than if it were indeed a sketch in the window frame. But he only half repented. Standing gazing at the figure, he began to have a feeling as though his fleshly senses were failing him, as though the substance slowly was draining out of the shape of things. Lifting his voice a little, he said, "And you won't even think about turning yourself in?"

But Cam did not answer.

Ames reached into his pocket. "Here's the money I've got, if you want it. It's fourteen dollars."

Cam stirred, a listless movement. He turned around but he did not say anything. Ames put the money on the table.

"I guess I'll go on now," Cam said.

"You'd better go on back home."

Without quite looking up, Cam crossed to the table and took the money. He stepped to the door, brushing past Ames, and opened it. But there he stopped. Although his eyes caught light again, there was no longer any illusion of ferocity. "Ames, I always tried to be what she wanted."

"I know."

Cam's gaze shifted to a point somewhere behind Ames.

"Where *are* you going?"

Cam did not reply. He turned and went out, and Ames had been left standing there until long after the sound of descending feet had become mere phantom steps in his ear.

Reliving those moments now, Ames experienced again that initial brief sense of deliverance. Cam was gone. Where he had been there was silence. And as before, except with greater intensity, the feeling that displaced his relief was one mingled of pity and throttled rage. He kept on standing at his window until he saw the hearse pull up at the curb in front of the house.

It was about nine o'clock when they brought Cam's body in and, under Aunt Minnie's garbled and contradictory directions, banked the flowers around the coffin and finally opened it. When they did, Ames imagined that this was what had released again, as if from out of the coffin, the drowning scent of flowers. From the hall he watched Aunt Minnie, a shrunken, child-size figure in lacy black, standing with hands on the coffin edge and with palsied, bent, white head. Later, when the parlor was empty, Ames approached for a look at him. Except his stillness and the hue of his skin, he was like himself. It was himself got up for an occasion, in tweed coat and dark red tie and auburn hair swept neatly back from his clear, chiseled forehead. Handsome. No, he was more than that. He was beautiful, and for these moments it became in Ames's mind the most obvious of certainties that any kind of unseemly act had to have been impossible for his brother.

Ames knew that his mother never had come for a look into the coffin. Right up until time for the funeral the door to her room stayed shut, and when she entered the crowded parlor, on his arm, followed by Aunt Minnie and a few family members from Montgomery and Nashville, he did not see her give even a glance toward the open lid. Except for one striking interval in the hall preceding her entrance, she kept throughout the funeral the same look of pale, abstracted serenity, with dry eyes wandering over the flowers or pausing for moments of incurious scrutiny on the natty and eloquent young preacher. At the cemetery there were only different objects for her gaze. The acres of gravestones in sun or heavy shade, a few low vaults, a sculptured figure of Christ or of an angel perched on taller monuments here and there. At the last moment, when the family withdrew, she allowed herself to be led away without even a sign that she was conscious of the coffin suspended over the open grave. Except for that incident in the hall, there had nowhere been a break in her demeanor.

But that incident lingered with Ames. He had seen his mother's remote pale face when the door to her room opened, and then he had seen it change like a face suddenly come awake. Lucius was there, in dark blue, double-breasted coat, with black hat held in both hands against his stomach. She walked straight to him and, gripping his coat under each arm, hid her face deep in the hollow of his shoulder. For many seconds she stayed this way, while Lucius, holding the hat against her back, with his free hand gently patted her. "Now, Miss Hester. Now, Miss Hester," he said in a deep voice that could not have been heard at more than a few steps' distance. When she turned away from him, Ames saw her face. He remembered that her eyes were glistening, but it was more than this. What he had seemed to see in the moment before her expression dried up was like a flush of tremulous joyfulness.

After the funeral she went back into her room, and Ames did not have to confront her again that day. The fact did not help him resolve anything. Intervals he was forced to spend with kin and callers downstairs only seemed distracting, and the isolation of his room through the long ambiguous night left him as uncertain as before. Sometimes, remembering Cam in that coffin, his whole frame would ache with the pity of it. Then his rage would come, burn for a while, and he would know exactly what envenomed words he would say to her. For wasn't it all her doing? But again the passion would drain out of his heart. He would go away, for good this time, without confronting her at all. The thought of his father came to mind. Had his father been notified, even? When a slow cold daybreak began to smear his east window gray, he got up and dressed himself. But then he lay down on his bed once more.

At noon he still had not seen her. After a breakfast which Aunt Minnie finally puttered into existence, he had waited a little while in the kitchen. His mother had not appeared, and soon he had thought of some excuse. What he had done with the hours since, was hard to recall in detail. A lot of walking here and there in town, a pointless stop at the bus station, an extended walk through Meadow Hills along a road from where he could see Libby's house in the near distance. Her house was one of two sights this whole morning that had really engaged his attention. The other had brought him to a halt. He stood in front of Irving's Restaurant and looked at the jag-edged six-foot space that had been its plate-glass front.

Now he was standing, for no good reason, under a tree on Bell Street. The sound of his name startled him. He started again to see, pulled up at the nearby curb, the sheriff's car and Monk Venable's face in the window.

"I thought that was you, boy. Let me talk to you a minute."

The face that Ames presented felt as if blood had discolored it, but there was no escape. And even as he moved to comply, Monk opened the door and, slipping back under the wheel, beckoned him into the car.

"I hadn't seen you in a long while," Monk said as Ames got in. "Right off, I wasn't sure it was you."

Ames had to risk a moment's encounter with the small, quick blue eyes. They looked at him kindly, from a face netted with unremembered creases.

"How's Miss Hester holding up?"

"I don't know. As well as you could expect, I guess." The kindliness of Monk's scrutiny had a little diminished Ames's tension.

"That's pretty well, then," Monk said. "Because that's much of a woman, your mama. You ought to know it, too."

Ames forced a nod.

After a pause, Monk slowly shook his head. "A young boy like that."

Ames gazed through the windshield at a yellow leaf tumbling down the air from a maple tree. He weighed his question. "You know about how it happened?"

"Yeah. I had to go look . . . He was full of that old 'shine. Rafe Quinn's, I expect."

Monk fell quiet, sliding his stubby fingers along the wheel, and Ames relaxed still more. Monk knew nothing, it seemed. The event had passed, was buried, and not a soul was any the wiser. Except his mother and himself . . . And Pike Handley.

"I ain't been able to get my mind off of it, quite," Monk finally said. "Like there wasn't enough trouble around already."

Ames hesitated. "Something new?"

"Oh, all this stuff. I can't even see no end to it. Getting uglier all the time."

"It'll end," Ames said.

"Yeah. Maybe. It won't, though, long as that bunch of whites keep pushing them on. We might could have settled it with the colored folks."

Ames kept silent.

"But that bunch wants trouble. Setting *out* to have it. And even got some town white folks kind of halfway with them. Even Kirk Qualls." Monk shook his head.

"There *are* people who want to see them get their rights," Ames suddenly said.

"Huh?" Monk looked at him from the corner of one quick, blue eye. "Yeah, well, their rights is one thing. I try to see they get them, too, the best I can—whatever those folks are saying about me. But there ain't no right to break the law. Or put other folks up to it. Or go around making trouble. And that's just what those folks are doing as hard as they can go."

"There's a right to have equal justice," Ames said. "You can't sit there and tell me we have it. That's what they're trying to start." Ames did not know why his anger should have taken this futile occasion. But there it was, clear in the tone of his voice.

"Well, they are sure God taking the wrong road about it." Monk's wrinkled face might have indicated sadness instead of anger. "Like they was just calculating what'd provoke people the most. All this mixing in the homes. Some of it out in public, too."

"Why not, if they want that?" Ames said, still conscious of his foolishness. "That's a clear enough right, isn't it?"

Monk seemed to think about it a moment. "Naw. Not right now in Cameron Springs, it ain't."

Ames held his tongue. Monk looked at him without even a trace of hostility. "You seen that white girl going around with Pitts?"

"That's their business."

"Umn." Monk shook his head. "It's liable to end up mine, too, if I can't stop it."

"What girl?" Ames said.

"That Delmore's daughter."

Ames looked straight ahead through the windshield.

"Still got fresh scars on her. She's the one got cut up in that bombing. I know Pitts. And this don't sound like his idea. You know that girl, don't you?" He looked at Ames, keenly.

"Yes."

"Well, she's got to be stopped. Even if I have to arrest them."

"You haven't got any right to arrest them," Ames said. "They're not breaking any law."

"You know better'n that."

Gazing straight ahead, Ames managed to keep still. Presently, with a slight shifting of his posture at the wheel, Monk said, "You look out after your mama."

"All right," Ames said and got out of the car.

Watching Monk drive away he thought about Libby and Pitts. The surge of revulsion that now returned he smothered deliberately. It was what they all felt, what all of them were taught from birth—their heritage. It was this that, perhaps, he should warn Libby against. He thought of Cam. Then pity, bearing that last image of his brother, came back again. And then his mother, the slow rage welling up. He turned toward home. Nevertheless, when finally he approached the house, he was glad to think that Aunt Minnie would be present.

He entered, by deliberate choice, at the front door. There in the silent hall, he stopped. Fragile sunlight, tinted like honey, fell from the high west windows into a parlor restored to perfect order, every chair and ornament back in its inevitable place. The flowers, even to the last lingering scent of them, were gone—as if there had been no flowers. Ames experienced a moment of confusion. The memory of yesterday came back quickly enough, yet differently somehow, as if he had recalled it across a span of time. He listened for sounds in the house, but, except the clock, there were none. His mother's door was open. Approaching quietly, he saw that she was not inside and saw, also, that her bed was tidily made and the room straightened. It was as always.

He went to the kitchen and, finding no one, came back and stood at the foot of the stairway. In a manner as if his steps might fracture something, he started up, climbing until he reached the bend halfway to the top. He knew where she was.

He thought he had known, but now, from just outside the doorway, he could see that she was not in the room. Standing around on the floor were large pasteboard cartons, some of them already filled with articles of clothing. Everything was bare—chest of drawers and tabletop, the mattress on the bed, the walls on which triangular marks palely showed where the patterns of colored banners had hung. Already it was no one's room. The thought gave an added weight of desolation to his spirit.

It was this very desolation that drew him into the room, among the filled and half-filled cartons. In one he saw Cam's silver cups, lying as if simply dropped among the banners and sweat shirts and an oily baseball glove. He was still gazing at them when he became conscious of a broom leaning in the open door of the big closet, and then of his mother, little more than a silhouette in the bad light, standing at the small dusty window. She was looking out, and he thought he might still make his escape. But it was too late. He did not know how he could tell that she knew of his presence and that in a moment she would speak to him.

19

There had been a stretch of time, hours, when all the functions of Hester's body seemed to be virtually suspended. Her consciousness, like the images fixed or passing in a mirror glass, was whatever thing impinged upon sight or hearing, without before or after. Her window curtains, tightly drawn, held a flush of unchanging lavender light. A sheen lay upon the tall, mute footposts of her bed, and cracks in the ceiling plaster were a script that never made advance toward saying anything. Comb, brush, and pin box stationed in that order on her dressing table were pin box, brush, and comb when looked at in reverse. There had been voices, but these were sounds escaped into her ears, as if from doors pushed slightly ajar and quickly shut again.

One face, Aunt Minnie's, had been present sometimes, and forgotten questions which Hester could not even recall voicing answers to. A teacup steamed on a tray. Her lips were burning. But this had been like a preface, finally. The lavender flush in her curtains was gone, the cracks in the ceiling had vanished. She thought it was deep in the night and yet her lips still tingled. So did her scalp and forehead, though she did not feel feverish. Something had happened. She made an audible sound with her mouth and afterward was sure that another almost like it had come back in response. Was that Aunt Minnie's breathing? But Aunt Minnie was not in the room. Staring into the darkness Hester did not know when or how it was that she could see her comb and brush lying in a different arrangement on the dressing table. She touched her hair. It felt as soft as down beneath her fingertips. Someone had combed it for her. Was it then, or later, in a dream, that she saw her mother standing beside the bed?

But had it been a dream? Lying wakeful in the cold depth of night, she was more and more certain that there had been someone,

someone by whom she had been touched and handled, even kissed, like a child. Who else but her mother? There were such things: all her life she had known this. It was a small doubt, hardly worth the proving, that made her, feebly, get out of bed into the frosty air and creep into the hall and back to Aunt Minnie's door. The door was open. She could hear Aunt Minnie's sleeping breath. Moon rays through the rear window had partly dissolved darkness in the room, and soon she could see the bed where Aunt Minnie lay and could see, beneath the old lady's black nightcap, a fringe of hair as white as cotton lace. She had been gazing tenderly at it for a moment when she realized that the sound of breathing had stopped.

"Hester?" A quavering sound.

"Yes, Aunt Minnie."

"Do you need something, child?"

"No, Aunt Minnie." She paused. "Were you in my room a little while ago?"

"No . . . I think I've been asleep."

"Were you there earlier?"

Aunt Minnie was quiet for a moment. "Not since ten. And I heard it strike midnight . . . I expect you've been dreaming, dear."

"I don't think I was . . . I think Mama was there."

"Oh no, dear."

"I think she was. She was standing by my bed. She touched me. I think she kissed me, too."

"She loved you very much . . . But you shouldn't stand there in the cold."

Hester came through the door and, stopping beside Aunt Minnie's bed, gazed down at the fringe of white hair below the cap. "I'm sure it was her. I think she came to tell me that . . . that everything is all right."

"Yes, dear. It could be. I expect it was her." The old lady had struggled up onto an elbow. She extended a shadowy, faltering hand, and Hester took it, held it in her own, feeling the bones like twigs beneath flesh as fine and dry as old satin. "But you'll catch your death standing there. Please go back to bed."

"I'm not cold, Aunt Minnie." Still holding the old lady's hand, she sat down on the bed beside her and presently closed the hand in both of her own. So softly that she was not sure Aunt Minnie would even hear, she said, "Do you think everything is all right?"

Aunt Minnie did hear. "It will be, child. God will make it all right."

"And you think it was Mama? Come back to tell me? Haven't there been things like this before in our family? At Fountain Inn, there were."

"Oh yes." Aunt Minnie's head was back on the pillow. Beneath the white fringe her face was dim, and the stillness that had come over her seemed to mean that she was falling asleep. Hester pressed her hand. The hand appeared to have no pulse and Hester, in a little start of panic, squeezed it hard.

"Oh yes," Aunt Minnie faintly said. "There were such things. We had an uncle . . ."

After a second Hester said, "They saw him after he died, didn't they?"

"Yes. In the hall . . . upstairs. He was standing . . ."

Hester waited, remembering that hall. Even at noon there was twilight, and darkness in the corners behind the great bureau and the rolltop desk that her grandfather used. To see a spirit there, motionless, like a stain upon the gloom, had required of her no effort. Hester believed that she, too, had seen her great-uncle there. And others also, perhaps. They were never far away. Sometimes she had heard, or almost heard, their voices, a secret sound like lips giving shape to faint exhalations of breath. And always there was the sense of never being quite alone. "Did you ever see him?" Hester whispered.

But Aunt Minnie was asleep. Hester sat for a while gazing at the dim face, holding between her own a hand as weightless and fragile almost as a shadow. Gently she laid it down upon the cover and softly got up from the bed. Moonlight at the back of the room fell like rays of luminous yellow mist. It was easy to believe—in fact she was sure—that her mother's spirit abided somewhere near.

She had dreamed through the rest of the night, and when morning came it seemed that with a part of her mind she was still dreaming, walking in pastures, lolling in green shade beside the fountain. But there was the other part, where thought smoldered like a coal lodged in the tender matter of her brain. Sometimes her attention would come to focus here, until she could not endure it any longer. Then a sort of lunge would set her free, send her back into the fields and to the fountain.

But in time she would learn to live with thoughts of that night. For what she had done had been done in an agony of her spirit, in defiance of every instinct. In defiance of herself, then, in behalf of something dearer and greater than only herself. If it was true that her deliberate act had been the final cause of his, it was also true that she, her hand, had relented. And as for the feelings that he had read in her, had read *before* those moments in the car, how was she to blame? How could she have hid these feelings, how have gone on hiding them from his eyes? It would not have been possible. And even had it been so, there would have been no bearing such a life, such an evil in her house.

No, he was part of a mystery. He was part of her fate, like something sent in malice to bring ruin upon her, upon her family, upon all that she held dearest and most worthy. To bring extinction, this was the word. And in its wake, over the ashes, only triumphant mockeries to be remembered by. Then what if she had put a blemish upon her soul? Would not this agony purge it at last? A truth she never had perfectly realized now was clear to her: that this was not a world in which goodness could keep itself without a stain. More or less, according to one's luck, one sinned and bore it, and trusted—whatever one had to trust. It was the trusting that mattered.

Hester thought that these were the things her mother had come back in the night to tell her. She needed only time. Meanwhile the fields were there in her mind. There was the long driveway to the house, and the oaks and the lush boxwoods. And a powerful scent of flowers. It was a long time before she understood that the scent was not in her memory but a presence here in this house. Then she expelled the fact from her mind. From her window she gazed out over her garden of shrubs, observing, at intervals when the vision drifted back into her eyes, how frost in the early sunlight had tipped the leaves with silver.

She saw Ames, like a not quite real intruder, passing through. Soon she heard him in the hall, but even after she had called to him and knew that he was standing behind her in the room, it seemed that she could not perfectly grasp the sense of his fleshly presence. Not until she heard his voice. It was a faint shock, and after a moment she turned and looked at him. She could not read his face. Thin, thinner than in the past, with a shadow of whiskers over the cheeks, its grimness seemed to her like a veil obscuring the truth behind it. Pity and affection together started up in her breast. Now she would give him the love he was due. He would be the one. An image of her farm at Rainbush came into her mind.

But he had not responded to her words: this was not the time. Instead, questions he asked had seemed almost as if intended to punish her with thoughts of yesterday. For a long while afterward, she sat there blind at the window, unable to wrench her mind's gaze from the sight of a stiffened arm and fingers reaching shy of the floor.

All day she had kept her thoughts averted from that moment when she must go into the parlor where eyes waited and sit down before a coffin in which *he* lay. But there in the hall, as her door swung back, was Lucius. It was this that had seen her through. The minister droned his piece, a hymn was sung, and through the netted bank of flowers appeared the blue and silver of a coffin. These things were starkly real, assailing her eye and ear. But also real were those moments with Lucius out in the hall behind her. His coat had a soapy smell. Its texture lingered on the flesh of her cheek. On her back, on one of her shoulder blades, was the place where his hand had gently patted. And his voice, speaking her name, had a resonance as of echoes called from the deepest abyss of her memory.

At the graveside, surrounded by all those acres of stones and gleaming shafts and bent and mournful angels, there were intervals when her attention made perfect its escape. Far down the slope by a cedar tree she could see the plot where the Camerons were buried. In soundless, flower-scented vaults, with beards and old white tresses and immaculate eyelids shut, they lay remembering. She knew what they remembered behind those lids. And Lucius was a part of it. His voice recalled it still in her ears, and so did his face just now, where he stood in mourning, hat to chest, beside a gray headstone. She had continued to regard him until a gentle hand was laid upon her arm.

"I feel that I oughtn't to go yet, Hester."

"It's all right, Aunt Minnie. I'll be all right."

"Ames will be here, won't he?"

"Yes, he'll be here." And he would, although it was past noon, and Hester had not seen him since the funeral yesterday.

The old lady's eyes, made unsteady by the palsied movements of her head, sought to study Hester's face. Behind her, holding open the front screen door, the cabman stood with her black suitcase. "I'll always be there if you want me, you know," she said. Leaning upward she kissed, with lips like satin, the cheek that Hester offered. "God bless you, dear." Then she was gone and the door was shut.

After she heard the cab drive away, Hester opened the door and took down the wreath of evergreen. She held it for a moment. There were still a few flowers standing about in vases here and there. One vase held carnations, red and white ones, which she loved. She had to steel herself. Finally she took all the flowers from their vases and took them out back and, without looking squarely at the process, dropped them beside the garbage can. Opening the parlor windows for a little while expunged in the cool, dry autumn air the last hint of flowers. Someone had put her furniture back, but certain pieces were not properly in place. She set them right. Then, with an expectation of some kind of contentment, she seated herself in the big mahogany chair.

The contentment was fleeting, but she had not expected much—not yet. Only time could bring this, when she had learned to silence the cries that came from a depth yet too great for her answers to reach. No, she thought, they never would be wholly silenced. It was right that she should suffer, and there was one part of her that had no desire ever to be rid of the pain. It came upon her now, in fact, that she feared the thought of losing it, as if this might be the loss of that which justified her act. So let it rage for now: time would bring it in measure. She could bear it. Life, as she had always known, was duty.

A duty was waiting now. The thought that it must be done had come over her in the night and dogged her all this day. What use to put it off? But the mere intention to rise from the chair seemed to exhaust her strength. Besides, at any moment Ames might come. He might come into the parlor where she was and talk or sit in silence with her until their common grief had dissolved the last of that grim expression from his face. What would she say to him? She planned some words. She spoke them half aloud and for a long time sat waiting as if she expected an answer to come back.

But Ames did not appear and that duty still waited. It was to be done. Heavily she got up from the chair. In the room behind the garage there were pasteboard cartons. She made two trips, dragging the cartons behind her up the stairs, and afterward waited outside his door for the blood to stop assaulting her heart. She unlocked and opened the door. Segmented by columns of light from the west windows, the room was like a sinister dream that she must enter. To get across the threshold took a long time. It took still longer before she could lift her hand against the room's perfection.

The banners, first. She stripped them relentlessly from the walls and dropped them into the same carton in which, next, she put the china pieces and the cups arranged on the chest and table. Into other boxes she put his clothes, carefully folded, his shoes and toilet things. She even took the cover from his bed. Last, she turned to the shut closet. After staring for a little while at the rubble, the filth on the floor, she got her broom from the hall. Dust rose into her nostrils. When it seemed about to stifle her she opened the little window at the back and stood with her face in the cool autumn air. She closed her eyes. The long breaths she drew recalled the scent of fields at harvest-time and filled her mind with the vision.

She had heard Ames come into the room, but a minute or two was required before she could isolate this fact. A glance behind her through the door showed him standing among the cartons, head bent down, solidly there. Anxiety seized her and kept her at first from speaking. Then she said:

"I was afraid maybe you had gone."

"Not yet."

The flatness of his voice did not relieve her distress. After a moment she said, "I wanted to get this over with."

"What are you going to do with it all?"

"Give it away."

"Who to?"

It came to her at once. "The Negroes."

"The Negroes," he repeated in a voice still perfectly flat. "The cups, too?"

She stared through the window at yellow leaves. "I don't know."

"Hadn't you better keep them?"

She did not reply.

"Wouldn't it look funny? Your not wanting to keep them, to remember him by?"

She closed her eyes again.

"Well, wouldn't it?"

"I would like not to remember him," she said. She heard him move, but the tone of his voice did not change.

"Do you think you can just erase him?"

Erase him. She opened her eyes in time to see a leaf from higher up on the elm tree come reeling zigzag down across her gaze. Her lips had been open to speak, but a different impulse made her say, "Let's talk about you. And your future."

There was silence behind her. Holding her eyes fixed upon the leaves she said, "Have you thought about what I said to you yesterday?"

"What?" his voice finally said.

"About the farm."

"The farm?"

"That house could be renovated, you know. It has four bedrooms. So when you marry—"

"This is not 1857."

It was a little as if he had shouted. For a space his meaning evaded her grasp. Then it stung her. "Why do you say that?"

"Skip it."

She tried to ignore his tone. Forcing herself, she said, "Why do you? I know it's a human way of living."

"Instead of a real living, you mean. Why do you think they're all leaving the farms?"

It was only that he did not understand. In sudden passion she turned to face him, advancing as far as the door. "But they'll come back, don't you see? They will have to. People can't go on living like this."

"Like what? With enough money so they can live like people?"

His grimness was a shell that she had to break through. "Without real ties. Without a sense of things . . . of the past. That's what keeps us human. The way we live is not human anymore."

Did she not see his harsh gray gaze waver a little bit? Behind that rigor of expression something already had given way. "Please think about these things. I want you to live a real life."

There was a long pause, without any change, and she could feel how tight her fingers were clenched. Then there was a change—in his eyes, first. They seemed to brighten as they looked at her. *"He* had a real life, didn't he?"

Ames's meaning was like a thing that took a moment to unfold. She had to draw a breath with which to say, "Please, let's not—"

"Talk about it?" he interrupted. His mouth suddenly looked as if it had got cramped at the corners. Then:

"You never want to talk about things. You just erase them. Then you don't have to blame yourself. For anything. Not even poor, crazy Cam."

The same kind of lapse occurred, as if his words needed time in order to be understood. She put a hand on the doorjamb. In not much more than a whisper she said, "You know what he was . . . what he did to us."

"He was what you taught him to be." Ames's eyes, cold gray, did not even blink.

She said, "I taught him decency. And respect. Always. And he perverted it."

Ames's lips parted, then shut hard against something already in his mouth—thin lips, clamped together like halves of a shell. She saw them open again, releasing a voice that was unexpectedly hushed:

"You taught him drivel. Old South drivel. And the main thing was nigger-hating. Except a few pets."

"I taught him what I taught you," she said, like speech at the end of an exhausted breath.

"But *he* swallowed it . . . all of it. Whatever he thought you wanted, he did. *Anything."* His mouth shaped a sound that did not come. Then he added, "No matter what."

The succeeding hush was an emptiness, as if the breath needed to speak these final words had used up all the air in the room. She seemed to feel one thing only—intermittent tides of cold or hot blood in the flesh of her neck and cheeks. Her eyes never left him. She saw the change when it happened in his face, and she watched his expression harden again. His lips, that had been open, once more pressed tight together. His gaze drifted from her. Turning, he left the room and left her standing with only the doorjamb, where now her shoulder rested, for support.

That he should think such things, should speak them to her—things which, for their ugliness, she would not allow even her own mind to repeat. On the lips of a son whom she had conceived in her own body and borne in pain and loved and raised to manhood. And this, now, was what he thought, what he saw when he looked at her: not his mother but a cruel and monstrous parody of herself—an evil woman. Did he really believe this of her? No, he could not, not in his heart, for his own eyes never had seen it. Did she not know where it came from? It was what *they* in their hatred saw, what the likes of Horace Delmore invented in their malice. Ames would come back. With bowed head, in shame, he would stand before her and try to unsay it all. This was why she had waited in that room, seated on the bare mattress because her legs would not support her any longer.

But he had not come. She had heard him in his room for a while and heard when he passed through the hall and descended the stairs, but even then she had thought that he would come back. At last, so that it might be easier for him, she had made her way downstairs and sat waiting in a chair not far outside her bedroom door. For an hour, perhaps, she had waited, tensely holding to her faith that finally he must appear. But he had not come and the clocking stillness of the house, grown ponderable like fear, had driven her out into her garden.

Here was chill declining sunlight and the muted tingle of cricket voices falling over her consciousness like shades of oncoming sleep. She knew that he would not be here. The slow sweep of her eyes to discover him, in the summerhouse or out among the shrubs, was like an act performed in a kind of trance. Where pale sun slanted down through the west door, she sank into her chair. Already she was cold. Her body trembled, but soon she willed it to be still. Could he not be hidden somewhere among the foliage, watching her? And could he not see her suffering and understand that his vision of her was merely an evil dream, a nightmare shaped for his eyes by those who hated her? For how could such a self as that feel what she had felt, what she was feeling? If he could but see into her heart, into her mind, or know what she had known in the night when spirit hands and lips had been laid upon her. Why could he not see? . . . But he was gone.

A little later she had a moment of uncertainty about this fact, for it seemed to her that she heard, though barely heard, a sound as of footsteps on the back porch. She lifted her head. Her spirit trembled. But the sound had no sequel and again there was only the tingle in her ears. The sun, about to set, was slipping behind a tissue of filmy cloud. The light paled, and leaves of the shrubbery, suddenly without shadows, stood out in separate, bleak detail, like leaves printed upon her mind's eye. She closed her lids. But now it seemed that there was the smell of gardenias somewhere and, to shut out the scent, she confined herself to breathing only through her mouth.

"Miss Hester."

Even her alarm was a feeble thing. It did no more than lift her head upright and fix her eyes where Hollis Handley stood at the entrance to the path. He held the green hat in his hand, mournfully, gazing at her through the lattice. Something that would have sounded harsh receded from her tongue. She watched in helplessness, in a sort of incredulity, as he advanced to the door and stopped and stood regarding her with the same mournful expression. For just a second, when he did not speak again, she allowed the thought that her own fancy was mocking her with his image. Then he said:

"I just come by to pay my respects. Knowing how you bound to feel, in your loss."

She did not answer. What stood in his wide brown eyes was like innocence, and thoughts of what might lie concealed fell emptily at thresholds of her mind.

"Me having a boy, too. And them good friends. I can feel it for you same as it was mine."

Which was to tell her . . . ? A chill came over her body, but again she willed her trembling to stop. The hush persisted. He stood with his head still bowed a little in sympathy for her. The sun had gone down. Clouds gathered there in the west made first twilight wintry pale and bleak.

"Lonesome for you here," he quietly said. "Your other boy gone on back."

"How do you know?" she whispered.

"I seen him going in the bus station."

She waited.

"And I seen the bus come out. He was on it."

She gazed into the shrubbery, and it was a while before she heard anything.

"Time like this, a body needs some company," Hollis Handley said. She saw him turn.

Numbly, not quite believing it, she watched him take a chair from the yard and place it in the summerhouse not very far from her own. She thought then that she would get up, but she did not. And afterward, as he sat holding the green hat sorrowfully on his knees, it seemed to her that she had tried to and failed. The fat, gold-spangled tie brightened in the bleakness of growing dusk. He was speaking. His voice, kept low and mournful, sounded less abrasive than before. He was speaking about her summerhouse and the board shingles that still were lacking. He would get them for her and put them on, for nothing. And all the while she was thinking that now she would rise from her chair. But dusk grew into night and, though her body's trembling was beyond all power of her will to arrest it, still she did not get up.

20

Ames closed the book—momentarily he had forgotten which book—that had been lying open on the desk before him. At the foot of the stairs he paused in front of the letter boxes on the wall. It was habit. He had known there would be nothing and there was nothing in his box. The thought of his freedom did not lift his mood. He walked down Benton Street where the gusty afternoon wind was stripping leaves from the elm trees, then up Fischer a block to Valento's Restaurant. It was dim inside, only a few people, a little talk and clattering. He had finished his coffee and got up from the table before he saw Libby.

He had wished to avoid her, or thought he had. Yet now when he saw her nodding to him, only her face clearly visible from within the tall corner booth, he realized he was not sorry. All of a sudden he was conscious of a desire for even the kind of wary and painful intimacy he felt with Libby. And of something more besides. There was a certain clarity in her presence, as if her straight hard gaze, her father's eyes, sheared away the knots and webs in which his own thoughts nowadays seemed to be always tangled. For the moment, at least, she made him able to look at things with some of her boldness.

Watching him as he came up to the booth, her eyes were now a little veiled by her show of sympathy. "I wanted to tell you how sorry I was to hear . . ." It was only then that he saw her father, dressed in a dark suit, sitting opposite her in the booth.

Horace Delmore did not say anything, but he gave a slow nod of sympathy and extended his hand, a wide tense hand that gripped Ames's for a second only. There was nothing for Ames to do but sit down, beside Libby, and say the things that he must, that he could, say. Already he regretted that he had not devised an excuse to hurry on. He imagined that he stumbled in what he said and that Horace Delmore's eyes regarded him with an intensity that might have seen through to the secret thoughts rising in his mind. Once he saw the muscles knot in the heavy jaw. Later, in the awkward silence that had fallen, admitting voices from another booth, he observed the impatient gesture with which Horace Delmore crushed out his cigarette in the ashtray. But Libby said something quiet and kindly then. Her father nodded in sympathy once more, and Ames felt almost reassured. He would leave now. Probably they wished it, too. He was not certain whether it was an anxiety just to know or a feeling of real solicitude that made him linger yet a moment, rehearsing his words, and finally say:

"Did Sheriff Venable ever talk to you?"

She was looking straight at him with eyes that could have been her father's. "Did he talk to you about that?"

"Yes. He mentioned it. He told me I ought to warn you."

Horace Delmore lit another cigarette. Libby said, "You would think we were stupid fools. He talked to Daddy."

Her father dropped his dead match into the ashtray.

"He even threatened to arrest me," Libby said. "And Wendell, too."

Smoke drifted from Horace Delmore's lips. His intentness made it a little hard for Ames to say, finally, "He does have a point, you know. About the danger." He looked at Libby, at the scar on the cheek next to him.

"Do you think that's his real reason?" Libby's face had the same ironic expression that it had worn that night at the fraternity house.

It was her father who answered. "I doubt it." He paused, as if to wait just an instant for a reply. "He's just another piece of the town, Glenn. It's not the danger he's worried about, it's the fact that a white girl and a black man are occasionally together like two human beings. And he intends to use his office to stop it, if necessary. I hope he does try it. It would be our chance to expose him in the press. And I don't mean just the *Cameron Springs Herald,* either. We could make a real thing out of it . . . Do you know him well?"

"Fairly well," Ames said. "He's been sheriff since I was a child." He hesitated. "I don't think he's as bad as you believe." He was conscious of their eyes, but he added anyway, "Most people think he's tried to be fair."

Libby's expression had not changed. Horace Delmore let smoke drift from his slightly pursed, thin lips. Rising, it clouded his eyes for a second.

"Has he? You might try asking some Negroes. Like Wendell Pitts. You would get a different answer." His thick middle finger had a wide gold band. "Is it even conceivable that he couldn't have found out something about any of these incidents? Not to mention that savage lynching, after nearly two months. No, I'm afraid his 'fairness' is for whites only, like the restaurants. He's nothing more than an agent for the whole rotten system—a nigger-hater with a badge."

After a pause, Ames said quietly, "I believe you're misjudging him."

This time there was no response, only their silence. Why, Ames thought, must he always be defending, maintaining some small point against a whole that his own mind now had discredited. Not even maintaining it. He said, "It's still dangerous, anyway. It's waving a red flag, you know. Especially for Pitts."

"Wendell knows that. And so do I," Libby said. "We are very, very careful. Anyway, Wendell says they wouldn't need this excuse to get him if they had the nerve. He knows the situation better than any of us."

"Maybe," Ames said. "But how would you feel if they did get him?"

"That's a risk we have to take."

She had quit looking at him. She was looking at her fingernails, unpainted, rounded like a boy's. So was her profile like a boy's, with strong prominent bones and short-cropped hair that did not entirely cover her ears.

"Why is it necessary, though?" Ames said. "Remember, you're not exactly safe, yourself."

"All right. Someone has to take these chances, the Negroes have taken theirs long enough. It's necessary because we are only doing what we have a perfect right to do. People have to commit themselves if we are ever to have a decent society here. This one is not even human."

Ames's mother came to his mind. The thought made him look still more intently at Libby's face, half imagining that he saw familiar lineaments. Horace Delmore said:

"As her father, naturally I worry. But she's right. Someone does have to take these risks. I wouldn't interfere if I could, except to caution her. It would be cowardly of me."

Ames said nothing. In a quiet broken only by the undertone of voices from another booth, he felt depression closing in with a weight somehow greater than before.

"It's still hard to tell which side *you* are on, though." Horace Delmore spoke in a level, not-quite muted voice.

Slowly Ames lifted his gaze to meet him, through smoke that wreathed up in front of the quizzical eyes. Even now his tongue resisted, but he forced it to say clearly, "Yours." It had almost added, "I think." And something had prevented Horace Delmore from looking quite satisfied.

"Maybe this is not the time to talk about it, Daddy," Libby said in a voice unexpectedly softened. But if Horace Delmore paid any attention, its effect was only to delay his next question for a moment.

"Your father is alive, isn't he? Does he agree with your mother?"

"I don't know," Ames said.

A second or two went by.

"I thought probably you saw him sometimes."

"No . . . I haven't seen him since I was a child."

Libby was beckoning to a waiter who was in sight, and this was the end of it. A minute later he was outside alone walking toward the fraternity house, pondering the idea.

But it was another two days, in the evening after supper, before he got up suddenly from his desk and proceeded to shave and put on the clothes he would travel in.

The odor of cooking cabbage, like the stale breath of all these mean little houses facing each other in tight ranks along the street, was what made Ames pause at the corner. The sign said "Bandy Avenue," all right. Up and down in diminutive front yards there were some shedding maples and hackberries, but these did little to relieve an atmosphere of depression that would be called squalor in a few more years. Yet this was where his father lived. And without even a telephone listed, so that Ames had had to find out his address in the city directory at the courthouse. Now he wished he had not come.

For why had he come, come by bus these two hundred miles to see a man so little known to him that Ames had not even been certain whether Memphis was the right city? A long-established notion was all he had had. "In Memphis," he seemed to remember hearing his mother say. Just as vaguely he seemed to remember her tight lips when she said it, and this, he guessed, was why he had long ago almost ceased wondering, or even thinking, about his father. There was no picture of him that Ames had ever seen, and all the image the years had left was of a smallish, jaunty man, given to jokes and teasing, and of whom Ames had been fond. Would he know him now at all? And what could he say to this stranger? Standing gazing down the street at the ranks of little houses, he realized that his coming here had been a pointless venture.

But he did not turn back. He set his feet in motion, walking, because there was not any sidewalk, on the shoulder along the edge of the pitted, asphalt street. Some of the numbers on the dingy houses were faded, but he could read enough of them, and then, halfway down the block, he stood before the one he was looking for. An old Ford was parked in front, not many feet from the small porch. His heart was beating. He stepped up onto the porch and knocked.

After a little he knocked again. Now there were footsteps. The beige curtain moved and a woman's face appeared through the glass. "What is it?"

"Is this where Thomas Glenn lives?"

The face looked sallow, with loose flesh along the jaws. The door opened, but only a little way. "What do you want with him?"

"I just want to talk to him."

She continued to look at him distrustfully. "Who are you?"

Ames swallowed. "I'm his son. Ames."

Her lids drooped faintly as something crossed her face. "Well, you might as well come on in," she said and opened the door for him.

There was an obscurely rancid smell in the tight little living room, two chairs, a frayed sofa, a table with a purple vase and a bright peacock feather in it. Only this, the feather, he thought, was his father's touch.

"You might as well sit down there on the sofa."

He did, but the woman kept standing. Fleetingly he thought that she must have been rather pretty a few years ago, before the flesh had puffed her face and the polka-dot housedress that was unevenly taut around her body. "Is he here now?" Ames murmured.

"No." Her eyes were a pale, diluted blue. With a look of decision they turned away from him and she said, "I might as well tell you. You all were bound to find out. Tom's dead. Been dead going on three months. Died of heart attack."

Ames's faintness of spirit gathered in the room like dusk coming on too fast. Beyond her was the bright feather in the vase.

"I know I don't have no claim, except living with him ten years. But he didn't leave nothing much. This little old house and that old car out there. A few hundred dollars. Took the biggest part of that to bury him. Look like I ought to have it, seeing you all are rich."

He was hearing her, but he was also gazing at the feather. Its bright presence in the desolation of the room was like pain that filtered her voice to his ears. But she was arguing with him.

"I took care of him all these years. Put up with all his drinking and his fooling, losing jobs. No matter, I loved him. I'd do it over again, too. And not for nothing he had, either, but just him . . . I know he meant for me to have it, though . . . what little there is. He same as told me so, several times."

"You can have it," Ames said. He drew his gaze away from the feather, to her feet that were shod in loose, broken slippers, a man's slippers. He was conscious when her feet moved, and that now she had sat down in the creaking rocker opposite him. A shrill voice out in the street shouted something indistinct.

"It ain't like I was trying to keep something not mine by right," she said. "Even if I wasn't his wife."

"It's yours," Ames murmured. But maybe she did not hear him.

"I ought to been his wife. But she wouldn't never let him go. It wouldn't have cost her a thing to, either."

It was his mother she was talking about now. He was also conscious that her tone had changed. He asked, "What did he say about her?"

"Said he tried hard as he could to, for *several* years. Till he gave up. He said she said divorce was 'wrong.' She wouldn't do nothing 'wrong.' "

Her tone brought his gaze up. Her face no longer spoke of a vanished prettiness: at one corner her mouth was set in an ugly twist. She was not looking at him, but, apparently, at a dull chintz curtain on the window beside him. He said, "What else did he say?"

The curl on her mouth was still there. "What he thought of her . . . I know it's your mama, though," she said, looking hard at him.

"What did he say?" Ames stooped his head, waiting.

"All right. He said he hated her guts. He told me sometimes he wished he knew some kind of way to bring her down and rub her face in dirt for the way she was. Her and her 'right.' He'd get to thinking about her sometimes when he was drunk and call her names I couldn't say to you. Said he wished to God he never had seen her."

Ames, his head stooped, waited. When she spoke again her tone had altered.

"I wish to God it'd been me. He wouldn't have been like he was. I'd have gave him what a man needs. He did me wrong plenty of times, but I never held nothing back on him, I let him be. And he loved me for it, too, even if he did do like that . . . But he came to me too late."

Her voice went out on a sad, pining note. Ames heard the rocker faintly creak.

"I know she's your mama, but she made him like he was," the woman said, still quietly. "He was a good man in his heart . . . he could have been. But he couldn't be no kind of a man, with her. She took it out of him, all but what she wanted. Then when he kicked back, she sent him off . . . Sent him on to me."

Ames thought of answers—about the divorce, at least, she had been deceived—but he kept still.

Presently she said, "I don't reckon you believe me, but your daddy wasn't any bad man . . . whatever *she* might have told you. He was a man with a loving heart."

Softly Ames said, "I wouldn't know. I hadn't seen him since I was a child. Not even once."

In the pause he heard the rocker creak again. Her voice was gentle. "It wasn't him not wanting to, though."

"Then why didn't he?"

"Because of her. He said he went back several times, but she was so ugly to him, like he was going to dirty you up or something. He just gave up on you . . . like he did a lot of things. Figured she had poisoned you against him, anyhow . . . Wait a minute." She got up from the chair. With loose heels flopping she walked out of the room, and then he heard a drawer open. When she entered again she held something out to him. It was a snapshot. "He used to look at that long at a time," she murmured.

He held it to the light. Obviously the picture was of his father and himself, standing side by side, with a billow of shrubbery for background. His father, a jaunty smile on his face, wearing a loose hunting jacket, held his hand. His own thin face, which was about level with his father's hip, had a slightly puzzled but not displeased expression. It seemed to Ames that he remembered his father looking just this way, in the same hunting jacket, and he fancied that he could remember this very occasion. Wasn't it a summer afternoon? The memory hung there in a silence of his mind. For some minutes he sat gazing at the picture, gazing through it and beyond into a summer scene of real green leaves and birdsongs where a breathing man and boy stood hand in hand. The warmth that now had stolen into Ames's blood might have come from a pressure of living flesh upon his hand.

"He always wished he had a picture of the little boy, too." Then she said, "I'm glad he never had to know about that."

"You know about it?"

"Somebody sent a wire. It wasn't her, though. Somebody in *his* family."

Their words had shattered the little scene in his memory. Her feet in the loose slippers, naked swollen ankles, stood there on the floor close by him. Faint scent from her body suddenly oppressed his breathing.

"You know," she said, her tone going hard again, "she wouldn't even send him a picture of him. She wouldn't even do that." One of her feet stirred. At length, "He kept up with you all, though, best he could. He knew about your little brother being such a good ballplayer. He always wanted to go see him play."

Ames looked up at her. The blueness of her eyes looked even paler, more diluted than before. "He never saw him, then? Since he was a baby?"

"Nothing but just newspaper pictures."

Ames's gaze drifted away from her, out the window into the street where a boy was riding past on a bicycle. And now? He looked at the picture again. He got to his feet and held it out to her.

"You can keep it, if you want," she said.

He regarded her, the sagging flesh, the fallen color of her eyes. "I'll have a copy made," he said. "And send this back to you." And then, "I want you to have everything else he left, too."

She looked grateful, smiling sadly at him. Her last words to him as she let him out the door were, "He's buried right there at East Lawn. If you want to go see it. It's way over toward the far left corner." And when he looked back from the street he saw her standing in the doorway watching him with an expression that made him think of hunger.

Ames found his way to East Lawn Cemetery, flat, treeless ground with hundreds or thousands of little white headstones that looked all alike. After a time he gave up searching for the grave and headed back, passing again, just before nightfall, through the same neighborhood. Soon the mean houses gave way to yet meaner ones where, in the light of distant streetlamps, flimsy dwellings leaned for support on their own crowded ranks. There was broken glass and tin cans in the street. There were odors of garbage and, more persistent, an acrid smell like the gases from burnt-out coal. Several times he was hooted at by groups of Negro boys, which reminded him finally that there was some danger in his walking here. But he paid the fact only a little attention. In a small park where, besides refuse, there was an empty bench under a tree, he sat for an hour or more watching the cars pass by. Depression, like something on the tainted air he breathed, half befogged his consciousness.

Later there were streets like lighted canyons between blank warehouse walls, a few loiterers at corners, occasional cars whose occupants sometimes eyed him in passing. Uptown at this late hour it was not much different, only more light, neon now, and plate-glass windows displaying unreachable shiny wares and manikins in postures of stunned inanimation. Wedged in along a street he wandered down was a dull brick church. Its steps mounted from the sidewalk, and at the top a tall iron grille like a jail door barred entrance to the black and soundless vestibule. He lingered here for a while, then walked on back to the bus station where faces in raw fluorescent light had the stark expression of prisoners in solitary.

21

"Tick" went the sound. With a faint start she turned her head in time to see the leaf flutter down the pane and slide from the ledge into the shedding fig bush outside her kitchen window. Wind, stirring the branches, was stripping the brown and russet oak. Soon the tree would be bare, its naked limbs accenting the gray of a leaden winter sky.

"Old winter going to be coming early this year."

She started again, for it struck her that Lucius had been conscious of her secret thoughts. She looked sidelong at him, seeing the gray knobby head bent low over the bowl of soup, which he was ladling noisily into his mouth. But he could not know, he could not even guess at the thoughts that ran sometimes like fire along the circuits of her brain. He was the same. The difference was in herself, he but reflecting, mindlessly sensing, the strain with which his presence lately had afflicted her . . . Or had he somehow fathomed more than this? Could he have glimpsed, obscurely mirrored in the lenses of her eyes, an image of his undershot African jaw and depending lip from which the soup dribbled and thick flattened nose? Inscrutable blackness. She could not tell. But how could she love—had she ever loved? —what was unknown to her, and ugly? . . . And yet she had, she did! Her gifts, her kindnesses, her efforts in his behalf through all the years were a thousand testimonials to this fact. It was real. Her doubts would pass.

"You want me to move them other little boxwoods at the corner?" He did not look up at her. The sounds of his eating continued, picking at her nerve strings. She gazed out of the window.

"No. You had better wait until next month." She hesitated. "You can go home when you are through with your lunch."

Perhaps it was only that he had finished just while she was speaking, but the noises had stopped. She thought he was watching her. Because it seemed as if her hands might start to tremble, she folded her arms across her bosom, tightened them. A little while passed and she heard him, only once, make a faint movement. If only he would go now. What use to deceive herself?

"I was you, I wouldn't have that there Handley fooling around here no kind of way. He ain't nothing *but* trash."

She drew her arms still tighter. But her throat was too tight. She succeeded in murmuring, "He is not quite through with the summer-house roof yet. He has to find a few more shingles."

"I wouldn't let him on the place, I was you."

She knew that he was staring at her, merely staring. When would he go? For another minute she stood there. Then, without explanation, she turned and left the kitchen.

From her bedroom she heard when he went out, and it was only then that she grew fully conscious of her reflection in the dressing-table mirror. She was seated here, the comb in hand, her image in focus now. It was the same face, her eyes were playing tricks again. It was only her thinness, the way her flesh sank in shadows around the cruel prominences of bone. And her pallor. When would the color come back? The most strenuous of her exertions, the scrubbing of floors or woodwork, brought only the fleeting blood to her cheeks and forehead. In the mirror she would watch it drain like the flush of life from her face. A face she would hide if she could. An impulse made her take old rouge from a bottom drawer and set about tinting a cheek. The effect quickly stopped her. It was a lie, a cold corpse's face. Erase it.

Yet who was there to see her? Except *him,* when he came. For whom, then, was she combing her hair, stroke after stroke after stroke? Her hair had been one of her points once, a rich shadowy chestnut as fine as any down. The trouble now was not the gray in it. She watched the hairs divide on the ebony teeth and close behind without a hint of luster. Where was its life? For all her combing it would not whisper. Nothing whispered to her, and no one had combed her hair in her sleep that night. The room had been empty, as silent as now. She stopped her combing and listened.

The sound she soon heard was no real sound, in spite of times in the night when it had seemed to be. Overhead, behind the door she had locked, where stood the cartons of banners and clothing and cups, the padded restless tread of his feet was obscurely audible. But this she was able to silence. It was the knockings at her doors, because some of them were real, that always afflicted her with a cold paralysis of attention. All but a few of them went away after a little while, and she had had several glimpses of ladies departing down the sidewalk, hats visible over the hedge. The knocks, the real ones, at the back doors were those that would not finally go away.

That furrow between her eyes. Even in twilight her mirror would record it, like a groove left by a chisel in a hard colorless mask . . . And yet, at that last moment in the car with Cam, she *had* drawn back. Her agony was real, her whole soul screaming outrage. Who for his own self only would put that self on such a rack as this? It was not herself she had done it for: it was for *them,* for all her people, against a posturing enemy who did not mean to leave intact even the tenuous threads of common memory. Had she not, then, given herself? . . . at cost of her own self purged this house? Her fear, therefore, her helplessness in the face of this man's evil, was nothing more than fear of the knowledge he possessed. Only this was what so haunted the stillness in this house. His voice, its meaning barely veiled behind his intonation, would repeat it if she listened:

"I wish I knowed how to handle that boy. Can't get nothing out of him. Drinking all the time. It's some times when I get to thinking I'll just go and let them catch him, it might be for the best." Sadly shaking his head as if he had not noticed anything, as if her very eyes had not stiffened in their sockets, he put a foot on the ladder leaning against the summerhouse and added, " 'Course I raised him like a son and been fond of him. But it ain't like he was blood of mine. He's my dead wife's boy. He's just going to have to straighten out, is all there is to it."

A lie, a mere bluff? Was it not a fiction, concocted only here of late, that Pike was no blood of his? So how could he really mean that threat? At times, however, moments when she surprised his gaze upon her, she was certain that he did mean it. Not that the gaze was one she could perfectly read, because his lids, the membranous lids that looked as if they might only darken vision, would quickly curtain his eyes. But still there was time to see in them something that almost made her shudder. Did he not hate her? These were also the times when she was sure that he did hate her, and therefore that, being what he was, his threat was not merely bluff.

But this opinion came and went, and there were long intervals when she was convinced that the threat was an idle one. Yet the fear never left her. It was like something she drew in with her breath, or a thing unremittingly crouched to spring at the sound of any knock on her door. Those that came at the front door, once her frenzied ear could trace the sound, fell like blessed reprieves in the silent house. For always his knock had been at the back, the kitchen door. Until last night. The hall door this time, a tapping on the glass. She had seen his face at the pane and seen him take the hat from his head. The little hat again, instead of the shapeless felt he wore about his daily work. She had stopped at a little distance, planting her feet. But his face was patient, deferential, as if he was prepared to wait in courtesy for any length of time on her decision. Not this door, not her hall!

"What is it?" she had said, uncertain whether her voice would carry through the glass.

His face had gone mournful. His lips shaped words that just did reach her ears. "Can't talk much out here, Miss Hester."

What could he have to tell her? Nothing. "I'm getting ready to go to bed."

"Just want to talk to you for a minute."

There was something? She did not know. She took the three steps forward, like charmed steps, and unlocked the door. Air that came in as she drew it ajar was like a cold effusion from his body. "What do you have to tell me?"

There was pressure, physical now, gently pushing the door against the weight of her hand. No, he could not enter her hall. But the pressure kept on, until she could only retreat and, standing with her back to the staircase, watch him enter, hearing her own voice say, "Do you have something to tell me?"

"Nothing special, Miss Hester. I just wanted to talk to you a little bit. That's all." His gaze wandered past her down the hallway. "Know you get lonesome in this big old house by yourself."

"I am very tired," she murmured, feeling not only tired but helpless, feeling herself pressed back against the staircase as if the nearness of him had ponderable weight. He gave no sign of having heard her speak. His eyes were roaming again, measuring eyes that seemed to study walls and doors and cornices. He said:

"Seem like my painting job is holding up pretty good."

She had not known what he meant—or had not known at first. She watched him move on past her into the hall and there, in front of her bedroom door, stop and turn his head about in scrutiny. "Is getting a little dark, though. Doorframes and all ought to have another coat now." She watched his neck twist in the loose collar, light reflecting on his scalp among the sparse and rusty hairs. "Come look and see if I ain't right."

She had held back for only a moment. She remembered approaching within a step or two and gazing sightlessly up at the doorframe. All she had been conscious of was him, the bulk of him in tight tweed suitcoat and spangled tie and small hat with which his hand gestured, standing at the center of her hall. There was scent, some lotion upon his body. "Won't cost you a thing, neither, Miss Hester," he had said. "I wouldn't think about charging *you* nothing."

But there had been worse to follow, there had been the sight of him squarely planted upon the frail love seat next to the wall. His hat rested upon one knee and his eyes, lifted because she had continued standing, regarded her with a sort of dewy brightness. It was a lie, what he had said: "You know, my granddaddy, he helped build this house. You didn't know that, did you? It was right before the war." For it was not "right" before the war, it was ten years before, and slaves had done the work. All that he said, or meant by what he said, was lies. "Yes'm, our old folks, they put things up to stand here. Wasn't none of this junky propping up and painting over, like they're doing now. Our kind, they done it for good. Now you take these-here folks nowadays . . ."

And she, while his voice went on, had stood with her hand for brace on the back of the tall armchair, feeling exhaustion slowly drain the will that had kept her sinews drawn as tense as wires. Even so she could not clearly remember how or when she had managed the surrender that had allowed her finally to sink down into the chair. She vaguely recalled that he had urged her to. "You're looking tired, Miss Hester. Why don't you just set down in that chair and be easy?" But it would have needed more than this. The threat again, the thought of Pike—had he not in some way recalled it to her mind? Or was it merely the gathered weight of oppression that his voice created, suggestions which a tired will could not in that hour expel from her imagination.

"Now you and me, Miss Hester, we're the same kind of thing. You come from rich folks and I come from poor ones, but that ain't no real difference. That's just skin-deep. It's a matter of what you hold to makes the difference. Now, ain't it?" He had paused, his eyes wide, dewy, waiting upon her answer.

"I don't know," she had murmured helplessly, her hands placed tight together upon her lap. Then, as now, just as if a second self had stood outside observing the first, she had been able to see her own person upright in the chair facing this man across the little distance the hall afforded. A gentleman and lady alone together—figures to astonish, and repel, the spirits who had used to inhabit this house. Her own eyes, amazed, looked on from the parlor door or, from up the curving staircase, looked down at the pair of them seated as if rapt in a spell that his appalling voice had conjured. She could still hear it, saying:

"Yes, you do, too, now, Miss Hester. It's what people hold to makes them alike. And we both of us holds to the old folks' way, we ain't forgot them. I ain't and I know you ain't, either. They ain't just old dry bones for us. And we mean to stand up for them." His eyes, open wide, looked for her concurrence.

"You look around at these people the way they're acting nowadays, you wouldn't think it ever had been any old times. That Delmore's crowd and that newspaper fool—all them big shots around town. They don't care nothing about that monument or nothing else old-timey. They wanted it blowed up. Letting niggers come in their houses. Setting right down beside of them. What you reckon the old folks would have said about that?"

The question was asked of her. She met it in the only way she could, with the same blank gaze that already had frozen itself upon her face. Hollis Handley waited, leaning a little toward her.

"You know what they'd have said. You know what they would have *done,* too. Wasn't none of this nigger-loving then. They knowed where a nigger belonged at. Where the good Lord put them—in the cotton field. It wasn't no foolishness then about what the Lord meant. Black was black. You and me, we know it, but these folks don't. *Act* like they don't. It makes them feel good. Truth is, they hate them bad as we do."

"It's *not* the truth," she suddenly said in a voice smaller than she had intended.

Hollis Handley, with that effect of only clouding his eyes, let his lids fall shut for a second. "What's not?"

"That we . . . that *I* hate them."

A moment passed. He quit looking at her and with a thumb and finger gave a little shaping squeeze to the crown of the hat on his knee. Quietly he said, "You know you ain't no nigger-lover, Miss Hester," and went on shaping the crown of his hat. "You know you ain't nothing like that crowd—you and me."

"I don't hate them," she said, barely said, for exhaustion had come down with a kind of swoop. "I am very tired."

For all the response he made, her voice might have gone unheard. She thought of rising, but the will was not there. Now she noticed that even from her posture the rigidness was gone, that she was no longer sitting quite erect in the chair. When he looked up at her she saw him as through a wavy pane of glass, distorting the movement of his lips:

"That ain't the idea I got from that boy of yours. I used to hear him talking to Pike."

That pane of glass muffled his voice, made grotesque his lips' motion.

"I'm satisfied he thought you was right in behind him when he done that thing. It wouldn't be right to go back on him now."

His face writhed. He was something inside her mind, an evil something, reading with malice all her most secret thoughts. "It's not true," she said, hearing her voice afterward.

"Aw, Miss Hester, it ain't nothing to be ashamed about. Not with me. We didn't tell them to kill that nigger. They done that by theirselves, we didn't even know it. We can't help what our boys does.

Hating somebody ain't the same thing as killing them . . . Else we'd have done killed them all off by now."

She seemed to remember that a long pause had followed this, minutes of silence in which she had tried to summon her denial. It had come too late. Before she had managed even to draw herself erect in the chair again, he was on his feet mumbling apologies for having tired her. Then he was gone, and the words she had meant to deny it with lay unspoken upon her tongue.

It was all a lie. A thousand acts of hers belied it. Depravity never failed to see its image everywhere, as this man saw his own in her. Or, with a terrifying shrewdness, pretended that he did? She looked again at her face in the mirror. It was merely a drawn, exhausted face, and time would restore it. For when had she failed in charity to them? Her charities were too many to count, and so were the Negro faces that had smiled blessings upon her for the food or clothes or money she had brought. Only weeks ago, in fact. The woman, with old melted eyes studying Hester's face, had known her finally, had known the family lineaments and, speaking in a voice that Hester must have heard in childhood, had talked of her grandfather Cameron and the house at Fountain Inn.

Hester saw that her face in the mirror had brightened with the memory. Upstairs there were clothes already packed and waiting. Abruptly she took up the comb. A few more strokes and then, with hurrying accurate fingers, she drew and pinned her hair behind in the accustomed bun. Rising from the table, she was left with a glimpse of a face no longer strange to her.

And yet the stairs took all her breath away. The door, as if these two weeks' time had sealed it shut, presented her with a barrier beyond her tremulous strength. Even so she barely paused. At her touch the door swung back, exposing with a violence the stripped and desolate walls, the cartons on the floor, the motes of floating dust that seethed like a dizziness in her brain. Still she entered, and stopped beside a carton filled with clothes.

She had sat down on the bed, finally, for the giddiness made by dust motes swimming inside her head had seemed to threaten her balance. Her eyes, as long as she held them open, were fastened upon a garment spilling from the carton closest by. It was a white T-shirt. It was printed upon her lids when she shut them, and somehow the image, as if it possibly could retain some vestige of heat from his living body, seemed warm against her eyes. Imagining, she let the warmth increase, let it spread along her veins, suffusing the flesh where he, no bigger than this bare pillow on the mattress beside her, had lain cradled in the hollow between her breast and thighs. She could all but feel him there. Drawing the pillow to her, enclosing it with her body, she lay down across the bed and knew again, in the swooning dark behind her tight-shut lids, the shape of his small body and downy head. Safe again, shielded by her body. The room, as of old, was hers and sunshine from the tall windows fell in streams of dusty gold upon the bed where they lay. Sounds grew out of the silence. Her mother's voice, some other like it? Those in the distance, a drowsy-faint and resonant undertone, were voices of Negroes moving out to the fields. Clink of harness, creak of well rope drawing water from cool depths of the earth. And roosters. Their cries echoed over the land like bugles from the sun.

But what, all of a sudden, had shattered her peace? There were footsteps. They were mounting the stairs. For a moment her arms grew tense around the sleeping child, holding him closer. But she was sitting erect on the bed when she heard the determined steps approach her door, saw the knob turn.

Standing there in a collarless and slightly wrinkled sport shirt, her husband looked first at Cam, then at her. His face went wry. She could see that his eyes had fastened on the hand with which she was holding shut the dressing gown above her breast. For a space he said nothing. Then:

"Lack of modesty was never one of your faults."

She did not answer. She could see the hints of crimson at the corners of his eyes.

"Sorry to intrude. I just thought it would be nice to come up and renew acquaintance with my son."

"You can see he is asleep."

"Well, he can go back to sleep, can't he? He doesn't have anything else to do."

She only looked at him.

"I have a part in him, too, you know. As little as you may like to think about that." He stepped around to the other side of the bed and, bending, so that she could smell his whiskey, with a small grunt picked up the heavy child. Restraining her impulse, she watched him anxiously.

"Don't worry, I won't drop him. I won't even get him dirty," he added dryly, stopping in the middle of the floor. "See there. He remembers me."

She saw that the little boy was smiling up drowsily into his face, and she tried to put away a different kind of anxiety.

As if he sensed her feeling he said, "I don't guess he's old enough yet for me to be a bad influence, is he?" He jiggled the boy a little, producing a wider smile.

But it was herself he was really attending to. He was waiting for her answer. She would not be baited. She merely looked on, her anxious feeling undiminished, observing her little boy's face, then his. There was no likeness. Not a single feature was the same. Once she would have been sorry and would have wished for little Cam something of the delicate handsomeness that, despite the loosening jowls and the pouch starting under his chin, her husband's face still had.

She watched him turn and sit down in a chair, placing the baby upright on his knee. "Getting to be a big one, aren't you?" But his attention was not really there, and soon he glanced at her over the baby's head.

"You look even more hostile than usual. Any new evil reports on me?"

"Should there be any?" she finally murmured.

"You never can tell. With a low fellow like me." He gave a sort of smile at the little boy on his lap.

She quietly said, "Are you trying to tell me I invented your infidelities?"

"Not exactly that." Still more sarcastically he said, as if to the boy, "My 'infidelities.' "

"What would you call them? Your unfaithfulness, then."

"All right." The naked glance he sent her did not match the tone in which, after a second, he said, "But you ought to admit you present some problems. I've often wondered what kind of a man could be what you would call faithful. An angel on a white charger, maybe. A Confederate angel."

Deliberately she bridled her contempt and only said, "Tell me what you have been faithful to. Even among your mistresses."

"I don't know." The small grin again, seemingly directed at the boy. "Myself, maybe."

"What is that supposed to mean? That you faithfully indulged your passions?"

"Skip it."

Again he jiggled the boy on his knee. Even through her bitterness she felt another pang to see the child's hand reach out and touch her husband's lips. Trying to ignore it she said, "You are determined to blame me, aren't you? For your own lack of manhood. As if I had shut you out for nothing. But you know it isn't true . . . Not until your behavior became intolerable."

"My behavior was intolerable to you from the start." He was looking grimly into the little boy's face. "Long before I ever jumped the fence. And it really became 'intolerable' when I got my 'Yankee' friends. That was—"

"It was not because they were Yankees. It was because they were loose, mocking, destructive people."

"Destructive of what?"

"Of everything. Everything decent and established."

Her husband, closing his eyes, put his head against the back of the chair and mumbled something inaudible.

With passion that was a response to whatever words he had uttered, Hester said, "And of you, too."

A little silence followed. Then her husband opened his eyes and, looking at little Cam, said, "Well, then, there must not have been much to me from the first." The small grin appeared again. "Just bad blood." Touching the boy under the chin he said, "Poor little fellow. Fifty percent bad blood."

A bubble of laughter came suddenly from the child. The sound reached Hester like a chill, freezing her heart. For the interval she could only sit with her gaze blankly focused on the small figure, hearing him cruelly laugh again, feeling the tension with which her hand held shut the gown above her freezing breast.

Her husband got up from the chair. He put Cam down on the

bed beside her and, with a last chuck at his ribs, said, "So you'd better look out. He'll be jumping the fence, too." He grinned crookedly at her. Then he went out of the room and shut the door.

At first she stared at the little boy, who lay as if startled by this abandonment. Then, despite his struggles, and now his cries, she drew him tightly against her once more. It took a while, but his struggles ceased. She had him warm again, drowsy, asleep against her breast in which the heart had now renewed its languid, measured beating.

For a time she had him. But in a little while, as by a process of following some complicated route whose turns were strange to her, she reached an understanding that what she held so closely in her arms not only lacked any warmth of its own but was not even flesh. She saw that she had, in a manner, been asleep and that this pillow was what she had taken for the small body of her son. She pushed it away. The cartons stood there on the floor, a white T-shirt spilling down. There was no warmth in it, and her husband's words came back to mind like a mocking prophecy.

She got up from the bed. The carton she seized was heavy beyond belief, and she had to stop many times for rest before she reached her car.

There was unexpected wind, bearing an edge of winter, and although she had shut tight the windows of her car, she felt it. Woods to either side of her shivered in the sudden gusts, shedding over the roadway leaves like missiles aimed directly at the lenses of her eyes. Some trees were already bare at the top. Their branches scored a film of arching cloud through which the sun, sheared of its aura, diffused a colorless sterile light.

There was a crossroads, a cotton field beyond. Confusion descended upon her. Letting the car coast to a stop, she sat scanning the roads and the field for some detail that would call this place to her memory again. In the field, clear to the horizon, dry stalks from which a few neglected bolls of cotton still were hanging rippled in buffets of wind. But nothing stirred in her mind. The landscape like an empty eye stared back at her. Yet it was not possible that she never had been in this place before. Her gaze struck the roof of a cabin down the road to her left, and in haste she turned her car that way.

But the cabin, again, had no feature she knew. It sat against the broad expanse of field, without a tree, without a movement to show that there was life about. And yet the small bare yard was swept, a proof of habitation. She glanced at the carton of clothing on the seat beside her. She looked at the cabin once more. The door was shut, and the sheen of flat silver light upon the windowpanes stopped vision from outside. Not from within. From there it would make concealment for an eye that could be watching, watching her expressions, studying her white face. Even above the throbbing of the engine, the stillness seemed to yawn upon her. Abruptly she put the car in motion, driving fast away down a bumpy rutted road that seemed as if it might lead into a country out of which she never would find her way.

But soon the road emptied into a better one, and with relief she recognized the place. Down this road beyond a naked chimney and then a beech woods was Bo Camron's cabin where she had left the money a month ago. As much as any, they would need these clothes. Turning right she went on.

The big mimosa trees were yellow now, and shedding. Their branches heaved in a gust that came as her car rolled to a halt. She waited a minute, but only the branches moved, the wind sounding. Where were they? Her gaze swept over the cotton field, returned to the cabin door and windows. She was suddenly cold again.

No, there was someone, a boy watching from near the cabin. Getting out of the car, she walked around to the other side and opened the door. Lifting her voice that sounded hoarse, "Here are some things for you. You may be able to use them," she said and gave one tug at the heavy carton. She let her hand fall, waiting. Wind whipped at her skirt and drafts of air tingled upon her flesh. But the boy had not moved.

"Come get them, please," she said, keeping her voice level.

The boy, a skinny fourteen or so, his black arms naked up to where the sleeves were torn off just below his shoulders, came silently forward. It was only to be expected that she did not know his face. She tried to recall it. She thought she did. "Aren't you Tull?"

"Ma'm?" He had stopped in the gate, his eyes evading her.

"You are not Tull? But he's older, isn't he?"

The boy's eyes were fixed on the car but his lips said something.

"Which one are you?"

"Ben," he mumbled.

Ben? It was foolish the way her mind cast about in a sort of desperation to recall the name. She said, "You probably don't remember me. I'm Mrs. Glenn. I've known your daddy since we were children."

The boy's eyes glanced at her. The wind flapped her skirt, a chill ran tingling up her body.

"Some of these clothes may do for you," she finally said. "I know they'll fit Tull. And maybe Lee, too. I don't know about your daddy, though. I doubt it. He's probably too big." Suddenly she heard herself. Briefly she added, "Take them, please."

The boy looked as if he was reluctant to move, but he did. He gave a slow tug at the carton, pulling it against his stomach.

"Is your daddy here?"

"Naw."

She swallowed it. "Is he still working for Mr. Barden?"

The boy stood still, his arms around the carton. "I ain't got no daddy."

She looked at him in confusion. Then she understood. "Oh, you don't live here, then?"

"Yeah, I lives here."

A noise, making her start, cut into the blankness his words had left. From just inside the gate a spotted dog stood barking at her. "Hush up," the boy said with a violence that sent the dog skulking back toward the cabin. It seemed a long time before she could get her scattered thoughts in order and now the boy stood with a hand on top of the carton, fingering a garment. It was the white T-shirt.

"What happened to him . . . your daddy?"

"Don't ask me."

"He's not . . . dead, is he?"

"I don't know. I ain't never even seen him."

She glanced around at the cabin, looked back at the reeling mailbox. The name 'Camron,' though peeled and faded, was there. "Isn't your daddy Bo Camron?"

"I don't reckon he is." His fingers lifted an edge of the T-shirt. "Naw, he gone from here. Been gone. They went off up north some place."

Been gone? "But his name . . ." she protested and let her voice die out. After a space she said, "When did they go?"

"I don't know. After we move in here, after picking time. The one before last."

"Two years?"

"I reckon."

She stood there and the wind came at her, humming in the trees. She looked at the cabin again, then out across the expanse of field where dead stalks with last white tags of cotton hanging rippled in the gusty tides of air. Clear away to the rim of woods there was nothing to be seen, no bonnets of yellow straw to dip and rise, no hint of a human shape. And suddenly this was a place she did not know. Had she ever known it, seen it as it was . . . and seen herself? Her heart lay like a stone in her breast.

"You still want me to take this stuff?" the boy said.

It was a moment before she could focus on him, on his hand that rested limp and indifferent over the edge of the carton. "If you want it," she murmured.

The boy gave a sort of shrug, as if to say that it was her decision.

"Take it on," she said, suddenly knowing that she did not feel anything beyond her impulse to be rid of him . . . and rid of this carton. She paused only long enough to see him lift it out of the car, his flat black face evading her as he turned. If there were thanks she did not hear them, or want to hear them. From the cabin windows eyes pursued her around and into the driver's seat. Quickly she was out of their sight, leaving behind her the cabin and the dead, windy cotton field for what would surely be the last time in her life.

22

Why doesn't Will bring on another log?" Aunt Minnie said with feeble but demanding petulance.

It seemed as if at any moment they might hear black Will's uncertain steps in the room and see by the fire's glow, as he bent down with the tremulous log, the strain in his wrinkled and desiccated face. Even here they would feel, issuing from his ragged coat, the cold of winter night outside, and shiver. It was not winter but it was cold. Hester leaned forward and with the tongs put two lumps of coal from the scuttle into the little grate.

"That's better, dear," Aunt Minnie said. But sometimes she said Margaret, or Ellen, the names of her dead sisters, and "dear" might have meant one of these as well as Hester. She was wandering badly tonight. Summoned on the telephone by Mrs. Torbert, Hester had come with a reluctance that had kept her standing, trembling with the cold, for many minutes on the walk outside this rear apartment door. Cruel or not, it had been a relief to find the old lady this way, withdrawn into a cocoon of shawls and blankets, vacantly staring into the fire and, in those first moments, gazing up as if Hester's body had not the substance to make it entirely visible. No need for Hester to veil her face against such scrutiny as this. In fact, seated there in firelight through long intervals when nothing but flames and shadows stirred, it had been her part to study Aunt Minnie's face.

But this had been an hour ago. Now, even when the old lady spoke, Hester did not look at her, did not have to look. As in an image cast by the fire on a surface of her brain, she saw the familiar lineaments, the family skull obtruding beneath the dry and haggard flesh. Eyes with none but inward sight, as blind as if shut to the world. Nose whose faintly arching bridge gave hint of rapacity. Cold: no warmth but from the fire, warmth retained by shawls and blankets only. Yet was it not her own likeness that Hester envisioned? No pity for that, no excuse of age.

"Why are we burning coal, Margaret?"

"Because it's all we have," Hester said in a voice pointlessly abrupt.

But Aunt Minnie did not notice her tone. "Oh I'm sure there's plenty of wood out in the woodpile. Will could go get it."

"Maybe he's tired. And cold. They get cold, too." Her harshness made no sense. But even the feeble stirring, the sign of discomfort wrought in the bundled figure beside her, did not bring any impulse to relent. She said, "Anyway, we are not at Fountain Inn. We are here, in the Torbert house."

After a moment, "Of course," Aunt Minnie faintly said. "Of course I know that, Hester."

Hush, Hester thought, emptily reprimanding herself. Why ask the vaporous question standing in her mind? But she did. "What was it really like there . . . at Fountain Inn?"

"At Fountain Inn? . . . Oh, it was lovely. But you were there, Hester. You remember."

"Down underneath, I mean? That a child's eyes never saw? How was it really?"

Her absurd question had brought what it could only bring, silence as blank as a curtain—and also had brought a sensation, quite palpable finally, of being alone again. Huddled deep in itself, the bundled form beside her seemed to have no life. Yet, as if the coiling tongues of flame kept shaping it in her eyes, Hester's question abided. In memory she drifted from room to room of that house, and into the yard, to the cabins. But the people were all like shadows, or timid ghosts that fled as she drew near. Until at last, rounding a corner that she had not known existed, she confronted the solid figure in her hall. All along he had been there, planted on the love seat or pacing about the house. "We're the same kind, Miss Hester, me and you. Money ain't no real difference. It's what you hold to."

He would be there tonight, waiting—every night. There was scent of him in the house, a musky-sweetish smell of lotion that faintly lingered in covert, unclean places, wafted out on intermittent drafts of air to her nostrils. Once, in spite of the weather, she had opened a dozen windows. But by this she had only admitted a chill that would not be driven out again. This was the odor of her house. She was obliged to breathe it. For he would keep on coming back. "I know how lonesome you get. With even your other boy done turned his back on you, like you wasn't even his mama." She shut her eyes.

He had touched her again. His hand had lain like ice on her wrist, burning, and yet she had endured it. She endured it still, as if a scalded place was left in the flesh where his hand had rested. Some print of it there? She examined her pale wrist in the fire's glow.

"I know your feelings, Miss Hester, same as I know mine. Look around, it makes you sick, sometimes, don't it? Black niggers and whites all getting in together. White gals, too. That Delmore gal running with that Pitts nigger, loving it up with him." He was standing above her, inches from her chair, the scent of him in her nostrils. "How long you reckon the old folks would have stood for it?"

Maybe she shook her head.

"You reckon they'd have held back a whole minute, Miss Hester?"

"No," she whispered. But her voice seemed more than a whisper in the room.

"What did you say, dear?" The firelight played on Aunt Minnie's shapeless figure.

"Nothing," Hester said.

"I'm sure I heard a voice." Then, "I think somebody called. It must have been Papa."

"No. It was me thinking out loud."

"He may want something. We should see about him."

Hester watched the fire. "He doesn't want anything. He's dead."

Aunt Minnie stirred. "Papa?"

"Yes. For thirty-five years. You're dreaming again." She saw the old lady's face now, the family skull beneath the tissue of dry and haggard flesh. Pity her.

"Oh, Hester . . . My mind wanders so, sometimes. I forget things."

Hester watched the fire and did not speak, thinking that the very source of pity had dried up in her. Somewhat later she heard, barely heard:

"Are you very unhappy, dear?"

Hester had no answer. Watching the fire, she let Aunt Minnie's question die out of her consciousness.

"I wish so much I could comfort you."

But soon she would forget, escaping into her dreams.

"I know Ames must be a comfort to you."

Ames? For an instant it had been in her mind to say that he also was dead, but this had been her old self darting back into life. Somewhere, then, in its own dim way, that self was still alive. "Yes," she coolly lied.

"I hope you pray a lot. I've been praying for you."

Hester should have said that she was grateful, but still she said nothing. What was there to pray for? For that old blind and deadly self to take up its life again? Or for this self, that was not anything at all?

"I think I want to go to bed now."

In silence Hester helped the trembling old lady into her nightdress and then to bed. Covering her deep in blankets, so that the small body made scarcely a mound in the surface, she turned back and replenished the fire with coal. "Good night, Aunt Minnie," she said. No answer came. Already asleep, or dreaming. Already miles and decades away. Shadow obscured her face, her slightly beaked and rapacious Cameron nose, and only some hair like a tag of cotton had any vividness in the firelight.

The air outside was bitter. Looking first for the car she had not brought, she set out walking along the soundless street. More and more slowly she walked, passing, it almost seemed, as if she were a ghost that vanished in the intervals between the pools of stark streetlight. At Maple she turned for what seemed no reason and walked until she stood in front of the church building. The dull brick front was faintly illuminated from a distance, but the wide doors under the arch were invisible in darkness. Why was the outside light not burning? This fact appeared somehow ominous, and the more she stared, the more it seemed as if the arch framed only a hollow place where carved oak doors had used to be. Then she remembered. They had been bent on moving the church. Yes. Perhaps already she was gazing into the darkness of an empty shell. If not yet, it would soon be so. She stood a little while imagining it bare, stripped of pews and pulpit and figured, stained-glass panes—a place where prayers would be flung back as echoes off the desolate walls.

Approaching her house at last, she stopped on the opposite corner. Light visible in windows and fan glasses around the front door was light she had left burning, but still she knew that he was there. Pacing the house or squatting on her love seat or a chair, he would be waiting—however long he had to wait. And greet her at the door. Incredible. When would it ever end, this penance that she could not bear?

Tonight she could not bear it, not yet a while. Entering by the driveway in back, she circled around to the garden on the other side of the yard and sat down on a chair in the summerhouse. There were sounds from the distance only, remote as buried sounds. Twice she saw his shadow pass across her curtained window. The numbness that finally stilled her body's shuddering was almost as welcome as sleep.

Sometime in the night, with a click of the back door shutting and faint steps on the porch, he left. In a stumbling race against exhaustion she made her way into the house and locked the doors and put out the lights and locked her bedroom door behind her. She did stop once, so still that her shivering ceased, before she continued to undress. After that she refused to look at the wrinkled place in the coverlet of her bed. One snatch of her hand pulled the covers back and, sinking down, she reached for the table lamp. But it was a long while yet before she could perfectly understand what was scrawled on the piece of paper lying under the lamp.

> Sorry I could not wate no longer for you tonite. I got some news you want to here—about Delmores gal and that nigger Pits. I will tell you when I come back tomorrer nite.

First daybreak had defined the footposts of her bed and made of her dressing-table mirror a gray smear on the wall. But though she waited for many minutes and heard the clock strike once, daylight seemed not to advance. Turn on her lamp, then? No, she would wait until her eyes could read by the natural light of day, for this would be only minutes now. But the minutes went by and the gloom was unrelieved.

She pushed back her covers suddenly. Out in the hall she found by touch the telephone book on the table and, returning, held it up to the window. But the pages were featureless. She felt an instant of relief. A moment later, however, and her hand was on the lamp switch. Light flooded, blurred the names, but her fingers went on turning pages until her eyes, focused now, discovered the page and then the name. She switched off the lamp and, in the dark hall, counted out with her fingers the numbers on the telephone dial.

Three times, then a fourth, she heard it ring, imagining its shrillness in the bleak dawn hush of a house like Lucius's. All at once she had to sit down in the chair, and this was why she missed the click over the wire of the receiver's being taken up. A voice, a man's voice, was in her ear. It was repeated, with increment, before she could produce a sound, in a voice that was strange even to herself. "Is this Wendell Pitts?"

"That's right." There was a pause. "Who are you?"

Just above a whisper she said, "Is everything all right?"

"Who is this?"

She gripped the receiver and felt her lips move once or twice before she said, "Please be careful," and quickly hung up and made her way back to her bed.

For some hours, sleep held her like a sort of cold swoon that never did extinguish a last flicker of consciousness. Something shook her awake. It was sound, and before her strained attention could locate the source she lay there in the expectation of hearing footsteps in the hall. The sounds were made by Lucius who was working near her window; she heard him grumbling. But the moment of comfort passed like wings. What time was it? The gray light told her nothing about the hour and at noon Lucius would be at the door for his lunch.

"Please be careful."

Those words were hers, in first dawn light over the telephone. The note was still there on the table. Starting up from her pillow she read it once more, then crumpled it in her hand. Suddenly it was as if time had stopped. Across the gray interval between her and night there seemed to be no passage. Did he mean only to torment her? Had there not been times, times when her back was turned upon him, when she had imagined the look of eyes gone as flat as stones in his head?

The thought was no comfort. With an abruptness that left her head vaguely swimming, she got up and seized her clothes. Minutes later she stood at the kitchen door spying out through the glass for a sight of Lucius. Softly shutting the door behind her, she hurried. His voice, "Come here a minute, please, Miss Hester," as if it had been a shout from among the shrubs, spurred her only the faster and, still pursuing, inspired the abandon with which she backed her car out into the street.

She did not remember having passed through town, and the turnoff beside the cotton field came up suddenly. Her image of the house, its every feature staring back in gray cloud light, was not less real than the building which now, through half-bare trees, started up in front of her. Nothing was unexpected. Turning in, she saw at a glance the familiar gaps where boards were missing in the wall, the windows where rags and cardboard sheets replaced the broken panes. But where was his car . . . or any sign of life?

Poised beside her car, she could hear no sound except of blood throbbing against her own eardrums. If he was not here . . . The thrust of her denial made her let go of the car door and hurry up to the steps and onto the porch. The door was open. Again she looked into the hollow and desolate hall, at the staircase winding upward in gloom to an equal desolation overhead. The rap of her knuckles on the loose screen door echoed like distant gunshots in the house.

She saw him before she heard his step. He seemed to come out of the gloom where the staircase rose, suddenly detailed, in overalls, his features vivid around a smile that stretched his mouth in welcome. "Never looked to see you here today, Miss Hester. A pleasure to, though." Approaching with hand reached out for the screen he pushed it open wide and held it. "My place ain't so fine as yours is, but it's home. Come on in."

"What did you mean by that note?"

For a second she was conscious of those lids through which his eyes seemed still to watch her.

"Aw, that," he said. "Come on in, I'll tell you about it."

"Tell me here."

"All the times I've took your hospertality?" Slowly he shook his head. "Naw, naw. Come on in and we'll have a talk." His back to the doorjamb he waited, would go on waiting.

She stepped across the threshold and turned to face him again. "What about them . . . the girl and Pitts?"

"Well." He let the screen swing softly shut. "Need to get us some chairs, first thing, though."

Holding back what might have been a plea, she watched him walk deliberately down the hall and, at a shadowy door near the staircase, vanish. She stood there hugging her breast against the chill, staring at naked laths in the wall and shards of plaster strewn about the floor. A hall like hers, a staircase like her own, and doors opening into rooms whose every dimension she knew by heart.

A thudding noise. He appeared out of the doorway carrying chairs in his hands. He placed one of them close to the wall, the other carefully at an angle to it. "This one suit you, Miss Hester?" He was holding it for her.

She sat down quickly. "Tell me, please."

"Aw, it ain't really much to tell. Just something I heard. I ought not to left that note."

"What did you hear?"

"Just some fellows talking. It might not mean a thing." He had sat down. His hands on his knees, he was looking at her. "You look like you're cold, Miss Hester. Why don't I make us a fire in yonder?"

"What did they say?"

Hollis Handley rubbed his knees. "I ought not to left you that note."

She felt that in a moment she might scream at him. He looked up at the ceiling, exposing to her those unexpected sinews in his fleshy throat. "Let's just forget about that. I'll make us a fire," he said, shifting as if to rise.

"You've got to tell me!"

He looked down at his hands. "Likely it wasn't nothing but talk. About they was going to get them . . . It ain't really none of our business, Miss Hester."

"How 'get them'?"

"Lay for them someplace. Said they know a place where they go to."

In the hush she heard her voice say faintly, "Kill them?"

"Now it's probably just talk. You know how folks carry on when they're mad."

For a long while she stared at the thick, motionless hands on his knees. "Who were the people?" Then, forcing her eyes in a gaze that would not quite stay fixed upon his, she said, "Or are there really any?"

His eyes went out for a second behind the lids. "What would I tell you a lie like that for? I ain't no liar, Miss Hester. You must not think too high of me."

"Then who are they?" she whispered.

Hollis Handley shook his head. "You're a heap better off not to know that. 'Cause if they was to do it, it'd make you feel bad, knowing them, wouldn't it? You know how you are, Miss Hester. Might make you feel like you ought to do something about it and you shore couldn't do that . . . Even if you was to want to."

She recognized that these words, the last ones, were left on purpose to dangle like a bait before her. But there could be no refusing it. "What do you mean?"

" 'Course you *wouldn't* want to, them being our folks." Hollis Handley looked up at the ceiling. "But even if you was to, you couldn't. Neither one of us could. 'Cause me and you ain't the only ones knows who killed that nigger."

She was only just aware that his gaze came down from the ceiling and settled on her face. "It's not true," she murmured.

He shook his head. "I'm afraid it is, Miss Hester. Hit me hard, too. I don't know how they found it out, but they did some way." He paused. "We ain't got any worry, though. It's our folks, and they shore ain't going to let it out. I wouldn't even have told you but just for knowing how you are."

"How I am?" she breathed, merely repeating, like words recalled from a dream.

"I mean you having such a conscience and all . . . So I'll just not name them to you. 'Cause it wouldn't be nothing you could do if you did know. Not one thing . . . Not this time, Miss Hester."

It was the look of his eyes that broke like a fierce and blinding light through the haze. For a moment afterward, as in a glare, she could see nothing before her. What she did see, through eyes of that bodiless self looking down from the winding staircase, was the strange and also familiar sight of the other Hester Glenn seated almost knee to knee with this appalling figure in the desolation of this ruined hall. A soundless place. It stifled sound, made a silence of the question that her mouth was trying to utter.

Yet his voice, as searing as the eyes that swam back into her focus now, answered her. "No'm, they ain't going to be setting around 'sleep in a car waiting for you to come turn the switch on them."

A time passed. Something kept defeating the impulse to shake her head.

" 'Cause that's what you done, ain't it, Miss Hester?"

Presently she did manage a shake of her head, or thought she did. If so, the denial made no impression.

"I figured it was," he said. "Turned the switch on him. Him laying in there drunk."

"It was not that way!" Afterward she understood that her voice had failed her. The words had not been spoken aloud. Repeating them, still she made no sound. There was a sound, but it was the creaking of the chair as Hollis Handley shifted and leaned a little toward her, squaring his eyes with hers.

"Killed your own boy. That's really something. It ain't none of the old folks ever did come up to that." He slowly blinked, but his lids seemed not even to interrupt the glare of triumphant hate in his eyes. "Naw, Miss Hester. It ain't *nobody* you can look down on."

What had followed this seemed to Hester afterward like scattered events in the aftermath of a blow. There were things he had said, letting drop the unction from his voice, deadly vaunting things whose tenor kept sounding in the chaos of her mind. She remembered contempt unveiled in his face, his lips mocking her name. Above her were gaps in a ruined ceiling and broken walls that seemed to be her own.

Had he spoken obscenities to her? It seemed that he had. Perhaps this was what finally had released her, had given her strength to rise from the chair and, half blindly, make her way to the door and out and down the steps to her car. He had been there, too, however, handing her in, leaning at the window saying, "No need to go running off, Miss Hester. What you want to run for?"

What was she running for? Where the gravel road met the highway, she had stopped and when the engine quit she did not start it up again. A drizzle was falling now, from a low arch of cloud that curtained out the skyline beyond the cotton field. In every direction it looked the same, without horizon. Whatever way she went would be the same, for this was where her fate had left her. The fate that her hands had made. Somehow had made. Hands that had shaped and guided a little boy and at last had turned a switch on him. Dangerous hands. "Somebody 'good' as you are, Miss Hester, other folks better keep their eyes open, hadn't they?" "Yes," was her silent answer now. But it was not only to others that she had been a danger. To herself, also: in the end her turn had come. For where was a way that she could change this self for another one?

Finally she started the car again and pulled out onto the highway. But she turned left, not right, and followed miles of glistening pavement to where a bumpy road led off uphill through woods to a ridge. It was miles yet, through misting rain, but at last she turned once more, then stopped beside a field. There was only sound of the drizzle whispering in weeds outside her window. Nothing. Not even a bird flew over. Her eye picked out foundation stones in the brown grass, the rotten fence, the post where the summerhouse had stood. But after a minute or two she was not looking anymore. Some way she had snagged her wrist. Blood was smeared down onto the heel of her hand and this was what she was looking at. When at last she raised her eyes, it was to start the car and turn around and set out driving deliberately back toward Cameron Springs.

23

The fine rain was still falling as Ames, again in a borrowed car, approached the outskirts of Cameron Springs. All the way down he had been rehearsing what he would say, how he would say it, but now, minutes from his destination, his confidence faltered. For might not Pitts, however Ames might veil its purpose, see through this intrusion? Ames being who he was and asking this particular question, could not the same thought come to Pitts as readily as it had to him? A woman, a white woman, Pitts had thought.

"He was pretty sure it was a white woman, from her voice," Libby had said. "She just told him to be careful and then hung up. It was barely daylight."

"And that's all she said?" Even this quickly the thought had come and Ames, fearing some hint of it in his face, deliberately had looked down.

"She asked him if he was all right, or something. Wendell called Daddy after it happened. He didn't think it was meant as a threat and Daddy doesn't, either. They think it's somebody with a bad conscience."

Still not wanting to meet her eyes, Ames had looked away across the cafeteria to where the line of students was edging along the counter. "No idea who?"

"There are probably a thousand candidates," she said, ". . . in that sick town." With the unpainted nail of an index finger, Libby silently tapped at the lip of her glass. "There is a threat somewhere, though, and this person knows about it. It might have to do with the meeting Wendell and I are going to tonight."

Ames looked at her now. "Are you still going?"

"Of course," she flatly said, her tone recalling the not too pleasant conversation they had had in this same place three days before.

"And your father won't object?"

"What do you think?"

He paused a second. "Or Pitts, either?"

"I don't think Wendell is any more of a coward than I am," she said dryly. "In fact I don't think he can be stopped by any threat that town has the guts to make."

Her dryness persisted in the manner with which she waited for his reply, waited with stern assured brown eyes trained on him and strong jaw locked with that knot of muscle that made her face so like her father's. And not only her father's, Ames imagined again. The image of his own mother that stood once more in his mind's eye seemed as if it might also have sprung from a likeness in this face.

Ames could not recall what his reply had been. Since that moment, in fact, he could remember very few things not connected with the purpose that had brought him back here to Cameron Springs again. These doubts had surprised him. Now, thinking of Pitts, there came an interlude in which his car rolled almost to a stop. The violence of a truck horn close behind startled him out of it, and after that he tried to ignore his doubts. Nevertheless, uncertainly turning out of his way, he did drive past his mother's house for a look that, after all, showed him only blank windows and an open garage where not even Cam's old car was any longer to be seen . . . Where was she? But he actually stopped only the one time, at a filling station on the edge of the Negro district, in order to look up Pitts's address.

Such numbers as appeared on the weathered little houses and mailboxes along Pearl Avenue were indistinct. But the need for scrutiny was a help, deflecting his doubts, obscuring the moment that waited for him at one of these houses down the empty, glistening street. Then suddenly he was there. Beyond a little stretch of clean, brown lawn, on the painted doorframe of a house larger than the rest, the number stood out in brass through the mist of rain. Along the street in front of and behind him he could not see anyone and from either direction the dusk was coming in. Wait until dark? Or give it up and drive away? For what except his fancy had wrought this intuition that something at last was about to be settled?

He did neither thing. Getting deliberately out of the car he started up the gravel walk toward the door.

"You looking for Mr. Pitts?"

Ames's startled eye found the Negro man, in a dark jumper, beside a privet bush across the fence. "Yes," he said, but his voice sounded too quiet for even this little distance.

"What you want with him?" Gathering dusk did not make indistinct the look of scrutiny in the black oval of the Negro's face.

"I've got something to talk to him about."

"Yeah, but who are you?"

Ames's name was almost on his lips before he thought to say, "I'm a friend of the Delmores. Of Libby," he added. "From up at the college."

The scrutiny continued for a space. "Wendell, he ain't got home yet. Look for him in about half a hour."

Ames hesitated. "Maybe I'll wait in the car."

"That be all right." But Ames had moved only a step back toward the car when the Negro said, "You a friend of Libby's?"

"Yes."

The Negro put a big hand on the paling fence. The shape of his lips grew suddenly distinct through the misty twilight. "You tell her she ain't doing nothing but just making him more trouble."

Mechanically Ames said, "How so?"

"Coming around here. Come here two, three days ago, by herself. Wasn't just that one time, neither. Been here *several* times. Riding around in the car with him. It ain't nothing going on with them, but that don't make no difference. You see that window yonder?" He lifted his hand to point to the dim window. "Got two bullet holes. Last one ain't been a week ago. Somebody come by at night in a car. He's got a plenty danger without her heaping it up for him. And it ain't a bit of use in it. Don't help nothing. She going get him killed."

Ames, facing him again, said, "Have you told him that?"

"Shore I told him." The Negro put both big hands on the fence. "You don't know Wendell. That'd be backing down for him. He won't back down. Be ashamed to in front of that white gal, anyhow. It's her doing. You try to tell him that, he gets mad. Say they got a right to. But that don't make no kind of sense. He keep on, they *will* get him. That gal's the one got to stop it."

"I've already tried to tell her," Ames said.

"Tell her some more. She want to get him killed, just keep on. It already is something working. He got a call on the phone daylight this morning warning him. It's something going on."

Ames hoped that the closing twilight had veiled his expression. Subduing his voice he said, "Who was the call from?"

"They wouldn't say. He says he knows it was a white woman, though. And I got a notion he's fixing to hear from her again, too."

On the end of a breath Ames said, "Why do you think so?"

The Negro nodded his round head toward Ames's car. " 'Cause it was a white woman stopped her car right there where yours is at a little while ago. Setting there looking at the house when I seen her. She drove off 'fore I could get close enough to tell much. Had a green car. A nice one."

It was dark now and, through the drizzle, windows on the street side of the house had a bleared and sightless look. Their light was cast from the hall, or perhaps from her bedroom beyond . . . where she would be. Doing what? Even the rain that he heard whispering on the car roof close above his head would not be audible to her there. Or audible only as drops which the wind might flick against her windowpane. Was she standing upright in the floor? Or sitting on the edge of her bed, in the glow of her table lamp, staring against the wall?

He did not know what he was waiting for. For the coming of an impulse that would lift him from the car, thrust him into her presence? But he knew that this could not be. What was it he had intended? Now he could remember only, in the moment when he had turned away from the Negro man at the fence, how the grip of this anxiety had shut down on his heart and sent him here. How long ago that seemed.

In a stark and sudden blaze of light, the interior of the garage appeared. It took him a second to understand that the headlights of his mother's car had come on and that already the car was moving, backing from the driveway. Out in the street it paused and then, rolling past him, afforded a glimpse of his mother's white face through the window. She turned at the corner, heading for the square. She had passed clear out of sight before his hand found the ignition switch.

Where the street emptied into the square, she had stopped. It was not because of traffic, for he could see, from where he in turn had stopped at a distance behind her, that the square was deserted. Yet she went on sitting there, her motionless head framed in the rear window, her light beams flaring on the otherwise darkened cannons and the pedestal that, all of a sudden, made him think of an altar with nothing on it. In motion again, she passed around the monument and entered Forrest Street.

Where was she going? Soon enough he thought that he knew. Trailing far behind her, ticking off each cross street as he passed, he saw her finally round the curve where Forrest changed to Quincey. Then he did know. And presently, just as if his knowledge had conjured it, her car turned left up the rise into Meadow Hills.

She wound ahead of him, topping the crest from where she must see, through the misty rain, lights blooming row on row along the slopes of what had been green pasture land. At the fork there, she paused uncertainly, but then went on, choosing the right road down. He saw her stop briefly in front of a house at the foot of the incline and, creeping, move forward again and stop before another house. The porch light was burning. It was the place. Coasting also to a stop, he saw her silhouette appear, standing in the gloom beside her car. She held there for a moment. Then, drifting like a shadow around to the walk, she slowly entered the light and mounted the steps and lifted her hand to the door.

He had watched her be admitted. Yet it seemed, before the fact could quite take hold, that he needed a space in which to stare at the shut door and the empty porch. He let his car roll down the slope and stopped in back of hers. Still another minute passed before the feeling of shame swept over him. He did not pause again.

Libby's face in the vestibule. He did not try to read her expression, and for an interval after that, he had not even a consciousness of her presence. What his eyes sought, and found in that same instant, was his mother. Her image, rather, reflected in a massive mirror that hung beyond the archway on a wall of the living room. A perfect image, yet dim somehow, like a faded familiar portrait of herself. Looking at him. She must have been looking at him, because her eyes, darker than her face, were gazing squarely at the mirror and because her lips were parted as if she had broken off in the middle of speech.

"Go on," Horace Delmore's voice said. Seated under a floor

lamp, he was leaning forward, toward her, with elbows on knees and strong tense chin thrust out as if in challenge. From the archway now, Ames looked directly at his mother, saw her eyes leave the mirror and for a moment, as though he were some unhappy riddle, linger upon him. The glass had not fully recorded her ashy pallor, nor shown, between her eyes, the depth of the crease that must have rent even the bone beneath her skin. And where, in so little time, could so much flesh have gone, that jaws and temples should make him think of the hollows in a skull.

"Please do go on." It was Mrs. Delmore, seated beyond her husband. Ames got an impression of bare, round, braceleted arms, a puckered and eager brow.

"I've told you all I know. That they plan to 'get' them." His mother had slightly turned her head to look at Mrs. Delmore. Now she turned toward Libby, who was standing intently just to the right of Ames. "To get you . . . and Pitts. If it is true." Her voice was clear enough, but there was a measured and fragile quality unfamiliar to Ames.

"To kill them, you mean?" Horace said.

It seemed a point of duty with her to squarely meet each face. "That must be what it means. If it is true."

There were knobbed brass andirons that gleamed from the fireplace and here, in the interval, she appeared to have let her attention come to rest. But it was not so. Ames knew, could sense, what a blankness stood before her eyes. And could he not detect, as by a sort of muscular sympathy, a stifled tremor of flesh and bone which the gray suitcoat buttoned so neatly across her breast barely did conceal?

"Who is the man that told you this?" Horace said.

Seconds passed before she looked at him. "His name is Hollis Handley."

Hollis Handley? To Ames it was as though an obscenity had passed his mother's lips.

"Who is Hollis Handley?" Horace said.

"He has a farm just out of town . . . off Grimley Road."

"But what is your connection with him?" This was Mrs. Delmore, an impatient voice. "You know him someway, obviously."

His mother loosely held a purse on her knees and her right hand, as if preparing a gesture that never came, slowly disengaged itself. "I know him because of his son. He was a friend of my son . . . Cameron."

In the stillness Ames was conscious of a movement, of Libby sitting down in a chair close by. It made him notice the tightness in his legs, but he could not take his eyes from his mother's face. Was she merely unable to get on with it? Or was the pain what she wanted, that she must let them draw the pieces one by one like teeth out of her head?

"But why would he tell you this?" Horace said. "Is he a part of your . . . 'movement?' "

She only shook her head.

"All right. But you seem to doubt his information. Why would he lie to you?"

Faintly she said, "Because he hates me." She hesitated. "But that is a different matter. I have no way to know whether he's lying. I just want to warn you."

"And that's all?"

But her gaze had come back to the andirons in the fireplace.

Mrs. Delmore said, "I think you could tell us more about this man that would be helpful. If you wanted to."

Ames saw his mother stir, a movement as if she might be preparing to rise from the chair. She did not. And when her eyes shifted his way, it was not to look at him. She looked into the mirror again, at herself, and Ames felt a stiffening of his own lips to see hers slowly part:

"His son was a friend of my son." She drew a breath. "They are the ones who killed the Stevens Negro."

It was a long hush. Her stark face was at the center, compelling every eye. Yet, out on a far margin of his mind, Ames kept being distracted by the fear that her limp hand might let fall the purse resting at an angle on her knees.

A little creaking noise made preface to a voice: "Are you certain of that?" Horace had partly straightened up in his chair.

"Yes." She was barely audible, but she had faced him again.

"How do you know it?"

"Because he admitted it to me. Not very long before he died

. . . I think I had known it all along, though, really. I couldn't face it."

Still intently watching her, Horace sat back in the chair. Mrs. Delmore said, "It's too bad you couldn't. I hope it would have prevented you from starting your 'movement.' "

Something tightened in Ames's breast. The woman's expression, the lifted brow reflecting her tone, gave hint of a certain exultance not far beneath the surface. Now he would have undone even the faint assent that his mother had acknowledged by her nod.

Presently Ames heard another creak of the chair. Horace, sitting now with his hands folded under his chin, said quietly:

"I take it that your son's death was not just an accident, then?"

The movement of her head was so slight that, from where Ames tensely stood, it could have meant either yes or no. But Horace said:

"You mean he took his own life?"

The tightness became a knot in Ames's breast. "It's none of their business, Mama."

Excepting hers, every eye turned on him—and then hers, too, for a little space. But there was not time to understand what had passed between them. In a voice somewhat flatter than before, Horace said:

"I was only trying to see it whole. This detail needn't go any further than us."

"Do you think people won't put two and two together?"

It was Libby who had spoken—to him, Ames realized, but he did not answer or even look at her.

"I'm not really trying to pry into your private misfortunes," Horace said. "I have no intention of mentioning this fact publicly. But it is part of the whole, isn't it?, when you look at it in context. His life is a perfect illustration of what a dehumanized society does to its victims. I have no doubt that your boy, when he murdered that Negro, had some kind of an idea that he was upholding society, carrying out its will. That's why he could bring himself to do it. The trouble is that really he *was* carrying out its will. This society trains people to do what your son did."

She had stopped looking at Horace. But it only appeared that she had not heard him, for now she gave a feeble shake of her head. "I was the one who trained him."

"Partly, yes. But you were doing its will, too, Mrs. Glenn. Don't you see, you're another one of its victims? It's not 'people' we're fighting against." Horace broke off, unfolding his hands. Then, "I'm going to go ahead and make this known—the sooner the better. You haven't told this to anyone else?"

She shook her head.

"Not the sheriff?"

She was still for a moment. "No . . . But I will. I'll go to him tonight."

"I wish you would put it off, Mrs. Glenn. Of course he'd be forced to act, now, but it would look like he had a hand in the matter. When actually he's done nothing at all—never intended to do anything. I would bet he knows who did it. At the least, my way won't give him any credit. And it might suggest the truth about him."

"Your way?" she said. "You mean . . . put it in the newspapers?"

"You must have expected that, Mrs. Glenn. I know it will be painful, but the papers will have it soon enough in any case."

"The sheriff *doesn't* know," Ames said. "He wouldn't hide it."

Horace looked at him. So did Mrs. Delmore, icily, and Horace said, "I think he would." Then, to Ames's mother again, "I know a great deal about Sheriff Venable, through the Negroes. More than you do, Mrs. Glenn. He's part of the system, too. He wouldn't be sheriff if he wasn't."

"Monk?" she said. "I've known Monk all my life." She had lifted her head. Perhaps because of her pallor, she looked a little as if she had spoken in astonishment. "You want me to help you hurt him?"

"To hurt what he *stands* for, yes. But you needn't worry it will hurt him with his own kind. They'll back him more than ever."

Still regarding him with that expression of dim astonishment, she said, "I won't do that."

Horace's mouth tightened. The bulge of his jaw caught a little highlight from the lamp above him. "What did you come here for, Mrs. Glenn. Only to warn us?"

She hesitated. "I don't know anymore . . . why I came here."

"Wasn't it guilt? You've confessed all this, when you didn't have to."

"As you said, you are the one who trained him," Mrs. Delmore put in. She had leaned forward, with wide blue accusing eyes, to say it.

"But what is your guilt worth," Horace said, "if you won't at least try to help out now. It's a small enough thing, considering."

"Let her alone." Ames's voice came out tight with the anger that had been mounting in him. And the look that was his answer in Horace's face goaded him to add, "Let's go, Mama."

Three steps across the plush, silent carpet put him beside the chair where, now, his mother sat with a kind of strained and tentative erectness. Horace's voice once more:

"It isn't really much to ask of you."

"She said no." Ames's hand closed on his mother's arm.

"Let her speak for herself."

"Come on, Mama." But he felt no response of her body—only her pulse beating in the thin arm he held. Looking straight at Horace, she said:

"I should have gone to him, not you."

"Come on." He felt a preparatory movement of her body, but Horace's voice stopped it.

"You are the one it's impossible to excuse."

This was said to Ames, and what he met in Horace's face was a look of flat contempt. It was the same in all their faces—in Libby's, where it had made a curl on the thin line of her mouth.

"I suppose you've known this all along, haven't you?" Horace said.

"He had to know it." This from Libby.

"Yes, I knew it."

"But he was your brother, wasn't he?" Horace said.

"That's right." The pulse he seemed to feel in his mother's arm might have been the blood of his own hand throbbing.

"And the man he murdered was a Negro. *They* are not your brothers, of course."

A hard rush of anger just for a moment distorted Ames's image of Horace's face. The words came crowding into his throat, stifling one another, and all Ames could manage to say was, "Maybe as much as they are yours. What do you know about it?"

"Oh my God!" Mrs. Delmore's grimace showed the whites of her eyes.

In a drawl of scathing mockery Libby said, "We just don't *understand.* Really you all just *love* Nigras, don't you? They make such nice pets."

"Some of us love them more than you love Pitts," he said, thrusting it at her.

"Meaning what?"

"That you'd trade him for a 'right.' Or a headline. If you get him killed, you'll chalk it up as a sacrifice. To righteousness." Abruptly turning back to his mother, he said, "Let's go," and felt her response to the pressure of his hand. Horace's voice, speaking to Libby:

"You see now, don't you? I had him pegged all along."

His mother had risen from the chair and was standing up beside him now as if she did not need his hand. But she was hesitating. Ames did not know why—unless it was to observe from this new angle the starkness of her face reflected in the mirror glass. Then he saw her speaking:

"I know what I've done. I was not anybody's victim. It's unjust of you to blame anybody but me."

She did not wait for his pressure. It was he who was drawn along, past the rigid figure of Libby, through the archway into the vestibule. In the sifting rain outside, he saw that she had no hat or coat, but only the purse that she carried with both hands against her body as if it was a thing of delicate value. They had passed beyond the aura of light from the porch, almost had reached her car before he was conscious of weight in the arm he held. It increased. He felt her start to tremble.

"Get in this side," he said, at the car. "I'll drive you home."

But he saw in the gloom the shake of her head refusing. "I'm going to Monk."

"That can wait till morning."

"It has to be now."

Except to hold to her still-trembling arm there was nothing he could do but walk with her around to the opposite door. Then, "I'll go for you. I can tell him as well as you can."

Holding to the door handle, she paused. She shook her head. "It has to be me."

"Why does it?"

Finally she murmured, "Because you don't know."

"What don't I know?"

In the dimness he could see her white face bowed and see how the rain had gathered like dew on her hair. "Get in the car," he said. "You're getting wet."

She did not move. "That I killed him."

"I shouldn't have said that to you. I didn't mean it."

"It was the truth."

He could hear rain falling with a sort of metallic whisper on the car's roof. "But you didn't really."

"He was asleep. I turned the motor on. I couldn't do it and turned it off, but he had waked up. He spoke to me. He said . . . He said just, 'Where are we going, Mama?' Just that."

She was still for a space.

"Later on, sometime, he did what I wanted him to do."

It seemed to take a long while—for the sound of the rain kept breaking in—before he got through hearing her voice. Then he heard it again:

"He obeyed me."

But all that Ames could muster to say, finally, was, "You'd better get in out of the rain."

Now she did get in, but afterward she only sat there under the wheel waiting, or not waiting, for him to speak. Still standing in the rain, beginning also to shudder, he noticed that the curtain across the Delmore's picture window was drawn back a little at one side. Someone was looking out, and he wondered vaguely which one of them it was. It would not be Horace. Somewhere in the house, in a voice as sure and commanding as a trumpet, he would be speaking into the telephone. At last Ames said:

"It's nobody's business, though." And after that, "I'll drive you home. Then I'll go find Monk."

"I have to do it."

"Move over," he said, and soon she obeyed.

All the way back, driving slowly in the rain and the click of windshield wipers, they did not speak. He noticed, when they reached the square and circled around the empty pedestal to the other side, that she kept her gaze fixed straight ahead of them. Faint light still shone in the downstairs windows. Almost too late it occurred to him that he ought to stop short of the garage. He did stop, and quickly extinguished the headlights, but he knew that nevertheless he had been too slow.

"You had better go on with me," he said. "You can stay in the car."

"No. Just let me sit here a minute."

But a minute passed, and others followed and he never heard her stir. A little wind had come up. He was conscious of branches and shrubbery riffled in the gusts.

"It must have been like a dream he was having . . . about me. I came in his dream and told him. And he did what I told him to."

Then she said, "He was doing my will."

Ames could find no reply.

At last she said, "Except I didn't make the world."

"Let's go in," Ames said and got out of the car.

The wind was gusting, and close by the walk a white camellia, newly bloomed, swayed in the darkness of a bush. He opened the kitchen door for her. Just inside, without switching on the light, she turned around so that he could see the pallor of her face.

"Will you be coming back?"

"Yes. As soon as I see him."

"It's your house, you know." She reached out and touched his arm, and then, with a movement that seemed slow in the dark, she shut the door upon him.

24

It was enough for Ames that he must remember the reality of what his own part had been—or had failed to be. For this, his cowardice, really, he could make not even a claim in his defense. But why must he keep turning and probing his memories of that final night? As certainly as he knew anything, he knew that he could not have stopped her—not even if he had had the foreknowledge with which his conscience kept charging him now. Foreknowledge? This was too much of a word. It was only hindsight that now would make of the dark anxiety in which he had driven away from the house that night a shape he ought to have recognized. Unless he had simply refused the vision? What of the moment when he had stopped where his mother an hour before had sat in her car with headlights flaring on the empty pedestal? But a horn had sounded behind him. And then the distraction of seeing, as he pulled out into the square, the sheriff's car appear from behind the courthouse and head up Forrest Street. Ames had followed it nearly to the city limits before he recognized that the driver was not Monk but Larch.

After that, it had been the thought of what he must say to Monk. And when he was there, in the confinement of Monk's little office, the sheer bulk of the words in his mind had left no margin for other thoughts. In the flat stillness, while from the other side of the littered desk Monk sat watching him, Ames listened to his own voice reeling it out—a tone as if this were some stale anecdote barely worth the telling. Except for the twitch of a muscle in a creased and wind-dried cheek, Monk had never moved. The only change had come in his eyes. Then, instead of shrewd, his expression was that of a man who watches from a distance of miles some incredible disaster. For a long time he did not speak, but finally, just at a murmur, he said, "Miss Hester?"

He had surely said other things, too, but Ames did not remember. In the utterance of her name, that formless anxiety once more had clutched at him. He knew that after this moment he had hurried and that, in the dark on the back porch walk, he actually had been brought to a stop by the sudden flooding of his heart. He remembered the sough of wind, the branches pitching, the shrubbery out across the yard like billows lashed in a gale. But the hall light was burning still. And when he entered, by the back hall door instead of the kitchen, he heard through the wall the innocent sound of water running into her tub.

It had lasted for a minute or two, this feeling of immense reprieve. He stood where he had stood times without number, almost serene in his sense of her vivid presence beyond the panels of her shut bedroom door. But there was something wrong. He heard a buffet of wind at the back door and he heard the water running. This was all. But the water kept on running. He felt again the tightness closing around his heart and presently he stepped forward and lifted his knuckles to the door. Softly, three times, he tapped, then waited. No sound but of water running. With force enough to raise echoes in the house, he knocked, and after that, straining it out of his throat, he called, "Mama."

The door was locked. He shook it, rattled it hard, calling her name. The flooding of his heart held him back for a space. Then with his shoulder he butted the door, rebounded. A second blow sheared the lock, and he stood in a room mellow with light from her table lamp falling across the flawless counterpane and onto her dressing table where lay, side by side in perfect symmetry, comb and brush and ebony pin box. Nothing awry. A room like a dream of itself. The moment held him quite fastened there, hearing only faint wind buffet her windows and, from beyond the shut bathroom door, water running into the tub.

He did not remember crossing the room to that door, but he did remember precisely the cool texture of the knob and what it had been like to feel the door give way to the pressure of his hand. He recalled, too, the curious and irrelevant feeling of shame at his brash intrusion upon her modesty—a feeling that was to be, in the next moment, involved with the shock of seeing her there. It must have been part of the reason why he had shut his eyes for a second, as though she had been naked. And why, after that, it seemed that his staring at her was in violation of every decency he had been trained to honor.

Yet only her arms, to the elbows, were naked, angling from her shoulders down into the tub. Her head rested cheek down on the rim, and the white stare of death in her eyes was fixed upon the wall. Except on her wrists where the vivid slashes were, and on her hands, there was not much blood. Even the tub showed only traces, a scarlet spray which the fall of water had splashed up onto the procelain sides. He remembered thinking that in some way it would make an important difference if he turned the water off. But when he came to do it, bending above her to twist the faucet handle, he saw the bright straight razor lying close to her hands in the tub.

A long time must have passed while he had continued sitting propped against the bathroom wall. A part of it, some minutes, was spent in a sort of incredulity that she could go on leaning there with her head in such a twist, her cheek on the hard porcelain rim. But for the rest he was thinking, as he since had thought so many times, how she must have felt to see her own life pulsing away in the swirl of reddened water. Maybe she had closed her eyes. Then, maybe, she had looked upon the scenes that she so often had tried to describe to them, to Cam and him: the procession of ordered trees and shrubs and the great house at the end, cabins, fields in summer haze and sounds of morning that must always have remained as clear as living voices in her ears. Perhaps it had all come very near as the life streamed out of her body. Yet—for his mind kept circling back to the same conclusion—he did not think that this was true. What he believed was that she had sat there, if less and less rigorously, with open eyes intent upon the sight of her blood swirling down the drain.

No, he could not have prevented it. And to wrestle the fruitless question of his foreknowing much or little was perhaps nothing except a diversion from the blame which he certainly bore. This blame was real. There was not even any question to turn about in his mind. Clearly he had deserted her, had fled, leaving it all in her hands. And then, from his refuge in an abstraction as great as her own, had condemned her. It was no use to tell himself that he could not have foreseen the shape of what he had condemned her to. But the vision had been waiting for him that night . . . As if the sight of her body had not been horror enough for a single hour.

It could have been a whole hour. He had the idea that while he was still sitting slumped against the wall on the bathroom floor he had twice heard the clock strike. That and sometimes the wind outside, but these were all he had heard—or would hear, even after the moment when he first became conscious of a living presence close to him. How, without making any sound, had the man got there? Warned only by the start of his pulse, Ames had looked up to see him standing in the doorway at a distance of not much more than an arm's reach. For many seconds, while Ames went on mutely staring up into his face, the man had not noticed him. He was looking at her, and only her, as if at a sight from which nothing could ever dislodge his eyes.

All at once he did see Ames, but still another moment passed before his expression changed. And this was the moment that Ames remembered far beyond any other. One flick of the reddened eyelids had made a blank of Handley's face. In the same instant he disappeared from view. The interval, although in Ames's memory it resembled one, had been no nightmare. The back door standing open, swinging in the wind, was proof enough that Handley had been present in the flesh. Even so there still were times when Ames felt less than sure, times when he fancied that he had seen only in his dreams such a look of malignant exultation.

This was what he had left her to. If he never would know the whole of the story, he was still able—by what he had learned from Lucius and what he had heard his mother tell the Delmores—to infer enough of it. He did not think that it was money, or anything else so simply human, that Handley had been after. What Handley had wanted, maybe *all* he had wanted, was what had been so clearly reflected in his face that night. For most of his lifetime, probably, in whatever he had for a heart, he had nurtured this hate. Then at last, among the carnage, he had seen his chance. So that night had been *his* night. So what did he care for the consequence which that same night had brought? According to Monk, he had not even troubled to inquire about his own son in the jail.

All this had happened more than a week ago. But if time in any degree had shaded these images in Ames's mind, it was only upon occasion. Nor had it helped, either, after enduring his comforters and seeing his mother into the ground, to lock up the house and hurry back to college. He had soon returned again. Why, when his presence seemed only to haunt the place? There were, he told himself, arrangements that had to be made. He would sell the house and go elsewhere, because now there was nothing to hold him here. Then why did he keep postponing it, letting the days go by while he tried, in spite of the silence, to read from old books on the sitting-room shelf, or merely sat, or paced about the house or through the yard? As if he were waiting for something.

On Tuesday, one of his "days," Lucius showed up. Standing in the kitchen, he wore still a shadow of that expression with which, after his look at her body lying in the coffin, he had turned to Ames and said, "It ain't Miss Hester."

Now, with just that dimness in his eyes again, he said, "You ain't thinking about selling this place, is you?"

"I don't know. Not yet, anyway," Ames said, realizing that in fact this was true.

"Reckon I better keep on coming around here, then."

"If you will . . . If you still want to."

"You ought to know I wants to." In a lowered voice he added, "It wasn't none of her fault . . . what he done. They all gone crazy."

But Ames did not answer. Presently, with a mumbled remark about some shrubs, Lucius turned to the door and put his hand on the knob. Gazing out through the glass, he said, "Keeping right on at it out there, too."

Ames took a moment to understand what he meant. "Out there." It was the way Ames also had come to think. This was so far true that, having discontinued even the newspaper, he had had no inkling of what Lucius went on to tell him. Two nights ago someone, with a shotgun, had made a try at Pitts. His aim had not been perfect, and Pitts, with a gap in his windshield and safety glass in one probably blinded eye, had escaped with his life. Libby, who had been in the car with him, was not injured. But this was not all. In retaliation, apparently, a white delivery man driving through the Negro section had been beaten savagely and now lay in the hospital with a badly broken skull.

So it was "out there," Ames thought. And he could go out and join one side—the one with all the truth—and help to annihilate the other. For this was the kind of war it was, under banners of past or future, with even the winner losing more than his humanity could stand.

Then what was he waiting for? That afternoon he sat down at the telephone and looked up the number of a real-estate man he knew by reputation. But this was as far as he got. And then, after pacing a while from silent room to room, he knew that this was as far as he would get. What else but this house was his own? It was no use to tell himself that these affections were a part of him and would be with him still wherever he went. This house was their abiding place. It was also something else. Here, at least for him, were intimations of a time when life exceeded the grasp of stiffened minds and wills. In the absence of any other church, this one would have to do.

No, he would keep the house. He would rent it for now, but it would still be his, still recoverable. And who could say—since a spirit that had lived once could live again—that much more than this was not recoverable.